CRASH

CRASH

SINNERS AND SAINTS
BOOK ONE

KATHY LOCKHEART

Editor: Susan Staudinger
Proofreader: Jovana Shirley, Unforeseen Editing, www.unforeseenediting.com

Cover design:
Model cover design: © By Hang Le
Photographer: Wanderer Photographer
Discreet Cover: Wild Love Designs

ISBN:
ebook: 978-1-955017-51-0
Paperback Discreet Cover: 978-1-955017-53-4
Paperback: Model cover: 978-1-955017-52-7

Published by Rosewood Literary Press

BLURB

Code blue in the ER. That's how I end up in his hospital. In my brother's best friend's care.

Dr. Blake Morrison is the star of every fantasy I've had since I was sixteen. Now he's the only one who believes something is truly wrong with me.

The only one who can save me.

But with each passing day, each failed diagnosis, I see him changing. The brilliant, controlled doctor is becoming something else. Something darker. More possessive.

"These symptoms aren't random," he growls. "I think someone's hurting you deliberately. And when I find them ..." His fingers clench. "They'll learn exactly how much damage a doctor can do."

His touch sets my heart monitor racing, and what's growing between us is more dangerous than any symptom. More forbidden than any diagnosis.

But as my mysterious illness worsens and time slips away like sand through an hourglass, **will the man who's saved countless lives lose the only one that's ever mattered to him?**

AUTHOR'S NOTE & INSPIRATION BEHIND THE STORY

I'm not going to lie. The inspiration behind CRASH was so emotional, it took me years to process the trauma enough to write about it. **Don't worry—the book is light and fun, and you will LOVE Doctor Blake Morrison, the obsessed hero who will burn the world to save Tessa.** But the heart of this story? It was born from terror.

In 2021, we plunged into a nightmare. First, a loved one went from healthy to dying within two weeks, and, get this...the doctors had NO IDEA WHY. I watched helplessly as he slipped through the cracks of a well-meaning system, and while his life was ultimately saved, our family was about to face another devastating medical mystery.

That same summer, **my healthy five-year-old suddenly lost control of his body. Convulsions. Swelling. Unbearable pain. Every day brought new symptoms, new fears, and we were bounced from doctor to doctor like a pinball. Meanwhile, he was deteriorating before my eyes,** and I cried myself to sleep every night, consumed by a mother's worst nightmare.

What if he never got better? What if he couldn't go to school, have a normal life? What if this was terminal, and they didn't figure it out in time?

I rolled up my sleeves and became a medical detective. Obsessively researching, losing sleep, spending every waking moment hunting for answers while waiting for the next appointment. But he kept getting worse.

I pinned all my hopes on a well-rated pediatric neurologist. This was it. This was our answer.

But when we finally saw her, she didn't listen to a word I said. "Something is wrong," I insisted. "Really wrong. His body is under attack." **She dismissed me with a wave of her hand. "I think your son is just an emotional child."**

That night, I hit rock bottom. I cried until I had no tears left, and then I prayed.

I begged God to take my son's illness and give it to me instead. **I prayed for just one doctor who would listen,** who would take this seriously, who would dig deep enough to find the truth.

And then... one did.

Weeks later, we got the call that changed everything. "I know what's wrong with your son," he said. "He has a rare genetic disorder. It's not curable, but it's treatable."

Within days of treatment, my son's body stabilized. The convulsions stopped. The swelling disappeared. He still has ongoing medical issues and will be on this journey for the rest of his life, but today, he's thriving in sports and living his best life.

But the experience haunted me. **As I shared our story, every single person had either lived through something similar or knew someone who had. This desperate hunt for medical answers, this struggle to be heard and believed, was a shared human experience that needed light shed on it.**

CRASH was born from that darkness. It's a fun read, but there's true heart behind every page. I hope you see yourself in its story, and I hope it reminds you that sometimes the most powerful thing we can do is refuse to give up.

. . .

P.S. CRASH contains content that might be triggering for some readers. For a full list of triggers, please visit my website at Kathy-Lockheart (dot) com.

To anyone who has ever navigated the labyrinth of medical uncertainty— whether seeking answers for life-altering conditions, fighting to validate symptoms, or simply searching for the diagnosis that remains just out of reach.

For those who've sat in sterile waiting rooms, collected folders of test results, and walked away with more questions than answers.

This is for you.

May you find a reflection of your journey in these pages and remember that your experience is real, your struggle is valid, and

your story matters.

You are seen.
You are heard.
You are not alone.

1

TESSA

Of all the ways to start my day, crashing to the ground and subsequently knocking myself unconscious wasn't what I had in mind. But little did I know, that in T-minus five minutes, that physical pain would be nothing compared to the emotional gut punch that was about to saunter back into my life. All six foot three of him, with his infuriatingly hypnotic muscles carved by unfair gods, a jaw that could start religions, and the kind of dominant energy that had the power to spontaneously combust every pair of panties within a five-mile radius.

Not that my brain was aware of any of that right now. It was too busy trying to reboot itself from my impromptu meeting with the sidewalk. Current status: rebooting basic human functions. Name loading ... 47%. Species identification ... 23%. Dignity recovery ... failing to launch.

My eyes flew open. Big mistake. Fluorescent lights stabbed my retinas with the enthusiasm of a thousand tiny assassins while some sadistic gremlin with a pickaxe played demolition derby inside my skull. The antiseptic smell burned my nostrils as voices floated around me, growing clearer by the second while a blurry room slowly sharpened into focus. Gray walls. Heart monitor. IV stand. Each detail a confirmation of my horrifying realization:

I'm lying in a hospital bed.

God Almighty, please no.

"Welcome back." A woman wearing navy-blue scrubs and a disheveled bun materialized before me. "I'm Amy. You're in the emergency room. Do you know your name?"

It took me a second to answer, on account of me mentally cataloging every embarrassing thing I could have possibly done while unconscious. The list was disturbingly long.

"Tessa Kincaid."

"Do you remember why you're here?"

Because apparently, the universe likes to get itself a huge bowl of popcorn and laugh as I twist in agony.

"Um ..." I closed my eyes, willing the fragments of memories to assemble into something less mortifying. "I was talking with a friend. Got lightheaded and ..." Right, then came the *I don't feel so well*, followed by my not-so-graceful descent into unconsciousness. "I ... fainted. Kind of." Not fully, but then the concrete slab smacked into my skull in the most unladylike landing, and, well, that finished the job.

The rest came in snippets. Muffled voices swimming above me. The wail of sirens. My body swaying in what felt like a boat in a storm but had to be an ambulance. My brain serving up consciousness with all the clarity of a drunk GPS, until one thought hit harder than that damn sidewalk:

"Which hospital is this?" I tried to keep my voice from non-shrieking level, like someone who hadn't spent the last two years actively avoiding one specific emergency room in Chicago.

The city had dozens of hospitals. The odds that the EMTs would've brought me to his were astronomical.

"Mercy Harbor," she answered.

F my life.

Calm down. This is fine. It will be fine.

Hospitals were big, and the chances of *him* being here, today, tending to this exact emergency room patient... Those had to be about as likely as me winning the lottery while being struck by lightning during a shark attack.

Right?

Nurse Amy focused on the monitor, her experienced fingers dancing across buttons with practiced precision as she repositioned a blood pressure cuff around my arm, which squeezed like it was trying to extract a confession.

"I'm going to recheck your vital signs and ask you a few questions, okay?" She placed a pulse oximeter on my right index finger. "Do you have any allergies?"

Only to good luck and sensible life choices, apparently. Side effects include spontaneous business failure, romantic disasters, and ending up in my crush's ER at my absolute rock bottom.

"No."

"Medical conditions?"

"No," I lied, the word sticking in my throat like old gum. I'd gotten good at that particular lie over the last year, and as for today's fainting episode, I preferred to follow up with my normal doctor about this. Not give this woman an excuse to keep me here any longer than legally necessary.

My phone buzzed with a message from my client, probably wondering why their wedding planner hadn't called them back this morning. But the wedding that could either save my business or sink it completely would have to wait until I convinced the nurse to let me go.

"Look, I haven't had any water today. I'm sure that's all this is."

"Do you faint often?"

"No," I said, channeling the same convincing tone I used when assuring a mother of the bride that rain on the wedding day was good luck. "I've never fainted before. Really, I'm fine."

She smiled, but didn't budge. "Dr. Hansen will be in shortly to examine you."

My shoulders dropped in relief when she said, "Dr. Hansen."

Not Blake. Maybe the powers that be were finally calling off their vendetta against me.

A movement caught my eye through the doorway: an elderly man lying on a gurney in the hallway, his weathered face drawn with pain, making my own discomfort suddenly feel trivial. Rationally, doctors and nurses knew better than I did about urgent care priorities, and it was probably presumptuous to interfere, but I couldn't relax until I knew he wasn't being overlooked.

"Nurse?" I called out softly. "Is someone checking on that gentleman in the hall? He looks like he needs help."

She gave me an appraising look, but, perhaps sensing the sincere worry in my tone, nodded and returned minutes later to assure me he was being well cared for, just waiting on next steps.

Only then did I let myself breathe easier.

Just as my muscles started to unclench, however, I heard it. His voice. That deep, rich baritone that had haunted my dreams for years. Outside my room, it rolled through the emergency room like a coming storm, my stomach performing a gymnastics routine worthy of an Olympic medal.

"Tessa." A redheaded female without a single wrinkle on her alabaster skin entered my ER room, white coat pristine against navy scrubs. "I'm Dr. Hansen." She glanced at my chart, then at the monitor. "How are you feeling?"

"Better." *Lying. Definitely lying.* "Ready to leave actually."

Dr. Hansen's exam went by in a blur of questions and vital checks while my body remained hyperaware of every shadow passing by the door, every echo of that familiar voice. My phone buzzed again with probably the tenth call from my client. At this rate, I'd not only lose their wedding, but my entire business. Still better than—

There. A flash of dark hair that was unmistakably his. Short, professional, but a little longer on top, imperfectly perfect. Lucky for my dignity, he had his back to me, but even that view sent my pulse skyrocketing.

Dr. Hansen's eyes narrowed at the monitor. "Are you feeling anxious?"

Only about the fact that the man who's starred in every romantic fantasy I've had since I was sixteen might walk through that door.

Oh, and as a bonus, he might discover the secret I've been hiding for the past year.

"Just ... eager to get back to work." I forced a smile. "Important client."

"Well, your pupils are equal and reactive, no signs of neurological deficit, and your speech is clear." She looped her stethoscope back around her neck. "But given the loss of consciousness, I'd like to get a head CT, just to be safe."

"How long will that take?" *Please say five minutes. Please say I can escape before—*

"Not long. And if the scan comes back normal, we should be able to discharge you."

First good news all day. I could do this. Hide in this room until the results came back, then execute a strategic escape that would make Navy SEALs proud.

"The attending physician will be in shortly to complete your exam."

Every organ in my body attempted to relocate itself. "I thought you were my doctor?"

"I'm the resident. Protocol requires the attending physician to examine you as well."

"Is that really necessary?" *Like, legally necessary? Constitutional-rights necessary? Geneva Convention necessary?*

"He can examine you while we're waiting for the CT."

He. Not she. My pulse quickened into a drumbeat of apprehension.

"Don't worry; it shouldn't delay your discharge."

Yeah, that wasn't exactly my concern here. But before I could ask which attending was assigned to this particular room, she disappeared, leaving me alone with my mounting dread.

I stared at the ceiling, mentally drafting my petition to the universe for a mercy rule. Like I needed another masterclass in humility right now. Between my failing business, my train wreck of a love life, and this mysterious health situation I'd been hiding, surely, I'd maxed out my quota of life lessons.

The thing about rock bottom though is that it looks deceptively solid until life decides to break out its jackhammer.

I could sense the disturbance in the force before it arrived. Like a wave, attention rippled through the space outside of my room with nurses pausing mid-conversation, casting hungry glances as they tracked a figure walking this way. Even the male staff reacted, straightening their postures as if the man's mere presence demanded a higher standard. The soft knock that came next might as well have been that jackhammer striking concrete.

The door slid open, and there he stood. Dr. Blake Morrison, somehow looking even more devastating than my memory had allowed. His dark hair was still that perfect mess that made my fingers itch to run through it, and his white coat did nothing to hide the athletic build underneath. But it was his eyes that undid me. Deep brown with flecks of gold, holding mine with a mixture of surprise and something else I couldn't quite read.

The fluorescent lights, hum of voices, and antiseptic smell all faded away, leaving nothing but him, me, and years of unspoken words hanging between us like suspended scalpels.

"Tessa?"

One word. That's all it took for my chest to tremble. He stepped closer, and I caught the familiar scent of his body wash ... the same scent that had tortured me two years ago, when everything had changed.

He glanced at the monitor, then back at me, his doctor's eyes too observant, too careful.

I wasn't sure what was worse: the way my heart still did backflips at the sight of him or the fact that, in about five minutes, he might discover my secret.

Either way, I was doomed.

2

BLAKE

The trauma bay doors burst open with a familiar bang that echoed through Mercy Harbor's ER. Male, mid-fifties, crush injuries from a collision. Another face joining the sixty-eight thousand patients who'd roll through these doors this year. Another shot at beating the seven percent mortality rate that haunted lesser doctors' dreams.

While most doctors hated those odds and, frankly, burned out from the stress of the unpredictable nature of this job, I thrived on the chaos. It kept my mind sharp, my reflexes primed, and challenged me in ways that made every other department feel mundane.

My best friend, Ryker, had once told me I had a savior complex. He hadn't been entirely wrong. Every life I saved in that ER had been an unconscious attempt to make up for that helpless moment when all I could do was watch my little sister's blood seep through my fingers, my untrained hands desperate but useless to help her. The metallic scent of her blood still haunted me in the quiet moments of a shift, but those minutes of powerlessness had changed me forever. Every saved life had become a whispered promise to her: never again. Never again would I watch someone I love suffer while I stood by, helpless.

But there was another side to that coin, one my colleagues with their white-picket childhoods and Sunday school memories couldn't understand. My path to medicine was born in blood, violence, and betrayal. Beneath this white lab coat, I wasn't normal, and sometimes, I wondered if that darkness was just waiting for the right moment to surface again.

"Multiple rib fractures, decreased breath sounds on the left," a resident stammered. "BP's dropping—"

"Push one gram of TXA and start two units of O-neg," I cut in, my hands already moving.

Around me, nurses and residents scrambled to keep up. A woman's hysterical sobs pierced the controlled chaos. Probably family.

"Ma'am, I understand you're worried, but right now, I need complete focus to help him. Jennifer, could you please show her to the waiting room? I promise we'll update you as soon as we can." I kept my voice firm, void of any panic.

Emotions were dangerous in the ER. They could cloud judgment and slow reactions, and in this department, every heartbeat counted. Every second meant the difference between life and death.

The monitors screamed a warning as the patient's oxygen levels plummeted. Other doctors might have hesitated, might have called for consultation, but hesitation killed more patients than any disease I'd ever encountered.

"Chest tube. Now." My tone left no room for debate.

The resident's hands shook as he handed me the kit, but mine remained steady. They had to.

"Vitals are stabilizing," a nurse called out.

I breathed a silent sigh of relief, watching the steady rise and fall of his chest, the beautiful sign that another person would make it home to his family. These were the moments that made the brutal hours worth it. A quiet reminder of why I chose this path.

And soon, hopefully, I'd become chief of emergency medicine, and I'd be able to shape the kind of ER that saved even more lives.

"He should have worn his seat belt," the resident muttered, typing notes into the chart.

I froze, my hands still steadying the chest tube. While I didn't allow emotions to cloud judgment in my ER, I sure as hell didn't tolerate disrespect either.

"See his wedding ring?" I snapped. "That's someone's husband who nearly died tonight. You think he won't wake up hating himself for not wearing that belt? He's facing months of PT, assuming he makes it through the night, and your medical insight is 'should have worn his seat belt'?"

The resident shifted, defensive. "I'm just saying—"

"You're not saying anything helpful." My voice dropped low, controlled. "In this department, we treat patients with dignity. They don't need lectures while they're fighting for their lives. If you can't manage basic human compassion, at least keep your judgments to yourself. Now get out."

"But the chart—"

"I said get out."

I waited until his footsteps faded before turning back to check the patient's vitals one last time.

Outside the room, my cell buzzed in my pocket. Normally, I wouldn't reply to a group text right now. Not even with the men I considered brothers, but the words *brain injury* caught my eye.

SINNERS & SAINTS GROUP CHAT

Axel: Blake, I had a date last night with a woman who I'm pretty sure has a severe brain injury. Need your professional opinion.

Jace: Wait. Axel cares enough about a woman to send a text about her? Someone check the apocalypse schedule.

Ryker: [sends GIF of pigs flying]

Me: What are her symptoms?

Axel: Being attracted to you. Evidently saw you at some charity function and begged me to give her your number. The nerve.

Me: I swear to God, Axel, if you ever use a fake medical emergency to get my attention again, I'll make sure your next hospital visit isn't pretend.

Jace: If you do, make it look like an accident, Blake. I know a good lawyer.

Axel: Someone is so testy before breakfast. Can I give her your number or not?

Me: I don't date. You know that. And even if I did, I'd never take sloppy seconds from you. Managed to live 35 years without an STD and don't care to get one now.

Axel: She's a model.

Me: Don't care.

Axel: A lingerie model.

Jace: Leave him alone, Axel. Some of us have better things to do than collect STDs. Like saving failing businesses. Or in Blake's case, saving lives.

*Axel: *eye roll emoji**

Me: I'm literally in the ER. With actual emergencies.

Axel: Perfect. You're already at work. Can diagnose her terrible taste in men. So, that's a yes then?

Me: I DON'T DATE.

No matter how up front I tried to be with the women I'd casually dated through the years, they always seemed to want more, so I'd given it up.

Axel: Who said anything about dating? Take a page from my book. Never spend the night with the same woman twice.

Me: A page from your book should include an STD warning label. Now excuse me. I'm WORKING.

Ryker: Blake, poker night this week. Don't even think about trying to reschedule again.

Jace: I need to win back last week's losses.

*Axel: The mighty Jace lost at cards. *laughing emoji* Now who needs a medical evaluation?*

Jace: If you miss this week, Blake, I'm buying your hospital. Not just to rearrange your shifts so you can make poker night either. As a bonus, I can name the STD wing after Axel.

Me: I have actual dying people to attend to.

Ryker: Bring them too. They can't be worse at cards than Jace was last week.

"Dr. Morrison?" A nurse materialized at my elbow. "Room seven needs an attending."

I nodded, already stepping through the controlled chaos of the emergency department, expecting to find another stranger whose life hung in the balance. But when I walked into room seven, a set of achingly familiar eyes made my feet stop dead.

Tessa.

3

BLAKE

Tessa Kincaid. My own personal torment since I was a teen, wrapped up in a five-foot-three package of sunshine and sass that had no business making my heart rate accelerate every time she walked into a room.

When I was younger, I told myself I noticed everything about her because that's what outcasts do: we watch from the shadows, cataloging details about the normal people. And in the Kincaid household, no one was more luminously, impossibly normal than Tessa. The way she'd dance through their kitchen, making pancakes at midnight, how her green eyes lit up like she'd mainlined caffeine whenever she talked about her latest passion project. How her small frame moved with a grace that made my hormone-addled teenage brain short-circuit, especially when she'd reach past me for the syrup.

At night, when insomnia kept me company like an unwanted best friend, I'd lie awake, analyzing every interaction. The way my stomach would drop when she'd brush against me ... completely accidentally, because why would Ryker's little sister touch the brooding mess who haunted their couch? The urge to check her room when I heard her come in late, just to make sure she was safe. The way I'd count the minutes until she came home from dates, pretending I wasn't listening for her car.

It was all just ... brotherly concern. After all, the Kincaids had taken in this stray when my own home became a war zone. It was natural to feel protective. Natural to want to murder any guy who made her cry.

So what if I'd memorized her laugh like a favorite song, or noticed how her hair caught the sunlight just so, or the precise shade of pink her cheeks turned when she was embarrassed?

The dreams I sometimes had about her were clearly just my subconscious taking the whole guardian role too seriously. And that white-hot rage when guys tried their luck with her? Pure big-brother instinct. Had nothing to do with wanting to shatter jaws when they made her smile in ways I couldn't. And if I happened to accidentally break the nose of the quarterback who tried to pressure her at homecoming? Well, he shouldn't have been standing where my fist was going.

Tessa was family, nothing more.

Even if, sometimes, late at night, in those moments between sleeping and wake, my mind wandered to dangerous territory, Ryker was my best friend, and I wouldn't do anything to jeopardize that.

Plus, Tessa deserved far better than me. She deserved someone who didn't have more issues than a medical journal, someone who'd kept my darkest skeletons hidden from her.

When I found myself having to remind myself of that, after I'd almost crossed a line, I decided to put some space between us. Two years of silence hurt like hell, but it made it easier to sell myself the brother-sister story.

But now, here she was in my ER, somehow more beautiful than my memories had preserved, making me realize that two years of distance hadn't done a damn thing to stop these unwanted thoughts of her.

I had less than thirty seconds to figure out how to be her

doctor without my unprofessional behavior destroying my career, my friendship with her brother, and any chance of Tessa ever talking to me again.

4

TESSA

Kill me now.

I mean, my God. It was cosmically unfair how Blake Morrison kept aging like a fine wine while the rest of us mere mortals just … aged. Those faint lines around his eyes had deepened since I'd last seen him, but in that infuriating way that made him look distinguished rather than older. Like time itself had decided to be his wingman, chiseling his features into something even more breathtaking than before.

And his body. Good Lord. Those dark blue scrubs were fighting a losing battle with muscles that made his teenage self look scrawny in comparison. Which was saying something, considering teenage Blake's body had been the star of approximately ninety-eight percent of my high school daydreams. Okay, fine. A hundred percent. Apparently, Dr. Morrison had found time between saving lives to become camera-ready for a Calvin Klein underwear commercial. Which was just rude. What …did he do push-ups between patients? Curl medical textbooks in his spare time?

Also, why did he have to succeed at EVERYTHING? Successful doctor wasn't enough. He had to go all *ER trauma savior in a sexy white coat* too. His stethoscope was probably made from the tears of every woman who'd fallen in love with him. And who could blame them? Blake had that whole brilliant-doctor-who-looks-like-he-walked-off-a-medical-drama thing going for him.

Not that he noticed. In true Blake fashion, he remained either completely oblivious to his effect on the female population or just supremely uninterested. This was the same guy who'd once asked me, with genuine confusion, why women kept finding reasons to bring him coffee in the hospital cafeteria. As if his face alone wasn't a walking invitation for cardiac episodes.

At least the universe had thrown me one bone today—exactly one—and had waited to stage its hostile takeover of my consciousness until after I'd showered and made myself presentable. If I'd landed in Blake Morrison's ER sweaty from my morning workout and looking and smelling like an armpit, I might have asked them to pull the plug right then and there.

Blake's stormy eyes remained locked on mine, and time ceased to exist. Every stolen glance from our teenage years rushed back—him watching me across my parents' dinner table, that scorching hot August afternoon by the community pool when he'd taught me to dive, his hands gentle on my waist, my skin buzzing beneath his touch. Or that one night by the bonfire, when orange embers danced into the ebony night, and he'd touched my hand, his lips parting like there was something he was working up to saying. Only for the moment to slip through my grasp the second he let go of mine.

Even now, all these years later, he looked at me with that same unreadable intensity. The one I'd spent my teenage years desperately decoding, wishing my brother's best friend saw me the way I saw him.

Back then, I'd told myself him going away to college would cure me of Blake Morrison, that four years of distance would finally shake him from my system. Wrong. Instead, his absence carved deeper hollows. I caught myself searching for him in every corner of my childhood home: the empty chair at Sunday dinners that had been unofficially his, the garage where he and Ryker had spent countless hours tinkering with that old motorcycle they never got running, even the porch swing where he'd sat with me the night before he left, promising to look after my brother at school. When Ryker's calls home were peppered with stories of Blake's latest adventures—the fraternity they'd both gotten into, the parties he'd attended—each word felt like swallowing shards of glass. Which was stupid. What did I want? For Blake to be miserable because he was too busy pining after me to have any fun?

Answer. Yep. Evidently, that selfish desire was exactly what my heart wanted.

Which was when I knew the truth. You don't spend years trying to forget someone who was just a crush. You don't feel physical pain at the mention of their name. Unless they've become part of your DNA, coded into every cell like a genetic memory you can't erase.

Honestly. If humans could choose who to have feelings for, it would make life so much easier. Maybe one day, big pharma could come up with a pill for that.

For people like me, who had feelings for someone who had never returned my interest. Blake had never been interested in anyone that I knew of, though, so I guess that was something. Rejection of all humans, not just me. The guy was massively guarded, to say the least, damaged by a traumatic childhood that he never wanted to talk about with me.

Well, except that one time I walked in and saw something I wasn't supposed to, but I digress.

"*You're* the patient that fainted?" Blake took a step closer, eyeing my monitor with worry.

"Not fully." Man, look at me go. Faking a smile, putting on my camouflage that had taken years to perfect. The one that said, *No feelings here.*

As Blake stepped to the edge of my bed though, it was hard not to notice the small silver scar cutting through his eyebrow.

When I was a teen, I would have known the story behind it. He would have crashed on our family couch, feet propped on the coffee table, telling us how he got it while Mom fussed over him with an ice pack. Now that scar was just another reminder of how much of his life had become a mystery to me. Another chapter in a book I wasn't allowed to read anymore.

"Does Ryker know you're here?"

I rolled my eyes. "I'm a thirty-three-year-old woman, Blake. My big brother isn't my keeper."

"Dr. Morrison."

"What?"

"I go by Dr. Morrison."

I smirked. "That's such a flex."

And then ... oh God ... there it was. That rare Blake Morrison smile, the one that made time stop. It was infectious, melting away some of the tension, making me remember the boy who used to sneak candy bars into my hospital room when I had my tonsils out.

"You did it," I said softly, a surge of pride warming my chest. "You're a doctor."

"This isn't the first time I've seen you after medical school."

Classic Blake, dodging praise like it was a physical attack. He'd always been allergic to compliments, as if accepting them might jinx everything he'd worked for.

"But this is the first time I've seen you in your natural habitat." My eyes wandered around the space, taking in the scene and the way he seemed to belong here. "It looks good on you."

Wonderful. My cheeks just incinerated, and his gaze was—yep—glued to them. Maybe he'd write a paper titled "The Curious Case of the Perpetually Blushing Patient."

"Tessa, we can catch up later." His tone shifted into that no-nonsense doctor voice that probably made interns quake in their shoes. "Right now, I need you to tell me about your head injury. When did it happen? How? Where?"

I fought an eye roll. The resident had clearly told him my skull wasn't split open, or I'd already be trapped in some machine with Blake hovering over the controls like an overprotective helicopter pilot.

But before I could answer, another nurse appeared, and I watched in fascination as Blake Morrison gave a practiced flick of his wrist, causing the nurse to retreat like she'd been caught stealing cookies from the break room.

The moment the door shut, he leaned against the wall, crossing those arms that strained against his white lab coat in a pose of pure authority. This wasn't my brother's best friend anymore; this was Dr. Morrison, the man who commanded one of the most prestigious ERs in the country.

"Tell me what happened," he pressed, his voice softer now, but no less commanding.

Okay, I could do this. One final interrogation, and I'd be free. The fainting was nothing. Just a classic case of me versus gravity, a battle I'd been losing my entire life whenever I stood up too fast. Nothing to do with my medical mystery at all.

But if Blake caught even a whiff of something wrong? God help me. He'd turn into a medical bloodhound, complete with the stubborn determination and inability to let things go. He'd want to start from scratch, consulting every specialist with a pulse, ordering tests I probably couldn't even pronounce.

Yeah, no. Not happening.

I'd already sacrificed a year of my life to this mystery. Watched my bank account hemorrhage even more money into medical bills while my client list shrank faster than a wool sweater in hot water. Hell, the stress of it all had even cost me my relationship. Though, honestly, good riddance to Eli and his WebMD obsession.

If something was seriously wrong with me, surely, one of the seventeen doctors I'd seen would have caught it. Instead of, you know, patting me on the head and telling me all my tests were fine while practically shoving me out the door.

I'd finally made peace with having a slightly defective body. Like a car with a weird rattle that mechanics can't find. Annoying, but not deadly. And I refused to let go of the control I'd fought so hard to reclaim over my life.

One teensy problem with my brilliant plan: stress had a way of making my symptoms throw a party. A very unwelcome, very noticeable party.

Like the wave of nausea currently throwing a rager in my stomach.

"So, you fainted." Blake's voice carried that same authoritative edge he'd used on the nurse, only now it was laced with something else. Concern? Irritation?

I swallowed hard against the rising nausea, plastering on my best this-is-totally-normal smile.

"I skipped breakfast and, well ..." I shrugged like I was discussing the weather. "People faint all the time."

"Not you." The words shot out like bullets. "Ryker's told me about every scraped knee and broken bone since you were ten. Never once mentioned fainting."

My heart stuttered. He remembered my medical history? But of course he did. Dr. Blake Morrison probably filed away medical details like other people collected baseball cards.

"First time for everything," I managed, aiming for casual and probably hitting somewhere around guilty teenager explaining a curfew violation. "But I've always gotten lightheaded whenever I stand up too quickly."

He paused, and I could practically see him rifling through his mental file cabinet.

"Has it gotten worse?"

"Look," I blurted out, suddenly desperate to escape those too-observant eyes. "I appreciate the concern, but I only came to rule out a concussion. I'm fine. Really."

Blake's jaw clenched, a muscle ticcing there that I definitely wasn't staring at. Not at all. After a few seconds, he pushed off the wall with grace, checking my monitor with a slight edge to his brows.

"Blood pressure's low."

"Always has been." *Please, just let me go. Don't look at me like that. Like I'm a tantalizing puzzle you're determined to solve, piece by maddening piece.*

"Could explain the lightheadedness."

Yes! He's totally buying there's nothing to see here! Almost home free.

"I'm going to examine you now."

The stethoscope slid from around his neck, and suddenly, Blake was leaning so close. The scent of his probably organic body wash did all sorts of unwanted things to me. The cold metal pressed just above my left breast, and I swear my treacherous heart skipped a beat.

Don't think about his hands. Don't you dare think about how many times you dreamed of him touching you. Just pretend the simple act of listening to my heartbeat doesn't feel more intimate than any first date I'd ever been on.

He glanced at the screen again, a flicker of ... something ... in his eyes.

"Your heart's racing."

Great. Now my feelings were literally being broadcast to him in high definition.

"Yours would be, too, if someone shoved cold metal on your chest," I quipped.

"Sit up."

His hand wrapped around my shoulder—warm, solid, confident—guiding me forward. That simple touch sent a flash of heat searing across my skin, and I silently cursed whatever twisted karmic event I'd done to deserve having him as my doctor.

"Deep breath."

I inhaled shakily, and because, apparently, I enjoyed torturing myself, I looked up. Bad idea. Catastrophically bad idea. His mouth ... God, his mouth was exactly as I remembered from all those forbidden fantasies. Soft yet firm, the bottom lip slightly fuller than the top, the kind of mouth poets wrote sonnets about and artists immortalized in marble.

Our eyes locked, and I felt the air between us shift, growing heavy with unspoken tension. Heat flooded my cheeks as recognition flashed across his face. He'd caught me staring at his lips like a woman starving for a taste, not a patient awaiting a diagnosis. Time stretched between us as his smoldering gaze dropped to my mouth, lingering there with an intensity that made my breath catch. One heartbeat. Two. Three. Until Blake finally cleared his throat, the stethoscope finding its way back around his neck with hands that weren't quite as steady as before.

Blake's eyes raked over my body, a frown tugging at the corners of his sinful mouth. "You look like you've lost weight."

"Stress." I shrugged, trying to play it off as no big deal. "And I need to do a better job of eating three meals a day."

Lies. The truth was, nausea had infected my life. It appeared with no rhyme or reason, and while I was lucky enough to not actually worship the porcelain goddess on a daily basis, the persistent queasiness had definitely done a number on my appetite. Hence the weight loss that apparently only Dr. Observant here had picked up on without so much as glancing at my chart.

Wait a minute ... my medical records ... would he have the authority to pull up all of my medical records? From all the doctors I had seen?

"Those circles under your eyes. How long have they been there?" His gaze narrowed, clinical assessment battling with something far more personal, more intense.

I shrugged. "Bad night's sleep. That's all."

"Insomnia?" He arched a skeptical brow.

"Try running a start-up." *Please, stop looking at me like that, like you can see right through me.*

Blake turned to the computer, his frown deepening as he scrolled through my chart.

"These tests aren't telling me why you fainted. I want to see the results of the CT scan."

Panic clawed at my throat. "Am I showing signs of a concussion?"

"No."

"Then I'd like to be released." I tried to keep the desperation out of my voice, but it clung to every word.

His head tilted to that dangerous angle I remembered all too well, the one that meant Blake was gearing up for a fight he had no intention of losing.

"Tessa, you could have cracked your skull open. We're finding out why this happened, end of story."

"Blake, I don't need more tests. I need Gatorade and a nap."

"You hit your head." His voice dropped to a low growl that made my skin prickle with awareness. "This isn't up for debate. We need to run tests to find out why this happened."

Tests. More freaking tests. Something snapped inside me, frustration boiling over.

"I've already had a CBC, comprehensive metabolic panel, thyroid function tests, iron studies, and cortisol levels checked. Everything's normal. I'm fine." The words tumbled out before I could stop them.

Blake went utterly still, realization dawning in his eyes like a slow-motion car crash. The brilliant doctor in him was connecting dots I'd worked damn hard to leave scattered.

"Why would a doctor order extensive endocrine workups and stress hormone panels on an otherwise healthy thirty-three-year-old woman?"

Crap. "She's just ... very thorough. Likes to cover all her bases."

His expression softened, concern etching into the lines around his mouth. "Tessa, you can trust me. If something's wrong, if you're sick or in trouble—"

"Nothing's wrong," I bit out through clenched teeth. I straightened my spine, channeling my best take-no-prisoners boardroom voice. "With all due respect, Dr. Morrison, I appreciate your concern, but right now, you're my physician, I'm your patient, and I'm formally requesting to be released. Immediately."

The transformation was subtle but instantaneous. Shoulders

squaring, jaw tightening, eyes hardening. Clearly, the formidable Blake Morrison wasn't accustomed to having control wrestled away from him. Several tense heartbeats passed before he spoke.

"Fine." The single word carried the weight of a thousand reluctant concessions. "One final test. Stand up and walk a few steps. Show me your balance isn't compromised. Then, and only then, will I release you. Provided your CT doesn't come back concerning."

Relief flooded my strained muscles, sweet as honey, but guilt followed close behind. I hadn't meant to be so harsh with him, to push him away when all he wanted was to help. Maybe I could make it up to him sometime. Grab a beer, shoot the breeze, do something normal people did. Not people with complicated histories and unspoken secrets.

I swung my legs over the bed's edge, feet finding linoleum.

"I'm sorry," I offered quietly, taking my first tentative step toward him. "I didn't mean to be such a ru—"

Oh crap. Houston, we have a problem. Namely that my head had suddenly transformed into a helium balloon, the room was tilting sideways at a decidedly alarming angle, and the edges of my vision were bleeding to inky-black-like watercolors in the rain.

I tried to turn around and make a desperate reach for the safety of the bed, but my rising panic only made the dizziness worse.

I'm going down. I'm going to face-plant on this unforgiving floor and shatter my nose, and Blake is going to have to stitch me back together like human Humpty freakin' Dumpty.

But suddenly, strong arms caught me mid-fall, and the world dissolved into disjointed fragments: the solid warmth of his broad chest, the steady thrum of his heartbeat against my flushed cheek, the gentle sway as he lifted me effortlessly, and the soft creak of the mattress as he laid me down gently.

"Tessa?" His voice cut through the encroaching darkness, urgent and achingly familiar.

Light crept back in, and when I finally managed to pry my

eyelids open, I caught the exact moment his relief transformed into something fierce and furious and protective.

"That's it," Blake snapped. "You just earned yourself a full workup and an overnight stay for observation." His jaw hardened. "With me."

5

BLAKE

"I want a CBC, metabolic panel, thyroid panel, pregnancy test, EKG, and get that damn CT scan of her head already. Pending the results, I may add an MRI." My voice was steady, practiced. Clinical. It had to be. The alternative was letting my control tremble. "Pull her recent labs." Labs that you don't run unless you suspect something is wrong with the patient, so what was Tessa hiding? "Page cardiology for a consult. Heart's always a prime suspect with fainting."

The intern's fingers stopped typing. Even before he spoke, I could see the question forming. The same questioning look I'd given attending physicians a lifetime ago, back when I thought I knew everything. Funny how life beats that out of you.

"Dr. Morrison, if I may?"

I pinched the bridge of my nose. Teaching future doctors was exhausting, and today of all days, I didn't have the patience for it. Today, when my past was lying in a hospital bed down the hall.

"Go on," I allowed, though every second spent explaining was a second not spent solving whatever Tessa was going through.

"Her symptoms could be explained by dehydration or low blood sugar. Is there a specific reason we're running such an extensive workup?"

"I'm thorough," I said defensively. Too defensively. *Control yourself, Morrison. You're not some green resident anymore.*

"Right, but hospital leadership has been—"

"Pushing back on unnecessary labs, I know."

Insurance companies had become a thorn in the hospital's side, declining to cover a chunk of services rendered. Doctors and patients were getting caught in the crossfire, but I wasn't going to let Tessa suffer because of bureaucratic red tape. Not her. Never her.

And, yes, I was painfully aware this could damage my shot at chief of emergency medicine. The position I'd sacrificed everything to earn. The board was watching every move, every decision, every dollar spent. One wrong step now could derail years of careful planning. But even with my career hanging in the balance, I couldn't stop myself from ordering these tests. Some things matter more than promotions.

"Our patient has fainted twice today. One of those episodes caused her to hit her head. Next time, she could be driving a car into oncoming traffic, risking her life *and* the lives of everyone on the road. It's imperative we get to the bottom of what's going on here."

I forced myself to look at her chart instead of the memory seared into my brain—the way she'd collapsed into my arms, pale as a ghost. The way her body had gone limp ... I don't think I've ever moved so fast in my life.

How long had Tessa been suffering? She'd lost weight since the last time I'd seen her ... weight she didn't have to lose. Her cheekbones were sharper, shoulder bones shooting out of her shirt like warning signs. Those dark circles under her eyes ... how long had she been fighting this battle alone? The Tessa I knew never fought alone. She was the one who'd sit with me during med school study sessions, forcing coffee and encouragement down my throat in equal measure.

My stomach clenched. I remembered her as that lively, bubbly girl who'd chase away everyone's shadows with that ridiculous laugh. Even now, sick as she might be, she was trying to mask it, probably not wanting me to worry. Always taking care of everyone else.

"Add orthostatic vitals," I added. "Let's see if there's a blood pressure drop with position changes. And check troponin levels to rule out cardiac ischemia."

"You're taking this one personally, Dr. Morrison." The nurse's chipper voice stabbed my eardrums.

Her knowing smirk said she thought this was some poignant moment, when the Grinch's heart grew three sizes. If she only knew how many times I'd let my heart grow, only to have it carved out of my chest.

"She is my best friend's sister. That's all."

And now she was my patient. I couldn't get emotionally attached to a patient. Not again. But how could I stay detached when it was her? This was Tessa.

Tessa, who'd left cookies outside my door during high school finals week. Who'd never once looked at me with the pity I saw in everyone else's eyes. Who somehow always knew when to push and when to let me be.

My anxiety began to wind down as the intern keyed in the last orders while I made fast work on another screen, trying to pull up any labs this hospital might already have in its system.

I wasn't normally on edge like this, but when I'd walked into the room and seen her lying in my ER, my heart had dropped into my gut. The only thing that kept me calm was knowing the resident had already examined her without raising any red flags. Still, I'd scanned her body from head to toe, noticing every detail that was slightly off. The way her hands twisted in the sheets—a nervous tell she'd had since high school. The exhaustion in her eyes that makeup couldn't quite hide.

The intern was probably right. The fainting spell was probably related to dehydration or low blood sugar, and I was probably overreacting. Probably letting old ghosts cloud my judgment.

Speaking of ghosts. One of my interns, Collins, was hiding in the corner. Again.

I sighed as I walked up to him and put my hand on his shoulder.

"Follow me."

6

BLAKE

I tried to ignore my buzzing pager as I guided Collins into an empty office. The harsh fluorescent lights highlighted the exhaustion in his young face. God, had I ever looked that young?

"I know you care about your patients," I started, choosing my words carefully. "But this is the second time this week I've found you crying in the halls."

"I'm sorry," he mumbled.

"This job is hard," I assured. "But you need to find a way to manage your emotions. If you can't, you might not be cut out for this. This might not be the right career path for you."

His shoulders rolled back, a look of offense rolling over him. "What else would I do?"

"You could consider research or pathology. Or even anesthesiology."

"Those specialties don't interest me. I want to work with patients."

"Your patients rely on you to stay sharp and focused."

"I am."

"Crying in the halls is not focused," I reasoned.

Freaking hell. The kid's waterworks reactivated right in front of me, tears welling up in his eyes like some kind of emotional sprinkler system. My hand twitched toward his shoulder before I caught myself. Comfort wasn't my strong suit, and it wouldn't help him in the long run. Instead, I shoved my hands into the pockets of my lab coat, ignoring the familiar ache in my chest that came with watching another bright doctor learn this lesson the hard way.

Collins looked at the floor, shoulders hunched. "I'm sorry."

"Look, I get it. Every case hits hard at first. But you need to find a way to channel that emotion, or it'll burn you out. The best doctors don't allow emotions to cloud their judgment."

"I'm an excellent doctor." His attention snapped to my face, a spark of defiance in his wet eyes.

"You are," I agreed. "But you're getting too emotionally attached to patients and their families."

He blew his nose, the tissue crackling with snot and awkwardness. "He just graduated college, and his dad—"

My pager buzzed again, and this time, the vibration seemed to travel up my arm and into my skull.

"All patients are important, Collins. Moms. Dads. Brothers. Sisters. Only children, the only living caregivers to someone who needs them. None of that changes how we practice medicine. We give each patient the best medical care we can."

He wiped his eyes with the same booger-laden tissue. Had the kid not attended Harvard Medical School and taken the course on germs and fungus?

"What if I don't want to be like you?" His voice found its strength and apparently he found his balls, too, based on his tone. "You're known as the Iceman."

"And my survival rates are among the highest in the department because of it."

Another buzz against my hip, the pager alerting me that a car accident patient was inbound.

"You're the most emotionally detached doctor I've ever met." He flung the accusation at my face like his job didn't depend on attendings like me.

"Somehow, I doubt that."

"Not all of us want to live that way."

"You have to maintain a detachment from your emotions." *The moment you care is the moment you fail.* "Emotions compromise your clarity. Distance keeps you sharp."

"You shell out medical information like a computer, completely detached."

For a moment, I saw myself in Collins's determined stance, in the way he was fighting to hold on to his humanity in this brutal profession. But that path led to disaster. I had the scars to prove it.

"And you need to do the same."

He took a deep breath, his spine straightening. "I respect you, Dr. Morrison. Tremendously. But I believe there's a better way to be a doctor."

Offense shot through me like a bolt of lightning. How dare this junior doctor disregard his superior's advice and have the audacity to suggest he had some for me?

"You have a point, so spit it out, Collins."

"May I speak freely, Dr. Morrison?"

"If this wasn't you already speaking freely, I'm quite intrigued by what the hell is about to come out of that mouth of yours."

His nervous gaze flickered back and forth like a trapped animal. "With respect, sir, I don't think you understand what it's like for the rest of us. You've probably always been hardwired differently."

"I learned the hard way, Collins. And this is me, trying to help you, but if you have it all figured out and don't want to hear it, then by all means, get on with your shift."

Pivoting, I strode toward the door.

"It's not easy for normal people!" he snapped.

The hairs on my arms prickled. Did my subordinate just yell at me? I turned, assessing his half-angry, half-panicked face. He was clearly aware that he'd crossed a line, but there were his emotions again, bubbling into tears.

And that's when all patience I had left finally snapped.

"You think it was easy?" My voice came out harsh. "I started just like you—caring too much, letting myself get invested." I paused, the memory still sharp enough to draw blood after all these years. "And you want to hear how that worked out for my patient?"

He wiped a tear from his cheek.

"When I was on my surgical rotation ..." I stopped, my throat suddenly dry. The memory of that day lived in my muscles, so I turned to the window, using the excuse of checking the ambulance bay to gather myself. "There was this sixteen-year-old girl who presented with broken ribs that punctured her spleen." The image of her young face crashed over me like a wave of ice water. "Now, I'd seen this sixteen-year-old a week prior, with a different sports injury, so I became particularly invested in her case."

My pager screamed against my hip.

"When it was time to operate, I was thrilled when they let me scrub in. Thrilled when I was allowed to handle part of the procedure myself, but do you want to hear what happened?"

Based on his swallowing, he could see where I was going with this.

"Emotion clouded my judgment. I wasn't fully present in that operating room because I was imagining her distraught parents and boyfriend waiting anxiously, imagining what I'd say to them if we couldn't repair all the damage and salvage her sports scholarship. So, my hands shook. And before anyone could stop it, I punctured an artery. She bled out."

The words suspended in time, my fingers curling into fists at my sides, fighting the emotion of that moment. The image and sounds of that girls' parents in the waiting room, crumbling into shrieks.

The hospital review board investigated the case and found evidence that the artery was supposedly compromised in the same accident that brought her in, so they cleared me, but I knew the truth. My emotional attachment diminished my focus. And from that moment, I vowed to keep an emotional distance from all patients because that detachment made me a better doctor. Empathy was a dangerous vulnerability that could cost lives.

"I ... I didn't know."

"Well, now you do," I said. "So, come on. We have a fresh patient inbound. You think you can keep your emotions in check long enough to help this one?"

Sometimes, I wondered if the greater forces of life—the ones the patients often talked about—liked to mess with me. Because after that speech I just gave Collins, the alarm that sets every doctor's soul on edge blasted through the emergency room. That horrible, mechanical screech that meant someone's world was ending.

"Code blue. Room seven."

My heart stopped as the room number registered.

Tessa.

7

BLAKE

I bolted down the hallway, my normally measured stride—the one I'd spent years perfecting to project calm confidence—replaced by frenzy. Every step felt like my heart might burst through my chest. The lights streaked overhead like shooting stars, each step echoing against sterile tiles with the sound of a countdown I couldn't afford to lose. Time warped around me, stretching and compressing with each ragged breath.

Not Tessa. Please, not Tessa.

At the nurses' station, my composure—the mask I wore like armor—crumbled further, my hip catching a computer screen, sending it crashing to the floor. Staff members called out, their voices a distant buzz beneath the roaring in my ears. I caught fragments of their concern—"Dr. Morrison?"—but couldn't stop. Wouldn't stop. I took another corner at full speed, my hand gripping the doorframe, and burst into the room that had become my waking nightmare.

The sight stopped me cold. The room was already chaos, with a nurse performing chest compressions on Tessa's too-still form while another squeezed the bag valve mask over her blue-tinged lips. The monitor's accusatory flatline pierced the air like a blade.

A lifetime of moments flashed through my mind in the space

of a heartbeat. Tessa's infectious laugh around a bonfire, understanding my obscure jokes when no one else did. Her small hand covering mine after my first med school rejection, her unwavering faith in me stronger than my own.

"You're meant to save lives, Blake," she'd said then.

I never imagined I'd be trying to save hers.

"I'll take over," I said, my voice cracking. Something that hadn't happened since residency. The nurse stepped back, and I positioned my hands on Tessa's sternum.

One. Two. Three.

Don't die, Tessa. Not you. I can handle almost anyone else, but not YOU.

Tessa's delicate frame jerked with each compression.

Ten. Eleven. Twelve.

Come back to me.

Twenty-eight. Twenty-nine. Thirty.

First cycle complete. How had only thirty seconds passed when it felt like years?

One. Two. Three. Four.

Don't make me tell Ryker his sister died under my watch.

Eight. Nine. Ten.

I should have checked on you more. Should have noticed something was wrong. Should have ...

"You will not die, Tessa. Do you hear me?" My voice betrayed me, rough with emotion I never allowed myself to show.

From the corner of my eye, I caught the startled glances between nurses—Dr. Morrison, always in control, now fighting back tears as he fought for a life.

"Fight, Tessa! I need you to fight for me!"

Twenty-nine. Thirty.

Sixty seconds. Protocol said two minutes of continuous compressions before checking rhythm, but each second stretched like an eternity. She should be back by now. Why wasn't she back?

One. Two. Three.

Stay with me, Cupcake. Please stay with me.

"Doctor!" The nurse's voice cut through my spiral just as the most beautiful sound I'd ever heard filled the room.

Beep. Beep. Beep.

I lifted my hands, every muscle in my body tense as I pushed my fingers to her artery, feeling a pulse, my eyes burning with the threat of tears.

I willed that rhythm to continue. If she crashed again—

Tessa gasped, the sound like music. Her eyes fluttered open, disoriented but alive. So gloriously alive.

"Tessa ..."

The nurse stepped back, giving us space as Tessa's chest rose and fell on its own. Everyone and everything vanished into a black hole, and all that remained was this: her breathing, her pulse on the monitor, her eyes struggling to focus. Like watching a butterfly emerge, fragile and beautiful and miraculous.

My own heart thundered against my ribs, my breath coming in short gasps that had nothing to do with physical exertion and everything to do with the fear slowly unclenching from my chest.

When her eyes finally found mine, they were filled with confusion. But they were open. They were seeing me.

"Blake?" Her voice was barely a whisper, scratchy and uncertain. "What happened?"

I pressed my forehead to her bed for a moment before pulling it back up and fixing her with a stare.

"Your heart stopped."

And mine nearly stopped with it.

8

BLAKE

"FUCK!"

The medical chart hit the wall of the on-call room, papers scattering like confetti. Not professional. Not doctor-like. But for one goddamn minute, I needed to not be Dr. Morrison. Not when my hands were still burning from the feeling of her lifeless body beneath them.

I slammed into the bathroom, bracing my hands against the sink, watching water spiral down the drain. My hands wouldn't stop shaking. Years of medical training, countless hours in emergency rooms, and I'd never felt this unstable after a code.

The last time I'd felt this helpless, I was seven years old. My sister, Faith, was five, and we were at our grandmother's house while our parents finished their holiday shopping. The kitchen had been warm, filled with the sweet scent of chocolate chip cookies and the sound of Faith's giggling. I could still see her, perched on her step stool, chocolate smeared across her cheek, oblivious to how our world was about to shatter.

Then the doorbell rang.

Some memories blur with time while others carve themselves into your bones until every detail haunts you. I can still see the police officer removing his hat, that slight tremble in his fingers telling me something was wrong before he even opened his mouth, the way his Adam's apple bobbed before he spoke. Then came Grandma's hand flying to her chest and that animal howl she made before collapsing, her heart giving out right there on her foyer floor with the news that her daughter, my mother, would never come home again.

That was the last day my parents' hearts had beat. The last day my grandmother's heart had beat too.

And now, Tessa's heart had stopped. On my watch.

My stomach began churning, like it hadn't been trained to be unaffected by ER traumas.

The reason I cared this much was because she was Ryker's family ...

Right?

I splashed cold water on my face, trying to wash away the image of her lying there, lifeless on that gurney. The cardiac monitor's shriek still echoed in my ears with that terrible, continuous tone that meant someone you cared about was slipping away.

I couldn't think about how, for sixty hellish seconds, I'd been that helpless seven-year-old boy again, watching someone I cared about slip away.

But Tessa's heart was beating now, and I would be damned if I let anything stop it again.

I couldn't save my parents. Couldn't save my grandmother. But I could save Tessa.

I had to.

Because the alternative was unthinkable.

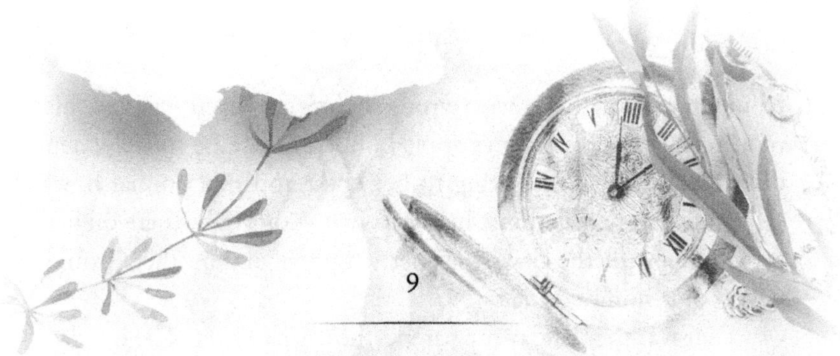

9

BLAKE

"She needs to be admitted to the ICU!" The words came out harsher than I intended, echoing across the busy nurses' station, where phones rang and monitors beeped in their endless symphony of emergency medicine. I wasn't normally this disrespectful to the ICU attending physician, but the image of Tessa's lifeless form was still too fresh, too raw.

Dr. Calloway adjusted his wire-rimmed glasses. "Dr. Morrison, I don't need to remind you that this hospital has strict criteria for ICU-level care, and this patient does not meet it."

"She was in cardiac arrest."

He planted his hands on his hips, regarding me with the kind of impatience reserved for difficult residents. As if coming down to examine Tessa had been a waste of his precious time. The second he finished his cursory exam, he'd shipped her off to a regular floor while I stood here, fighting for what she needed.

"Briefly," he emphasized. "Her pulse and breathing immediately returned to normal ranges. Her heart rate, blood pressure, oxygen saturation are all fine. As was her 12-lead EKG. Her arterial blood gases and cardiac enzymes all showed signs of stability. Her pregnancy test was negative, ruling out any pregnancy-related complications."

"Doctor—"

"Your patient is stable now. ICU beds are for patients requiring active life support. She'll receive careful monitoring in a normal room."

"Her heart stopped. I will not take the chance it will stop again." *I will not lose her.*

Calloway's eyes narrowed, his head tilting slightly in irritation. "You've never challenged my judgment on an ICU admission with such persistence before."

"She needs to be monitored. This is a healthy woman with no obvious explanation why her heart stopped." This wasn't just another case file or set of vital signs. This was Tessa. Flesh, blood, and years of memories.

"We've ruled out seizures and stroke. To be safe, we'll investigate cardiac arrhythmias, like atrial fibrillation, ventricular fibrillation and bradycardia, but it's also possible that dehydration, electrolyte imbalances, or hypoglycemia caused her issues."

"The statistics of this being a simple electrolyte imbalance are slim. She's a thirty-three-year-old otherwise healthy woman."

"Is she?" Calloway's tone shifted. "It sounds like this patient's had extensive blood testing recently. That's not typical for a young woman. Has she told you why she had that blood work?"

My jaw clenched so hard it ached. He had me there, and we both knew it.

"Right. Well, get your patient's full medical history. If she deteriorates, page me."

The dismissal in his tone as he walked away ignited something primal in my chest. My palm slammed against the counter, the crack splitting through the ambience of the ER. Nearby nurses jumped, their wide-eyed looks barely registering. Nothing could make this moment of helplessness worse—

"Tessa Kincaid?"

Every muscle tensed at the sound of an unknown male voice saying her name. My focus snapped to the other end of the counter, where a man stood. Mid-thirties, athletic build, expensive watch. Something territorial coiled in my gut.

"They told me she was in room seven, but it's empty?"

"She's been admitted," the nurse began. "She's in room—"

"I'm Dr. Morrison." I cut across the space between us before she could finish. "And you are?"

The nurse's eyebrows shot up at my tone. The stranger turned, all casual confidence and concerned expression.

"I'm Eli. Is Tessa okay?"

Eli. In all my years of knowing the Kincaids, I'd never heard of an Eli. Sounded like a name for a goddamned snake, if you asked me.

"You family?" I challenged, knowing damn well he wasn't. I knew every Kincaid, every shared holiday, every inside joke.

"No, I'm, uh ... her boyfriend. Well, ex-boyfriend."

My tongue swept harshly along the inside of my teeth.

"Did she call you?"

"The hospital did. I'm her in-case-of-emergency contact."

"Ryker is her emergency contact." The words came out automatically, but even as I said them, doubt crept in.

His head tilted back. "You know Ryker?"

A protective surge flooded my system, followed by something darker, something that felt dangerously like loss. When had I let myself drift so far from her life that I didn't even know this basic fact?

"I'll ask again. Why are you here?"

Every cell in my body perked up, ready to remove him if necessary. I might have lost the ICU battle—for now—but I would die before I let anyone who might cause her stress near her. Last I checked, ex-boyfriends had the word *ex* in front of them for a reason.

"He *is* listed as her emergency contact," the nurse confirmed quietly.

The words twisted in my ribs like barbed wire. This stranger had replaced Ryker as her most trusted person? When had that happened? How had I not known? I'd convinced myself keeping my distance was right, was what she needed. Now I realized I'd let her slip away entirely.

"Are you her doctor?" Ex-Boyfriend asked.

"I am." *And unlike you, I'm not going anywhere.*

"They said she fainted? Hit her head. Is she okay?"

Like hell I was sharing her personal information with this guy.

"Does this have to do with how sick she's been?" he asked.

The question stopped me cold, a jolt of adrenaline rushing blood to my ears until I could hear nothing but his voice.

"Sick?" I repeated.

"She didn't tell you?"

"Tell me what?" The words felt barbed, tearing at my throat.

"Tessa's been sick. Really sick. For a year."

10

TESSA

"I'm going to murder you." I glared at my best friend, Scarlett, as she entered my private hospital room.

She looked too beautiful to be among the sick and injured, with her long blonde hair cascading over her shoulders, a figure most women would go into debt for a chance to achieve, and green eyes that sparkled, unfazed by my dark sense of sarcasm. If anything, it made her smirk. Confirmation I was alive and well, I guess.

"I'm going to murder you, then bring you back to life, just so I can kill you again."

Our friendship operated on its own frequency where casual death threats translated to *I love you, but you just seriously angered me*, and we both knew the difference.

Scarlett plopped down in the corner chair with an eye roll, the leather squeaking beneath her. The sun streamed through the windows, casting everything in that strange hospital glow that made even the pristine white walls look institutional. The room itself was nice—nicer than some hotel rooms I'd seen—with its gleaming floors and state-of-the-art equipment, softened by abstract paintings in soothing blues and greens. But it was still a hospital room.

"Oh, I'm sorry. What's the proper protocol when your bestie's eyes roll back into her head like she's having an exorcism and she goes all rag doll on the sidewalk?"

"Let me have a mini coma," I reasoned, trying to ignore how the heart monitor's sticky pads pulled at my skin with every breath. "Always let me have a mini coma."

"Why are you being so weird?" Scarlett motioned around the room with a twirl of her finger, her silver bangles catching the light. "Obviously, doctors were worried enough to admit you, so it seems to me the words you should be hunting for are *thank* and *you*."

I adjusted the scratchy hem of the stupid hospital gown, the material crinkling like paper.

"Sorry," I said. "Thank you. I just ..."

My thoughts trailed off. It wasn't fair to be this rude to her. She did what any good human would've done when she called 911. And in fairness, I not only fainted again, but also suffered brief cardiac arrest. As soon as she heard that though, I knew Scarlett was going to launch into a lecture.

Scratch that. Based on the look on her face, the one I'd seen every time she caught me minimizing symptoms this past year, she was about to launch into a lecture right now.

"Look, I know you want to move on," she started. "But maybe this all happened for a reason. Maybe this is the universe's way of saying you have to keep fighting because if you don't know what you're up against, how do you know it won't kill you?"

Yeah, not the best time to tell her my heart stopped.

For the record, I wasn't taking the whole heart-stopping thing lightly. The memory of coming back to consciousness, of seeing Blake's face tight with worry, haunted me. Of course I was worried why my heart stopped; that's why I allowed myself to be admitted and tested ad nauseam by a cardiologist. And I would follow up with my primary care physician or said cardiologist after this to address any lingering questions about the strength of my heart, but as for my medical mystery, I wasn't having this conversation with Scarlett again.

At least being admitted meant Blake would hand me off to someone else. Despite growing up with him constantly at our house—my brother's perpetual shadow—I knew surprisingly little about hospital hierarchy. But he was ER, which meant once they moved me upstairs, I'd be someone else's problem. Cardiology or internal medicine. I didn't care which. Just ... not him. Not those careful eyes that had watched me as a teen, now trying to diagnose what was wrong with me. The universe owed me that much.

"I can't imagine ever winding up in the back of an ambulance again, but if I do, please at least tell the EMTs to take me to a different hospital," I added gently.

Scarlett's attention swept around the pristine hospital room. "What's wrong with this one?"

On cue, Dr. Blake Morrison ambled into the room, his white lab coat—I swear—looked somehow even more formfitting than before. So did his scrubs. In fact, his thigh muscles decided now was the perfect time to bulge against the fabric, competing with the broad plane of his chest and flatlands of his abs.

"Oh ..." Scarlett mouthed far too long, her right eyebrow threatening to arch.

"You just said that out loud," I chided.

"Right. Sorry." She stood. "You look like a very ... er, good doctor."

The microscopic hint of a curl to one side of his lips preceded Blake clearing his throat.

"I'm Dr. Blake Morrison. It's nice to meet you."

"Blake," Scarlett balked, her eyes bouncing to mine. "*The* Blake?"

"Scarlett ..."

Now she full-on smirked. And the little devil didn't even try to hide it. Instead, she eyed him up and down with a fresh holy-crap, mouth-drooling mannerism, then came over to "whisper" a goodbye into my ear.

"No wonder you wanted to stay in a coma."

"Goodbye, Scarlett."

She smiled, ambling out of my room with the wave of her hand. "I'll be back, Tessa. I'll bring you dinner, and you'll bring me details."

Look at her saunter out of here. I could see her mentally compiling a list of interrogation questions for later.

Great. Just great.

If my heart hadn't stopped, I'd walk out of here right now, but cardiac arrest had a way of keeping you planted.

"We need to talk." The edge to Blake's voice made me freeze.

Oh crap.

"Did my tests uncover something?" Was it something bad all along, and all those other doctors had been wrong?

"Tests thus far have been unremarkable."

Unremarkable. A word I'd heard so many times before. I wondered if med schools taught doctors terms to replace *the tests came back normal so I don't know what the hell is happening with your freakish body* to make it sound more scientific.

"Then what's with the funeral face?" I asked.

He stepped toward my bed and stared down at me the same way he'd done when he told me he'd been accepted into a medical school that would make family visits much less frequent.

"Why didn't you tell me you've been sick for a year?"

11

BLAKE

"Why didn't you tell me you've been sick for a year?"

Tessa's eyes widened, but not with guilt. With something worse. Fear. The kind that made my medical instincts scream that I'd missed something critical. And, God help me, I should have seen it sooner. The slight tremor in her hand as she adjusted the pulse oximeter, the way she subtly shifted to hide her discomfort, the shadows under her eyes. All classic signs I should have focused on more before her heart stopped.

My pager shrieked. Emergency room. Of course. But the residents were capable of first assessments.

I couldn't remember the last time hot tears had pricked the backs of my eyes like this. The tightening in my throat, the heat flashing through my chest ... these weren't sensations I allowed myself to feel anymore. But watching Tessa lie there, knowing she'd been suffering while I remained oblivious ... I deserved this pain.

Every symptom she must have experienced, every test she'd endured, every doctor who'd, according to Eli, dismissed her. These weren't just medical facts anymore. They were my failures. Each one a time stamp of when I should have been there, when I should have noticed, when I should have helped.

Because I was the one who'd stopped answering texts, who started missing her family's holidays. Who created this distance between us, all to protect her, though she'd never know the real reason why.

"When did the symptoms start?" I pressed, but a nurse entered with medications, the door whooshing open on pneumatic hinges.

"Dr. Morrison, pharmacy has questions about—"

"Not now." My voice carried an edge that made the nurse pause, the IV bags in her hands swaying slightly. Before she took the hint and left.

"What?" Tessa clutched her sheet to her chest like armor, as if cotton threads could shield her secrets from my medical scrutiny.

"You've had extensive blood work." I moved closer, desperate for answers. "Why—"

The sound of footsteps entering turned the question to dust in my mouth.

"Tessa!" His voice struck my spine like a reflex hammer as Eli—the alleged ex-boyfriend—bulldozed his way into her room. The sharp scent of his expensive cologne corrupted the sterile hospital air as he went right to her side like he belonged there. Like he had the right.

I watched his hand grip hers, saw his lips press against her forehead, noted the obvious intimacy in their shared gaze. Each gesture felt like acid in my veins.

A quick glance at the monitors showed her heart rate stabilizing at his touch, and that observation hit harder than any kick to the ribs could have.

"God, I was so worried when they called me," Eli said, and the genuine concern in his voice made it worse somehow.

I assessed him with clinical detachment. Or tried to. How long had they dated? What did she see in him? Based on what I could see, he was nothing special. Not even close to what she deserved.

"I'm fine." Tessa offered him a weak smile and patted his

hand. A gesture I'd seen her give me a hundred times before, back when I was the one she trusted.

I wanted to snap his fingers off.

"How did you know I was here?" she asked.

Another sound joined the chorus of music notes, this one warning of a low IV bag that needed changing. Just one more interruption in a day full of them.

"In case of emergency," he replied.

The IV pump's alarm grew more insistent, its digital display flashing red.

"Oh ... right." She gripped the sheet tighter with her left hand. "I forgot to change that. I'm sorry."

"Don't be." Eli swept a fallen hair off her forehead with the casual intimacy of someone who'd done it a hundred times before.

My own hands twitched, remembering how she used to fall asleep during movie nights, her head on my shoulder, and I used to sweep her fallen hairs back into place.

"I told you, I'll always be here for you. Always."

The way he said it—it sounded to me like maybe he was the one who broke up with her. What kind of a moron would let someone like Tessa go? Then again, who was I to judge? I'd preemptively done the same thing, albeit for different reasons. The reasons that kept me awake at night.

"If you'll excuse us," I cut in, my doctor voice sharp enough to slice, "I was about to complete an exam." *And find out what the hell has been going on this past year.*

"Doctor," Eli began, "you have to help her." His voice cracked with an edge of fear as he snapped his focus to me. If his fear wasn't about Tessa's health, I'd have rather enjoyed it.

"Eli—"

"I thought you were getting better," he added.

The words choked me with their implications. Better? Just how sick had she been?

"I was." Her voice was small, defeated in a way I'd never heard before. The sound made my ribs threaten to splinter.

When I watched him pull up a chair to her bedside, his palm settling on her arm with casual possession, the room became an inferno.

This was the arm of a girl who used to be the epicenter of my own personal snow globe, the two of us warm and safe inside our bubble while the world spun outside. I knew her favorite food—mac and cheese with extra breadcrumbs—how she liked to sprinkle cinnamon across the whipped cream on her hot chocolate, and the way her eyes lit up when she found a new romance novel. I knew she hummed when she was happy and went quiet when she was truly upset. I knew her.

Or I had. Now, with absolute crushing, heartbreaking clarity, I stood on the outside of her snow globe, watching this stranger occupy the space I'd willingly abandoned.

The irony wasn't lost on me. I'd stepped away to protect her, only to leave her unprotected when she needed someone most. If I hadn't pushed her away ... I could have helped her.

What if it's too late?

"Please," Eli pleaded. "Someone has to get to the bottom of this. She can't go on like this."

"Eli ..." Her voice wavered. Another tell I logged away. Fatigue? Fear? Both?

"No, you have to keep fighting, Tess."

Tess. I wanted to shock his heart for using that term of endearment.

"I need to examine her." I moved to the bed, removing my stethoscope with an edge that made Eli finally seem to get the message, assessing me, then Tessa.

"Oh, right ..." Standing up, he added, "I'll be just outside, okay?"

His lips pressed to her forehead again, lingering a moment too long.

I wanted to cut his lips off with a ten blade. And something about the gesture set my teeth on edge too. A nagging sense of unease that I couldn't quite shake. Was he having trouble letting her go? Was she afraid of him?

Once he finally left, I turned my attention back to her, and that's when I saw it.

A jagged line on her skin that would change everything.

12

TESSA

"Where'd you get this scar?"

Blake's thumb trailed over the white line on my collarbone. The one so faint that I'd managed to hide it from my brother and family for years. But today wasn't a casual family gathering with the blessing of distraction. Today, I was being examined.

Closely and intensely.

Not ideal for someone harboring a secret since nineteen. Yes, a different secret. A bigger one really. God, could I catch ONE break? Managing my medical mystery was draining enough brain power without Blake excavating that buried chapter of my past.

"I forget."

The moment those words left my lips, his expression darkened.

"It's not from a car accident," he said. "Your brother would've told me."

Uh-oh.

"When can I leave? I really need to—"

"And if it were a simple accident, a fall or something, you wouldn't be twisting your fingers right now. You only do that when you're hiding something."

My pulse stuttered. "I do not."

"I spent nearly every afternoon at your house, watching you, Cupcake."

Cupcake. The pet name he'd called me for years, providing no explanation for where in the world it came from. Normally, that name made me turn into a puddle of goo, but I had bigger things to think about right now.

"Three failed history tests. Three times you twisted your hands in your lap when your parents asked about grades."

Teenage Tessa would've melted at those words—*every afternoon, watching you*. Probably would've filled pages in her diary about how Blake Morrison saw her—really saw her—in a way no one else did.

But adult, secret-keeping Tessa recognized this for what it was: a ticking bomb waiting to explode.

"Tessa." Blake's voice yanked me back.

No way could I sell my cover story to an ER doctor trained to read injuries. The whole Tessa-versus-concrete-stairs tale wouldn't hold up to his scrutiny. Only long gaps between college visits had kept this scar hidden when it was fresh.

"How much longer until I can leave?"

"Dodging only confirms what I'm starting to suspect." His voice rumbled with something dangerous like the sound of a predator scenting blood.

"My *extremely* old scar has nothing to do with why I'm in the ER today." I forced steel into my voice. "So, if you don't mind—or even if you do—I'd like to get on with whatever testing will get me out of here. Please and thank you."

Blake's thumb swept across his lower lip, and when he spoke again, his voice was hauntingly soft, vibrating with barely contained fury. "Someone did this to you."

My stomach plummeted.

"No," I lied, my tone too high-pitched to be believed. "No one did this to me. Now, about those tests ..."

His attention dropped to the floor, jaw working. After a few seconds, his gaze snapped back to mine, a terrifying current radiating from him, like the charge before a storm.

"I'll find out who did this to you," he vowed with a silent threat lacing his words.

13

TESSA

Heat crept up my neck as Blake stood there, looking at me with those damn eyes like he had the right to know all my darkest secrets.

"You don't get to do this," I said, my voice quieter than the storm building inside me.

Two years of swallowed words rose up like bile in my throat. The gentleness in his touch, the way his fingers had traced my scar, the way he made me feel like that scar was all that mattered to him. It was everything I'd once craved, everything I'd forced myself to forget.

And now, it was all rushing back.

God, I was an idiot. One knock to the head, and I'd let myself forget how this story ended. How many nights had I stared at my phone, watching those three dots appear and disappear as he typed and deleted, typed and deleted, until finally ... nothing.

"Do what?"

"Act like my protector, like you care."

His brows furrowed in unjustified confusion. "I do care."

Yeah, that's what I thought once upon a time too.

Pinching the bridge of my nose, I swallowed down a fresh lump in my throat. I felt like a terrible person. Blake just saved my life. The right emotions were to be nothing but grateful and kind to him, but my heart disagreed. It kept a record of every slight, every silence, every moment I'd waited for him to remember I existed.

"I thought so too," I said. "But turns out, I was someone you could just discard."

He recoiled as if I'd slapped him, hands clenching at his sides. His eyes searched mine, confusion and something deeper darkening his features.

"Tessa, I never discarded you." Something rippled across his face. Pain? Regret? But it disappeared too quickly to read.

"Bull," I said. "And the least you can do is tell me why."

Blake's hand found the back of his neck—his tell for emotional distress. If he thought I was going to break the long, long silence that elapsed? He was wrong.

"Can't we leave the past where it belongs?" he questioned.

Belongs? How insulting.

"No." The word shot out like a bullet. "You don't get to push me away and pretend I never existed without explaining why."

His Adam's apple bobbed, and it took him for-freaking-ever to finally speak.

"Everything I did was to protect you."

A harsh laugh escaped me, echoing off the sterile hospital walls. "Protect me? By blowing me off?"

Something shifted in his expression—just for a heartbeat—but it was enough to make me wonder if there was more to his abandonment than simple rejection. A reason he wasn't sharing.

But if we had any hope of moving forward—and I had no idea if I wanted to move forward, by the way, let alone if he did either—we had to talk about this.

His career, however, disagreed.

His pager buzzed, and the way his shoulders tensed told me he couldn't ignore it. Part of me wanted to grab his arm, make him stay and explain himself. But he was a doctor. Saving lives would always trump my wounded heart.

And the way he kept inching toward the door, like a trapped animal seeking escape, only twisted the knife deeper.

"Just leave," I said.

Blake's chest rose and fell as he appeared to hunt for the right words.

Did he look pained, hurt even? Yeah.

But welcome to the party, Blake.

Then, just like he did two years ago, he did what he did best. He left.

14

TESSA

"You kicked him out?" Scarlett raised her brows, lounging in the corner chair she'd claimed as her territory.

The leather squeaked as she shifted, watching me pick at the dinner she'd brought. My favorite Caesar salad from Giovanni's, the one with extra crispy croutons that usually had me fighting for every bite. The sun was starting its leisurely descent in the sky, painting orange stripes across my hospital bed.

"When you put it that way, I feel like an even bigger bitch than I already feel." The plastic fork scraped against the container.

"Oh, please, you have every right to be upset." Scarlett's bangles clinked as she gestured emphatically.

"Upset, yes. But I didn't handle myself as well as I wanted. I'd always envisioned having a calm conversation about what happened, not some emotional blowout."

I pushed the lettuce around the black plastic container to make it look like I was eating. At least my clients had been cool about rescheduling our appointment today.

Focus on the positive, Tessa.

"How long ago did he leave?" Scarlett checked her rose-gold watch.

"Five hours." Five hours of replaying it all in my mind,

wishing it had gone different. Five hours of anger receding away like a wave and regret taking its place. Five hours of staring at the same spot on the wall where he'd stood.

"You're being too hard on yourself." Scarlett waved her hand, her purple nail polish catching the fading light. "If you ask me, he deserved a verbal beatdown."

Maybe. Maybe not.

"I feel like I just ruined any shot of us being friends." Great. Another lump in my throat. "I still care about him." Greatly. "He's … family and always will be." The admission hung in the air.

"Families fight. I'm sure it will be fine."

I pushed my uneaten salad away, the wheels of the hospital tray squeaking in protest.

It felt like anything but fine. What if that was the last time I'd ever see Blake? If our relationship was going to end completely, I wanted it to have gone differently.

"I doubt he'll ever speak to me again." The words choked out in absolute despair. A complete contradiction to the nurse's bubbly smile as she practically bounced into the room, her white sneakers squeaking against the floor, clearly unaware of the depressing atmosphere she'd entered.

"Someone sent you a gift." The short nurse with spiky black hair carried a silver gift bag, the tissue paper rustling with each step.

I eyed Scarlett, who held up her palms defensively.

"My gift was the salad and the amazing company."

The bag was cool to my touch, the metallic paper crinkling under my fingers.

Inside was a black coffee mug with white letters that read, *I Came to the Hospital and All I Got Was This Lousy Mug*. Stuffed inside the mug was a single serving of powdered hot chocolate and nestled in the tissue paper was a note.

. . .

Tessa,

You used to love hot chocolate before bed, extra whipped cream with just a dash of cinnamon sprinkled on top. "Life's little luxuries," you'd say, curled up with one of your romance novels.

I hope this makes your hospital stay a little more bearable tonight.

For the record, I NEVER stopped thinking about you. In fact, I had to stop myself from calling you every single day for the last 687 days. You deserved better than my silence. After a thorough self-examination, I've diagnosed myself with Acute Chronic Jerkitis. Recommended treatment plan: Extensive groveling, followed by a lifetime of making it up to you.

Blake

P.S. Ask the nurse for hot water. I remember how you like it scalding hot.

P.P.S. The chocolate is from that fancy place on Michigan Avenue you used to drag me to.

I smiled, a warmth spreading throughout my body that had nothing to do with hospital temperatures or IV fluids. Blake was a very busy doctor, and even if he'd had a break in patients or his shift had ended, he'd taken the time to get me this.

"I don't mean this to sound rude," Scarlett started, her eyes narrowing at the nurse. "But why are you grinning like that?"

"I've just never seen Dr. Morrison smile before."

So, she knew it was him that gave the gift.

"Every nurse and female doctor in this building would donate a kidney to get him to smile at them like he did with you." She smirked.

I blushed. "Well, I'm an old friend."

She patted my leg. "Honey, I don't know who you are, but I've worked with Dr. Morrison for years, and I've never seen him like that with anyone. I don't know who you are to him, but *old friend* doesn't sound like it cuts it."

Then, like some cosmic timing I couldn't have scripted better, Blake edged into the room, his arms hanging uncertain at his sides. The sunlight caught his dark hair, turning the edges almost golden, and for the first time today, his doctor mask was completely gone. In its place was just ... Blake.

My Blake, his voice all deep and dramatic as he said, "Can we talk?"

15

TESSA

"I, er ... have an emergency date with a television." Scarlett stood and patted my shin. "I'll call you later, okay?"

"Thank you, Scarlett. For everything." *For being there, for not judging, for understanding.*

"Don't mention it." She walked off with the nurse, and behind Blake's back, she gave me an exaggerated thumbs-up and mouthed, *Good luck.*

I didn't need luck; I needed a time machine to transport me back to the before. Before I ruined everything between me and Blake. Before I learned how it felt to be carved out of someone's life. Before my stupid heart decided to stop beating in his ER.

Once she was gone, Blake took a tentative step closer, his eyes flickering to the empty chair, a muscle working in his jaw. "Did the boyfriend leave?"

"Ex-boyfriend." I focused on smoothing nonexistent wrinkles from my blanket rather than the way his jaw tightened at the word. "And yes."

He nodded, uncertainty playing across his features, visible in the slight hardening of his chest, his eyes more vulnerable than they'd been earlier.

"You're right. We should talk about what happened between us," he suggested.

I could only hope that talking about everything wouldn't make it worse because the truth was, I couldn't bear to lose him twice. Not today. Not when my body had already betrayed me in the most fundamental way possible.

"I owe you an explanation." His voice dropped low, intimate. "I never meant for our friendship to stop, Tessa. I never stopped caring about you."

He opened his mouth like he was about to launch into some speech, perhaps one he'd practiced multiple times in his head, but his damn pager beeped. Again. He looked at it, his face saying it all.

"Dammit!" Blake said. He looked visibly frustrated, hands sweeping through his hair. "This conversation is too important to rush."

"It's okay," I said, forcing a smile. "Go."

"How about we have coffee when you're discharged?"

I eyed him.

"We can talk without interruption."

"Sure," I agreed.

He reread the page. "I have a few minutes before I need to leave, and we need to go over your medical history. It'll help us figure out which tests to run."

He pulled up the chair Scarlett had vacated, the legs scraping against linoleum, making it clear he wasn't about to take no for an answer either.

I swear, my freaking body could feel his presence, even with my eyes closed. Some kind of current existed in the space between us, pulling me into his orbit, no matter how much I fought it.

"Now, please," he said, sinking down, resting his elbows on his knees as he leaned closer to me, "tell me everything."

It wasn't lost on me: his word choice, how he'd flipped from medical jargon to Blake speak.

“It’s a little ironic, don’t you think?” My lips curled into a sad smile.

“What is?”

“You’ve never wanted to tell me anything about your life. But now you’re asking me to tell you everything about mine.”

He’d never talked about his sister, Faith, or why she’d wound up in a different foster home than him. A different school district, so I’d never even met her. And he never talked about the years of darkness that must have surrounded that chapter in his life.

Would he ever open up to me? It was a stupid question really, one my heart shouldn’t be wondering right now.

His face tightened. “This is different.”

“Is it?”

“Your heart stopped beating.” His voice cracked slightly on the last word. “So, yes, this is very different.”

That was fair. Childhood trauma wasn’t exactly the same thing as listing medical symptoms.

“I’m sure you have more important things to do right now than listen to my medical history. Can’t a nurse get it from me?”

“I prefer to do it myself,” Blake replied.

“Why?”

“Why what?”

“Why *you*? You’re getting paged, you probably have a hundred patients to attend to, so why would you waste time with something as mundane as taking my medical history?”

“Tessa, for nearly two years, I’ve wondered if you were okay. Now I know you weren’t, and nothing else in my life matters until I understand why.”

Heat bloomed across my skin.

“I can’t focus on anything else. I can’t help any other patient. I can’t even breathe right until I know what’s been happening to you.”

Warmth spread to my neck and flooded my cheeks.

“Now, we can dance around this all night, but I’m not going anywhere until you tell me what’s going on.”

Once again, I had to remind my stupid lungs to keep breathing. If I fainted one more time, he'd probably admit me for a year.

"I don't want Ryker knowing about this," I clarified.

His dark eyebrows shot up. "You've kept this from him?"

"That's why I changed my emergency contact. He's not my keeper, but he still acts like he is."

He scratched the side of his face. "Yeah, Ryker would probably set up a medical command center in your living room."

That pulled a genuine smile from me.

"There's another reason you don't want to tell me." Blake eyed my twisting fingers. "What is it?"

It took me a second to find the right words.

"Once people find out that you're not feeling well, it becomes all they see. Every conversation starts with: How's that going? What are the doctors saying? What's the next step? It's like your whole life gets put on hold and these medical questions define who you are."

And if Blake and I had any chance of rekindling our friendship, I didn't want my illness to be the excuse for our speaking terms. I wanted our friendship to be genuine, not reborn out of pity or obligation.

"I found that out quickly with Eli."

Blake's slight flinch at the name didn't escape me.

"He meant well, but his constant questions and passionate opinions about what I should do ..." I trailed off, remembering the suffocation of constant concern that snuffed the life out of our relationship. "Sometimes, you need to compartmentalize. Put the dark stuff in a box under the bed and just ... be normal. Laugh about movies or books. But the minute people know something's wrong, you lose that privilege forever."

Blake's shoulders rose with a deep breath.

"I don't want *you* to look at me differently." My voice came out smaller than intended.

Despite everything, Blake was still my rock. Even through two years of silence, I'd known that if I ever truly needed him, one call would bring him running.

"It's okay to be vulnerable sometimes, Tessa. It's okay to lean on people; it doesn't make you weak."

"Says the man who refuses to lean on anyone. Ever."

His lips twitched. "That's not true. I've leaned on you and Ryker."

"We're the exception to the rule; you never let anyone else in."

And never told us *why*.

"In college, I even made a few more buddies." His attempt at lightness fell flat.

"On accident," I teased. "Ryker made you join that fraternity."

Something dark flashed in his eyes, and suddenly, I could feel the chasm opening around him. The one he always disappeared into when conversations strayed too close to his secrets. But what secrets could he have from college? I thought all his secrets preceded our time with him?

When he cleared his throat and looked down at his hands, I recognized the move like an old dance step. That throat clear was his involuntary SOS signal when conversations threatened to expose too much.

"Tell me everything, Tessa." His voice was gentle but firm, doctor mode sliding back into place like armor.

I paused, the weight of my own secrets pressing against my chest.

Finally, I took a deep breath, feeling like I was about to step off a cliff.

"It started a little over a year ago ..."

16

TESSA

"It started with the flu," I said, fidgeting with my hospital blanket. "The usual symptoms. Fever, body aches, chills, and a cough." I paused, remembering how simple it had seemed back then. "But the cough wouldn't go away, so I went to my primary care physician. She ran blood work, did a chest X-ray ..." I shrugged. "Thought I had viral bronchitis. Said it needed to run its course."

Blake nodded encouragingly.

"But it didn't get better." My voice caught. "My cough wouldn't go away, and then the fatigue came. The fatigue became debilitating like I was going through each day on sleeping pills. Brain fog set in, and I was just so physically exhausted that I couldn't work out anymore. It took every ounce of energy just to get through my day." I let out a bitter laugh. "Eventually, I couldn't even manage that. I'd collapse on my couch the second I walked in the door."

Blake's face tightened, but he remained silent, letting me continue.

"I thought maybe it had turned into a secondary infection, like pneumonia, so I went to urgent care. They ran the same tests, got the same results: blood count normal, chest X-ray clear." I rubbed my temples, the memory of that frustration rising fresh.

"They ruled out strep, Covid, and pneumonia and sent me home."

I shifted in the hospital bed, avoiding Blake's intense gaze. "I started thinking maybe I wasn't trying hard enough to fight it off. So, I bought all these healthy foods, premium vitamins ... you know, doing everything you're supposed to do. Vitamin C, rest, the works." My lips twisted. "It worked at first. I started to feel better, with the chest stuff at least. And the fatigue started to decrease too."

That false hope that it was behind me was cruel.

"A few weeks later, the nausea and stomachaches started." I closed my eyes briefly. "First, I blamed the new vitamins. And I stopped taking them. Went back to my old ones. When that didn't work, I quit vitamins altogether, thinking maybe I'd irritated my stomach lining. Just tried to wait it out."

Still leaning forward in his chair, Blake repositioned his elbows on his knees. I could see him processing everything with his doctor's mind, but his eyes ... they held something else. Concern? Guilt?

"I just didn't feel right. I started getting headaches and itchy skin."

"Itchy?"

I nodded. "Started taking an antihistamine, figuring I must be getting into something I was allergic to."

"Did it help?"

"It did. With the itching. But then the stomach pains got worse. When my heart started feeling like it was beating too fast, my doctor sent me to a cardiologist."

"What did they say?"

"Heart was fine."

Blake's lips thinned.

"Six months in, my symptoms became more bothersome. I kept having flushing episodes. By that point, I was convinced it was something in my diet since I was still feeling nauseous, so I saw a GI specialist, who said I had some markers of IBS. He suggested a lifestyle change and put me on a special diet."

"Did it help?"

"Not at all."

Blake's hand twitched like he wanted to reach for mine, but he held back.

"You know what that gastroenterologist did?" My voice took on an edge. "In my follow-up appointment, he kept checking his watch, like I was wasting his precious time. When I insisted something was wrong, that I couldn't live my life like this anymore ..." The memory made my ribs burn. "He looked me dead in the face and told me I was just getting older."

Blake's expression stilled.

"I told him he was wrong. That I didn't feel like a woman in her thirties, that I felt like I was ninety-five." I laughed, but there was no humor in it. "He just dismissed me. Told me to go to the ER if things got worse."

I took a shaky breath. "The physical exhaustion, the nausea ... it was taking its toll emotionally. My primary care suggested depression." I met Blake's eyes. "But I wasn't depressed before I got sick. The despair came after. After months of symptoms, after being told everything was normal, after struggling just to get through each day. I saw a psychiatrist to rule it out anyway," I continued. "They agreed with me. The exhaustion and despair were consequences of whatever was wrong, not the cause.

"By month eight, I started having dizzy spells. Especially when I'd stand too quickly. So, my doctor sent me to a neurologist. Who found nothing and suggested it was hormonal, so he sent me to an OB-GYN. Who found nothing and told me I should see a lung doctor since my lingering cough came back.

"Months of being bounced between doctors, all pointing fingers at each other." I blinked back tears.

Blake massaged his hands harshly.

"So, I took matters into my own hands." I straightened slightly. "Tracked everything: food, products, places I went. It was an overwhelming task, and I'd review it every night, every week, but I found no patterns." My shoulders slumped. "I started to worry that maybe my new apartment had hidden mold or something, but then there was about six weeks where I felt better. Started hoping maybe it had just been a virus all along. But then …" I closed my eyes. "Everything came back with a vengeance. My flushing was more intense, sometimes accompanied with a feeling of throat tightening, and I'd have a hard time catching my breath."

My voice cracked as I admitted something I'd never said aloud before. "You don't know how many times I cried myself to sleep. I knew I was sick, and it felt like no doctor believed me."

Blake's warm hand covered my own, his eyes meeting mine. In a deep, tender tone that seemed to reach into my very soul, he said, "I believe you."

My eyes stung. His belief, after a year of dismissals, felt like the first real breath I'd taken in months.

"Why didn't you call me when this started?" The question came out soft, laden with a year's worth of missed chances and what-ifs. His eyes held mine, filled with something that looked dangerously close to regret.

"Because you might have said the same thing every other doctor said. That nothing's wrong."

And of all people to not believe me, I couldn't handle that from Blake Morrison.

Blake's beautiful lips thinned. "Something *is* wrong, Tessa. I would never have dismissed you like that."

The fierce protectiveness in his voice took me back to a hundred different moments: Blake stepping between me and anyone who dared to hurt me, Blake showing up at my door after every breakup with ice cream and terrible movies, Blake's fists clenching whenever someone made me cry. That same protective fire still burned in his eyes, only now it wasn't aimed at high school bullies or boyfriends; it was aimed at every doctor who'd failed to fight for me.

"And all these symptoms ..." Blake's voice shifted slightly, doctor mode tempering his earlier tenderness. "Did you ever have problems with fainting before today?"

I shook my head, watching his expression grow more focused.

"All right, give me one second." Blake left the room and came back, sitting in the chair. "Bought us a few more minutes. Residents are managing that patient." He leaned forward. "Now tell me everything that happened today from the time you woke up until you landed in the emergency room."

I drew a steadying breath. "I woke up at my normal time after a good night's sleep, got ready." My fingers traced invisible patterns on the blanket as I recounted the morning. "Scarlett met me at my place for our prescheduled breakfast date. When Scarlett and I went outside, I dropped my cell phone. I bent down to pick it up and stood up too fast ..." I swallowed hard, remembering the world tilting sideways. "That's when I half fainted."

"Did you feel sick when you woke up?"

I rubbed my temple. "Not today, no."

"So, it came on suddenly?" His brow furrowed together.

I nodded.

His expression changed, like something about that bothered him.

"So, it was acute." He rubbed his jaw. "Odd."

"My whole medical history is odd."

Blake then asked precise, targeted questions, each one making me feel less like a hypochondriac and more like a puzzle he was determined to solve. Finally, he clasped his hands together, his expression settling into something that looked dangerously like hope.

"I'd like to take advantage of you being here for the night," he said. "With your permission, I'd like to order an MRI of your head and chest." He leaned closer, his eyes intent on mine. "And I want to order more labs today to look for markers that might have been missed. I'll consult with some of my colleagues and put a rush on the orders." His lips curved into a small, reassuring smile.

"With any luck, by morning, we'll have some answers as to what's going on."

Peace. It began to settle into my bones.

But the thing was, that MRI was evidently about to come with sedation, thanks to my claustrophobia. Combined with the painkillers already floating through my system, that cocktail would loosen my tongue and unlock the vault where I kept my darkest secret of all.

And if that secret slipped free, it wouldn't just hurt me; it might destroy everyone I'd spent years protecting.

17

BLAKE

"Let's go with 2 milligrams of Midazolam," I said. "Once she's sedated, we'll proceed with the MRI."

Chuck, my charge nurse, gave a professional nod. We'd done this dance countless times, helping claustrophobic patients face their tube-shaped demon. Minutes later, I stood in the fluorescent-lit hallway outside her room, wrapping up a call. Through the half-open door, I watched Chuck introduce himself—his first interaction with Tessa since the nursing shift change—and when he reached up to adjust her IV, Tessa flinched.

Flinched.

Away from his hand.

That flinch set my pulse on fire, every hair on my arms standing on end.

Chuck didn't seem to notice, administering the fast-acting sedative.

But I did. I caught every microsecond of that involuntary reaction. The slight crinkle of her face, the instinctive withdrawal, the sharp intake of breath. Time stretched, and suddenly, I couldn't hear anything over the furious blood screaming in my ears.

I ended the call, forcing myself to breathe while every muscle in my body felt wired, primed for a fight with no target. In fact, I had to count to twenty, just to make myself move into her room without scaring her.

"Blake!" Tessa's voice came out slurred, a loopy grin spreading across her face.

Jesus.

"You look grumpy," she said, words swimming together.

"And you sound like you're feeling no pain." Despite the rage churning in my gut, I nearly smiled.

Evidently, she was adorable when loopy, but that earlier flinch haunted me.

Flinching meant history. Flinching meant someone had taught her to expect pain. Was it the same bastard who'd marked her collarbone?

"They'll be here to bring you to the MRI soon," Chuck said, excusing himself.

"Come closer." Tessa patted her hospital bed.

I shoved my hands deep in my coat pockets, hiding their angry tremors as I approached. My fingers itched to trace that scar again, to decode its story.

She blinked with the exaggerated care of the heavily sedated.

Note to self: Tessa was a lightweight.

"Can I tell you a secret?"

I studied that damning scar. "I'm counting on it."

"Back in high school, I thought you were the hottest guy I'd ever seen."

She wouldn't remember this confession tomorrow. The medication mix virtually guaranteed that.

"Cupcake, I thought you were the most beautiful girl I'd ever seen."

Her eyes went wide. "You did?"

"Still do."

"I could never get a read on you." She flopped her head sideways, fidgeting with her IV line.

"That boyfriend of yours in high school," I said carefully, "did he hurt you?"

Tessa giggled, waving her hand dismissively. "He was a teddy bear. Couldn't even work up the courage to kiss me."

Jealousy that had been buried in a shallow grave started to unearth itself.

"Then who, Cupcake?" My voice came out rougher than intended. "Who gave you that scar?"

Her smile vanished, glazed eyes drifting to the wall. "I don't like thinking about that."

"Dr. Morrison?" A nurse appeared in the doorway. "They're ready."

"One minute." I held up a hand, not looking away from Tessa. "Answer my question."

She pressed her lips together, stubborn even through the haze.

"The MRI machine is overbooked today. We need to go now."

"One. Minute." Each word came out clipped.

The nurse planted her fist on her hip. Just my luck. One of the few not intimidated by me.

"There's an ICU patient waiting," she pressed. "We need to move."

"A name, Tessa."

But Tessa had retreated into silence. Goddammit.

The nurse wheeled the chair to the bedside, actually shooing me aside as she transferred Tessa into it.

"I shouldn't have gone to that party," Tessa murmured.

I blocked the wheelchair's path, my heart suddenly a battlefield.

"Doctor—"

"Go get whatever damn patient is next. Come back for her."

"That'll take too long," the nurse objected.

"Just give us a couple of minutes," I snapped.

The nurse arched an eyebrow, looking between me and my

patient like she was calculating whether this battle was worth her time. Apparently not.

She spun on her heel with a muttered, "Two minutes," that sounded more like a threat than a concession.

I crouched before Tessa, forcing gentleness into my voice, even as acid burned through my veins. "What party, Cupcake?"

Tears welled in her glassy eyes, and something primitive in my chest howled at her pain.

"I shouldn't have had three beers at a frat house," she whispered. "I knew better."

My muscles coiled tight, bracing for impact.

"He said he wanted to show me his book collection. I knew better than that too."

Every cell in my body went cold.

"Who?" I fought to keep my voice steady. "Who wanted to show you his book collection?"

"It's not like I just met him," she said. "I had class with him. We'd talked before. I thought ... I thought I could trust him."

"Tessa." I brushed hair from her face, touch featherlight. "Tell me what happened."

Her lower lip trembled. "He ..." She looked down. "He pushed me down. I told him no, but he was so strong ..." She sniffled, unable to go any further.

I tilted her chin up with my finger, my other hand fisting at my side. "You don't have to tell me more. But I need his name."

"You don't care what he did?"

I care more than my next breath.

"I won't make you relive that hell. But I require a name."

"He didn't ..." She tugged at my white coat like a child. "A guy mistook his door for the bathroom, so he got interrupted. He hurt me, but he didn't fully ... *you know.*"

"If you think that lessens his punishment, you're wrong. His fate was sealed the moment he touched you."

"I don't want you to see me as damaged goods."

Fresh rage exploded through me. She'd been the victim of

something unimaginable, and now *she* lived with a scarlet letter on her self-esteem?

"Listen carefully." I cradled her face. "Nothing, nothing, could make me think less of you." When she pressed her forehead to my chest, I kissed her crown, breathing in the scent of her. "Knowing you survived this? It only proves what I've always known about your strength. Now. Please. A name."

"Why do you want to know?" She pulled back, eyelids growing heavier.

Damn. Should've gone with 1 mg.

"Police said they can't prove the letters are from him."

I lifted her chin. "What letters?"

She tilted her head. "In movies, they have handwriting experts. How come they can't do that?"

"Focus, Tessa. What letters? Did he contact you after?"

"Are you going to find out why I've been sick?"

I exhaled slowly, trying to find my patience. "Working on it. What's from him? Did he contact you?"

"He was so handsome," she mumbled, playing with her IV. "Could've had any woman. He didn't need to ..." Her lip quivered again.

"Name, Tessa. Give me his name. Now."

Shit. Too harsh.

She tugged at my stethoscope. "Why? Do you think you know him?"

No. But he'll know me tonight.

"One way to find out. Tell me his name."

"Eric Voss."

The name etched itself into my brain like a patient's time of death. A moment where everything after would be measured as before and after.

Eric Voss. I'm going to fucking end you.

18

BLAKE

"Ryker, I need advice," I said into my phone.

"Nothing I can do. Your face will always be ugly."

"Your humor never gets old. Now, I'm serious. For the next minute, you're my lawyer. I just wired you twenty bucks to make it official."

"The hell?"

"I'm about to do something illegal. If I get caught, I need to know my odds. Prison won't stop me, but Knox says it's something I should avoid."

"Blake." His voice sharpened. "What the hell is going on?"

"Can't tell you."

"Then how exactly am I supposed to help?"

"By speaking in hypotheticals."

"I can't defend you without details."

"Fine. I'm going to hurt someone."

"Who?"

"Can't say."

"Then why are you hypothetically going to hurt this hypothetical person?"

"Does it matter?"

"Does motive matter in prosecution? Yes, motive fucking

matters. If you can't tell me who, at least tell me why. Because if a prosecutor can trace the motive—"

"Hypothetically speaking," I cut in, "if someone had attacked one of your family members, would that information fall under attorney-client privilege? As in you could never breathe a word of it? Especially to them?"

A pause.

"Did someone in my family show up in your ER?"

Yes. And lucky for me, my shift just ended, and I have a few hours before Tessa's labs will come back.

"Answer the question," I said.

"Yes, it would be privileged."

"And you'd never be allowed to tell this family member you knew? Because finding out would cause them severe emotional distress?"

His shoes clicked against what I assumed was hardwood flooring. "I won't tell Tessa. You have my word. Now what the fuck is going on?"

"In college, a guy assaulted her."

The pacing stopped dead.

"What did he do?" His voice had gone Batman-level low.

"Don't have all the details." My grip tightened on the steering wheel. "But he hurt her. Bad. Left a scar." Physically and emotionally.

"And you're going to confront him."

"She wouldn't want me to."

"He's in Chicago?"

"Saved me airfare."

"You're leaving now?"

"Already driving."

"Pick me up."

"Why?"

"To make sure you don't murder the guy. You do that, you're definitely screwed."

Unless they never find the body.

"A criminal attorney getting caught doing what I'm about to do would be spectacularly stupid."

"On the contrary. My expertise will be useful. Hypothetically." Something metallic clanked. "Plus, I have a bat."

I put my turn signal on. "I'll pick you up in twenty minutes."

The bastard wasn't home. Four hours of watching his door, imagining every way I could make him pay, and nothing. The disappointment tasted bitter, but maybe this was the universe's way of stopping me from crossing a line I couldn't uncross. Based on how Ryker's fist had become a regular passenger against my car seat, neither of us would've shown much restraint.

The drive home was silent, heavy with all the things I couldn't tell Ryker, and dammit if I didn't feel like shit for keeping this from my best friend. How his baby sister had confessed her darkest moment under sedation. How she still blamed herself. Ryker had the bare minimum—the legal framework he'd need if things went sideways. Nothing more.

Still, the guilt of betraying Tessa's confidence sat like lead in my stomach. She trusted me as her doctor, as a friend, trusted me with a secret she'd kept buried for years. If she ever found out I'd told Ryker ... Christ. The thought of losing her trust made my chest burn.

Worse, if I got her brother roped into something that would land him in prison, she'd suffer more than she already had.

I couldn't allow that to happen.

Wouldn't.

The next time I visited Eric Voss, I'd come alone.

And next time, maybe I'd worry less about landing myself in prison ...

For now, I needed to get back to the hospital and check on Tessa.

19

TESSA

Eli: How are you feeling?

Me: Fine. Thanks for being there yesterday.

Eli: Need anything? I make a mean chicken soup.

Me: I'm good. Though ... did I leave my pink work binder at your place?

Eli: Yeah. Want me to bring it to the hospital?

Me: Being discharged today. Could you drop it at my place? Under the mat if I'm not home.

Eli: Work. Always work with you, Tess.

Me: Don't start.

Eli: You scared the hell out of me yesterday.

*Me: Just a fainting spell. *eye roll emoji* Add it to my list of stellar life choices.*

The typing bubble appeared, disappeared, appeared again.

Eli: Your mom's wrong, you know. About having to choose between your career and ... everything else.

I stared at the screen, fingers hovering over the keyboard.

Me: Can we not do this right now?

Eli: Sorry. It's just ... seeing you like that ... I keep thinking about all the things I should've said.

Me: Eli ...

Eli: Just know I'm here. For whatever you need. Even if it's just someone to bring you more color-coded binders.

20

TESSA

"Morning," I called out as Blake strode into my hospital room, the early morning sun dappling through the window.

My half-eaten breakfast of scrambled eggs and toast sat, forgotten, on the tray beside my bed. The dark circles under his eyes suggested he hadn't slept, and the manila envelope in his hand made my stomach clench.

"What is it?" I sat up straighter, my gaze fixed on the envelope. "It's bad, isn't it?"

His silence spoke volumes. When Blake Morrison was at a loss for words? That never spelled anything good. My throat became unimaginably drier as I watched him stride across the room and sit on the edge of my bed, the weight of his unspoken words feathering across my skin.

"Your test results," he started, then methodically recounted everything he'd run, all the doctors he'd consulted with at the hospital to ensure he hadn't missed anything.

That's when I realized where this was going.

"It all came back normal," I spat, though my anger wasn't directed at him. It was at my body. My biggest traitor, systematically attacking me physically, mentally, and emotionally, skilled at hiding all evidence from medical experts.

"I'm sorry," Blake managed.

"Don't be." I wiped away a tear I hadn't realized was there. "I don't know why I got my hopes up for a hot second that this time would be any different."

Maybe because my heart stopped. You would think that if your heart literally stopped beating, there would be a trace of some goddamned explanation for it lingering in your body for them to find. But nope.

"I'm not giving up," Blake added.

My gaze snapped to his, anger flaring. Again, not directed at him.

"Blake, I really appreciate everything you've done for me. But you've probably run more tests in the last few hours than have been run in the last year combined, and none of them have told us anything."

"Tessa, I know this is frustrating—"

"Respectfully, you don't know." I pushed myself straighter in the bed. "You're a good doctor, and I know there are tons of great doctors out there, but you don't know what this feels like as a patient. You don't understand the catch-22 of enduring a medical mystery." I pressed my palm against my forehead, fighting back tears. "You want answers so desperately, but at the same time, you pray each test comes back negative. You don't *want* Lyme disease or some horrible heart condition. You don't want lymphoma or stomach cancer. But with each negative result, you're another step further from explaining why your body is betraying you, until finally ..." My voice cracked. "You can't decide which is worse: getting a diagnosis that could change the rest of your life or never getting one at all."

Blake moved closer, his expression softening. "Tessa—"

"No, you need to listen to me." My voice trembled, a year of pent-up emotions unexpectedly deciding now was the perfect time to finally explode. "You don't see how many nights I've cried myself to sleep, wondering if maybe I'm imagining things. If maybe this is all in my head. If maybe this is just me getting older." I twisted the blanket between my fingers. "And then having to find the strength to get up and keep advocating for myself, keep insisting something is wrong, only to be told repeatedly they can't find anything."

Blake's eyes intensified. "But one thing has changed, Tessa. Your heart stopped this time." His voice dropped lower. "And the fact that we don't know why should terrify the hell out of you."

"So, you want me to feel afraid? Is that it?"

"I want you to find that fire in you," he said gently. "I want you to get to the bottom of this."

"You don't know what it feels like to have your life completely disrupted by some physical ailment that no one can seem to pinpoint."

"Pinpointing something going on in the human body is much harder than people realize."

"Clearly," I said.

"Tessa, there are thousands of possible explanations, and you have to hear me when I say this: ruling stuff out gets us that much closer to the truth."

"Really? Because from where I'm sitting, none of these tests have ever even pointed my doctors in the right direction. In fact, it feels all compartmentalized. If I have a problem with my skin, they send me to a dermatologist. If I have a symptom with my heart, I see a cardiologist. But no one can seem to put these puzzle pieces together to figure out what the source is, and you know what? After a year of going through this, I have finally accepted that the human body is complex, and mine just doesn't function properly."

"You need to find out why."

"Do I? You have no idea what this has cost me, Blake. Not just the physical pain or emotional toll. Do you know how hard it is to launch a small business when you can't even promise people you'll show up? I have lost clients over this, Blake. I had to spend money on marketing to capture those clients, and then they understandably fired me because I kept missing appointments. As if that weren't financially hard enough, do you know how expensive health care is? My premiums are absurdly high, and so is my deductible. Money I don't have to be spending on this. But more than all of that right now is, I just want to move on with my life."

Freedom—true freedom—was learning to live with this condition. Moving on, even if it didn't have a name.

"And if your heart stops again?" His voice was sharp with barely contained anger, the kind that came from fear. "Damn it, Tessa, you're talking about risking your life!"

"I'm risking my life? I tried everything in my power to get to the bottom of this, Blake. I ran the ball down the field for a year through twists and turns and hailstorms and rocks being thrown in my face, and you're asking me to go all the way back to the beginning. I don't have that in me. And maybe that makes me sound weak. Hell, maybe I am weak. There are warriors who charge on with medical mysteries for years, but I don't have that in me anymore. And that is my choice. If you want to judge me for deciding that I want to move on with my life, go ahead."

"I'm not judging you, Tessa. I'm scared."

"I was, too, for a while. But fear has a short shelf life with me. If there was something dangerously wrong with me, they would've figured it out by now."

"Dangerous? You went into cardiac arrest."

"The cardiologist said I was probably dehydrated and extremely low on electrolytes, which they have supplemented."

Blake's jaw clenched, and he stood up. Started pacing.

"He's coming up with the best hypothesis he can because the truth is, he doesn't know, Tessa! It is not normal for a thirty-three-year-old woman's heart to stop beating."

"I will follow up with the cardiologist. I will wear that remote monitoring thing that he wants me to wear. And if, by some chance, those heart results finally answer the question? Great. But otherwise, I'm done."

"How can you be this reckless?"

Reckless. Was he not listening to a word I said?

"You want to know what happened at my last appointment? I met another patient in the waiting room. She'd been chasing *her* medical mystery for three and a half years. Her cousin? Twelve years." I stopped, hoping that would sink in for him. "For some people, that might be inspiring, seeing and hearing about people with such a strong will that they'd stop at nothing to get answers. But for me? I saw the next twelve years flash before my eyes: spent in doctors' waiting rooms, explaining my symptoms over and over. Going literally bankrupt, just to be told I'm getting older, or hormonal, or depressed. That everything is fine. In that moment, I made a decision. No more. I chose to reclaim my life. I chose to learn to live with the symptoms, just like a lot of people do with medical conditions."

His voice softened as he reached for my hand. "You're not in this alone anymore. That's the other thing that's changed. For the last twelve months, you've been going through this alone, and I'm sorry. I didn't know, but if I had known ..." His thumb traced circles on my palm, sending shivers up my arm. "I would've knocked down your front door and held your hand through the entire process. I would've gotten you the best doctors in the industry on your case, and I wouldn't have accepted no for an answer until we got to the bottom of this."

He squeezed my hand gently. "So, let me take over now. Let me shoulder this burden for a while. Let this become my fight."

"Blake ..." I looked away. "I don't want this to be your fight."

"Let me take this from you mentally and emotionally," he insisted. "You focus on your work and whatever else you want to focus on in your life. All I ask is that if I need to run a test, you let me run it. That's it."

Blake took my chin, tilting it up.

"Let me put this another way." His voice was low and intense. "I will not stop until I get answers. It will become exceedingly more difficult for me to do that without your cooperation. So, have some compassion for me. Cooperate." His thumb brushed my jaw. "I will be investigating this with or without your help because I will not let you drown in this ocean, Tessa. And I can promise you this: I will not rest until I figure out what's hurting you."

I swallowed hard, the intensity of his gaze leaving me breathless. His eyes dropped to my lips, and for a moment, I forgot to breathe. My heart thundered in my chest, a surge of affection mixed with a flicker of fear. Was I just a medical mystery to him? I didn't want to be just a case for Dr. Blake Morrison.

"Even if I considered this," I started, "I wouldn't be comfortable with this going on indefinitely. There would need to be an end date."

He seemed to consider this. "A year?"

I laughed. "I was thinking a week."

"Test results alone can take two. And I might need follow-up testing. Six months?"

"One."

"Tessa."

"One month, final offer."

He let out one deep-ass breath. "Fine. One. Give me four weeks. You go about your normal life. Run your business, go out with friends. Do everything you want to do. Just give me four weeks."

I chewed on my lip, considering his words.

Four weeks. To either find answers or finally close this chapter of my life. And all I had to do was agree to work with the one person who could complicate everything.

I met his gaze, finding both determination and something else there. Something that gave my body a whole bucket of symptoms that had nothing to do with my medical condition.

"Four weeks," I whispered.

His answering smile was both a victory and a promise.

If only I knew the side effects that were about to come along with this ...

21

BLAKE

"Stacy, is it?" I ducked into what had to be the most depressing basement office in Mercy Harbor.

The redhead spun so fast that her glasses nearly flew off. "Dr. Morrison? I mean ... you're actually ..." She fumbled with her frames. "What can I do for you?"

"Heard you're the billing wizard around here."

"I ... manage the department, yes." Her cheeks turned the same shade as her hair.

"Perfect. Need you to look up a patient." I leaned against her desk, pretending not to notice how she edged her chair back. "Tessa Kincaid."

After I spelled it out and rattled off her birth date, Stacy's fingers flew across the keyboard like she was defusing a bomb.

"Here's what I need." I dropped my voice. "Every bill that goes to her address? Show a discount. After insurance, make her portion exactly 1.64%. You'll send the difference to me."

"I ... what?" She blinked owlishly behind those frames.

"The hospital won't lose a dime. I'll cover it. I'll come down each week and pay the bill in person."

The words *in person* did something to her pupils. She turned to her screen, clicking through menus. "We could just zero it out ..."

"No. She'd notice that. Same with round numbers. Trust me, 1.64% is specific enough to make her think it might be legit."

"But won't she still—"

"If she calls to question it? Feed her something about income brackets or insurance adjustments. Pull it off, and there's a bonus in it for you."

The look she gave me was downright predatory. Christ. Maybe I should've specified cash bonus.

"We'll make it work, Dr. Morrison." She practically purred my name.

I straightened, already heading for the door. "Perfect. And, Stacy? This conversation never happened."

Now it was time to run more tests and figure out what was wrong with Tessa.

22

TESSA

"This really wasn't necessary," I mumbled, sinking deeper into Blake's Mercedes-Benz E-Class, trying to ignore how the buttery-soft leather seemed to embrace me like a lover's arms.

The contrast to my own car's torn vinyl seats felt like a metaphor for everything in my life right now: held together with determination and duct tape. In contrast, everything about his vehicle breathed success. From the hand-stitched leather that probably cost more than my monthly rent to the gleaming wood trim that caught the fading sunlight like liquid amber.

The ambient lighting only made the differences between our lifestyles more pronounced. While my car offered two settings—serial killer shadows or police interrogation—Blake's Mercedes painted the world in whatever shade of luxury he desired. The soft glow caught the sharp line of his jaw, turned his dark eyes to midnight pools, and made everything, and everyone, look like they belonged in a world where people didn't have to choose between paying rent and fixing their transmission.

"We've been over this." Blake's fingers flexed on the steering wheel, the movement drawing my traitorous gaze to his forearms. Now wearing fitted black pants and a long-sleeved shirt that clung to every hard-earned muscle, he looked like he'd stepped out of a luxury-car commercial. "My shift ended, and you didn't have a car at the hospital. End of discussion."

"Oh, is it the end?"

He glared at me.

I forced my voice to lose its bite. Not easy, considering the argument we'd gotten into over said ride situation. I called an Uber. He canceled it. I flagged down a taxi. He waved him off.

"You're helping me," I started. "A lot. An important fact that I'm going to take into consideration with the tone of my response."

"Here we go." The corner of his mouth twitched in amusement.

"I appreciate everything you're doing for me. I really do. Major brownie points for taking eighty percent of my blood and passing it around to all your doctor friends to try and identify the defect in my body."

"But?"

"But I want to be very clear where that line ends. You are helping me with my *medical* issues. Not my driving issues. Not my work issues. Medical only. Okay? So, please, don't slip back into your bossy self."

"*I'm* bossy?" His eyebrows tried to high-five his hairline.

"Infuriatingly."

"This from the woman who used to barricade the kitchen and declare martial law whenever you were baking?"

"You and Ryker used to eat all the cookie dough!"

"And threatening my life with a wooden spoon. How'd that work out for you?"

Heat flashed through my body at the memory. He'd grabbed that spoon with a devilish smirk, but I didn't release it, so we locked in a silent battle of wills, our chests nearly touching. With flour dusting his black T-shirt (he knew exactly what that shirt did to me, damn him) and desire making my fingers itch, something shifted between us and the playful banter evaporated into something raw and primal. Blake's gaze dropped to my mouth, and when he stepped forward, the air crackled with possibility. I wanted that kiss with an intensity that scared me.

Cut to my brother yanking that spoon from his grip, shoving Blake back, and giving him a death glare that could have frozen the North Pole. Probably killed Santa and all his elves too. Apparently, we weren't the only ones who noticed the kitchen had turned into a powder keg of sexual tension.

"We're getting off topic. Point is, don't get all bossy on me, Morrison."

His mouth curled again. I swear, he looooooved pushing my buttons.

Shelly McBride's latest text popped up with yet another issue. Who knew wedding planning was less champagne and more battlefields?

"Why do you keep checking your phone?" Blake asked.

"I'm googling *how to escape overprotective men in moving vehicles*. The results are concerning."

"Hilarious. Question remains."

"I missed a meeting yesterday with my client. There's a situation I need to handle."

He seemed to digest this. "Ryker said you started that event planning business."

"Wedding planning," I corrected.

Irony was a wicked witch with a possible vendetta against me. *Thirty-three-year-old woman, who hasn't even come close to finding her soulmate herself, plans everyone else's happily ever after. I should put that on my business cards. Maybe add some tearstains for authenticity.*

"I'm sure your clients will understand you taking a few days off."

I seriously tried not to roll my eyes. "I've burned through a zillion days off this past year in medical appointments and illness alone. Not all of us can afford to miss work anytime—"

"Our heart stops?"

"Swim lane, Morrison. I can't take any more time off work, and I can't afford to lose this client."

My only client.

"Tessa." The way he said my name—soft yet commanding—made my stupid pulse skip. "You need to rest."

"I did. All night. Will have a gigantic fat hospital bill to prove it."

"Yet you look exhausted." His gaze swept over me while I pretended every inch of my skin didn't cheer him on, all shouting, *Look here! Look at me!*

"Turns out, hours of beeping machines and a hovering cardiologist aren't exactly a spa treatment." Plus, my chest still hurt. I got lucky. No cracked ribs from the CPR, but my bones were still yelling at me.

"The cardiologist suggested staying another night."

"When someone *suggests* they add another twenty grand to your already-bankrupt-inducing bill, the choice isn't difficult."

Oof. Blake's face turned into granite.

"Trust me," I assured. "If I thought death was still lurking nearby, I'd be demanding the penthouse suite."

I drew in a steadying breath, wincing at the twinge, which, of course, he noticed. His eyes slammed into my ribs with the same force as chest compressions, and then that sexy mouth of his converted itself into a dash before returning to the road.

"Look, I know you care. And, again, I appreciate everything you're doing. But this—the hovering, the second-guessing, the swooping in to save me from myself—this is exactly what I asked you not to do. I need my doctors to give me the facts, and, yes, I even need your medical opinion. But the final call? That's mine. Can you respect that?"

The muscle in his jaw ticced, and his fingers tightened on the steering wheel until I thought the leather might crack. For a moment, I thought he'd argue. But he released a breath that seemed to carry the weight of our entire complicated history.

"Fine," he said finally, though the word seemed to cost him.

Hallelujah. I could hear the angels singing.

"Thank you."

Blake shifted, his shoulders tensing, eyes darting to me in quick glances.

"So," he said, "do you want to stop at a coffee shop before I drop you off?"

I raised my eyebrows, realizing he was referring to *the talk.*

"*Now*?"

"We agreed to go once you were discharged."

My phone buzzed for the fourth time in an hour. The bride's name flashed across my screen.

"I didn't mean the literal *moment* of being discharged," I clarified, staring at the wedding disaster emails that kept coming in. "And I should probably rain-check that."

"But you said—"

"I know." I rubbed my temple, already feeling the pressure of missed appointments mounting. "And we need to have this conversation. But I've got a panicking bride, and I already missed her meeting yesterday. I need to deal with this crisis, and when you and I talk ..." I met his eyes. "I want to actually talk. No distractions, no checking my phone every two minutes because work is imploding."

Right on cue, my phone lit up again.

"Shelly. Yes, I'm looking into the catering issue right now ..."

The bride's voice trembled through the speaker, panic evident in every syllable as she explained how the caterer was suddenly balking at her menu requests.

"I'll pull up the contract right now. Don't worry; he put this in writing. He can't change it, and we won't let him."

Her grateful sniffles filled the line before she hung up.

Blake's jaw tightened. "Just over twenty-four hours ago," he said, his voice dangerously quiet, "your heart stopped beating. And now you're jumping back into work like—"

"Like I'm running a business that could make or break my entire future," I cut in. "This client could change everything for me, Blake. Everything."

My small business—the one I'd dreamed of since I was a girl and confidently rambled about to Blake, his eyes actually sparking with interest—was on the brink of bankruptcy. That's right. Despite my business skills and meticulous planning, I'd managed to start, run, and drive a business into the ground in less than two years. Currently, I was giving it CPR, and if it died, I'd have to say goodbye to a dream I'd had my whole life. And worse, suffer the massive financial strain of those loans for years to come. Future Tessa would probably be living off ramen noodles well into her fifties.

But this client—this one could change everything. A high-end client, with an influencer list that could bring in years of brides waiting around the block, trying to book me. I would not fail. Period.

Blake's Adam's apple bobbed as he swallowed whatever lecture was brewing, until, finally, he parallel parked in front of my rented townhouse.

That's when it hit me.

"How do you know where I live?" I'd moved here after we'd stopped talking.

Blake unfastened his seat belt with deliberate slowness. "Ryker gave your address to me when you moved in."

"What? Why?"

With casual elegance, Blake slid out of his luxury sedan, came around, and opened my door with old-world charm that felt dangerous in its familiarity.

"Because I asked him for it," he said simply, extending his hand.

See? This was exactly what I didn't want: him to look at me like I was too weak to stand on my own. I shifted out of the way and stood up of my own accord, dodging his hand altogether.

And now, I had to act like I didn't notice his handsome, knowing smirk.

On the sidewalk, Blake's broad frame seemed to curve toward me like a protective wall, his shoulders angling to shield me from the street. When he looked down at me, the height difference between us had never felt more electric.

"Again, why? Why did you want my address?"

"The day we stopped talking." His voice softened. "I made two promises to myself: I'd respect your space, and I'd always know where to find you if you needed me. Ryker's been helping with the second part."

Respect my space? Did he seriously just say that? Did he not remember what happened two years ago?

I should have called him out on it, timing be dammed, but unfortunately, my heart was too busy putting its spotlight on the other thing he'd said. *If I ever needed him.* As in, no matter what, he'd always come running if I did.

My soul danced in celebration at those words. Somewhere in the hospital's data cloud, little blips representing my heartbeat were bouncing across a screen. The electrodes itched against my skin with a constant reminder that my every heartbeat was being monitored, analyzed, and transmitted from the small device clipped to my waistband straight to my cardiologist's watchful eye.

"Well," I started, "thank you for the ride, and for ..." The words lodged in my throat like unspoken promises. How exactly did you thank someone for refusing to let you die? For seeing past your stubborn denials to the truth underneath? "Everything."

"You sure you're okay, Tess?" Blake's worried gaze settled on my face.

I flashed a reassuring smile. "If I feel off, I'll call the cardiologist right away. I feel fine though; you don't need to worry about me."

But I could see that was exactly what he was going to do today, until those lab results came back at least. I opened my mouth to reassure him again, but before I had the chance, life threw a fresh complication at me.

"Tessa!"

God Almighty.

If he found out about my neighbor, Blake would totally overreact ...

23

TESSA

Blake's entire body tensed, jaw tightening as his gaze locked on to my front porch.

"Who's that?" Blake growled.

"Just a neighbor," I assured.

"He's standing on your porch, waiting for you to come home."

"He's harmless," I said quickly. Too quickly.

Blake's dark eyes snapped back to me. "Why do you feel the need to qualify that?"

Damn. "Eli was always bothered by Sebastian, too, but he's just ... well, he has a little crush on me. It's not a big deal."

Blake's voice dropped lower. "People who keep insisting something's not a big deal usually know damn well it's a very big deal."

"Not in this case." I fumbled for my keys. "Now, if you'll excuse me, I—"

"I'm walking you inside."

"That's not necessary."

"This isn't up for debate." The words came out with all the immovability of a mountain.

I bit back a groan. I knew that tone. It was Blake's I'm-not-changing-my-mind voice. Fighting it would be like arguing with gravity. And the last thing I needed was a scene that would make this situation even worse. I just wanted to get inside, shower off the hospital smell, and deal with my latest work emergency before it exploded into something unfixable.

"Tessa." Sebastian shuffled forward as I approached my door, his voice pitched high with anxiety. "You never came home last night! I was so worried."

"You know there are laws against stalking," Blake snarled.

Sebastian's eyes widened like a startled rabbit's, darting between Blake and me.

I shoved Blake through my front door before he could terrorize my neighbor further. "Sorry, Sebastian. He didn't mean to be rude. If you'll excuse me, I'm in a hurry."

I yanked Blake inside my home to prevent him from giving Sebastian PTSD, shut the door, and sagged against it, exhaling slowly.

"You didn't have to be mean to him."

"And he doesn't have to monitor your comings and goings like an amateur surveillance team."

"He's harmless."

"Yet you've felt the need to clarify that. *Twice*." Blake put his hands on his hips, his shoulders rounding at the movement.

"He's socially awkward, that's all." I dropped my keys and phone on the foyer table with a clatter. "Being mean to him doesn't make social situations easier."

"You don't find it concerning that he's camping out on your porch?"

"Like I said—" I started toward the kitchen, desperate for a drink of water.

"Socially awkward but sweet?" Blake's voice dripped skepticism. "You're starting to sound like a broken record, Cupcake."

The nickname hit like a sucker punch. He didn't know it had this magical power to transport me into a girl who would gladly let him be bossy. In bed.

Domination, sign me up.

"I really need to take a shower."

Blake's attention finally swept through my shoebox of a home. I watched his assessment through new eyes, seeing my place the way he must. The kitchen was barely more than a hallway, with three tired cabinets on each side showing battle scars from previous tenants. My apartment-sized appliances huddled together like apologetic afterthoughts, the refrigerator's persistent hum serving as background music to my professional inadequacy.

The "dining room"—a generous term for the corner where I'd wedged a secondhand table—had disappeared under an explosion of wedding planning materials. Seating charts and fabric swatches spilled across the surface like evidence of the successful career woman I was trying to become. The living room didn't fare much better, featuring a love seat that had seen better days and a 32-inch TV balanced precariously on a garage-sale end table that wobbled if you walked too heavily past it.

My bedroom door stood open at the end of the hallway, just large enough for a queen-size bed that served as a daily reminder I'd chosen ambition over square footage. The whole place screamed *temporary situation*. Except I'd been telling myself that for a while now.

Blake's presence made everything feel smaller, more provisional too. His broad shoulders and success-story swagger belonged in some sleek downtown high-rise with floor-to-ceiling windows, not this glorified starter home, where I played at being a grown-up.

"You've lived here for what, a year and a half?" he asked.

"Yep." I kicked off my shoes, surprised to find I wasn't self-conscious about my home like I usually was with visitors. This was Blake. He knew me. Knew this wasn't my endgame.

"And you didn't have any health issues before moving in?"

"No."

He nodded, gaze tracking along the walls like he could see through them. "Seen any signs of mold or mildew?"

Oh. Now I saw where this was going.

"No. Eli had the same concern, so we both went over this place with a fine-tooth comb."

But Blake was already in full diagnostic mode, his eyes cataloging every crack like a potential symptom. "Mind if I take a look around?"

A look around. In my private residence. The teenage girl in me wanted to race ahead of him, hiding evidence of my decidedly unprofessional life. The reading glasses with the pink rhinestones I'd bought during a late-night Amazon spree. The collection of unicorn coffee mugs that my best friend kept adding to as a joke. And, dear God, please don't let there be any underwear lying around.

But he was looking for mold. Nothing else. And if I didn't let him satisfy his doctor instincts, he'd never let it go.

"Knock yourself out."

I shadowed his inspection tour, partly to prove I was fine, mostly to run interference before he stumbled across anything mortifying. Like my battery-operated boyfriend in the nightstand drawer. His physician's focus took him through my kitchen first, those capable hands—hands that had literally restarted my heart—running along cabinet edges and pipe joints, checking for moisture. In the bathroom, he examined the caulking with the same intensity he probably gave surgical sites.

His lips twitched as he took in my shower curtain, covered in cartoon cats wearing tiaras. "Nice decor."

"Judge all you want. Princess cats bring me joy."

That earned me a low chuckle that did dangerous things to my insides. But it was nothing compared to what happened when we reached my bedroom. Instead of mold, his attention caught on my collection of throw pillows, each embroidered with a different romance novel quote.

"*A duke in the streets, a demon in the sheets*?" he read, his voice rough with amusement.

I snatched the pillow from his view, but it was too late. He'd already spotted the book on my nightstand, and I bet my stupid heart monitor logged the moment he picked it up in those big, capable hands. The contrast of his masculine fingers against the pink floral cover—complete with a couple locked in an embrace against an impossibly rosy mountain backdrop—sent an inappropriate chill through my core.

"What's this one about?" The corner of his mouth lifted in that devastating half smile that undoubtedly made the nurses and female doctors swoon.

"Same as all the others," I managed. "Love."

"Ah, but you once gave me a twenty-minute lecture about how each one tells a unique story."

He began thumbing through the pages and—oh God—found my highlights. And my margin notes. Including the *OH MY GOD, THIS IS SO HOT* I'd scrawled next to a particularly steamy scene.

I lunged for the novel, but not before his eyes caught the passage in question.

That smile of his grew three sizes. "Getting her pussy eaten in front of city lights, eh?"

My cheeks burned hotter than that ridiculous pink cover. "Did you find any MOLD, Dr. Morrison?"

His laugh—deep, rich, and entirely too knowing—filled my bedroom, making me acutely aware that we were alone. Next to my bed. My very unmade bed, with sheets still rumpled from my fitful sleep two nights ago.

His gaze drifted to those twisted sheets, and I swear the temperature in the room rose ten degrees, making my lady parts start her engines.

No. False alarm. He's not coming inside.

Oh my God. I mentally cringed when I heard those thoughts in my own head.

"You okay there, Tess? You look like Ryker did when your mom found his browser history."

"Gross." *Nothing kills inappropriate thoughts like bringing up your brother's porn habits.* "No mold in here. Moving on."

I pretended not to hear his soft chuckle as he followed me, pretended not to be aware of the heat of his much larger body behind my own. Pretended Blake wasn't the one I'd fantasized about doing those things to me in that romance novel.

"So, where's the rest of your porn library?"

I spun around so fast that I crashed right into his chest. His hands shot to my waist to steady me, and suddenly, I was engulfed in his warmth, his scent a mixture of body wash and something uniquely Blake that made my toes curl.

"It's not porn." I pushed away from him, but the damage was done.

He'd switched to that casual stance, hands at his sides, that somehow made him look even more devastatingly attractive. Like a *GQ* model who'd wandered into my home by accident.

"I saw the words *cunt* and *cock.*" Blake arched a brow, his voice dropping to a tone that should be illegal. Based on the fresh smirk on his face, he'd said it to incite that fresh smoke from my cheeks. "I'm not a literary scholar, but I don't think that was *Moby Dick*. Although ..."

Glaring at him, I turned with a huff. "No mold. No mildew. I appreciate—"

"The CPR? The lifesaving? The literary criticism?"

I glowered at him, but he'd shifted back into doctor mode, his expression turning serious as his gaze swept the walls again with renewed intensity.

"The thing about mold and environmental toxins is that they're insidious. They hide in walls, under floors, in air ducts. Places you'd never think to look until it's too late."

"Are you suggesting my home is what's making me sick?"

"I'm saying we can't rule it out." He ran his fingers along a dark spot on my drywall, and I tried not to notice how his shirt pulled across his shoulders. "Environmental factors can destroy a healthy body from the inside out. Sometimes so gradually that you don't realize what's happening until you're in the ER."

"My symptoms weren't gradual," I reminded him. "It started suddenly with an illness."

"Still doesn't mean it's impossible."

"*Anything* is possible at this point," I replied. "Maybe I got infected by a pink elephant that blew a loogie through my bedroom window."

His glare was so delicious that it took everything not to smile.

Instead, I cleared my throat. "In any case, I can't afford to move, and even if I could, my lease doesn't end for another six months. I see no signs of mold, but your concern has been noted."

His jaw ticced as he looked around my small space again, and I recognized that expression. The one where he was gearing up for a fight.

Not happening.

"Now, if you'll excuse me," I said before he could launch into another chapter of his argument, "I have to get to an important meeting with the caterer."

His features tightened. "In *person*? Tell me you're joking."

"It has nothing to do with romance novels, I assure you."

"You just got released from the hospital."

"Keyword being released." I opened the front door, praying he'd leave before he discovered my special collection. The one Scarlett had strict instructions to burn if I ever actually died.

"Tessa, you need to rest."

"I will. It's one meeting."

"Your heart stopped yesterday." The reminder came with enough intensity to make my actual heart skip.

"And look at me now. Fresh as a daisy."

"You need to stay home."

"Again, your opinion has been noted. Now if you could go before bugs invite their friends, I'd appreciate it."

His jaw set in that stubborn line I remembered all too well from residency.

"I put a rush on your labs." He stepped on the front porch. "Should have the results soon. When I call, you'd better answer. Because if you don't, I'll assume you're unconscious and bring the entire ER to your doorstep."

So bossy.

"And where are *you* headed?" Why the hell did I ask that? Hello, my only goal was to get him to leave.

And why in the world were my lungs deciding to threaten a strike if he said anything about another woman? Blake probably had a thousand women he was dating. Surely, he'd grown out of his aversion to the female species and discovered what his body was capable of doing to the opposite sex.

"I have ... an engagement."

"He said cryptically."

Look at his coffee-colored eyes assessing me. Was he being deliberately mysterious just to mess with my head?

"I'm glad you're okay, Tess. I want you to text me when you get back home from your meeting." His attention swept to the neighbor's door. "Safe."

The reason I watched Blake saunter to the car was *not* because he had the hottest ass I'd ever seen, nor was it because I savored the way his broad shoulders stretched out that shirt. I was simply making sure he didn't have a run-in with my neighbor. *That's it.*

Okay, fine, yes, I was also massively wondering what kind of "engagement" had him looking worried.

And why did I have a feeling it had everything to do with me?

24

BLAKE

I stood frozen on the mansion's doorstep, my hand hovering over the brass knocker. Each visit here felt like crossing an invisible line between the life I showed the world and the darker one I shared with my chosen brothers.

Stone walls rose before me, crowned with weathered gargoyles that seemed to keep watch over our secrets. The sprawling estate on Chicago's outskirts had become our sanctuary. Our Sinners and Saints Club, as we'd dubbed it with dark humor. Beyond the iron gates, the distant silhouette of the penitentiary loomed. A perpetual reminder of the night that brought us together and why we chose this particular haven.

A place where five men—bonded not by blood, but by the kind of tragedy that reshaped souls—could speak freely about the nightmare that had shattered our college years. What should have been a time of late-night parties and cramming for finals had instead become a nightmare that changed our entire lives.

I caught my reflection in the window. Exhausted eyes, tension in my jaw. Beneath that, something else lurked: the weight of falling for my best friend's sister.

Ever since I'd driven to Eric Voss's home, intending to break his bones for breaking Tessa, an unwelcome realization had infected me faster than a staff bacterium. My feelings for Tessa were not brotherly at all.

I knew now, without a shadow of a doubt, that I was falling for Tessa.

Hell, beneath my cloud of denial, I'd been falling for her for years.

Tonight, I needed to hide these feelings from the one person who knew me better than anyone: Tessa's brother. Ryker had warned me multiple times through the years that if he found me with his sister, he'd dig me a shallow grave. The problem was, Ryker could read me easier than Tessa read romance novels, and the last thing I wanted to do was cause even more problems for Tessa right now.

I'd thought about skipping our weekly poker night. But after promising Tessa to keep quiet about her illness—and, yeah, the guilt of telling Ryker about Voss was still eating at me—I knew I had to show. Especially given our text exchange before Tessa landed in my ER, where they'd practically strong-armed me into committing to game night. If I bailed now, Ryker and the others might know something was up.

Ergo, here I stood. Ready to put on the performance of a lifetime.

Inside, firelight flickered across mahogany walls. Three of my four brothers hunched over the poker table in the corner, their faces illuminated by the overhead lamp.

"Just in time to see me wipe Jace's ass," Axel said, tossing chips into the growing pile with the casual confidence of someone about to lose spectacularly.

"Like hell." Jace's eyes glinted with the same focus he usually reserved for saving failing companies. He methodically arranged his chips, each stack precisely aligned. "You know, Axel, poker's a lot like business. The guy making the most noise usually has the weakest hand."

"Is that the wisdom that made you a billionaire?" Axel rolled his eyes. "Because I'm pretty sure it was your trust fund."

"The trust fund got me in the game," Jace countered, his voice taking on that quiet intensity that made boardroom executives squirm in their seats. "Everything since then? That's all about knowing when other people are full of shit." He glanced at Axel's chip stack. "Like right now."

"Pretty rich, coming from a guy who wears cuff links to poker night," Axel said, but I noticed him subtly rechecking his cards.

Jace's mouth quirked up slightly. "Presentation matters. Another lesson from the business world: people underestimate the well dressed." He pushed a neat stack of chips forward. "Raise."

"Christ," Ryker muttered. "And this is why we should've capped the buy-in."

The problem with playing poker against a billionaire CEO like Jace was that your *all in* was his pocket change.

Despite his witty remarks, Jace's posture seemed a little more withdrawn than usual tonight, perhaps still haunted by that family business he'd acquired last month. The one where he'd promised all hundred fifty employees they'd keep their jobs, even though the board demanded cuts. It had been quite a battle, but Jace had saved every single one of them.

Jace caught my eye across the table, his expression unreadable, save for the slight tightening at the corners of his mouth. His tell, if you knew to look for it. Unlike Axel's brash confidence or Ryker's calculated plays, Jace approached poker like he did business takeovers: patient, methodical, waiting for others to reveal their weaknesses before striking.

"You seem distracted tonight, Blake," Jace said, voice calm enough that the others paid no attention to it beneath Axel's trash talk.

The observation wasn't accusatory, just Jace's typical perception. He'd built his fortune reading people's vulnerabilities after all. I shrugged it off, but there was something in his knowing gaze that made me wonder if he saw more than I wanted him to. If anyone in our group understood keeping secrets the most, it was Jace.

Ryker looked up, and our eyes met.

An unspoken question passed between us. *Any luck finding Voss?*

I gave a subtle shake of my head.

"Scotch?" He stood, already reaching for the crystal decanter.

"Can't. Have to head back to work after this."

"Another marathon shift?" Axel whistled. "Man, this chief of emergency medicine thing has you working like a resident again."

Sitting down, I shuffled the second deck of cards. The familiar motion helped steady my hands, giving me something to focus on besides Ryker's concerned glances. If he kept looking at me, he might realize Eric Voss wasn't the primary cause of my turmoil tonight.

"Speaking of your questionable life choices ..." Axel smirked. "Whatever happened with that nurse that asked you out?"

This again. First that stupid text about the lingerie model, now this?

"What's with the sudden interest in my love life?" I challenged.

"What love life?" Axel's deadpan delivery made him laugh, but Ryker was preoccupied, and Jace, well ... he didn't date either. Presumably because of his dark past. His was far darker than mine, and that was saying something. With what Jace had been through, it was a wonder the guy hadn't become a serial killer instead of a corporate savior.

"Anyone who's in a committed relationship, raise your hand." I glanced around the table. "Right. That's what I thought."

They'd notice something was wrong soon enough; they knew me too well not to. These were the only people besides Tessa I'd ever truly let in, and it hadn't happened easily. Back in college, Ryker had been my only friend, dragging my antisocial ass to fraternity events despite my protests. Through him, I met Knox,

Jace, and Axel. But what cemented our bond was tragedy. Watching Knox being led away in handcuffs, headed for prison.

Charged with murder.

The fraternity we'd belonged to preached brotherhood, but when those police lights painted Knox in red and blue, that brotherhood shattered. Innocent until proven guilty wasn't their motto. Instead, they gave us an ultimatum: denounce Knox or get out.

That wasn't brotherhood. Brotherhood was what came next: four of us united, standing guard over our fallen friend. We formed the Sinners and Saints Club that night, understanding that the line between the two wasn't as clear as most people thought. Sometimes, good men did terrible things for the right reasons. Sometimes, the worst sinners were the ones hiding behind respectability.

Our mission was simple. Protect each other, especially if or when we'd get knocked down, and offer redemption should society, or our loved ones, ever write us off. We'd all been judged, condemned, or abandoned at some point. We knew what it was like to face the darkness alone.

Three sacred rules governed everything:

1) Absolute loyalty. We'd seen how fast the world turned its back on people who fell from grace. Each of us carried darkness, violence we were capable of when pushed too far. I'd proven that the night I saved my sister, Faith. Knox was living it now. But in this club, we didn't run from that darkness. We stood together in it, knowing that sometimes the most righteous acts looked like sins to the outside world. So, no judgment. No abandonment. Ever.

2) Protection. Attack one of us, you attack us all.

3) Unbreakable connection. This wasn't just a club; it was our chosen family, our life sentence. Regular check-ins, no matter where life took us. No man left behind, no brother forgotten. In a world where people disappeared from each other's lives so easily, we chose to anchor ourselves to each other.

Which made hiding these secrets about Tessa feel like betrayal.

"Earth to Blake." Axel's voice cut through my thoughts. "You going to play or just fondle those cards all night?"

My phone buzzed. Tessa's name lit up the screen.

*Tessa: You told me to confirm when I was all locked up and safe in my place for the night. Considered not doing it, just to prove you're not the boss of me. But I figured I owe you for the whole saving-my-life situation. So, here I am, being a good little patient. Happy now, Dr. Control Freak? *eye roll emoji**

I smirked.

Ryker's eyes narrowed on the phone, then snapped to my face. I tried to school my expression, but it was too late. He'd seen something there, something that made him set down his scotch with deliberate care.

"Who was that?" Ryker asked.

I met his gaze, saw the unwavering loyalty that would turn to fury if he knew the truth. That his sister was my secret patient, fighting a medical mystery I prayed I could solve before it was too late. That I was breaking the only promise Ryker had ever asked of me, to stay away from Tessa's heart.

The promise was born from experience. Back in high school, Ryker had another close friend, Tuck. Tuck had a sister who Ryker fell for hard, and for a while, everything seemed perfect. Until it wasn't. When the relationship crashed and burned, Tuck chose his sister's side. Just like that, a friendship was fractured, leaving scars that never fully healed.

So, when it came to Tessa, Ryker's rule was absolute: never date my sister. He couldn't bear to lose either of us, wouldn't risk our friendship imploding over something as preventable as romance.

"No one." I shoved the phone in my pocket without responding to Tessa. "Who's dealing?"

But from the way he studied me—really studied me now—I knew his radar was officially up.

25

TESSA

The late-spring breeze carried the sweet scent of blooming roses across the garden terrace, but all I could focus on was keeping my breakfast down. Wrought iron tables dotted the brick patio, their delicate scrollwork casting intricate shadows in the morning sun, which was the perfect setting for future wedding photos. If only I could appreciate it.

"Are you okay?" Shelly, my picture-perfect bride-to-be, leaned forward in her chair, her perfectly manicured fingers drumming against her designer handbag.

"Absolutely." The lie tasted bitter on my tongue, mixing with the acid already creeping up my throat.

"You don't look so good." Her eyes narrowed, scrutinizing my face with the same attention to detail she'd used to select her thousand-dollar centerpieces.

I didn't feel so good either. For the last twenty minutes, the nausea I'd arrived with had been building, like a volcano threatening to erupt. I needed to end this meeting. Fast. Without letting Shelly catch on to just how bad things were getting.

I could pull this wedding off. I had to. The majority of my payment wouldn't come until after the big day, thanks to the contract structure I'd stupidly agreed to nearly a year ago, when I was healthier and optimistic. If I didn't see this through, all the work I'd already done—countless hours of vendor negotiations, design consultations, and meticulous planning—would be practically pro bono.

"I'm great." I forced a smile, willing my hands not to shake as I shuffled through my portfolio. "Now, about the catering menu. We got that all sorted out. The caterer tried raising concerns about ingredient prices, but between you and me, I think he was fishing for a higher fee."

Shelly's perfect brows remained furrowed with concern. The last thing she needed was to worry about her wedding planner dropping the ball. This wasn't just any wedding; this was a merger of political dynasties, with a guest list that read like a who's who of Chicago's elite. I would rather turn into a human icicle than let her down.

"He knows you and James will be bringing in substantial business connections," I continued, swallowing hard against the rising bile. *Oh God. Just get through desserts and dresses, Tessa, and then you can run.* "As for the dessert menu, I looked over your vision board and—"

"I don't mean to be rude," she interrupted, subtly inching her chair away from me. "But if you're coming down with something, maybe we should reschedule. I don't want to get sick."

"I don't have the flu," I assured her, even as guilt gnawed at my insides alongside the nausea.

Maybe this was wrong. Maybe I was being selfish, desperately clinging to this job. This wasn't just her wedding day; it was a carefully orchestrated social and political event that could make or break careers. It wasn't her fault that losing this contract would financially destroy me. It wasn't her fault that I'd turned down three other weddings to focus entirely on hers. And it certainly wasn't her fault that I was battling some mysterious illness that came and went like an unwelcome ghost, growing more unpredictable by the day.

"You have a sheen of sweat on your forehead, you look pale,

and there are dark circles under your eyes." Her tone was gentle but firm.

Fantastic. Apparently, the extra-coverage foundation I'd carefully applied this morning wasn't doing its job. I pressed my trembling hands flat against the cool metal table, anchoring myself as my stomach swirled.

The truth was, my symptoms were like a cruel game of Russian roulette. I never knew when they'd strike or how bad they'd be. If I admitted I wasn't healthy enough for this commitment, it meant I wasn't healthy enough for *any* job. And if I couldn't work ...

No. I refused to watch my carefully built business crumble while doctors scratched their heads.

"I'm fine," I insisted, my voice steadier than I felt. "Now—"

"Look." She crossed her arms, her diamond engagement ring catching the sunlight. "You canceled our last appointment without explanation, and now this ..."

My heart thundered against my ribs. I could see the doubt blooming in her eyes like the roses surrounding us, threatening to destroy everything I'd worked for.

"That was a personal emergency," I said softly, omitting the part about being in the hospital with my heart deciding to take an impromptu vacation.

I hadn't even told my brother about that particular incident; I certainly wasn't going to share it with a client who was already questioning my reliability.

I could do this job. Most of it could be handled remotely. Hell, I could coordinate with vendors from my bed if necessary. Blake was running tests, and I trusted we'd find a way to at least manage my symptoms. I had to believe that.

"I'm fine," I repeated, even as bile inched up my throat. "If I'm being honest, that emergency cost me some sleep. But I promise you have my complete attention."

My eyes darted to the restroom pavilion across the garden.

Sixty feet. Just sixty feet away. The nausea was cresting, but I just had to hold on for—

"I've already renegotiated with the caterer to add the dessert bar for free after his pricing stunt. The bridesmaid dresses will be ready two weeks early, we're getting six dozen bonus roses at no charge, and your gown alterations are right on schedule."

Shelly's expression softened slightly, a cautious smile tugging at her lips. "If you're sure ..."

"I'm more than sure." I beamed, trying to casually gather my materials as my stomach turned into a hurricane. "This is the most exciting wedding I've ever planned, and it's going to be absolutely spectacular." I made a show of checking my watch. "Now, if you'll excuse me, I need to meet with the venue's billing office. Would you like to join me?"

As expected, Shelly wrinkled her nose at the mention of administrative tasks. The moment she declined, I made my goodbyes, promising updates and striding toward the restroom pavilion with all the casual grace I could muster.

Inside the mercifully empty bathroom, I barely made it to the first stall before my body betrayed me again. As I knelt on the cold tile floor, retching until there was nothing left, something inside me finally shattered. Months of holding it together. Months of doctors staring at test results, telling me nothing was wrong. Months of needles and scans and bills leading to dead ends, all while my body aged decades in minutes.

While I burned and ached and forgot what it felt like to be normal.

I couldn't take this anymore.

The first sob caught me off guard. The tears came hot and fast, streaking mascara down my cheeks as weeks of carefully maintained composure crumbled. I pressed my forehead against the cool tile wall, shoulders shaking with the weight of everything I'd been trying so desperately to outrun.

God, I was so tired. Tired of my body becoming a minefield of symptoms I couldn't predict. Tired of waking up each morning, wondering if today would be the day it all fell apart. Tired of smiling through meetings while my insides revolted. But most of all, I was tired of being afraid. Afraid of what was stealing my life piece by piece, afraid of losing everything I had left, afraid of the question that stalked my sleepless nights.

What if I never get better?

My fingers clutched the cool porcelain of the toilet bowl as another wave of nausea hit, leaving me dizzy and spent. Through blurred vision, I could see the pristine tiles of this picture-perfect venue bathroom. The same venue where, in a few weeks, Shelly would be taking photos with her bridesmaids, all smiles and champagne and a happily ever after.

The unfairness of it all hit me like a gut punch. I didn't need to be rich. Or happy even. I'd settle for just feeling *okay*. For being able to exist without pain and sickness. Was that too much to ask? Why did some people get everything—looks, money, success—while some of us sobbed on bathroom floors, trembling with violent episodes of vomiting? Why did *my* bar in life keep getting lower and lower until simply feeling *okay* felt as possible as landing on the moon?

Why did this have to be so hard?

I hated feeling sorry for myself though. Anytime I did, I felt like a terrible person because all I had to do was turn on the news and see what other people were going through in this world for me to realize that some people would kill to have the life I had. Feeling sorry for myself was ungrateful.

I was alive. And I would get through this.

After I wiped my mouth and washed my hands, my phone buzzed with a text. One that left me with a kernel of hope that maybe, just maybe, he might have found something that would tell me what was going on.

Blake: Test results are in. We need to talk.

26

BLAKE

I hurled the stack of test results across my office, watching the papers scatter like frustrated thoughts. My intern had printed them out, as if seeing the results on actual paper might somehow make them tell a different story. They didn't.

The harsh glow of my computer screen mocked me as I read through the list again:

Electrolytes: Normal. Glucose levels: Normal. Kidney function: Normal. CBC: Normal. EKG: Normal. Cardiac enzymes: Normal. Chest X-ray: Normal. Urinalysis: Normal. Liver function: Normal. Thyroid panel: Normal. MRI: Normal.

"Not one fucking test tells me why she's sick."

Dr. Johnson stood in my doorway, his disapproving gaze fixed on the mess of papers carpeting my floor. He drew in one of his signature condescending breaths—the kind that made me want to remind him that I wasn't his resident anymore.

"You're getting too emotional on this one," he drawled.

My head snapped up. "She's a family friend." I started pacing, deliberately stepping on the scattered reports, each crunch under my shoes feeling like another dead end.

"This is why you shouldn't treat someone you have a close

relationship with," Dr. Johnson chided. "You need to hand her off to someone else."

"To whom exactly?" I spun to face him, heat rising in my chest. "Immunology? No markers for immune deficiency. Primary care? She's exhausted those options. Cardiology's looking at everything heart-related, but that doesn't explain the last year of her life. Which specialty would you have me abandon her to?"

The words *abandon her* hung in the air between us. Because that's what it would be: abandonment. I'd seen the defeat in Tessa's eyes when she told me about every doctor who'd dismissed her symptoms, every specialist who'd sent her away with a clean bill of health and an implied pat on the head. Every doctor who'd tossed her to someone else when they came up short for answers.

Johnson tapped his fingers against my desk, staring at the screen. "Her presenting symptoms are two fainting spells and cardiac arrest, correct?"

"Most recently. This started a year ago with some kind of flu followed by a viral infection in her chest. A lingering cough."

He peered at me over his rimmed glasses, his voice taking on that patronizing edge that made my jaw clench. "A cough."

"And rashes. Hives. Weight loss." My voice rose with each symptom. "She has circles under her eyes so dark that they look like bruises. It's like watching the life drain out of her while everyone stands around, saying she's fine."

My mentor clicked through screen after screen of test results. The clicks mocked me with each movement of his mouse, and I knew what he was thinking before he even opened his mouth.

"Doctors have been thorough," he said, finally breaking the oppressive silence.

"Collectively," I qualified. "One doctor orders one panel, then passes her off to someone else. Collectively, she's had a lot of tests, but none of them tell us why she's sick."

"But it does rule out a lot," he said, and I could sense where he was going with this too. Every muscle in my body tensed, not wanting to hear one word of it while he stroked his beard, his expression maddeningly calm. "The skin issues could be allergies. The cough and nausea, a cold or flu. Fainting spells often stem from dehydration, which can trigger cardiac events. As for fatigue ..." He shrugged. "She's in her thirties. It comes with the territory."

Something inside me snapped. This was my mentor, the brilliant doctor I'd looked up to for years, suggesting that being tired was just part of being in your thirties.

"This is exactly what she's been through for the past year," I said, my voice deadly quiet. "Every doctor dismissing her symptoms while she gets worse. No one taking the time to step back and see the whole picture. You know how medicine works. We're all in our silos. The pulmonologist looks at lungs, the cardiologist at hearts, but when something's cascading through someone's entire body—"

"Have they ruled out depression?"

I stopped cold. "Tell me you're not one of those doctors."

"And what kind of doctor is that?"

"The kind who, when they can't find an answer in their precious textbooks, decides to blame the patient. Make them think they're being irrational, or old, or just complaining too much." I stepped closer, fury making my words sharp. "Just because we don't have the answer doesn't mean it doesn't exist. It's arrogant to think any of us has all the answers."

Johnson's face tightened. "You asked for a second opinion. I took time out of my day to review her records, and you have the nerve to call me arrogant?" He jabbed a finger at my screen. "This woman has had more testing in the past year than most patients see in a lifetime. Take it as a win that they didn't find something terminal."

"I won't—"

"I'm not finished," he snapped. "You know what's arrogant, Dr. Morrison? Thinking you're smarter than every doctor in this hospital. It's a quality the board likes least in candidates for chief positions."

He let that threat hang in the air for a moment before turning on his heel, leaving me alone with the scattered papers and the weight of Tessa's trust.

I stared at the test results littering my floor, seeing them through new eyes. This is what she'd faced. Dismissal after dismissal while something inside her continued its quiet ravaging. My fists clenched at my sides, anger mixing with a deeper resolve.

I would not let this go. Whatever was destroying Tessa's body, whatever had slipped past every test and specialist, I would find it. Even if it cost me everything.

But first, I had to break the news to her. After all the needles, the scans, the endless questions she'd endured at this hospital, I had to tell her we were no closer to finding her an answer. Or a solution. The thought of crushing her hope made me physically sick.

"Blake?"

Tessa's voice—that sweet voice that haunted both my dreams and nightmares—cut through my dark thoughts. I spun to find her in the doorway, and for that one precious moment, suspended in time before she registered the devastation on my face, I cataloged every detail of hers.

Bright, hopeful eyes that still held traces of the vibrant woman I remembered from before all this began. A smile—God, a genuine smile that made my heart stutter—and the way her body unconsciously leaned toward mine, as if some invisible thread kept trying to pull us closer together. It was only then that I recalled the text I'd sent her, and I silently cursed myself for not warning her this was bad news. For letting her walk in here, carrying that beautiful, fragile hope.

If I had, I wouldn't have had to watch it all crumble. Her lips fell, her shoulders crumpled as if under some invisible weight, and her eyes began to water as she whispered, "Did they find anything?"

The tremor in her voice shattered what was left of my heart.

After seeing that smile on her face, this was harder to tell her than any diagnosis because I was the one that got her hopes up. I made her get back into the fighting ring. And now it was *my* glove that was about to knock her out.

27

TESSA

Blake stood in his office, a sterile shrine to modern medicine with its gleaming white furniture and endless rows of medical texts, where sunlight drifted through the window. It was the kind of light that made everything look softer, more intimate—even the man himself, who'd forgone his usual white coat and scrubs today in favor of a crisp blue button-down with the sleeves rolled to his elbows. But what struck me most were the papers scattered across his pristine office floor like confetti.

"I have bad news, Tessa."

God Almighty, it's happening. My worst fear was finally materializing. Every time I'd imagined this moment, it played out the same way. They'd finally figure out what was wrong with me, only to say, *Sorry, turns out you're dying. Maybe if we'd caught it sooner, you could have had the life you always wanted. You could have planned that sunset wedding you used to dream about, felt the weight of your newborn against your chest, seen your name splashed across magazine covers as Chicago's most successful entrepreneur. But sadly, you should probably look into the economy package at the local funeral home.*

My heart thundered so erratically that I was pretty sure the cardiologist monitoring me was already reaching for the crash cart.

"The tests all came back normal," Blake announced.

I pressed my palm to my chest, letting out a whoosh of relief that made my knees weak. A smile crept across my face, slow at first, then spreading like wildfire.

"Oh my GOD, Blake. Don't do that to me!"

"Do what?" His brow furrowed in that adorably confused way that made him look more like a puzzled golden retriever than the brilliant doctor I knew him to be. The one who probably hadn't scored below a 98% since kindergarten.

"Look like you're about to tell me I'm dying!"

To think, I'd had that pity party from barfing. If this didn't put things in perspective, nothing would.

"This is bad news, Tessa." He swept his arms toward the paperwork on the ground. The sight of straitlaced, perfectly pressed Dr. Blake Morrison, the man who probably ironed his socks, having thrown what appeared to be a full-on tantrum made my heart dance.

I pressed my hand to my forehead, my smile growing wider.

"You seriously need to LEAD with, *You are not dying, Tessa*. For a minute there ..." I shook my head, almost giddy with relief.

It was astonishing how everything could change in just a few seconds. Like I'd had a loaded gun to my head, someone's finger pulling back the trigger, and just when I'd braced for my doomed fate, the gun vanished, and I was told I had another chance to live.

This was the second time I'd felt it. The first time, when my heart had stopped beating, I hadn't fully experienced the fear like this because I'd only learned about the danger after it was over. This time, I'd seen the gun, felt its cold barrel against my temple, heard the click of the hammer that should have been my last sound.

"You know what?" My smile widened. "THIS was the shock I needed. Thank you."

Without thinking—and that was probably good because if I'd thought about it, I never would have done it—I leaned up on my tiptoes and kissed his cheek. Blake froze, and a current of warm electricity snaked through my body at the feel of his skin against my lips. He smelled like coffee and something woodsy and expensive, and for one dangerous moment, I wondered if he'd taste the same way. It was a thought I had to actively push aside to stay focused.

"Here I was, feeling sorry for myself after throwing up at my meeting."

His whole demeanor changed in an instant, doctor mode snapping into place like a shield. "You threw up?"

I waved my hand dismissively. "Had a full-on pity party. You should have seen me, sobbing on the bathroom floor of that fancy place. Really added a certain *je ne sais quoi* to their marble tiles."

"Today?" His voice sharpened to a scalpel's edge. "You vomited today?"

"No one likes a Debbie Downer," I continued. "And that wasn't even the first time. I mean, damn, when I think about this past year ..." My voice trailed off, realizing the joy I'd let this steal.

That was the worst casualty in all of this, wasn't it?

Blake stepped closer, close enough that I could see the flecks of gold in his eyes. Definitely not helping my heart rate situation.

"Tell me exactly what happened when you got sick today."

But I was riding my wave of perspective, determined not to let it crash.

"I haven't just felt sick this past year; I let myself feel depressed over this."

"People don't *let* themselves feel depressed, Tessa." His voice softened, and something in it made me look up at him. Bad idea. He was giving me that look—the one that made me feel like I was the only person in his world. "That's not how depression works; it's not a choice. You're going through something terrible, and it would take a toll on anyone. Even someone as strong and cheery as you."

My cheeks warmed at his words. He saw me as strong? And

cheery? I *had* been cheery my whole life, hadn't I? The proverbial happy person who always saw the silver lining. Until my health started slipping away and I'd let my happiness and cheer slip away right along with it.

Until now. Now, I felt her return—the old me, the happy me, throwing up or not.

"To think of all the times I'd cried myself to sleep." I shook my head at my past self. "All those wasted nights I should have been counting my lucky stars I wasn't dying."

Blake's entire body went rigid, like someone had replaced his spine with steel. "You've cried yourself to sleep?"

"So many times that I lost count," I said absently. "But the point is, this whole time, I've been feeling sorry for myself; I've been taking all the other moments of my life for granted. I'm still here. And, sure, my body doesn't feel like the epitome of health, but think of all the people hooked up to ventilators who'd wish to be in my shoes. Or people fighting terminal illnesses, or facing atrocities around the world, or not here anymore. They'd all wish they could be in my shoes, Blake."

"Stop doing that." He reached for me, then seemed to think better of it, his hand falling back to his side while the ghost of that *almost touch* lingered between us like static electricity. "Stop telling yourself that your suffering needs to be justified by someone else's pain."

"This is the universe shaking my shoulders and making me see how much I still have, not just what I've lost." The words tumbled out faster, higher, riding that desperate wave of forced optimism. "I needed something to snap me out of my funk, and this was it!"

His face tightened, and I could read the worry there plain as day. He thought my feelings were temporary, but he didn't want to burst my bubble. If I was happy, even artificially so, he wanted to preserve it like a rare butterfly under glass.

"I'm not done with this, Tessa." The quiet determination in his voice cut through his office.

"I know."

"I want to run more tests."

"Figured as much."

"Talk to me about vomiting today." His doctor voice was back, all business.

"In what way? You want to know what color it was?"

He fixed me with a look that could have melted steel. "There is nothing funny about this."

"Disagree. I shall find the humor in this from now on."

"Tessa."

"It was brown," I relented.

Dear Diary. You know how I've had a massive crush on Blake Morrison since basically forever? Today, I talked about the color of my vomit with him. #RelationshipGoals

"You had no breakfast."

"Bingo." I forced myself to focus on anything but how his forearms looked with his sleeves rolled up.

He sighed, running a hand behind his neck, and for a moment, I let myself notice how the movement made his shirt pull tight across his biceps. He caught me looking, and I quickly averted my eyes, suddenly fascinated by his collection of medical journals.

"Okay, look." His voice had that tone that meant he was about to say something I wouldn't like. "There's one variable we haven't ruled out yet."

"Only one?" I arched an eyebrow.

"I'd like to hire a professional environmental inspection company," he said.

"What, pray tell, does a professional environmental inspection company do? By the way, they could seriously use a marketing person to help them shorten that name."

"Perform a visual inspection of the property, looking for any signs of water damage or mold growth."

"We already did that."

Blake leaned forward, and the intensity in his eyes made my

esophagus spasm. "And now a trained professional will. They'll have tools that measure moisture with meters and infrared cameras. They'll also collect samples and send them off to a lab."

Labs. It had been my experience that anything with the word *lab* in it wasn't cheap. Or quick.

"How long would that take?" I tried to ignore how close my body was to his. Close enough that I could feel its heat.

"When I did it a couple of years ago, I got my results back within ten days." His fingers drummed against his bicep. "Could be longer, could be sooner. Depends on how backlogged the labs are."

"And after that?"

"After that, we'll know if your environment is causing your health problems." The drumming intensified.

I narrowed my eyes. "But? Because I definitely heard a big *but* in your voice, Blake."

He winced. "They can't squeeze us in for a couple of more weeks."

"Which puts us at three and a half weeks until we find out if this is causing me problems?"

"Correct." The word came out clipped, like it physically pained him. Like watching me suffer was somehow harder on him than the actual suffering was on me.

I took a deep breath, bracing myself for what I knew would be the biggest hurdle. The one that had been lurking behind all my medical decisions this past year, like a loan shark waiting to break my kneecaps.

"How much do they charge?"

"This is a question we need answered," he said firmly, suddenly finding his desk calendar fascinating.

"And yet my bank account will ask again." I pressed my lips together. "How much will this cost?"

Blake's jaw tightened, a muscle jumping beneath his skin in that way that made me want to reach out and smooth it with my thumb. "Will it influence if you go through with it?"

"Unless the company is willing to take an IOU on a Post-it Note?" I let out a laugh. "Yes. It might influence whether I can do it."

"Then let me worry about it."

I straightened my spine. "Absolutely not. I'm not having you swoop in and fund solutions to my problems, Blake. How much?"

"It's not swooping. It's a gift." The smile he attempted didn't reach his eyes. "I never gave you a birthday gift this year."

"Our birthday gifts are in the $30 range." I fixed him with my sternest look. "I know this is well more than $30, so how much is it?"

"I can *loan* you the money if that's what it takes." His voice had gone quiet, gentle, like he was trying to coax a scared animal.

"I don't borrow money from people. You know that." Only banks, and that was all tapped out. "Is it $300?"

Blake suddenly developed an intense interest in his computer screen.

"$500?" My voice climbed an octave, approaching dog-whistle territory.

He examined his pen holder like it held the secrets of the universe.

"A thousand?" The word came out as a squeak.

Blake finally met my eyes, grimacing. "Shouldn't be too much more than that."

A bubble of hysterical laughter escaped me. "Too much more than that? Do you seriously think I have $1,000 sitting around?"

"You need to get better." His voice was thick with frustration and something else that made my chest tight. Fear. Blake Morrison was afraid for me.

"Which is why I've drained my bank account on medical bills." I ran a hand through my hair, wishing I hadn't when I caught his eyes following the movement. "But at least my medical bills are partially covered by insurance. This wouldn't be covered by insurance, right? Unless you can somehow convince them that my townhouse is actually a very large, very expensive medical device?"

His silence was all the answer I needed.

"I have to think about it."

"Tessa ..."

I held up my palm. "Blake, these are my decisions. I hear you loud and clear. There is a chance that my townhouse has mold that is making me sick. But we've both looked at it thoroughly and seen no signs of it, so spending $1,000 to confirm it isn't something I can afford right now."

"I can't let you say no to this." He paced behind his desk like a caged tiger. "Your environment might be making you sick, Tessa. Would you pay $1,000 to get better?"

"If I *knew* that the thousand dollars would get me better, of course. But this is a low probability—"

"You don't know that."

"Well, you don't know that spending another thousand dollars is going to get me better!" I shot back. "And if you want to do more medical testing? I need to save that money for that because, again, insurance doesn't cover everything one hundred percent, Blake. This has drained me dry. I'm one copay away from selling organs on the black market. And before you ask, no, you can't pay for those either."

His eyes blazed, like he was trying to go all Superman laser on me. "We have to eliminate as many variables as possible, Tessa."

"I have! Here."

My hands dug through my satchel for the little notebook I carried everywhere—my constant companion through this nightmare, filled with more details about my daily life than my high school diary. I pressed it against his chest, trying to ignore how solid he felt beneath my palm.

"Every morsel of food I have eaten. Every product I have put on or near my body. Laundry soap, makeup, everything. And you'll notice that list got smaller and smaller as time went on. I've kept track of everything, trying to figure out what might be making me sick, and I have carved out everything I possibly can. But I cannot carve out having a roof over my head, so unless you have a better option—"

"Move in with me."

I jerked my head back, blinking rapidly, certain I'd misheard. But the intensity in his eyes, the way his whole body seemed to lean toward mine like a compass finding north, confirmed it. He actually meant it.

The air between us crackled with something that felt dangerously close to possibility.

"Absolutely not." The words came out as barely a whisper, probably because all the oxygen had suddenly vacated the room.

"Tessa—"

"Look, I really appreciate everything you're doing for me, but this is going too far." I ran my hands down my pants, trying to pretend warmth hadn't flooded my body at his offer. Unwelcome warmth at the thought of waking up in his space, breathing his air, being surrounded by him.

He stepped closer, his voice gentle but urgent. "My place has been tested and is clean of any environmental factors that could be making you sick. Diagnosing what's going on with you is like a science experiment. We need to remove as many variables as possible."

"Why don't I just move into a petri dish while I'm at it?" I tossed my hands into the air. "Live in a bubble? Breathe only fresh oxygen out of a tank?"

"That's not fair."

"No, none of this is fair," I agreed. "But I get to decide how much this impacts my life from this point forward. I am not moving out of my place, and nothing will make me change my mind."

As it turned out, "nothing" was going to happen in forty-eight hours.

And it would change everything.

28

BLAKE

"Who wants to play a game?" The stack of papers hit the conference table with a sharp crack, silencing the whispered speculations.

Eight interns jolted in their chairs, the smell of hospital-grade coffee and nervous sweat hanging in the air while the fluorescent lights cast shadows under their eager eyes. Eyes that followed my every move like they were watching a cobra about to strike.

"A game, sir?" Martinez's voice cracked.

"Call it a competition." I circled the table. "I need help with a case."

The air sparked with sudden attention.

"Have a bit of a medical mystery on my hands," I continued, noting how their spines straightened at my tone. "And I need to solve it as soon as possible. The patient is a close friend of mine."

Eight heads snapped up so fast that I thought I heard cervical vertebrae crack.

"Yes, I have friends. Despite hospital rumors, I don't actually freeze people with my gaze."

"A *close* friend?" Rhet, perpetually testing my patience, wiggled his eyebrows like a cartoon villain. "That why the rumor mill says you were smiling at a patient?"

The *normal* me would've kicked his sorry ass out just to maintain order, but Tessa needed his irritatingly brilliant mind on this.

"Stop trying to impress the other interns," I snarled. "I saw you practicing your confident-doctor walk in the parking lot at 6 a.m."

Rhet's face went from cocky to corpse pale in record time.

"Now." I tapped the papers. "This patient ..." I watched their expressions shift from amusement to focused intensity. "Her heart stopped beating in our ER. Healthy hearts don't just quit without reason. There's an underlying condition here, hiding behind a year of seemingly unrelated symptoms. And if we don't crack this ..." I let the silence stretch, heavy and meaningful. "She might die."

I had to swallow the bile that came up every time that thought thundered through me.

What if Tessa was dying? Contrary to popular belief, there were plenty of things that could kill a person that were hard to diagnose, and one look at Tessa, you could see the toll this mystery thing was doing to her body. Almost like it was eating her from the inside out.

"The winner gets to be more than just another clipboard-carrying lab scout."

Time to dangle the real prize.

"Solve this ..." I paused, letting the tension build. "And you'll present the case at Grand Rounds."

Grand Rounds was an event where medical cases were presented to hospital leadership, attendings, and peers. It was rare for interns to get this chance. Rarer still for them to be invited.

The room fell so quiet that you could hear the hum of the fluorescent lights.

"Let me be clear what that means. You'll have every department head, every attending physician in this hospital, watching you break down one of the most fascinating cases I've seen in my career. Presenting will boost your reputation within the hospital. Every department head will know your name." I pressed my fingers to the files in front of me. "But that's not all. The intern who cracks this becomes my apprentice for a week."

A sharp intake of breath from two interns heightened the anticipation in the space.

"That means no more fetching labs or typing notes. For seven days, you'll be doing real medicine. Hands-on experience you can't get anywhere else. I'll teach you everything I know: every trick, every technique, every shortcut I've learned in my years of practice."

I watched skepticism transform into raw hunger in their eyes. Some were already pulling out their notepads, pens hovering eagerly over paper. Others sat perfectly still, as if afraid any movement might cost them their shot.

Now we were getting somewhere.

"Who's interested?"

Every hand shot up like they were spring-loaded.

"Oh, and one more detail." I leaned my palms on the table. "Every department head has this case too. Different rewards, same race. But they're drowning in meetings and paperwork while you've got fresh knowledge and hungry minds."

"We're competing with department heads?"

"Terrified?" I asked, arching an eyebrow. "Good. Fear makes you sharp. Beat them, and your name becomes legend in these halls." I checked my watch. "Clock's ticking. Shall we begin?"

The sound of frantically flipping papers filled the room. Eight minds racing against time, against each other, against the hospital elite.

Perfect.

Game on.

29

BLAKE

SINNERS & SAINTS GROUP CHAT

*Axel: Jace, my man, just watched you announce that merger. Your company's getting so big. You know what Freud would say about your obsession with size? *eggplant emoji**

Jace: Axel, saw you on the arm of yet another model. The fact that no one will sleep with you more than once says everything about your skills.

Axel: Please. I have a LINE of women. A LINE.

Jace: Yes, waiting for their antibiotics after one night with you.

Ryker: It's 7a.m. I haven't had coffee yet. I will murder both of you. As a criminal attorney, I know how to get away with it.

Axel: Jace, at least I have social skills. When's the last time you left your office for something other than our poker nights?

Jace: Yesterday. Spent sixteen hours at my law firm's headquarters, finalizing the details that will save thousands of jobs at my latest acquisition. Unlike your dating history, I actually finish what I start.

*Axel: *yawning emoji* Boring. Aren't CEOs supposed to be cutthroat? You're like the Santa Claus of corporate takeovers.*

Jace: I am cutthroat. Just ask the executives I fired last week. I just prefer destroying people who actually deserve it.

Axel: You owe me ten grand.

Jace: Improve your poker skills.

Ryker: Blake, any movement on the chief position? Hospital board still dragging their feet?

Me: Moving slower than Axel's brain after a night out.

Axel: Speaking of medical advice ... hypothetically ... if a supermodel had this weird rash ...

Me: Stop. Whatever you're about to ask, the answer is no. And get tested. Again.

Axel: You're just jealous I'm living the dream while you're all stuck in your sad, sexless lives.

Jace: The dream of being patient zero for the next pandemic?

Ryker: I'm muting this chat. Some of us have actual work to do.

Axel: Says the guy who just spent five minutes reading about my sex life.

*Me: *Your alleged sex life.*

*Axel: *middle finger emoji**

Jace: He's just mad because that rash is definitely herpes.

30

TESSA

I was about to die a very public death. Professionally, that is.

I stared at Chicago's most influential bride as she dropped her bombshell.

"You want to change the wedding date?" I tried to keep my voice from panic-level shrieking as we sat in the gleaming interior of Le Petit Café, where the scent of fresh croissants usually calmed my nerves. Not today. "We're more than halfway done with the planning," I reminded her, ticking off on my fingers. "Florists, caterer, venues—all with signed contracts."

"I don't want it to be next June." Shelly twisted her hands on the marble tabletop, avoiding my gaze. A cappuccino sat untouched before her, its foam design dissolving into nothing. "I want it to be this July."

"*This* July?" The words came out as a strangled whisper. "As in seven weeks from now?"

"That's the one." Her shoulders hunched forward, so unlike her usual camera-ready posture.

Do not laugh out loud at the audacity of it, I commanded myself. Part of being a wedding planner was dealing with unreasonable and unattainable requests from the bride and groom. But this? This was impossible.

"Shelly." I leaned forward, lowering my voice. "This is supposed to be the wedding of a lifetime." As an influencer with millions of followers, Shelly knew this, but perhaps it bore repeating. "There are politicians and Wall Street executives, massive influencers ... they'll all be there. Which means we can't afford anything less than perfection. People like that will be looking for something to criticize."

Especially with Shelly. She attracted a massive following, and with great success came ruthless trolls. One slipup, and that slip would be the headline on the front pages of gossip columns. Yes, including *Page Six*. And right next to it? My name and my shattered reputation.

I might as well engrave a headstone for my business right now. *Here lies Tessa's dreams, murdered by impossible deadlines.*

"Yes, it has to be perfect," she said, her manicured nails drumming against the table. "And it has to be in July."

"There won't be any venues available." The words tumbled out as I ran my fingers through my hair. "And that doesn't even factor in—"

"I'm going to stop you right there." This was the curtest Shelly had ever been with me; my spine stiffened at the icy tone frosting her words. "Something has come up, so it has to be in July. Period. And I need you to make that work."

I studied her, only now noticing how tense she seemed—her shoulders rigid, face tight.

"Oh my goodness!" A redheaded teen materialized at our table, practically vibrating with excitement. "You're Shelly McBride!"

McBride. Ironic, considering the circumstances.

"I am." Shelly's face transformed instantly, her media-perfect smile sliding into place as she posed for a selfie with the fan who gushed for over a minute before finally leaving us alone.

"Something has come up." I repeated her words softly, trying to imagine what could possibly derail a wedding that had more sponsorship deals than a Super Bowl commercial. "Are you ...

expecting? Because if you are—" The wedding was a year out. She could get her pre-baby body back in time if that's what worried her.

"I'm not pregnant," she said, her voice barely audible over the café's espresso machine hiss. "My dad ..." Her voice cracked, and her eyes welled with tears. Tears she tried to force away with a clearing of her throat. "It's pancreatic cancer."

My heart plummeted. Before I could respond, another fan approached, this one clutching her phone like a lifeline.

"Oh my God, I thought my friend was wrong, but now that I'm here—" The dark-haired girl babbled on, oblivious to our tension. "Can I just tell you what an inspiration you are? Your *dress like a million on a budget of less than fifty* posts? Oh my ..."

When she finally left, I reached across the table. "Shelly, I'm so sorry."

"Let's go for a walk?" she suggested, already gathering her things.

I nodded, following her into the warm late-spring air of Michigan Avenue. The shadow of skyscrapers fell across us as horns echoed through the steel canyon and the "L" rumbled overhead. Here, at least, pedestrians were too focused on their own destinations to notice us.

"He has to be at my wedding," she said, twisting a tissue between her fingers as we walked. "He has to walk me down the aisle. I've dreamed about this since I was a little girl, and if he's not there ..." Tears tracked down her carefully contoured cheeks.

I placed my hand on top of hers, our footsteps slowing. "Of course," I said gently. "He has to be there."

She let out a deep breath of relief, as if this part of the battle was behind her. But I knew better.

"You know," I ventured, "we could pivot. Organize a justice of the peace, get you married by next week if you want."

Her posture stiffened. "No," she said firmly. "I'm not willing to sacrifice quality. It still has to be perfect; it just has to be earlier."

My stomach churned at the impossibility of it all. Perfection in seven weeks? I might as well try to teleport to the moon.

"Doctors seem confident he can make my wedding in July," she added. "That gives us time to move everything up."

Now I understood, with crushing gravity, what she expected. Perfection. The same stakes were there. Her brand and mine would be in shambles if all those same high-end guests came to a disaster. Influential guests that would probably reorganize their lives when they heard why the wedding was moving up to July. Shelly's father was a powerful politician. The last chance to see him? People would reschedule an organ transplant to make that.

"Okay, listen," I sighed, stopping her near a towering glass building that reflected the afternoon sun. "I hate to say this, but you're taking a huge gamble on me. I want this wedding to be everything you've dreamed of, and while selfishly, I want to keep working with you"—*hello, bankruptcy court*—"I have to put your needs ahead of my own. Other wedding planners have hundreds of weddings under their belt and can probably handle a curveball like this without missing a beat. Many of them have exclusive contracts with florists and venues they can leverage." Me? I was running on desperation and sheer will.

"I know it's a challenge, but I want *you* to do it." Shelly grabbed my hands, her eyes intense. "I fell in love with you, Tessa. Your vision. Your talent. I don't want anything to change, except the date."

I swallowed hard. "I want to," I started, but she cut me off.

"This isn't just about you. One day, a female clothing designer chose *me* to promote her brand. She could have gone with anyone more experienced, but she chose me and gave me my big break. I saw that same talent in you, and as you know, this whole wedding planning journey has gone viral."

Don't remind me. It was an asset then. Now it's a Titanic*-level liability.*

"I'm getting messages from aspiring female entrepreneurs. They're watching you, Tessa. Looking on to see you pull off the wedding of the century, and if you do, it will tell them whatever dream they have in their heart, they can achieve it too. This is bigger than just us; it's hope for all the aspiring businesswomen who need a win when big corporations keep crushing the little guy."

Well, crap. When she put it that way ...

"Speaking of big corporations," she added, lowering her voice, "you know another big problem."

"Once Upon a Lifetime," I muttered, the name tasting as delicious as vomit.

Chicago's largest wedding planning company had been trying to crush me since day one. Evidently, it wasn't enough that they planned thousands—yes, thousands—of weddings a year. They were sharks, securing an almost monopoly by bullying out any budding competition. Like me.

Moving the wedding date would be massive news with Shelly and her influential father. Maybe they wouldn't be that ruthless if they knew the reason it was moving was because he was dying?

But the churning in my stomach told my sixth sense that they wouldn't give two craps; all they cared about was winning this wedding planning war they'd created. And even without their interference, the impossibility of planning a wedding in mere weeks made my vision blur. A wedding of a lifetime? I needed to hire a leprechaun for good luck.

My heart started to race, and nausea exploded, along with sweating palms. Nerves? Or another health crisis?

I pinched the bridge of my nose. "Shelly, I need to tell you something."

Panic flooded her eyes. "Don't say no," she pleaded, gripping my arm. "I can't start over with someone else."

"The other day, when I missed our meeting ..." I forced myself to meet her gaze. "I was in the ER."

Her eyes widened. "Are you okay?"

"Yes," I assured her quickly. "Well, sort of. I've been sick for a while, and doctors can't figure out why. It's only fair that you know that. It didn't start until *after* I took you on as a client," I assured.

Shelly chewed her lip, clearly calculating this curveball. "Do you think it'll interfere with wedding planning?"

"I want to say no," I continued, watching pedestrians stream past us on both sides, "but the truth is, I don't know what to expect. You need to understand what you're getting yourself into if you continue with me."

Rapid breathing, darting eyes. Shelly had entered full panic mode.

"How sick?" she asked.

"They've ruled out the really scary stuff, but—"

"That's good," she cut in. "Because no one else would be able to take me on."

"I'm sure they would." God, this was so unfair. I'd earned this job, sacrificed everything for it. But this was her wedding, and she deserved the best. "People would probably cancel other weddings to make it happen." I hated admitting it. "One call, and you'd have ten wedding planners booked by the end of the day."

"But ... you and I have been through so many details together."

"I'd be happy to transition everything to them."

"So, you're quitting?" Her voice cracked.

"Not at all. Shelly, I want this wedding. Truth be told, I need it, but this isn't about me; it's about you getting the best chance at having the wedding of your dreams. You deserve nothing less."

To this, her eyes watered. "See? This is why I want you, Tessa. Do you know how many people are cutthroat, bottom-line, greedy assholes?"

Sadly, I did.

"But you're the kind of person who will give up her dream to make someone else's come true. That's why *you* deserve this wedding under your belt."

And this was why I'd been thrilled to have her as a client. Despite how demanding she could sometimes be, Shelly was one of those female entrepreneurs who wanted to bring others up with her—the kind that paid it forward to underdogs like me.

"Are you sure?" I asked. "Because you don't have an hour to spare if we have any shot of pulling this off together."

Shelly nodded.

I blew out a breath. "Okay. I'll do whatever it takes to make this your dream wedding, Shelly."

She hugged me, and as she did, it struck me again how lucky I was. Not just to have a client like Shelly, but also that I didn't have pancreatic cancer. Shame on me for feeling sorry for myself during pockets of this past year. I would do everything in my power to pull off the wedding of her dreams.

Even if it meant caving in to the bossiest man on the planet. Blake's warning about my home echoed in my head. Maybe he was onto something. Maybe my environment *was* the culprit. After all, I hadn't been sick before moving in, and just the other night, I'd felt fine arriving home, but after sleeping there, I'd thrown up at that last meeting with Shelly.

Yes. My environment was suspect, and I couldn't wait weeks to find out if it was making me sick.

Which left me with exactly one option.

With trembling fingers, I pulled out my phone and fired off a text to Blake.

Me: That offer to live with you still on the table?

31

TESSA

"Holy shit." The words escaped before I could stop them, hanging in the air of the most extravagant space I'd ever seen.

"Do you like it?" Blake asked, setting my pathetically small suitcase down with a soft thud. The sound echoed through his foyer—because, yes, he had an honest-to-God foyer bigger than my entire bedroom.

An abstract painting hung above an elegant table that probably cost more than my entire building, its bold strokes of crimson and gold catching the late afternoon light.

"Do I like it?" I swept my gaze around, trying not to gawk like a tourist at the soaring ceilings and floor-to-ceiling windows showcasing a glittering city view. "Have you ever met a human being who doesn't?"

He shifted his weight, and I caught something unexpected in his expression. Was that nervousness? The great Blake Morrison, brilliant doctor and owner of this spectacular penthouse, actually seemed to care what I thought.

"I don't let many people up here," he admitted.

"Seriously?" I spun around, unable to contain my disbelief. "If I lived in a place like this, I'd host dinner parties every weekend. Hell, I'd invent reasons to throw parties."

"Well, I work long hours." He shrugged.

I cocked my head, studying him. "And if you didn't? Would you host parties then?"

His pause told me everything I needed to know.

"No," he finally admitted, the corner of his mouth twitching. "I suppose not."

I returned to taking in this alternate universe, where even the baseboards sparkled and everything looked like it had been plucked straight from an architectural magazine. My fingers itched to trail along the foyer table, though touching something that probably belonged in a museum felt sacrilegious.

"Seriously though ... this place is ..."

"Pretentious? Obnoxious?"

I smirked, meeting his gaze. "I was going to say incredible. Though I have to ask, don't doctors usually have a zillion dollars in student debt?" At least in the first couple of decades of their careers.

Blake rubbed the back of his neck. "Friend of mine is a savvy businessman."

"Jace," I said, memories flooding back of my brother's endless stories about his infamous college friend. The guy was practically a legend, showing up in business magazines before he'd even graduated. "Your guardian angel of investments?"

"He let me in on something when I probably should've been using that money to pay off my loans." Blake's eyes met mine, a hint of that old rebellious glint I remembered from high school. "Looks like it turned out well."

So, this must be why my brother lived like a king. My jaw clenched. *Thanks for the heads-up, Ryker. Thanks for letting your own sister in on this little gold mine.* But who was I kidding? He knew exactly why he'd kept quiet. I would never have risked my business savings on a gamble, no matter how much of a "sure thing" it supposedly was.

Blake shoved his hands into his jean pockets—and sweet mercy, those jeans should be illegal. They hugged his hips in a way that made my mouth go dry. Not that I was noticing the way every stitch got to touch him places I never had. Definitely not.

I drifted toward the statue on the foyer table, drawn to the way the light caught the wooden caduceus—twin snakes coiled around a winged staff, the ancient symbol of medicine. It looked like an artifact that belonged in a museum, not perched on Blake's entry table.

"My mentor gave me that when I finished residency," Blake said, and something in his voice made me glance over. He was looking at the statue the way most people looked at old family photos. "He said great doctors were like those snakes. Always adapting, always healing." His fingers ghosted over the wood, barely touching. "I've thought about moving it somewhere safer."

"It's beautiful." Just like the career he'd built. Just like his home. And just like his heart.

"So," he said, rocking back on his heels, "want the grand tour?"

"Before we do that—"

He held up his palm, stopping me mid-sentence. "Let's skip the part where you thank me profusely and tell me how guilty you feel for 'invading my space' and promise to be a ghost." His impression of my voice was terrible and oddly endearing.

"How did you—"

"Know exactly what you were about to say?" Those dark eyes locked on to mine, seeing straight through me, like they always had. "Because you'd rather perform heart surgery on yourself, using a rusty spoon, than accept help from anyone. You're infuriatingly independent like that." His lips curved into a dangerous smile. "Some things never change."

"You're one to talk," I shot back.

"At least I never moved next door to a stalker."

"My neighbor isn't a stalker!"

"Please." Something flickered across his face. "I saw how he looked at you, Cupcake. And I didn't like it."

The sudden intensity in his voice shifted the air between us, making it harder to breathe. I'd always known Blake had a darker side, one I'd seen glimpses of through the years in bloody knuckles after fights and sharp comments that didn't quite fit his polished doctor image. Most people would be put off by that edge to his personality, but it had always drawn me in, made me want to unravel all his complicated layers.

"So," he said, his casual tone a stark contrast to the tension crackling between us, "should we do a panty count to see how many your neighbor snatched, or should we get on with the tour?"

I crossed my arms, going for stern but probably looking more ... Jell-O-like. "I'll only stay here on one condition."

Blake arched an eyebrow, amusement dancing in his eyes. "Funny, I thought the suitcase implied we were past the negotiation stage."

"Whether you acknowledge it or not, this is a huge favor, and I need to contribute something."

His lips curved into that smile that had always spelled trouble. "Oh?"

"Not that." I ignored the heat crawling up my neck, and other places, at his suggestive tone. "Get your mind out of the gutter, Morrison. I meant something useful."

"Such as?"

"I could clean—"

"Have a maid."

"Cook dinner—"

"Personal chef."

I frowned. "I can't just ... live here. It doesn't feel right. It's unbalanced, and that makes me uncomfortable."

The playfulness drained from his face as he took three steps closer. Close enough that I caught the spicy hint of his body wash mixed with that uniquely Blake scent I'd recognize anywhere.

"You want to know what you can give me?"

I nodded, my throat suddenly dry at his proximity.

"Give me this." His voice dropped lower, softer. "Coming

home to lights on instead of darkness. Having you here, in my space, making it feel less like an empty house and more like ..." He ran a hand through his hair, messing up those perfect dark strands. "Just ... be here, Tess. That's more than enough."

Holy shit. Hello, backflips in my stomach.

"Blake ..."

"Besides," he added, his casual tone returning as he stepped back, breaking the spell he'd accidentally cast, "you're actually doing me a favor. Now I won't lie awake at night, imagining you breathing in toxic mold."

"You worry about me?" The words slipped out.

"Only when you do stupid things. Like moving next door to Norman Bates."

"He's not—"

"And now," he continued, talking over my protest, "I won't be distracted at work, wondering if your creepy neighbor is building a shrine to you in his basement."

I couldn't help but smirk. "That's a bit dramatic."

"I'm a doctor. We're known for our dramatic flair." He flashed that heart-stopping grin. "Almost as dramatic as wedding planners who refuse to accept help from their dearest friends."

Dearest. My stupid heart latched on to that word, hoping I meant as much to him as he did me.

"Fine. But I'm at least doing the dishes."

"Touch my dishwasher, and I'm changing all the passwords in this place to components of the periodic table. Now, can we get on with this tour, or do you need to list more chores I won't let you do?"

"A tour." I shook my head, studying the endless hallway before us. "At my place, I could do an entire tour in twenty steps or less, but this place? I'll need hiking boots."

"Don't worry; I had my assistant stock some emergency provisions in case you get lost between the kitchen and your bedroom." He started walking, expecting me to follow. "Living room first."

He swept his hand out to a sofa that looked like it was crafted from clouds. "State-of-the-art entertainment system, every streaming service known to mankind, and ..." He grabbed a remote, pointing to a distinctive green button. "One-click access to those god-awful romance movies you love so much."

"Says the guy who exclusively watches people getting dismembered in horror films."

"Those are educational. Some of us actually need to know where the arteries are."

"Pretty sure *The Texas Chain Saw Massacre* isn't included in med school curriculum."

"Shows what you know." He pressed the remote into my hand. "And before you start with the guilt spiral, I changed the purchase passcode to your birthday. Figured you couldn't forget that one."

My stomach did a perilous little twirl. He'd gone out of his way to change his passwords, just because he remembered how much I loved movies?

"Kitchen next," he announced, leading me into a space that belonged in a magazine. "Had my assistant stock your favorites."

Assistant?

He opened the fanciest refrigerator freezer I had ever seen. The thing was so organized; it looked like it belonged in an appliance commercial with glorious colors of fruits and vegetables on the left, lean proteins, eggs, yogurts on the right. And then some of my favorite foods. Including dark chocolate squares—the kind from that Michigan Avenue chocolate shop—on the lower shelves, the ones that much shorter me would have no difficulty reaching.

Guilt etched across my insides.

"Blake ..."

"If you're about to launch into your *you shouldn't have done this* speech, remember our deal." He opened a cabinet, revealing more of my favorites. "No more sorrys."

"I just don't want to be in your way. You work such demanding hours and—"

"Exactly. We'll be like two ships passing in the night." He leaned against the counter, his height making the massive kitchen seem somehow smaller. "Just making sure you have everything you need."

He pointed to a paper held to the fridge by a magnet shaped like a scalpel. "Numbers for the personal assistant and chef."

"I didn't know doctors got personal assistants."

"She's not from the hospital. I hired her directly. She handles the errands I'm too busy for."

"Like preparing for unexpected houseguests?"

"Like making sure said houseguest doesn't starve to death because she forgets to eat when she's working." He pushed off the counter.

I followed him down the hallway to a guest bedroom that made five-star hotels look like highway motels. A king-size bed dominated the space, draped in a gloriously fluffy comforter in shades of silver and cream that practically begged to be touched, while a crystal chandelier cast soft shadows across plush carpeting that sank beneath my feet. The air itself smelled of lavender and fresh linens, making the space feel both luxurious and somehow intimate.

"I have a few rules."

I arched an eyebrow. "Rules?" Totally fair, but totally unexpected. "Like what?"

"Your ex-boyfriend, or any current or future boyfriend, is not welcome here."

Okaaaaay …

"Why?"

"Because I'll be tempted to shove his face into my fireplace."

Trying to act like his flash of jealousy wasn't super welcomed in my lower belly, I carried on with a joke. "And hospital boards tend to frown upon that?"

"I don't want to ruin my perfectly good fireplace. Plus, I need to be able to think clearly; this is my safe space, and I'll be working after hours on your case here, so if you're going to meet a man, meet him outside these walls."

I smirked. "Don't worry. My only boyfriend right now requires AA batteries."

Holy crap, did I just say that out loud? I bet *my* face looked like it had just been shoved into the fireplace. His, on the other hand, looked ... ravenous.

He had to clear his throat and rub the back of his neck.

Looks like I'd finally said something that made him squirm.

"I wish you hadn't told me that."

Yep. Totally squirming. Shame on me for enjoying it.

"Why?"

"Because now I'm going to constantly be craning my ears to see if I can hear *that* coming from your room."

My neck flushed with heat, his eyes drifting across my skin. It took him several seconds to break the sexual tension and move onto something else.

"Look." He gestured to the bookshelf. "Had my assistant grab all the best-selling porn from the nearest bookstore."

"It's not porn!"

"Really?" He moved to the bookshelf, plucking a novel from the highest shelf with those doctor fingers that I definitely wasn't staring at. "Because this blurb implies the monster has two massive cocks."

"I know what you're doing." I snatched the book from his hand, trying to ignore how his low chuckle and heat from his very close body affected my insides. "You're trying to distract me so I don't feel weird about all of this."

"You seriously think a little food and some books are the most fascinating thing in this penthouse right now?" His voice dropped an octave. "You just admitted to having a vibrator, and you have a porn collection. I'm busy wondering how many of these books have anal."

"I'm sure if I looked at your internet browsing history, your porn collection would be pretty interesting too."

He smirked, holding this thread of ... desire tightening between us for a few beats before stepping around me. But did he take his eyes off me as he did that? No. No, he did not.

"Come." He waved his hand for me to follow. "No pun intended."

I followed him down a hallway so massive that it probably needed its own postal code. We passed door after door, all standing wide open, except for two: one at the far end that he'd breezed right past—*interesting since he'd been so eager to show off everything else*—and this one, where he now stood, waiting.

"Your office." His hand hesitated on the knob. "You mentioned being on a tight deadline with this wedding planning. I might have asked my assistant to do some research about what a wedding planner needs in their workspace."

"Blake ..."

"If you hate it, we can undo everything. If we missed something, we can add it." He opened the door, and my jaw nearly slammed on the ground.

The office wasn't a room; it was a dream materialized. Hardwood floors gleamed beneath pristine walls, adorned with elegant art pieces that somehow perfectly captured the essence of romance and celebration. An oversize window bathed everything in soft afternoon light, making the space feel almost magical.

My mouth fell open even wider as I took in the distinct stations he'd created. A primary desk boasted dual Apple monitors, flanking a brand-new MacBook Pro with an absurdly large bow perched on top. Bookshelves lined with every wedding magazine in existence stretched toward the ceiling. A cozy consultation area featured two plush chairs, separated by an end table that belonged in a museum.

Everything, from the pastel pinks to the silvery grays, blended into what looked like a headquarters for a seven-figure boutique wedding planning agency. Not my struggling business that was one canceled wedding away from disaster.

"Blake, this is too much."

"Nothing is too much for you, Tessa."

Based on the way his gaze latched on to mine and his mouth fell open slightly, he hadn't meant for that profession to slip out. I wasn't sure what to do with it. What to make of it. Was I picking up on desire? Like deep desire or simple hormonal desire?

Blake broke eye contact, and suddenly, I needed to fill the space with words. Lots and lots of words.

"You had your assistant import all my files from my iPad?" I finally managed, spotting my color-coded system on the massive wall monitor, displaying project deadlines and contact lists.

He'd asked for my ipad, and I'd handed it over, presuming he wanted to see my digital tracker of foods, which was more organized than my handwritten notes. Because, yeah, at one point, I'd kept both.

"That's why I borrowed it." He shifted his weight. "Not just to snoop through your medical history."

"Though you definitely did that too."

"Doctor-patient confidentiality prevents me from commenting." His smile turned sheepish. "We can change anything you don't like."

"Blake, this is ..." My eyes burned as I struggled to find words big enough. "No one has ever done anything like this for me."

"It was one phone call, Cupcake." But the way he said my nickname—soft and intimate—made it feel like so much more. "I just wanted you to have a space where you could work comfortably. You can have clients come here for meetings, use the chef for dinner presentations. Consider it your headquarters."

I blinked rapidly, fighting back tears that threatened to expose just how much this meant to me. When he'd offered to let me stay here, I hadn't expected this level of thoughtfulness. Hadn't expected him to seem so ... happy about my presence. Like having me here wasn't just convenient, but celebrated.

Which was incredibly flattering and dangerously complicated. Because now, every smirk, every laugh, every heated look was making it harder to remember why we'd always kept that line drawn between us.

And somehow, I had a feeling that line was about to become very, very blurry.

32

TESSA

I woke to the smell of fresh coffee and ... were those pancakes?

My stomach went from zero to hangry in approximately point-three seconds. I launched myself out of bed, made a quick pit stop in my private bathroom to ensure I looked less walking zombie and more functioning human, then ventured into the hallway.

And there it was again—that one mysteriously closed door in a sea of open ones. Even Blake's bedroom door stood wide open, his bed already military precise in its making. Of course it was. The man probably saved three lives before I hit my first snooze button.

Rounding the corner into the kitchen, I stopped dead in my tracks. A woman I'd never seen before stood at the stove, humming.

For a second, I froze, a dark, terrible feeling snaking through my chest.

Who was this woman in Blake's private residence? I thought he said he didn't let many people here, so was this woman special? She moved around the space like she freaking belonged here.

"Good morning, Tessa," she sang out as if we were old friends. "Dr. Morrison was very specific about your favorites."

She slid three perfect pancakes onto a pristine white plate, creating what could only be described as breakfast art—golden syrup cascading just so, fresh berries arranged with gorgeous precision, and a butter pat melting into a perfect golden pool.

"You're Blake's chef," I breathed, relief washing over me.

Wait, did I just use the word *relief*? Why did that word invade my psyche?

"Indeed. I'm Maria. And let me tell you, making something other than egg whites and organic protein shakes is a delightful change of pace."

She placed the plate—my own personal carbohydrate heaven—at the breakfast bar.

"Dr. Morrison thought you'd be more comfortable here than the formal dining room. But if you'd prefer—"

"This is perfect," I assured her, climbing onto a stool.

And that's when the universe decided to test my ability to maintain basic motor functions. Blake strode in, wearing nothing but workout shorts, his tattooed torso glistening with sweat that—you guessed it—made his muscles look even more impossibly sculpted.

"Morning," he said, still catching his breath. "Sleep well?"

My brain chose that exact moment to go on strike. Complete system shutdown. My mouth forgot how to work on account of the eye candy in front of me, and Blake's brows furrowed as he pressed his palms against the opposite side of the breakfast bar, concern flickering across his ripped abs.

Okay, fine, concern couldn't technically be on his abs, but those abs. Look at them—all ready for a photo shoot.

"What's wrong?"

I blinked rapidly, trying to reboot my brain. "Oh ... nothing ... just ... you're here, not at work, and working out, and ... I have pancakes."

Good God. Was that the same brain that graduated college with all *A*'s?

Blake seemed to evaluate me, probably wondering if I'd had a mini stroke, while Chef Maria's shoulders shook slightly with poorly concealed amusement.

Desperate to escape my own humiliation, I glanced down at my food and noticed a tiny white plate next to it that contained three mysterious pills.

"That's a medical-grade, high-absorption multivitamin," Blake explained. "Along with vitamin D and a probiotic. I'd like you to take them daily."

I eyed the little white dish. "I prefer my multivitamin. It's a chewable gummy."

"A gummy." He choked. "Do you know how many artificial colors and flavors are in most of those things? The absorption rate is practically zero."

"It tastes like candy, and I don't like to swallow."

The words hung in the air for one mortifying second before a smirk played across his annoyingly perfect jawline. He approached slowly, like a predator who knew exactly how distracting his presence was.

"Learn to swallow," he murmured.

And then he did the most unexpected thing: he kissed the top of my forehead.

Once again, my brain short-circuited, spiraling with questions. Did he actually just do that? Was he seriously acting like that forehead kiss was no big deal? And my personal favorite traitorous thought: Damn, girl, those lips were warm and firm as hell. Imagine them sucking on your—

Get a grip you pathetic, easily distracted brain cells. Blake isn't the first hot guy you've seen. Act like the adult you are, not some teenager meeting her celebrity crush backstage.

I squared my shoulders, scowling at the pills.

Was I comfortable with this? He meant well, and he was a doctor who knew all about, well, vitamin stuff, but he was being quite bossy. Maybe even crossing a line.

"The agreement was for me to stay here to avoid potential mold exposure," I reminded him, pulling my plate of heaven closer. "I didn't see the page of our agreement that outlines you taking control of my diet."

I took a bite of pancake and let out an involuntary moan that made Chef Maria snicker.

"You think *this* is me taking control?" Blake arched an eyebrow, gesturing to my breakfast masterpiece. "If I had my way, you'd be on nothing but lean proteins and organic vegetables."

I pulled my plate closer and scooted my stool a couple inches away from him.

"So help me, if you even think of taking this away from me after letting me taste it, I'll stab your doctor hand with my syrup-covered fork."

He stared at me, perhaps questioning my sanity. Or considering calling my bluff.

Not a bluff, I silently warned with my stare back, shoving another bite of syrup-drenched carbs into my mouth.

He rolled his eyes. "I'm simply asking you to take vitamins that will actually benefit your body. Vitamin deficiencies are linked to countless medical complications."

When he put it that way ...

"Fine," I conceded. "I'll try."

"Try hard," he growled. "Or I'll have Maria crush them into your smoothie."

"I'm not five years old."

"So, you *can* swallow?"

My entire face burst into flames, inciting a ridiculously sexy smirk from him.

"I'm heading to work," he finally said, mercifully changing the subject. "But I'll be back for dinner."

I glanced at the clock, confused. "Thought you worked thirty-hour shifts?"

"Day off."

"And you're going in?"

"Have some things to look into."

"Me," I thought. "My labs."

"I have a team working on this. Want to check their progress." He paused. "Maria, make fettuccine Alfredo tonight. Fresh bread, grilled chicken."

Maria's eyebrows shot up. "But tonight's brussels sprouts and—"

"Warm bread," he specified. "And a Caesar salad."

My fork stopped halfway to my mouth. That was my favorite meal, the exact one I'd mentioned during a casual conversation years ago. More surprising than his perfect memory was his willingness to deviate from his rigidly controlled diet.

"Maria, make sure Tessa eats whatever she wants for lunch."

Maria nodded, a knowing smile playing at her lips.

"Call if you need anything, Cupcake."

Oh, I had needs. None of them appropriate to voice out loud.

Once he was safely out of earshot, Maria smiled. Cleared her throat. "Would you like me to make you a cup of coffee?"

"Tea would be great."

She frowned. "I'm afraid Mr. Morrison doesn't have tea, but I'd be happy to—"

"I brought some," I clarified. "Brought a few things from my place."

"So, no coffee in the mornings?"

I had no idea what Blake had told her about my staying here, but given she was partly responsible for what I ingested while under this roof, she deserved some explanation.

"I cut it out when I started getting sick. Figured green tea might be ..." I shrugged. Might be what? Magic that erased my problems?

"Did it help?"

I frowned.

"I'm sorry."

"Don't be." I waved my hand. "Tell me. How do you function when he walks around like that? Because I'm going to need survival tips."

She smiled, cleaning up the mess. "I'm afraid you'll need to get used to it if you stay here; Dr. Morrison frequently wears no shirts."

Well, that should have been disclosed before I'd moved in here. Hello, you big distraction.

But him being comfortable wearing no shirts brought me joy because no one knew his history of hiding his skin.

"Is he always like this?" I wondered aloud, finally picking up the first pill.

"No," she answered thoughtfully. "I've never seen this side of him."

"Really? I figured he always acts like a massive control freak."

"Loving," she clarified with a smile. "I've never seen him act loving like this before."

I froze mid-swallow.

"He's normally ..."

"An Iceman?" I supplied, remembering the hospital whispers.

"I was going to say serious and rigid."

"So ... an Iceman."

"I would never describe my boss in unflattering terms," she said diplomatically. "But this softer side? It's refreshing." She patted my arm. "I hope you stick around, Tessa."

Later, heading back to my room to shower, I passed that mysterious closed door again. Logic said it was probably just an office, full of confidential medical files and boring paperwork.

But something in my gut said there was more to it. And why did that only make it more intriguing?

33

TESSA

Let me clarify, I didn't intend to wind up nearly naked, drenched, and in Blake's arms. All I meant to do was take a shower. A simple, normal-person shower. The universe, apparently, had other plans.

What else was new?

First order of business was letting the water warm up, a task I thankfully hadn't gotten completely nude to do. Though "thankfully" felt debatable as I stood here in my pink matching set. If only I'd left more than a bra and panties on. Like a hazmat suit.

I stepped into what had to be the most ridiculous shower I'd ever seen—less bathroom fixture, more spacecraft command center. Silver showerheads gleamed from every possible angle, floor to ceiling, like some sort of chrome polka-dot collection. Was this a shower or Blake's attempt to re-create NASA's mission control? And more importantly, where was the damn handle?

Squinting at the main showerhead—at least the one positioned where normal showerheads lived—I found exactly nothing helpful. No lever. No dial. Not even one of those fancy digital panels rich people love so much. I stepped out, circled the glass enclosure like a frustrated shark, then went back in. The steam from my rising blood pressure was going to fog up these pristine walls before any actual shower steam got the chance.

I couldn't see anything visually, but figuring maybe the showerheads had some kind of an invisible switch, I began inspecting it around the perimeter. My fingertip had barely brushed the metal when an explosion hit me.

I screamed as approximately seventy thousand jets of water attacked from all directions. Up, down, in my eyes, in my crotch—places water had no business being this aggressively shot. The force knocked me back against the tile, hands flying up to protect my face as I sputtered.

"Tessa?" Blake's voice boomed over the water's roar.

Because this wasn't mortifying enough.

Seriously, if there was a way to look regal while being violently assaulted by jet streams, I was for sure not pulling it off. I swatted the water like a swarm of bats. Through my waterlogged lashes, I caught a glimpse of broad shoulders, defined abs, and—thank God—dark shorts before Blake reached for something I couldn't see. The assault suddenly ceased.

I stood there, panting, dripping, my matching set now thoroughly transparent. A fact Blake seemed very aware of, if his darkening eyes were any indication.

His chuckle started low—a rough sound I hadn't heard since high school.

"Here." He grabbed a fluffy towel and wrapped it around my shoulders, his fingers lingering a moment too long. "You look like a drowned rat."

"Your shower tried to murder me," I accused, fighting a shiver as his hands rubbed warmth back into my arms through the fabric.

"It's touch-activated." His voice had dropped an octave, something that definitely wasn't helping my composure.

"And apparently set to DEFCON 1."

His eyes sparkled with amusement, and he reached past me to demonstrate the proper technique. I tried—really tried—not to notice how the water had made his shorts cling to every muscle or how droplets were trailing down his bare chest like they were living my dreams.

"You should really put a warning label on this thing," I managed, my voice embarrassingly breathy. "*Caution: Shower may attempt assassination*."

Blake smiled an honest-to-God genuine smile, rubbing my shoulders, trying to warm me up, and as his hands moved in slow, steady strokes, I found myself leaning into his touch, craving more of that warmth. More of him.

The laughter faded from his eyes, replaced by something darker, more intense, as his movements slowed, his gaze raking over the planes of my face, sending sparks through my nerve endings. The bathroom seemed to shrink, the steam wrapping around us like a cocoon, making everything feel more intimate, more electric.

I watched, transfixed, as a droplet of water traced its way down his neck, disappearing into the hollow of his throat. My fingers itched to follow its path, to explore every inch of skin on display, and when I dragged my attention back to his face, I found him studying me with an expression that made my breath catch. Part wonder, part hunger, all heat.

His hand slid from my shoulder to my neck, awakening every cell in its path. His touch was tentative, like he was giving me time to pull away.

Time seemed to slow, marked only by the steady drip of water and the increasing pace of my heartbeat as his stare found my lips.

Every breath between us felt charged, heavy with years of wanting, of almost moments and might-have-beens, dissolving like fog on the glass.

I tilted my face up slightly, willing him to lower his lips to mine, to claim my mouth with his own. The tension between us was like a live wire, one pulse away from exploding, and somehow, I knew that if we kissed, it wouldn't stop there. Couldn't. After years of fantasizing over Blake Morrison, I needed him, all of him, a fresh throb pulsing between my thighs to accentuate the point.

On the outside, this moment would look like a perfect romantic breaking point: two half-naked people, dripping wet, my nipples visible through the thin fabric of my bra beneath the towel that loosened around my shoulders, which could so easily be dropped. But inside our minds was an ocean of reasons.

I could see his playing out in the features of his face, could see it when he shifted back slightly, could hear it when he cleared his throat.

It was then that his attention drifted to the scar on my collarbone, the one he'd noticed in the ER.

His entire body tensed, just like mine had done all those years ago when I'd seen something on his body that he never meant for me to see. Something that had changed everything between us. Intricate patterns of ink now laced around his torso, a beautiful canvas of elements that cohesively blended together. On him, the tattoos looked like they belonged there, like they'd always painted his skin, but I remembered a time when his skin told a different story ...

34

TESSA

The memory hit me with startling clarity—standing in Ryker's doorway, seventeen and clueless about how one moment could change everything between us.

I'd opened the door to discover Blake. In the middle of changing.

His head snapped up, muscles tensing beneath skin that made my breath catch. In all the time he'd spent with my brother, I had never seen him shirtless, not even during pool days when the summer heat assaulted us, when the air conditioner couldn't keep up. He'd always kept his shirt on, which I'd found strange. I mean, it was clear that beneath his fitted shirts, Blake had the kind of muscles other guys dreamed of, with curved arms and a flat stomach that hinted at defined abs. Any other guy would look for every excuse to show off that body, but Blake always hid it.

Always.

Standing in my brother's bedroom, I understood why with heartbreaking clarity.

"Get the fuck out, Tessa." Blake's voice shattered the silence.

Two things struck me with that one sentence. First, he'd never yelled at me like that before. Not once. Second, he'd also never sworn at me before. This wasn't the Blake I knew, the one who'd save me the last slice of pizza every time he came over. This was a cornered animal, wounded and terrified.

Other people would probably be offended by his death glare, his cutting tone, but I sensed those were tools in his belt to push anyone away who'd gotten too close to seeing what was all over his torso: scars of various sizes and colors, scars that didn't belong on a teenage boy's body. Each one looked like a cry carved into his skin.

"Blake," I whispered, stepping forward instead of back. "I—"

"Don't." He stepped back, but the movement only emphasized the scars, making them stretch and shift, like pale rivers across his skin. "Just ... don't."

I thought about everything I knew about Blake's past: parents dead in an accident he wasn't in, bouncing between foster homes. One of which he'd only ever described as "bad." That word echoed in my mind as I took in the unnatural lines carved into his skin. How many nights had he lain awake, carrying these marks alone?

"Get out!" he snapped again.

But I didn't. Instead, I shut the door behind me, not knowing what had come over me. Maybe it was his eyes, eyes clearly riddled with pain. Or maybe it was the way his chest heaved as his breathing quickened or how incredibly vulnerable this huge, muscular guy now appeared, but something inside me told me not to leave him. That leaving him was the worst thing I could do right now.

He might be Ryker's best friend, but he'd been in my life for years, too, forging a friendship of our own. One that suddenly felt more fragile and more precious than ever before.

I closed the distance between us, drawn by the raw vulnerability in his eyes, a storm of defiance and desperation that made my heart ache. When I lifted my hand toward the jagged line across his ribs, Blake flinched but held his ground. Our eyes locked, and I watched the war play out in his features: trust or retreat, stay or run. His breath came in short bursts as my fingertips found his skin, tracing the raised ridge of his largest scar—a chapter of his story written in flesh and pain.

"Who did this to you?" I whispered, my vision blurring.

Why? How could they? The thoughts burned in my chest like acid.

He was silent for several seconds, and I was afraid—so afraid—he'd run and never come back, that I'd never see him again.

But instead, he spoke to me, his tone so low that I almost couldn't hear it. "I couldn't stop him. I couldn't—I was too ..." His voice cracked, and with it, something in my heart cracked too.

"You survived," I said firmly, looking up to meet his gaze. "That's not weakness, Blake. That's courage."

A tear escaped down my cheek, and Blake caught it with his thumb in a gesture so achingly gentle that it made my chest tighten. I wanted to tell him he didn't need to comfort me, that I should be the one wiping away his tears, though his eyes remained dry. Something twisted in my gut at the thought that maybe he'd shed all his tears long ago, in dark rooms, where no one had been there to catch them.

"I don't want anyone to see," he admitted quietly. "Every time I see them—"

"I see strength," I interrupted, my fingers hovering near the largest scar. I'd touched him before without asking, carried away by instinct and emotion, but I shouldn't have done that. He deserved the dignity of being asked, of having control over who touched these marks of his past. "May I?"

After a long moment, he gave a slight nod, and something shifted between us: a wall crumbling, a bridge building. My fingertips traced the raised line across his rib cage, feeling its texture, its story. This wasn't just skin I was touching; it was creating trust.

"I don't ever want to feel that weak again." The words seemed to cost him something to say.

"They don't make you look weak." I placed my palm flat against his chest, feeling his heartbeat racing beneath my hand,

strong and steady despite his apprehension. "They make you look like a warrior."

For a moment, I saw something shift in his eyes, maybe a glimmer of relief or understanding. The muscles in his jaw relaxed, just slightly, but it felt enormous.

"Please don't tell anyone."

Swallowing the thickness in my throat, I shook my head.

"I would never do that to you," I promised. "Never."

Now, years later, those scars were hidden beneath beautiful ink. He'd chosen to write over that chapter of his story, but I'd never forget being the one who'd read it in its original text, written in scars and trust.

BLAKE

I remembered that intimate moment when Tessa found my scars and how instantly, and unendingly, my feelings for her intensified.

Which terrified me.

It scared me that Tessa could shoot me a smile from across the room, and it would ignite the air in my lungs with chemistry and desire. It scared me how helpless I was around her, my eyes constantly seeking her out, my ears straining for even a whisper of her angelic voice. But mostly, it scared me that my heart dangerously, recklessly dared to hope I could somehow be worthy of her.

As if someone could surgically remove the darkness that lived in my bones.

The harder I fell, the faster I ran.

History had taught me that everyone leaves. Foster families had mastered the art of rejection, each one finding increasingly creative ways to tell me I wasn't quite what they were looking for. The door always clicked shut behind me with the same hollow finality.

So, I'd fought against my feelings for her. Hid them behind sarcasm and a foul mood, willing the unwanted feelings to go away because after a lifetime of collecting rejections like medical degrees, I couldn't survive another.

Especially not from Tessa. If she pointed to the door, whatever was left of my soul would splinter into dust.

The problem? With other people, my defenses were reinforced with steel and sarcasm, but they might as well have been made of paper when it came to her. Fighting these feelings became exhausting. Like a drowning person trying to swim against the current to save themselves. Wild and desperate, yet infuriatingly ineffective.

I suppose it was only a matter of time before I'd lose the fight with that current.

That moment came two years ago when I'd had enough alcohol to dent my shield of better judgment. After staring at her across the room the entire night, after thinking about all the what-ifs, I couldn't stop seeing her for what she was: a radiating ball of light, like the sun drifting through a party, unaware that she was illuminating everything in her space.

Later that night, I tucked a strand of hair behind her ear, my fingers lingering a moment too long. When she leaned in, the whiskey told me it meant something. Funny how alcohol has a way of making you forget every scar, every rejection, every reason you're not good enough.

Especially for someone like Tessa Kincaid. Cupcake.

The kiss was soft, sweet and everything I'd imagined. For three seconds, I believed in miracles. Then reality crashed back like a cardiac arrest—her eyes wide with horror, three fingers pressed to her lips like she needed to erase the taste of me. She stammered something and fled, leaving me standing there like the idiot I was.

Her texts came later, filled with gentle letdowns and kind rejections, ones I couldn't face at the time. Not in depth anyway. All I could do then was merely read them, not knowing how to respond.

But now. Now here she was. In my home.

More specifically, my bathroom, dripping with water and temptation ...

Making me wonder, why *had* she run away that night? Her texts had been elusive, more apologetic than explanatory. She'd been the only one I'd made an exception for—liquid courage or not—and she'd run away from me, just like everyone else. Why?

Maybe I misread everything from her all these years. Every look, every word, every touch. Maybe we weren't as close as I thought.

I wanted to ask her about it. We'd never had that talk like we'd agreed to, and I needed to know. Why had she run from me? And why hadn't she told me about this scar when she was lucid?

If she hadn't been medicated, would she have ever told me about it?

She probably didn't remember that I knew.

And now that I thought about it, standing here, pretending I didn't know who'd done this to her felt like another betrayal to Tessa.

A betrayal I needed to come clean with.

35

TESSA

My fingers hovered over his chest, just like they had that day I'd found his scars. The tattoos were gorgeous. An artful maze of elements flowing together, telling a new story, but beneath them, I knew every ridge, every line of the original chapter.

"No one else knows what's under there, do they?" I asked softly.

"No." Blake's thumb traced the raised line along my collarbone, and something shifted in his expression—that familiar crease between his brows that always meant he was wrestling with something. "Tess, do you remember telling me about this?"

His question, its implications, stole the air from my lungs.

"What?"

"When you were sedated," he said quietly, his gaze tentatively navigating from my left eye to my right, "you told me what happened that night."

My head spun. The bathroom walls seemed to close in, steam suddenly too thick to breathe, and in the span of a few heartbeats, several emotions charged through my veins.

Panic. Pure, premium, grade-A panic. This was the secret I'd guarded for years, planned to take to my grave. I'd spent a tremendous amount of energy hiding it from everyone, from the clothes I chose to the topics I avoided.

Every family gathering had this pulse, threatening to shatter the unbroken image my family had of me. Family dinners were a tug-of-war between the mundane in front of me and the horror in my head. *Tess, can you pass the potatoes? He throws me on the bed. Tess, do you need a refill, dear? He rips my shirt. Tess, how is your semester going? He shoves his sweaty hand over my mouth, as if anyone could hear me scream over the bass of the music, thumping through my body like a warning. Fight. Fight. Fight.*

Crashing right behind panic was *shame* because I knew better. The mistakes I'd made that night that put me in his room, that gave him the ability to try and ...

I was so much smarter than that. I'd seen enough news stories, thank you very much.

Which leads straight into *anger*. Women shouldn't have to be warned—constantly—about the dangers of men. Maybe, just fucking maybe, if police had—oh, I don't know—arrested that guy, he'd have been deterred from doing it again. I bet he'd done it before and then did it again after. Based on his creepy letters, he was probably still doing it to this day, and how many women came forward, asking for help? Why would they bother? Where did it get me without some smoking gun?

In fact, last I researched, out of a thousand sexual assaults, it was estimated that only six resulted in the perpetrator being incarcerated. Six. Out of a thousand. If my math was right, that meant these assailants had a 99.4% chance of getting away with it scot-free. Why the hell *wouldn't* some asshole go around raping women? I really hoped those statistics were wrong.

And then the hardest emotion hit. Sadness. Less so for me. My attack was interrupted. I had the privilege of having access to therapy. I got better. But my sadness was for the other victims who had it much worse than I ever did.

Which would then make me feel guilty. Why did I get away? Why did I get off so easily when others didn't?

"Tess. Breathe."

It wasn't until this moment that I realized I was hyperventilating.

"Sit."

He guided me to the toilet—seat down at least—and squatted in front of me while I had, well, whatever the hell this was.

"Head between your knees."

I complied while he rubbed my back.

"I'm sorry," Blake said. "Maybe I shouldn't have said anything. I felt like it was a lie, pretending I didn't know."

His words anchored me, giving me something to focus on besides the chaos in my head. In. And out. The gentle pressure of his palm matched my breathing rhythm, the vise around my chest slowly loosening.

When my lungs finally remembered how to work properly, I attempted to stand, to escape this moment of weakness, but Blake's arms caught me as I swayed. The concern in his expression made me feel absurdly delicate, less like an able-bodied adult and more like a baby giraffe standing for the first time.

I couldn't meet his stare though. Couldn't bear to see pity or horror in those eyes that had always looked at me like I was unbreakable.

"I didn't know what I was saying," I claimed, looking at the ground. "I was drugged."

"You don't need to hide from me." His voice carried the weight of old wounds, and his finger tilted my chin up until I met his eyes. "Not from me, Tess."

"Well ... it was a long time ago." The words felt hollow, rehearsed from years of telling them to myself.

"Stop."

"Stop what?"

"I can feel you pulling away. Don't shut me out."

I tried to turn away again, but his hold on my arms was sure.

"Did you look at me differently after you saw my scars?" His question held an edge of challenge.

"That was different."

"Was it?" His thumb brushed my cheek. "You said you saw me as a warrior. It wasn't until I saw your scar that I finally understood what you meant."

Something in his voice made me look up. The understanding in his eyes—not pity, not horror, just pure recognition—melted the ice that had formed around my chest. The steam wrapped around us like a cocoon, and I felt the fortress I'd built start to crack.

"You see me as a warrior?" It was so anti-feminine, caring this much what a man thought of me. But this wasn't just a man. This was Blake. My Blake.

"More than you can imagine."

Do not cry. You've done so much crying that you could seriously charge for water.

Blake dragged his knuckles down my jaw, looking heartbreakingly pained.

"I've been going through every memory," he said, "trying to pinpoint when this happened to you. Then, today, it hit me. That weekend Ryker and I were home from college for your dad's birthday. You came in late, went straight to your room. Ryker thought it was just some boyfriend-breakup drama, but ..." He set his jaw tight. "Something felt wrong. After Ryker fell asleep, I went to your door."

"I told you to go away." The memory surfaced, sharp and clear.

"But I could hear you crying. It was ... brutal to hear your pain. I wasn't sure what to do, so I just ..." His voice roughened. "I sat outside your door. All night. Just in case you needed me."

The sob that escaped my throat surprised us both. I had no idea that when my palm had been pressed against that door, wishing he was there, he actually was. I remember the confusing thoughts and feelings that first night and how I wanted to tell him what happened. Him, only him. Wanted his arms wrapped around me, my face buried in his chest as he assured me everything would be okay. And I remember how I'd wanted to tell him that I went down swinging.

"I fought back," I said, the words tumbling out. "When he got interrupted, I grabbed a bottle. I got cut, but I got away, and later ..." My voice cracked. "Later, I remember thinking you'd be proud of me for fighting back." I smiled. "Isn't that pathetic? That I wanted you to be proud of me for that?"

Blake's chest rose sharply. "I am proud of you. And I wish you'd let me in that night."

"I almost did." The confession felt like letting go of something heavy I'd carried for years. "I wanted so badly to just ... feel enveloped by your warmth."

His Adam's apple bobbed, like it pained him to hear that I'd been suffering. "Why didn't you?"

"I was overwhelmed, processing it all. And I couldn't let Ryker find out, so I just ..." I swallowed hard. "I pressed my hand against the door, wishing ..."

"I *was* there, Tess." His voice was rough. "Right there on the other side. The whole night."

It was strange how history, in that moment, actually rewrote itself. Thinking about the darkest night of my life, I'd always remembered how alone I felt. Scared. Violated. But knowing now that Blake had been there with me, a mere three inches from my palm, it changed something about that night. It lessened its darkness somehow.

I'd always known I could trust Blake—him, with his own scars, his own battles—to understand in a way no one else ever would.

"You always made me feel safe." My fingers found his jaw, traced the familiar line of it.

Blake pulled me to his chest, wrapped his arms around me, like I'd longed for him to do that night. His chest was just as warm as I'd imagined it would have been. A sanctuary where nothing existed except his skin, the beat of his heart beneath my ear.

"I wish you would have trusted me with it back then." He

kissed the top of my head. "I wish I'd held you because I would never have let go."

Never let go? What exactly did he mean by that? It felt significant.

As significant as these raised scars, which also ran along his back. Here was someone who understood both strength and vulnerability, who'd seen my worst moments and still looked at me like I was something precious.

"I'm sorry I wasn't there to protect you."

The moment stretched between us, heavy with years of almosts and not-quites. Steam curled around us, and I became acutely aware of everything: the cling of fabric to my wet skin, the warmth radiating from his, the way his chest rose and fell with each breath.

Pulling back, Blake dropped his eyes to my mouth, lingering there with an intensity that reminded me why he was the one I wanted to run to that night. Ghosting his thumb along my lower lip, he stared at my mouth with unmistakable longing, and instantly, I could feel the heat of him everywhere. But there was something else in his eyes. Doubt? Fear that kissing someone with my history might be triggering?

I wanted to tell him I was fine. At least in the sex department, I was, thanks to the aforementioned therapy. But I didn't have the chance.

He gave me a weak, reassuring smile before stepping back, being way too much of a gentleman for the thoughts currently charging through me.

Thanks, hormones.

After a moment, he swiped his thumb across his lip.

Not helping with the throbbing between my thighs.

"I'm glad you're here, Tess." He motioned to the shower with his chin. "If you need anything ..." The words hung there, weighted with possibility.

And then he left, looking at me over his shoulder one last time before vanishing into the penthouse's hallway.

It took a serious second to shake off the I-almost-kissed-Blake-Morrison moment. My lips still tingled with the ghost of possibility, sending my mind spinning through endless what-ifs.

But on the upside, it seriously improved my mood.

My steps felt lighter as I showered, dressed, and adjusted the heart pad device—the one Blake always reminded me to keep on. Where was he now? Probably at the hospital, reviewing patient charts, maybe thinking about our moment. Or maybe not thinking about it at all.

I distracted myself with unpacking, sorting through the mail I'd brought. Bills mostly. Healthcare, to be specific. Then one envelope stopped my heart cold.

I tossed it onto the dresser like it was an infectious spider.

Seconds later, my phone buzzed, making me jump. A smile tugged at my lips when I saw his name, my shoulders instantly relaxing. Even through text, Blake had a way of making me feel safer.

Blake: You okay?

Me: Why wouldn't I be? And where are you?

Blake: In my car. Your heart rate spiked.

Me: You're watching my heart rate?

Blake: You knew about the monitor.

Me: For my CARDIOLOGIST. Also, isn't that considered texting while driving? #Dangerous. Don't you work in an ER where crash victims are taken?

Blake: Answer the question.

Me: Saw a spider. No big deal.

Blake: I'll call an exterminator. The humane kind that won't make you sicker with chemicals.

Me: That's overkill.

Blake: Fine. I'll help the spider fill out a rental application.

I caught myself smiling. This was one thing I loved about Blake. He'd let me have my deeply emotional moments, he'd let me freak out and panic, but then he'd slide back into his normal self. Wonderful, sarcastic, normal him.

This was why I felt safe with him.

The joy of that realization almost made me forget about the envelope waiting like a bomb on my dresser. A smarter person would stop opening them. But since the police refused to take action, these twisted letters were my only window into my tormentor's increasingly unstable mind.

36

BLAKE

Me: You have a meeting near my penthouse today, right?

Jace: What, do you have a tracker on my phone? #CreepyAF #StalkerVibes

Me: You mentioned it last week. Need a favor.

Jace: Here we go. Can't wait to hear this. What, did you forget your favorite shoes? Or did you run out of hair product for that meticulously disheveled look?

Me: Tessa's at my place.

*Jace: Really? *smirking emoji**

Me: Not like that, dude. I'm helping her with something. And wipe that smirk off your face. I can see it through the phone.

Jace: I bet you are "helping" her. With your extensive "skills." Is that what the kids call it these days?

Me: She's not responding to me though. Can you check on her, please?

Jace: I'm sure she's fine. Probably saw your name on her screen and decided to preserve her sanity.

Me: Won't be able to focus on work until I know that for a fact. She hasn't answered her cell in hours. I'm getting worried.

Jace: Don't you have an employee or neighbor you can ask? This is a mile in the wrong direction for me. Some of us have actual work to do, not just playing doctor.

Me: Not friendly with neighbors.

Jace: You're not friendly with anyone. That's your personal brand.

Me: You gonna make me beg? Because I'll send a voice memo of it and you can use it as your ringtone.

Jace: Fine. Jesus, you're pushy. When I see her, I'm going to tell her to answer her fucking phone next time. Or invest in a better friend.

Me: Yell at her, and I'll dislocate your teeth. And ruin your perfect smile for your next Forbes cover.

Jace: Your gratitude is overwhelming. Truly heartwarming. Is this how you speak to all your organ donors?

Me: Only the pretty ones. Text me when you see she's in one piece.

Jace: Yes, Your Majesty. Anything else? Need me to pick up your dry cleaning while I'm playing errand boy?

TESSA

I didn't hear the door open. Didn't hear the man come into Blake's penthouse and didn't hear him come up behind me. Reason being, I was blasting music while making Blake blueberry cupcakes. It was the least I could do to say thank you, right? So, I'd sent the chef home and planned to have this all cleaned up long before Blake returned from his shift.

I was swaying my hips and singing loudly to the music while stirring the batter in an oversize silver bowl when it happened.

A hand came down on my shoulder from behind.

Instinct took over. I spun and slammed the silver bowl on top of his head so hard that he wobbled and dropped to the ground, where blueberry batter splattered all over the floor, the pristine cabinets, and the countertops.

The guy looked vaguely familiar. Handsome, with piercing

green eyes now narrowed in pain, broad shoulders straining against a business suit that looked like it cost a fortune, but was now stained in blueberries and what appeared to be blood.

Grabbing a butcher knife, I held it out in front of me, my heart pounding in my ears louder than the bass from the speakers.

"Jesus," the guy snarled, wiping batter from his eyes to reveal a murderous glower.

"Get out." My voice was steadier than I felt.

He glared at me, rubbing a now-bleeding spot on the side of his head. Based on the amount of blood seeping between his manicured fingers, the guy could use some stitches. His zillion-dollar watch was now splattered with purple goo too.

Had he lifted it from his last break-in?

"Why the fuck did you hit me?"

"News flash: women don't want to get assaulted by home invaders. Leave, or I'll cut your balls off." I gestured with the knife to emphasize my point.

Blood dripped over the batter in a grotesque kaleidoscope of tans, crimson, and purples.

How dare the guy look angry at me for defending myself!

"That's the last time I'm doing Blake a favor," the guy grumbled, getting to his feet with as much dignity as one could muster while covered in blueberry batter.

I froze. "Blake?"

"Just perfect." The guy pulled his hand away, which was soaked in blood. "Now I'm going to have to stop and get stapled up. *And* change my damn suit."

"Blake sent you?" The knife lowered slightly in my grip.

"How the hell did you think I got inside? Magic?"

Well, I hadn't had time to think actually. Just react.

"I'll be sure to tell him you're just fine." The guy grabbed a handful of paper towels, wadded them up, and pressed them against his head wound.

"He sent you to check on me," I realized.

God, of course he did. My phone was charging in the

bedroom; he was probably trying to get ahold of me, and now that I was looking, I did recognize blueberry face.

"You're Jace," I realized.

One of Ryker's college buddies, one I hadn't seen in ages. Maybe if I'd bumped into him in a coffee shop, I would have recognized him faster than, you know, in the middle of fight or flight.

"I'm so sorry. I thought you were ..." Not important. "Here, let me help you with that."

"I got it," he snarled, holding his palm out to me to keep me at bay. "Next time, answer your phone, okay? And maybe turn down the music so you can hear someone announcing themselves."

"I'm sorry," I called out after him as he walked toward the elevator, leaving a trail of blueberry footprints on Blake's pristine hardwood floors.

But he just held up his hand like, *Whatever*.

I sighed, staring at this mess. Blueberry-staining batter mixed with a little blood was splattered all over the ground and walls. Blake was going to be furious. And somehow, I'd managed to assault one of the most powerful businessmen in the city with breakfast ingredients.

BLAKE

I opened the emergency room door to find Jace. Blood spilled down his temple and soaked his shirt—a custom Armani embellished with purple stains visible beneath the blood.

"What the fuck happened?"

The nurse immediately shot her eyes to me. I wasn't using my doctor voice; I was using my brotherhood voice.

"What happened is, it turns out, your houseguest is just fine. So was I until I checked on her. I have a board meeting in three hours, Blake. I'm in the middle of acquiring a company worth half a billion, and instead of prepping my strategy, I'm sitting in your ER with my brain possibly leaking out."

"Tessa did this to you?" I couldn't keep the hint of pride from my voice.

"If you ever have an intruder, you should send her in to protect you. She's five foot nothing and nearly decapitated me with a mixing bowl. A mixing bowl, Blake." He winced as he shifted the ice pack. "I have security teams that couldn't react that fast."

"What did you do, sneak up on her?"

Jace's eyes narrowed. "You're taking her side? I'm the victim here. I have plenty of enemies: corporate rivals, that senator whose company I took from him. Yet it's your petite baker who managed to assault me."

"You must've scared her."

"I'm showing up with a bloody head, and that's what you have to say to me? My PR team is already drafting a statement about a 'minor household accident' because I can't exactly tell the *Wall Street Journal* that I got my ass handed to me by a cupcake chef."

"Oh, you're fine. That head of yours is too hard to do any real damage."

"Am I still stunningly handsome?" He pulled the ice pack away from his face, revealing a nasty gash and impressive swelling, noting my grimace. "Don't lie to me, Doctor. I need to know if I should cancel my *Forbes* photo shoot next week."

"Can they reschedule?"

"Great."

"Don't worry; once the swelling goes down, I'm sure you'll be beautiful again. At least it'll make it easier to tell you and Grayson apart now."

His identical twin.

"So, this will scar."

"Too early to tell."

"Great."

"So, she was okay?"

"You're still worried about *her*?" He pointed to the gash on his head. "I'm bleeding out in your ER while she's happily baking away like some disturbing Betty Crocker."

"You'll be fine. But do me a favor."

"Another one? Oh, sure. Sign me up. What'll it be this time, a compound fracture to my arm?"

"Don't mention this to the guys."

He cocked his head, wincing at the movement. "Ryker's going to kill you if you date his sister."

"I'm not dating her."

"Whatever." He rolled his eyes. "Just get me out of here. Fast."

"I'll call a plastic surgeon down so you look just as handsome as before."

"Yeah, well, watch your ass, Morrison. If she can do this with a mixing bowl, you should keep her away from your knives." Jace adjusted his ruined tie with his free hand. "And for the record, when you end up murdered in your sleep by Kitchen Ninja Barbie, I'm telling the detective everything. Right after I send flowers to your funeral with a card that says, *I told you so*."

37

BLAKE

SINNERS & SAINTS GROUP CHAT

Jace: Next acquisition I do, I'm going to need an IV drip of whiskey straight into my veins. Just spent twelve hours trying to save three hundred jobs because some trust-fund CEO thinks legally binding contracts are suggestions.

Axel: Trouble in corporate paradise, Mr. Fortune 500?

Jace: More like trying to stop some vulture capitalist from destroying families for a quick profit. My lawyers are as homicidal as I am right now. Speaking of prison ...

Axel: Smooth transition. But, yeah, anyone got Knox's new burner number? Been trying to add him to these chats.

Ryker: For the love of God, no more phones. He spent a week in solitary for the last one. We're trying to keep his record clean for parole.

Jace: Do you think he has a chance at parole this time?

*Axel: What, you think they won't release our favorite murderer? *grimacing teeth emoji**

Ryker: Call him that again, and I'll personally ensure you need a lawyer.

Me: How's he holding up?

Ryker: Better than any of us would. Says the prison book club is reading Fifty Shades of Grey.

Axel: No way.

Ryker: I'm kidding, moron.

Jace: Maybe we should just break him out. I've got the resources.

Ryker: Don't even joke. He needs to keep his spirits up, guys.

Axel: In that case, should I tell him about my mysterious rash?

Everyone: NO.

38

BLAKE

A scream shattered the night. Not just any scream. The kind that stops your heart.

Tessa.

I charged out of my bedroom, down the hall, bare feet nearly sliding on hardwood. My mind raced with every possible threat—intruder, accident, injury—while my body moved on pure instinct. In a more lucid moment, I might have remembered we were fifty stories up in a secured penthouse. But all I could process was that sound, that soul-ripping cry that made my blood run cold.

The darkness in her room disoriented me for a moment. When I turned on the soft lamp by her bed, I realized there was no intruder. No threat. Just Tessa, tangled in sheets, tears streaming down her face as she fought an enemy I couldn't see.

"No," she whimpered, one hand pressing outward against a phantom attacker. "Please stop."

My stomach dropped through the floor. Rage bloomed in my chest. Helpless, useless rage with nowhere to go.

"Get off me!" The raw fear in her voice made my hands shake.

"Tessa." I reached for her, then hesitated, worried my touch would make it worse. "You're safe. You're home."

She jerked away from my voice, still trapped in the nightmare. "No!"

Something inside me cracked, watching her relive this hell. I'd seen thousands of patients in pain, but nothing had ever cut quite like this.

"Tessa, wake up. It's Blake. You're safe."

Her eyes flew open, wild and unfocused. For a moment, she stared through me, still caught between nightmare and reality. Then awareness crept in, followed immediately by that mask she wore so well. The one that said, *I'm fine; everything's fine.*

"I'm sorry I woke you," she said, voice scratchy, embarrassment flooding her cheeks with red. "I haven't had a nightmare in a while."

Even now, she was trying to comfort me. Jesus.

"Something triggered it." Not a question. "Was it Jace? He didn't mean to surprise you in the kitchen."

We'd already talked about this, of course, when she'd apologized a million times.

"No." She twisted her fingers in her lap, gaze down. The tell I'd memorized years ago.

"Was it because of our talk?" Damn, why did I bring that up? Maybe I should have taken her confession to my grave. If this was my fault—

"No," she said.

"Then what?"

Silence.

"I'm fine," she insisted, but her voice wavered. "Really. I'm sorry I woke you."

Tessa lay back down, shifting the covers until she was comfortable, making it clear this part of the conversation was over.

But something had set her off, and for some reason, I believed her, that it wasn't our talk. But what then? What had infiltrated the safety of my penthouse and scared the shit out of her?

"Good night, Blake," she said gently.

I turned toward the hallway but stopped, watching her stare at the ceiling with that carefully blank expression I knew too well. My feet refused to move, understanding viscerally what it was like to lie there alone after a nightmare, trying to be fine.

"Sometimes, sleeping can be the hardest when you don't feel safe," I said.

When she clutched the covers together to her chest, something twisted in my ribs.

"I don't want to invade your space," I started. "But ... would it be okay if I lay with you? Just until you fall asleep?" She tensed slightly, and my voice softened. "I won't get any sleep, worrying you might be in here, unable to sleep alone."

Her voice was barely a whisper. "What if I can't sleep at all?"

"Then we'll be insomniacs together."

That earned me a ghost of a smile, and after a moment's hesitation, she shifted over, making room for me on the bed. After I shut off the light, we lay there in silence, but I could feel the tension radiating from her body, could sense her struggling to relax.

"Blake?" Her voice was quiet, embarrassed. "Would you ... would you hold me?"

My throat tightened. "Cupcake," I murmured, "I'd hold you every moment of every day if it meant you felt safe."

I reached for her, but again, hesitated. She was in a bed, perhaps not unlike the one she was assaulted in.

"You're sure?" I started. "I don't want to trigger—"

"I'm sure." Her voice wavered, and we both knew she wasn't being entirely truthful. The way she'd flinched from the male nurse was still fresh in my mind. But I understood what she meant. The nurse had been a stranger who'd moved suddenly, probably in a way that echoed her past trauma. With me, right now, she felt safe. "Therapy helped," she continued softly. "It's just the nightmares that still come, and for those few minutes after, everything feels ... raw."

My mind caught on the word *therapy*. This girl had been

through a war while I was evidently studying textbooks. Fucking A.

"Besides. *Your* touch would never trigger me." She nuzzled her face into my chest as if those words hadn't penetrated my soul. That *my* touch would be different. Safe. Even if all other men might scare her.

"Tell me what triggered this?" I kept my voice soft, though dread pooled in my stomach. Especially when she tensed.

"You'll freak out."

Despite everything, I smiled. "Stop trying to protect me from having feelings."

She traced slow circles on my abs, each touch sending warmth from my skin to my heart. "Promise you won't do anything rash?"

"Tessa."

She sighed. "He sent another letter."

Every muscle in my body went rigid with two more words: *another* and *letter*. I recalled what she'd been mumbling incoherently before her MRI. Something about police not being able to prove it was him, about wishing they used handwriting experts.

"What do you mean, another letter?"

The silence stretched so long that I thought she wouldn't answer.

When she did, her voice was carefully controlled, like she was defusing a bomb. "After I filed the police report, he started showing up on campus, demanding I drop the complaint. Then he went quiet. Long enough that when the letters began appearing, the police said there was no way to prove it was him. Especially since the first ones were typed, self-sealed, slipped directly into my mailbox. Untraceable." She drew a shaky breath. "Years later, when they turned handwritten, the police visited him, but again, no proof. No fingerprints. No explicit mention of that night. Just him, finding ways to remind me he's still out there, still watching."

My vision burned red. The only thing keeping me from

leaping up and hunting him down right now was the weight of her against my chest.

Knox was in prison with people like this predator. The type of guy who wanted control over his victim, and when she dared speak out against him, the only way for him to maintain a sense of power and control was to continue to dominate her through threats and fear. It was like reliving that attack over and over.

And putting Tessa through hell.

All while, evidently, keeping track of where she lived. He had to have her address to send that letter.

"Tess, have you seen him since the attack?"

Tessa yawned. "No. I just hate it when another letter comes."

A letter. How did he get her a letter *here*? She hadn't even had mail forwarded yet, just grabbed the stack of mail on her counter from—

I glared across the room at a piece of paper, a typed letter sprawled on her dresser.

Motherfucker. It took a massive—*massive*—amount of control to hold her until her breathing evened out, until I was certain she'd fallen into safer dreams. Only then did I ease away, tucking the covers around her shoulders, and then snatched the letter off her dresser.

I read it in the hallway. Twice, each word a bottle of gasoline to my wildfire of rage. How dare this piece of shit! The image of a man forcing himself on Tessa made me want to break every single bone in his body, find every nerve and cut it with a dull ten blade. Finding out he'd been taunting her this whole time, refusing to let her move on with her life?

Storming into my bedroom, I fired off a text to the guys. Time be damned.

SINNERS & SAINTS GROUP CHAT

Me: 911. Meet me at the mansion. Now.

Jace: It's 3:30 a.m.

Me: Yep, I can tell time.

Axel: If this is about your car getting keyed, I swear to God ...

Me: Nothing I can put in writing. You coming or not?

Ryker: Is Tessa okay?

Ryker didn't know she was staying with me—still didn't know about her medical condition—but he knew I was trying to find Voss. And knew Tessa was the only person in the world that would be worthy of a 3:30 a.m. 911 from me.

Me: She's safe. But I need everyone. Tonight.

Axel: I'm literally in bed with a supermodel.

Jace: Your cleaning service deserves hazard pay for those sheets. Now Blake said move, so move. And, Blake? You STILL owe ME a favor, don't forget.

Thirty minutes later, they arrived, looking like what they were: dangerous men dragged from sleep, running on loyalty and caffeine. Jace was the last to walk in, immaculate, even at this hour, in a black button-down with the sleeves rolled up, his tie loosened but still perfectly knotted. While everyone else looked like they'd been dragged from bed, Jace looked like he'd been calculating profit margins.

When asked, Jace kept the source of his injury vague enough that they didn't suspect where it'd come from. Luckily, they were distracted with wondering why I'd called this emergency meeting.

"I need your help." My tone made them straighten. "What I'm about to propose is unethical. Illegal. You can walk away. But I'm hoping you won't."

The temperature in the room dropped ten degrees.

"What happened?" Ryker's voice had that edge he saved for destroying witnesses.

"I want to ruin someone. Systematically. Completely."

Ryker's jaw locked. "He did something else to her, didn't he?"

My silence answered for me.

Ryker's fist found the wall. The lawyer who never lost control lost it spectacularly.

"Who?" Jace's voice was arctic as he reached for his phone, as if preparing to mobilize his financial empire at a moment's notice.

"The man who assaulted my sister," Ryker answered.

The room crystallized into something deadly. The guys who'd crawled through hell together slowly processed what was just said —someone hurt someone we loved—and now, their faces hardened, ready to drag someone else down.

"Tell us what you need." Jace's fingers were already hovering over his screen, his weapon. There was something lethal in his stillness, a darkness I recognized. The same kind that had lived in him since the day his father was murdered.

I'd tracked Voss down in terms of knowing his address and other intel, but without the ability to sit outside his place 24/7, I had yet to spot him, yet to physically get my hands on him.

"The guy owns a talent agency. Small but growing. His entire ego's wrapped up in it." I fixed on Jace. "Buy him out. Hostile takeover. Whatever it takes. I want him watching his life's work turn to ash."

A cold smile curved Jace's lips. "I know exactly how to destroy him. We'll start with his investors. I'll buy their silence, their shares, so fast that he won't know until he's bleeding out." His voice dropped lower. "I'll protect his employees though. Move them to subsidiary companies before the kill shot."

"Good. This is about him."

"I can have preliminary documents drawn up by morning," Jace continued. "By noon, I'll know every weak point in his financial structure. By tomorrow night, I can have rumors floating that will make his investors panic. Once they start selling ..." He looked up. "He won't be able to do anything to stop it."

"Good." I turned to Axel. "Your PR department still highly compensated?"

A predatory smile spread across his face. "Want me to dig up his skeletons?"

"I want you to find every secret he's buried and blast it across the internet. Make him radioactive."

"If you'd told me we were doing something this fun, I'd have shown up faster," Axel added.

"I've got contacts at every major news outlet," Jace added, his fingers already moving across his phone. "By the time we're done, his name will be poison in every boardroom from here to Tokyo. No one will touch him with a ten-foot pole." He looked up, and for a moment, I saw the wounded boy who'd lost everything, now a man with the power to make others feel that same loss.

In this moment, I think I appreciated Jace more than I ever had before. And trust me, I'd respected the hell out of him already.

You'd think a guy whose father was murdered would give up on life. Especially when it happened right in front of his brother's eyes. You'd think a guy who inherited hundreds of millions at eighteen would choose to coast. Globe-trot on private jets, sip drinks on beaches, collect supermodels like trading cards. And you'd think with all that money, he'd have just bought his way into business, but he took the time and energy to go to college.

"You can't run a company if you haven't paid your dues," he'd said once.

And that was Jace in a nutshell: a billionaire who still believed in earning his place. While other CEOs collected corporations like trophies, he spent his career saving struggling businesses from going under.

"Ryker, any evidence Axel finds with legal legs, build a file. Worst case, we take it to authorities. Get him shipped to prison. Preferably Knox's block."

"And best case?" Axel asked.

"Best case, I get my hands on him first," I said.

They understood instantly. Better yet, not one of them tried to talk me down.

"His name," Axel demanded, playboy facade burned away. "Give us his name."

"Eric Voss."

Jace was already making calls. Axel's fingers flew across his phone. Ryker's hand landed on my shoulder, solid as steel.

"He hurt your sister," Jace said to him, voice deadly quiet. "In forty-eight hours, Eric Voss won't know what hit him."

Brotherhood wasn't always about defense. Sometimes, it was about demolition. And Eric Voss? He was about to learn what happened when you hurt someone under our protection.

He didn't just pick the wrong girl to hurt. He picked the wrong family to face.

39

TESSA

I paced the penthouse like a caged tiger, my phone clutched in my hand like a lifeline. It was a wonder that I'd been able to get any work done today after Blake had snuck out. After he'd betrayed me by taking something that didn't belong to him, something that was so private that I couldn't believe he'd dared taken it.

All day, I'd had to be productive. Frantically searching for wedding locations that had any cancellations. Sadly, one other bride and groom had called it quits two days ago, so I'd snagged a coveted venue, one that my bride was thrilled about. It took hours to do the paperwork, do the tour, and then I came back to this empty place. Pacing.

When the elevator finally pinged, I whirled around, my heart leaping into my throat. Blake stepped out, and one look at his face made my stomach drop.

"Where were you?"

"Out." His tone was clipped, controlled.

"Did you take that letter off my dresser?"

"You're a smart girl, Tessa. You already know the answer to that."

"That letter was private!" With humiliating taunts from a sadistic bully.

Blake stalked past me toward the kitchen, his jaw set in that stubborn line I knew too well.

I followed him, my bare feet silent against the hardwood floors, watching as he retrieved a bag of frozen vegetables from the pristine stainless steel freezer.

"Give us a minute," he barked at his chef.

She scurried out, leaving dinner half prepared.

"Tell me you didn't beat someone up!" I said, though the evidence was literally right there on his hands.

He pressed the makeshift ice pack against his knuckles. "Voss proved more difficult to track down than expected. The punching bag at the gym took the brunt of my frustration."

Voss. He knew his name? When I'd told him about the attack, I'd also told him the attacker's name?!? File that in the *that can't be good* folder.

"With the hand you need to treat patients with?" I balked. "What has gotten into you? You're not some hotheaded teenager anymore, Blake. You're a board-certified doctor with everything to lose by going after ghosts from my past."

"That letter he sent you is very much in the present."

"He's not worth you risking your career by beating him up."

His gaze snapped to mine. "I intend to do more than beat him."

My neck sprang back. "Okay, I'm going to assume that's a heat-of-the-moment comment, and you don't actually mean that."

No response.

"This is not your fight."

He said nothing for a minute. Was too busy inspecting his knuckles, theoretically with his *doctor* lens. "The guy assaulted you. Now he's threatening you. You honestly think I'll let that go?"

"How have you made it this far in medicine with that temper? Last I checked, doctors weren't supposed to moonlight as vigilantes."

"Studying medicine never changed who I am, Tess." The way he said my name, low and rough, sent an avalanche of ice down my body.

That's when I realized how toxic I was being for him. I was his illness, infecting his world and his rational thinking, drawing him back to his teenage fighting days.

"I won't let you torch your career over me," I insisted.

Blake shook his head. "I need air."

He tried to walk away from me, but unlike two years ago, this time, I didn't let him. I followed him up a stairwell that led to a door, which led to, of all things, a rooftop terrace.

Seriously? Before me stretched a scene straight out of a movie: twinkling string lights draped between poles, ivory-wrapped railings framing the glittering Chicago skyline, and plush loungers arranged intimately around a stone fireplace. In another life, this would be the backdrop for something beautiful, like a proposal. Instead, the elegant setting was now the stage for what was shaping up to be the worst fight Blake and I had ever had.

"I don't understand why you turned back into this alpha, vendetta guy, stealing that letter and beating something until your knuckles are bloody. Is that all this is? Saving me? Because I don't need to be saved, Blake."

Here I'd been, thinking about our almost kiss, wondering what it meant, wondering what-if. Again. Just like I'd done so many freaking times before, and he wasn't thinking about any of that or me. He was thinking of victim Tessa, sick Tessa, who needed big bad Blake to put his cape on and rescue me.

Our feelings were on different frequencies, and it hurt.

"I don't understand why you're so upset?"

"You mean, aside from me being bad for you?" I snarled, cutting him off before he could come back with a retort. "This is what we've always done, Blake." I gestured between us, my laugh bitter. "One minute, you make me feel like I'm the most important person in your world, moving me into your penthouse, vowing to solve my medical mystery. But I know what comes next."

"And what's that?"

"Every other time I've let my guard down, you blow me off and make it clear how you really feel about me."

The moment the words left my mouth, I regretted them. I watched them hit like land mines, his shoulders tensing. Seconds later, his fists clenched, and he crossed the space between us in three long strides.

"You think I don't care about you?"

I said nothing.

"You're important to me, Tessa. How do you not know that by now?"

"Intellectually? Sure. But my heart has never been able to figure you out. Your constant push and pull, making me feel special one moment and invisible the next."

"You matter more to me than anyone else in my life."

"Really?" I couldn't keep the skepticism from my voice. "Then why wouldn't you return my calls? You made me feel humiliated!"

"*You* stopped returning *my* calls. I'd tried calling you, repeatedly, but after a while, I got the message loud and clear that you never wanted to talk to me again."

I laughed, the sound harsh in the night air. "I didn't answer your calls because before that, I'd sent you *dozens* of texts after that night I embarrassed myself."

"Is that how you see it? You embarrassed yourself?"

"Two months," I shot back. "For two months, you ignored me."

"What was I supposed to say?"

"How about accepting my apology?"

"You had nothing to apologize for."

"Your silent treatment said otherwise."

His jaw ticced. "I buried myself in work because I wasn't sure what to say to you."

"It takes two people to kiss, Blake." The words exploded out of me. "You kissed me that night, and I kissed you back. I know I left, but I tried to reach out to you. But you regretted it so much that you blew me off!"

"You think I didn't want to kiss you?"

"You made that perfectly clear when you ghosted me."

"I didn't ghost you. I took time to figure out what to say, and then you wouldn't take my calls."

"Because you blew me off for two months, and by that point, I was mortified!" The words burst out before I could stop them.

"You had no reason to be mortified, but for whatever reason, you pulled away from me, Tessa. *You* pulled away from *me*. That night was one thing, but when you did it again when I was trying to call you, it devastated me."

I wrapped my arms around myself, suddenly cold despite the warm night air. "Do you want to know why I ran that night?" I forced myself to meet his gaze. "That kiss ... it wasn't about you. I mean, it was about you, but my reaction wasn't." I squeezed my eyes shut, forcing the words out. "I hadn't been intimate with anyone since ... since the assault. I wasn't sure if it would trigger me, so I'd avoided it at all costs."

Blake went still.

"Deep down, I knew I was ready. My therapist had been telling me that for years, but I'd never ... you know, put it to the test. Dating just never felt right. Then that night when you kissed me ... God, everything felt perfect. It should have been the perfect moment to find out if I really was ready. But I panicked."

Which was ridiculous for several reasons. I wasn't scared of Blake. Nor was I the least bit uncomfortable around him the way I was with other men. Even with Eli, I'd felt a little unsettled. With Blake, everything had always felt natural and amazing, and when he kissed me that night? Also amazing. Theoretically, the second course of the kissing meal would also feel natural and amazing. But I'd panicked because what if I was wrong? What if I went to that next course with Blake and then fear kicked in or it suddenly didn't feel natural? Our friendship surviving a kiss was one thing. Surviving an abandoned night in the sheets? Sounded impossible. Ironic, I know. Considering me running away after that kiss ruined everything anyway. But there it was.

Drawing in a shaky breath, I continued, "If I did freak out when we were ... intimate, I would've had to explain why. And that meant telling you about my past. I was planning to take that secret to my grave. I couldn't risk anything happening between us until I was absolutely certain my past wouldn't come crashing in."

When I started dating Eli, I finally let myself try with him. And it was fine. Not *magical* fine, but trauma-wise, I was fine.

"Why didn't you tell me?" Blake's voice was gentle, filled with a tenderness.

"Because it was my secret to keep. I had that right, but I'm so sorry, Blake. I never meant to hurt you that night. I never meant for everything between us to fall apart. For two years, I've been trying to figure out how to explain that my anxiety attack had nothing to do with you, without having to tell you about everything else."

"Tess."

"No," I insisted, feeling his rejection all over again. "No pity. I'm fine. All healed. My point is, I know why I ran, but you ran for different reasons. You ran because I was disposable to you."

"Disposable?" He couldn't look more offended, or angry, by that word.

"I stopped the kiss. I tried to apologize for any hurt feelings or whatever, but you made it clear that you regretted that kiss more than I did. You discarded me, Blake. When I needed you the most, you just ... forgot about me!" I clenched my fists, all that rejection and sleepless nights assaulting my chest.

"You think I haven't thought about you"—his voice dropped to a dangerous whisper—"every moment since I first saw you?"

Heat flashed through me, but I ordered it to cool down.

"And every moment since that kiss? How do you think I got this scar?" He jabbed a finger at the small silver line slashing through his eyebrow. The one I'd noticed in the ER. "I walked straight from that party to the shittiest bar I could find. Picked a fight with the meanest bastard in there because getting knocked on my ass felt better than remembering how incredible your lips felt against mine."

The confession hit me like a hurricane. I'd spent two years thinking he'd walked away unscathed when, in reality, he'd sought out violence just to numb the pain?

He moved forward, forcing me to retreat until my back hit the concrete ledge. Behind me, only a decorative metal railing separated me from a fatal fall.

"I wanted that kiss, Tessa," he said, his voice rough. "I wanted more than that kiss."

I blinked, taking in three long breaths.

"What are you saying?" My brain ping-ponged.

His eyes locked on to mine, dark with an intensity that set my nerves aflame.

He leaned in closer, his breath heated against my ear as he whispered words that ignited my soul. "I didn't want to just kiss you that night, Tessa. I wanted to bury myself in you."

And then he crashed his lips to mine.

40

TESSA

His kiss was fierce and demanding, his fingers threading through my hair as his tongue pressed to mine. I melted into him, my fingers sliding through his silky strands, drawing him closer as need coursed through me like wildfire, settling between my thighs, where an unbearable pulse started to drum like a heartbeat.

Blake's palm found my breast, drawing a gasp from my lips.

Which made him stop for a second, his features falling into worry, perhaps that this level of intimacy was too much after my past.

"It's okay." I nodded, pressing his hand to my breast.

It took him a moment to accept the assurance, but when he did, his touch sent sparks racing across my skin.

Wrapping my arms around his neck, I pressed my body to his, feeling his desire press against my thigh. I rolled my hips slightly, drawing a groan from deep in his throat and matching it with one of my own.

Our kiss grew desperate in a symphony of sighs and gentle bites, of exploring tongues and shared breaths. In all my years of fantasizing about kissing Blake—that quick drunken moment, I decided, didn't count, not when I'd been too shocked to respond

—I'd never imagined it could be like this: raw, uninhibited, years of tension finally unleashing in a storm of sensation.

Standing on this terrace, with the city lights in the distance and gentle bubble lights floating over the space, I felt like we were in a magical garden.

His hand slipped beneath the fabric to caress my bare breast, and I arched into his touch, needing to feel him, all of him, all over my body. This was sweet torture, my body electric with pleasure but aching for more. When his hand traveled down my stomach to my waistband, I let out a soft whimper against his lips.

I didn't protest when he broke our kiss to slide my shorts and underwear down my legs or when he knelt before me, his eyes sparkling with promise as he waited for me to step free of them.

My pulse, my need, everything quickened at the intensity of his gaze.

He rose to claim my mouth again, his hands possessive as they explored my breasts, thumbs circling my sensitive peaks. My fingers mapped the planes of his chest, tracing the defined muscles beneath his shirt.

"You have no idea how long I've dreamed of this," Blake breathed against my skin, trailing kisses along my jaw and down my neck. In one smooth motion, he tugged my tank top up, exposing my breasts to the cool night air.

His mouth found my nipple, the wet heat of his tongue drawing a moan from my throat as I cradled his head, back arching while he lavished attention on each of my breasts. All the while, his eyes stayed locked on mine, sharp with desire, and then he lifted my hips and placed me on the edge of the terrace, the smooth stone cold against my ass.

The railing at my back was the only barrier between me and a long-ass drop, but I couldn't focus on anything except Blake kneeling between my thighs, his soft lips pressing kisses near my sensitive flesh. So close to where I wanted them to be that the pulse in my sex throbbed harder.

My fingers tangled in his hair as realization hit me. The city lights. The terrace. He might not have planned for this to happen, but he was re-creating that scene from the romance novel he'd found in my townhouse, where the heroine was pleasured against a backdrop of city lights.

And luckily for me, Blake didn't live in the heart of the city; he lived on the outskirts, on the tallest building for miles, making me feel free to enjoy what was about to happen.

Blake opened his mouth and hesitated, holding my eyes for one second before, finally, he swiped his tongue up my sex in a long, torturous lick.

The ache between my thighs intensified, becoming almost unbearable.

"You taste like heaven, Cupcake." His voice was rough with desire.

"Blake ..."

Pressing his hands on my inner thighs, he spread me wider, his gaze hungry as he took in the sight of me. "Gorgeous."

Another slow stroke of his tongue had me trembling, especially when he reached that sensitive bundle of nerves and began tracing lazy circles. When he slipped a finger inside me, I clutched the railing behind me.

"Tell me what you want, Tessa." His demand was both gentle and hungry.

"What ... what do you mean?"

"Tell me how you like to come."

He was asking for my *preferred* position, I realized.

"I ..." I swallowed as he licked me again, my shoulders pressing to the hard railing behind me. "I've only done it with my vibrator."

His eyes snapped up to mine.

"You've never come with a guy before?"

I bit my lip, shaking my head. With anyone else, this admission might have been mortifying, but Blake's expression looked ... honored. His mouth rose on both sides, and then he stared between my legs with an all-new intensity.

"I get to be your first." He licked circles around the most sensitive part of my flesh, his technique masterful, alternating between gentle suction and careful strokes that had me fighting to keep still.

"Oh God, right there," I pleaded as he found a particularly sensitive spot. "Just like that ..."

"Do you know what I've imagined doing to you, Tessa?"

I moaned as his tongue continued its sweet torture, the tension inside me building to unprecedented heights.

"I've dreamed of your mouth filled with me."

His words sent an unexpected thrill through me. I'd never experienced this kind of talk before, but I loved it.

"I've dreamed of being deep inside you."

He punctuated this confession by thrusting his tongue inside me, and I felt myself clench around him. I could feel his smile against my flesh before he returned to his earlier rhythm, licking and plunging his fingers inside of me.

"Ohhhh ..."

The pleasure built inexorably as he devoted himself to my satisfaction, letting me rock against his face as I chased my release. I couldn't believe this was happening, that after all these years, I was about to experience my first orgasm with a guy.

Best of all, that guy was Blake.

What a sight we were right now. Dark, handsome, and muscular Blake kneeling before my spread thighs, his face buried in my sex. Moaning, I felt my legs begin to tremble as I held his head to my sensitive flesh, riding a wave that was about to crash over.

When it hit, it was overwhelming. I fisted his hair, thighs quivering as my back arched against that cold bar while wave after wave of pleasure crashed over me. He groaned against me, the vibration only intensifying the sensation as he continued his movements, drawing out my pleasure until I was gasping.

When the last tremors subsided, he pressed a final kiss to my inner thigh before standing.

"That's what I wanted to do the night I kissed you, Tessa."

Wow. Two years of hurt, rewritten in one orgasm. Who'd have thought?

I stood, smiled, and reached for his waistband, wanting to return the pleasure he'd given me, wanting to show him how much this—how much he—meant to me.

His hand caught my wrist, gentle but firm, and my heart stuttered.

"Tess, I ..." The words seemed to catch in his throat.

Something flickered across his face. Fear? Uncertainty? But that didn't make sense.

"I thought you wanted ..." My voice trailed off as I watched him struggle for words. The silence stretched between us, heavy with everything unsaid, and in that silence, my hopes began to crumble.

Oh. The realization hit like a shotgun to the stomach. This wasn't some romantic breakthrough. This was just sex. This was him getting caught up in the moment, maybe finally acting on some long-held fantasy, and now he was stopping before it went too far, before it meant too much.

Just like that night, when he'd kissed me. And after, when he wasn't caught up in the moment anymore, when I'd reached out to him, he pulled away.

This time hurt so much worse.

"I get it," I spat. "Just getting it out of your system. Well, congratulations. Consider that box checked."

He jerked back as if I'd slapped him. "Tessa, that's not—"

"Save it." The burning in my eyes had nothing to do with desire now. "I'm not some naive girl anymore, Blake. I don't need you to let me down easily or make up excuses. This was just scratching an itch, right? Simple curiosity about what it would be like?"

My stomach clenched with pain and nausea, my heartbeat accelerating until I broke out in a cold sweat, and worse, my lungs felt like they couldn't get enough air.

"Tessa—"

"Thanks for the orgasm," I cut him off, my voice sharp enough to draw blood. "Now get out of my way. I have a bag to pack."

I made it all the way to my bedroom before I vomited, this time shaking on the bathroom floor. It felt like all my symptoms came crashing back, all at once.

BLAKE

What had I done? Of all times to surrender to temptation, I'd done it right after Tessa had shared something incredibly intimate with me. What was wrong with my twisted head?

I shouldn't have let that happen. Couldn't let it happen again.

And not just because I was damaged, my edges too sharp from past breaks to risk cutting someone as precious as Tessa, who'd already been through enough. Not just because she deserved better than someone who'd stand frozen in the aftermath of her vulnerability, unable to be what she needed. But because now that I'd had a taste of her, letting myself indulge in that single, devastating moment, I knew with absolute certainty that I wouldn't survive when she inevitably pulled away, leaving nothing but echoes and emptiness behind.

She'd explained why she'd done it two years ago, but that didn't change that it had happened. And that it would happen again. This time at a catastrophic level.

Maybe if I'd never met my foster mom, Sarah, I'd have been reckless enough to take the chance with Tessa, but some lessons brand themselves too deep to forget, and I'd learned mine well. The higher you let yourself soar, the farther you had to fall.

And Tessa. She'd be like surviving a fall from the moon.

I needed to reconstruct the distance I'd fought to create between us after my calls had gone unanswered.

But first, I needed to convince her to stay.

Her life depended on it …

41

TESSA

"You're not helping," I said, methodically folding another shirt and placing it in my suitcase with precise, angry movements. Each fold felt like drawing a line between before and after, between friendship and whatever mess we'd created tonight.

Scarlett wandered along my bookshelf, trailing her fingers across the spines. I was glad we'd had plans tonight. It was convenient she'd shown up when she had because now I had someone to vent to.

"I'm sorry, but I find it completely swoon worthy that he came back with bloody knuckles, wanting to defend your honor."

"You're missing the point, Scarlett." I slammed the latest shirt down harder than necessary.

"Oh, I heard the point." A smile played at her lips. "Especially the part where you said it was the best orgasm of your life."

Heat crept up my neck. Damn it. I had said that, hadn't I? In the middle of my rage-fueled pacing session, those words had slipped out. Now they hung in the air like evidence. "Can we not?"

"Right." Scarlett raised her hands in surrender. "The point. He hurt your feelings."

"It's more than that." I yanked open another drawer, probably with more force than strictly necessary. "He—"

"He's a total dick."

I shot her a look. "Don't do that thing."

"What thing?" Her innocence was too perfect to be real.

"That thing where you actually disagree with me, but say what I want to hear in this over-the-top way to point out how wrong I am."

"I would never." But her lips twitched.

"You're totally doing it right now."

Scarlett sat on the edge of my bed, tucking one leg under her. "Okay, fine. Do you want my honest opinion?"

"Is there any other kind?"

"Sounds to me like he's fighting his feelings for you."

I threw a balled-up pair of socks into the suitcase. "Don't romanticize rejection. I'm a strong, independent woman. If he doesn't want me, for any reason, that's it. Any possible romance over."

She studied me.

"What?" I demanded.

"Nothing."

"And yet you're looking at me like you've got a doctoral thesis forming in that head of yours, so just spit it out."

Scarlett leaned forward, her hair falling over one shoulder. "I'm not romanticizing rejection. You got hurt on that terrace, and that absolutely sucks. But this isn't some random guy from a dating app. This is Blake. Your history together is practically a novel of its own. Of course he's overthinking things."

"He wasn't overthinking when he went down on me," I muttered, then immediately wished I hadn't brought it up.

"That's exactly my point!" Scarlett's eyes lit up. "His control snapped. And the minute he got an ounce of it back, he started fighting the current again. If you want proof he's in love with you—"

"He's not in love with me." The words sliced through the air between us.

"Look at the evidence." Scarlett ticked off points on her fingers. "When you got sick, he moved you into his penthouse and personally took on your case on top of his already-excessive workload. He gave you your first orgasm." She paused. "And now his knuckles are bloody because of whatever your ex did."

Okay, I felt like a jerk; I told her Blake's anger was over an ex, but I really didn't want to be all, *Hey, FYI, I was assaulted in college and, you know, complications.*

I glanced at the window, where city lights blurred through the gathering darkness.

"I hate you for being rational right now," I said. "You know I need you to be my shoulder to cry on, not my voice of reason."

"Have you ever asked him why he doesn't do relationships?"

I stilled. "That's not what this is."

"That's exactly what this is. My question stands."

I shrugged. "I have a pretty good guess. His parents died in a car accident, so he's probably traumatized."

"You've been friends for years and the best you can give me is 'probably'?"

"What difference would it make?"

Scarlett's voice softened. "Based on everything you've told me, it could make all the difference. If you understood why he runs for the hills, maybe you could stop being so angry with him. Do you really want to lose Blake as a friend?"

The question stabbed me like a sword through the ribs. No. No, I didn't. Even through all this hurt and rejection and pain, Blake had been a constant in my life, someone I could go to outside of my brother and Scarlett. Too important to lose.

Scarlett leaned forward, her voice dropping to that gentle tone she used when she was about to say something I wouldn't like. "And for some reason, it sounds like if he explores a relationship with you, he's scared he'll lose you. Maybe you should ask him why."

I fidgeted with a loose thread on my sleeve. "What makes you think he's *afraid*?"

"Because every action says that he's in love with you, Tessa." Scarlett's eyes held mine, unflinching. "But every time you get too close to the fire, he backs off."

I blinked, hating that there was a possibility she was right because as I replayed the last several years, that push-pull I'd always gotten from him would make sense. But I didn't want it to make sense. Being angry at him and feeling rejected was simple, clean, black and white.

"Well, I can ask him some other day," I muttered, shoving another handful of clothes into my suitcase. "Right now, I need to get all my stuff and move out."

Scarlett arched an eyebrow. "And go where?"

"Home."

"I thought you said a preliminary inspector found possible signs of mold?"

I slammed a drawer shut. "Note the two keywords there: preliminary and possible."

"Tessa." Scarlett's voice had that mix of exasperation and concern that only best friends can perfect. "You can't sacrifice your health over your feelings."

"You're just a bucket of advice today, aren't you?" I snapped, then immediately felt guilty when hurt flashed across her face. "Sorry. I'm just ..."

"Come stay with me," she offered, gracefully ignoring my outburst.

A strangled laugh escaped me. "Your new apartment complex doesn't even offer parking. I wouldn't be able to leave for work."

"What about your brother?"

My hands froze on the pair of shoes I'd grabbed. "You already know the answer to that."

"He's going to find out eventually," she pointed out. "Might as well be now."

"Asked and answered." I shook my head sharply. "He would

literally drag me to specialists all over the country. I have a wedding to plan, Scarlett. On an impossibly compressed timeline. Or else my business? Kaboom."

"Then stay here."

"Absolutely not."

Scarlett's eyes narrowed. "How have you felt since you moved out of the townhouse?"

The question hit like a lie detector test at the worst possible time.

I frowned. "I felt sick after he rejected me."

She rolled her eyes. "Aside from that massive emotional moment, how have you felt since you got here?"

I said nothing.

"Yeah." She nodded slowly. "That's what I thought."

"It's probably just because I've been eating more regularly," I argued weakly.

"Or maybe because you removed the source that was poisoning your body." She stood up, crossing to where I stood by the dresser. "Listen to me. You can spend most of your time in your bedroom and office, avoiding Blake completely. But the most important thing is your health. If you go back to your place and get sick again, you won't be able to pull off this wedding."

"Why did you have to put it that way?" I snarled.

There had to be another option. Something I wasn't thinking of. Maybe Scarlett's apartment could work. I could spend a couple of days setting up a space ... well, I don't know, at her kitchen table maybe? And, hey, Chicago was known for its public transportation. Maybe I could Uber to all my appointments, somehow in a very timely manner?

Ugh. No, that wouldn't work.

I punched my suitcase.

"Stay," a deep voice bellowed from the doorway.

My heart did that stupid little jump it always did when Blake appeared. His presence filled the frame, and my eyes caught on his bruised knuckles before I could stop myself. Tomorrow, he'd probably have to explain those to his bosses at the hospital. Another thing I was screwing up for him.

I forced ice into my tone. "Eavesdropping? Yikes."

Scarlett cleared her throat dramatically. "Oh my God, I am suddenly parched. Like, Death-Valley-in-summer parched. I should ... water. Yes. That." She slipped past Blake with all the subtlety of a tornado in a trailer park.

Blake stepped into the room, and the air seemed to thin. "Tessa, I'm really sorry."

"Let me stop you right there." I held up a hand, hating how my voice wanted to shake. "I don't need the *sorry for giving you the wrong impression* speech. Message received. You work long hours; you don't do relationships. Done. See? We never have to talk about it again."

Something flashed in his eyes. Pain? Pity? So help me if it was pity.

"Don't leave. We can work something out where you never have to see me. I'll be like a ghost."

I looked at him then, really looked at him. At the tension in his jaw, the shadows under his eyes, the way his hands kept clenching and unclenching at his sides. And suddenly, I needed to reclaim some dignity from this mess, dignity that had absolutely nothing to do with living arrangements.

"I want to make one thing clear." I crossed my arms and approached him, chin up, shoulders back, like I was facing a difficult vendor instead of the man who'd turned my world upside down. "What happened on the terrace was a mistake. Just hormones. Nothing more."

His jaw ticced, and something darkened in his expression. The words hung between us like a gauntlet thrown, but eventually, Blake swallowed hard—hard, mind you—a muscle working in his cheek before he nodded.

"Good." I turned back to my suitcase, pretending to reorganize things that were already perfectly arranged. "We're both adults. Let's just pretend this never happened."

"Does that mean you'll stay?" The hope in his voice made something crack inside my chest.

"No."

I stared down at my half-packed suitcase, mind spinning through alternatives. My place with its possible mold. My brother, who would immediately take over my medical care and probably my entire life, and the energy I'd spend fighting with him every second to stop it from happening. Scarlett's tiny new apartment with no parking. Each option felt like choosing between different flavors of terrible and, more importantly, options that would ruin my chance to pull off this wedding.

"I can stay at a hotel," Blake offered quietly.

A hotel. God, if only my credit lines weren't maxed out, that'd be the perfect scenario for me to go to.

But no matter how mad I was at Blake ...

"I'm not kicking you out of your home."

He was doing a lot for me, and he didn't deserve to have to uproot his life even more than he had. Nor did he deserve to be loathed this much.

Goddammit. That inconvenient guilt charged back through my chest like a wrecking ball. Why couldn't my heart just pick a team? Team Be Furious with Him or Team Blake Has Done More for You in the Past Few Days Than Anyone Has Done in Their Life. *And even after you were mean to him, he's still doing nice things for you, so be grateful and kind.*

He studied me, and when he spoke, his voice was ... God, it was awful, hearing the hurt in it.

"Just ... think about it until morning?" he pleaded.

I looked up at him then, and for a moment, I saw something in his eyes that made my breath catch. Something that made me wonder if Scarlett was right, if there was more to this story than I knew. His bruised knuckles flexed at his sides, and the gesture was so perfectly Blake—violence wrapped in control, passion hidden behind restraint—that it made my ribs tighten.

"Fine," I said, the word barely a whisper. "I'll think about it until morning."

I didn't wait for his response, just grabbed my toiletry bag and retreated to the bathroom, but suddenly, I stilled. Turned. And kept my voice softer, void of all the hurt and anger.

"No matter how this turns out, I want you to know that I really am grateful for everything you're doing for me, Blake."

I met his gaze, his empathetic, impossible-to-stay-mad-at-him-forever gaze.

"If there's anything I can ever do to return the favor," I continued, "don't hesitate to ask."

His head slanted into the world's sexiest tilt.

"All I want is for you to get better, Tess. So, please, stay."

I bit my lip, then pushed the handle. The door clicked shut behind me with a finality that felt like the punctuation on everything we'd just said.

I pressed my back against the cool wood and slid down to the floor, drawing my knees to my chest.

Seven weeks. Could I survive seven weeks of this exquisite torture, of wanting something I couldn't have, of living with a man who'd drawn a line I hadn't even known existed until we'd crossed it?

I let my head fall back against the door and closed my eyes, breathing in the lingering traces of his body wash in the air. Some masochistic part of me wondered if he was still standing out there, separated from me by nothing but three inches of wood and an ocean of unspoken words. Like the night I'd been assaulted, I pressed my palm to the door while Scarlett's voice echoed in my head. *"Every action says that he's in love with you."*

God help me, but I was starting to think she might be right.

So, why did it feel like the closer he got to love, the harder he pushed it away?

42

BLAKE

"How'd it go, Romeo?"

Scarlett leaned against my kitchen counter like she owned the place, sipping water with an expression that said she'd been waiting for me. Perfect. Just what I needed.

"That well, huh?" She actually patted me on the chest as she passed by. The casual familiarity was jarring. Most people knew better than to touch me, but apparently, Scarlett hadn't gotten that memo.

"I screwed everything up." Clearly, I was more rattled than I'd thought, spewing this out to a woman I didn't know.

"If it makes you feel any better," she said, examining her nails with exaggerated casualness, "she said it was the best orgasm of her life."

I leveled my best glare at her. The one that made my interns squirm. She just grinned wider.

"We are not having this conversation." I pushed past her to the fridge, grabbing a beer. "I don't know you well enough to have this conversation."

"I don't think so." She plucked the beer from my hand and set it on the counter with all the authority of a kindergarten teacher confiscating contraband. "No drowning your sorrows until after we talk."

"We're not talking."

"Agree to disagree. You need to talk to someone."

"I have friends for that," I said, grabbing my beer, holding her gaze, and taking a long pull.

"Ryker." She cocked her head. "You and I both know you can't talk to him about this."

I ran a hand over my face. I didn't want to tell Jace, Axel, or Knox either. They could tell Ryker. And, hell, Knox was in prison. Let me show up with my little problems in life when the guy was fighting for his.

"I've never seen Tessa this angry," I admitted.

"Exactly." Scarlett's eyes sparkled with something that looked dangerously like insight. "She's angry because she has feelings, and when Tessa doesn't want to have feelings, she lashes out. Like a tiny, angry Chihuahua."

The mental image of Tessa as an angry Chihuahua nearly made me smile.

"I don't want it to be like this between us," I admitted. "I want things to go back to normal."

"Which normal?" She cocked her head. "The one where you both pretend you don't have feelings for each other? Because I gotta tell you, that ship has sailed, capsized, and is currently hanging out with the *Titanic*."

"I don't know you well enough—"

"To have this conversation. Yes, you mentioned that." She waved away my protest like an annoying fly. "And yet here you are, looking like someone kicked your puppy, which means you're terrified of losing Tessa."

Damn it. She was right. I hated that she was right.

"Can I give you some advice?"

"No, I'm good." I went to take another sip, but this woman, this fucking woman, snatched it out of my hand.

"Lucky for you, I'm feeling generous." She hopped up onto

my counter—actually hopped up onto my counter like it was a chair—and settled in like she was preparing to dispense wisdom. "You have exactly one get-out-of-jail-free card that'll make this all better. It'll be like magic pixie dust that erases everything that happened."

I pinched the bridge of my nose. "And what, pray tell, is that?"

"The truth." All the playfulness dropped from her voice. "Tessa's so angry and hurt right now that I don't know if she'll even bother asking you why. She's too busy being all *I am woman, hear me roar*. But she doesn't know why you push everyone away. Maybe if she did, it would heal that scab over her heart that you just created."

"I didn't create—" My words died as the truth of them hit.

Damn it. I had created that. I had hurt Tessa, the last person I ever wanted to hurt.

"I didn't mean to hurt her."

"Oh, I know." Her voice was gentler now.

"How could you possibly know that?"

"You know how, sometimes, two people can be in a tornado and not see things clearly, but somebody outside the tornado can see it plain as day?"

"Is this the part where you tell me you're the tornado whisperer?"

"This is the part where I tell you it's obvious you're in love with each other."

The words shattered my ribs. "We can never be together."

For several reasons, not the least of which was this: The darkness I'd feared was still inside me hadn't just surfaced; it had found fertile ground and was spreading its roots through my veins like poison. The part of me that had always been capable of violence, the part I'd tried to bury in sterile hospital halls and saving lives, now thirsted for blood. His blood. The man who'd hurt Tessa.

Some might call that romantic, this urge to hunt down her attacker. But they didn't appreciate the hunger that came with it, the way I caught myself imagining exactly how I'd make him suffer, planning it out with the same methodical precision I used in the ER. They couldn't see how my hands itched to hurt him, how I looked forward to it with a pleasure that should have sickened me.

I'd killed once before. I knew with bone-deep certainty I'd do it again, and this time, I'd enjoy every second of it. That wasn't protection or justice. It was darkness, wearing the mask of vengeance. And Tessa deserved better than a man who dreamed of blood.

In response to my declaration that Tessa and I could never be together, Scarlett just shrugged, completely unfazed by what should have been a conversation ender.

"Well then, if happily ever after is off the table, I guess you have two choices with Tessa." She slid off the counter and headed for the hallway, then turned back with a knowing look that made me wonder if she could see right through me. "Let this be the cancer that cuts her out of your life completely or be honest with her and save your friendship."

She paused. "Oh, and, Blake? Fair warning: if you choose option one, I will personally make sure every coffee shop in a ten-block radius knows to give you decaf for the rest of your life."

After watching her disappear down the hall, her words echoing in my eardrums, I looked down at my bruised knuckles, wishing they'd made a satisfying crunch against that bastard's jaw. The pain was a reminder of how far I'd already crossed my own lines when it came to her.

Maybe Scarlett was right. Maybe the truth was the only way forward.

But the truth could destroy us both.

43

BLAKE

The fluorescent lights flickered overhead as I strode down the ER wing, my white coat snapping behind me like a shield of ice. Another day in these sterile halls, now with the parade of interns trailing after me. The familiar routine should have been comforting. Instead, every step felt like an attempt to outrun what I'd done last night.

Years of carefully maintained control, shattered in one moment of weakness. I'd spent so long fighting it, forcing my gaze away when she'd bite those full lips, steeling myself against the way her clothes hugged her curves, pushing down the heat that would build whenever she was near. But last night, I'd finally let that wall crack.

The memory of her taste lingered on my tongue. The way she'd trembled beneath my mouth, vulnerable and trusting, as I'd drawn her first orgasm with a man from her. Damn if that knowledge, being her first, hadn't branded itself into my soul. When her trembling subsided and she'd reached for my waistband, everything I'd wanted was right there. I could have buried myself in her, made her scream my name until sunrise. Instead, reality had slammed into focus, and I'd done the hardest thing I'd ever done.

I'd walked away.

Without explaining why.

Maybe Scarlett was right; maybe honesty was the only way to salvage anything with Tessa now. Maybe I should have tried rather than coming into work early today.

But here I was, burying myself in cases with the kind of cold precision that sent interns scattering. Better they fear me than see through the cracks in my armor. Every time one approached with another theory about Tessa's case, my jaw clenched tighter. They seemed to think this was some kind of partnership, but as I'd explained an incessant amount of times, this was divide and conquer. If they had a question that would speed up their theory, fine, but wanting validation for every half-formed thought?

Wasn't the damn point.

"Dr. Morrison." Dr. Katie Chen matched my pace, her Harvard credentials practically radiating off her pressed white coat. Her eagerness grated against my raw nerves today. "About your friend's case—"

"Patient," I corrected, signing the chart a nurse thrust in front of me without breaking stride. Yes, in these halls, that's exactly what Tessa had to be. Not the woman whose lips I'd memorized from across rooms for years, fighting the urge to taste them.

"Of course. I was wondering about any history of strep throat?"

I shot her a sideways glance, letting ice creep into my voice. "If it's not in her file—"

"Childhood records," she pressed. "Even untreated cases. There are new studies showing long-term effects that could explain—"

I stopped abruptly, causing her to stumble. "What are you asking for?"

Her body stiffened at my tone. I wasn't trying to be an asshole today; evidently, it was seeping out of me like an oozing wound, thanks to last night.

"I need a complete childhood medical history, specifically focused on strep throat incidents, treated or untreated."

I resumed walking, my tone clipped. "You'll have it by end of day."

Two hours and three emergency consults later, Dr. William Parker materialized at my elbow as I reviewed lab results. Each case a welcome distraction from thoughts of Tessa, from wondering what she was doing right now. Had she moved out? Would she be gone by the time I returned? And if so, would she ever talk to me again?

"Sir—"

"Dr. Morrison," I snapped, not looking up.

"Dr. Morrison," he amended, clearing his throat. "Has the patient had any history of STDs?"

The lab results crinkled in my tightening grip. "Excuse me?"

"Given your personal relationship with the patient, I understand this is uncomfortable, but—"

"The point. Get to it." Ice dripped from every word.

"We need to rule out any STDs that went untreated for six weeks or longer."

"If she did, it'd be in her records."

I thought no one could upset me more than that whole STD thing, but it was the last intern who turned my world upside down. Rhet. The perpetual thorn in my side who was, infuriatingly, sometimes right.

"Dr. Morrison." He fell into step beside me near the ICU.

"Working on that confident-doctor walk?" I asked. "Still looking a bit lost puppy."

His cheeks reddened, but he pressed on. "The patient's records—"

"You have everything I have."

"Not a psychological evaluation."

"She was diagnosed with situational depression. Next?"

"Has anyone screened for factitious disorder?"

My nose found the tip of his in an instant, and I glared down at him. "Munchausen? You're suggesting she's doing this to herself?"

He glanced around the hallway, perhaps calculating the odds I'd slam him against the wall. Answer: high.

"You asked for help," he muttered.

"So, you decided to be an ass about it?"

"With symptoms this scattered, we have to consider—"

"She's not doing this to herself. End of fucking discussion." The words came out in a growl as I marched off.

"Then what about someone else?"

I spun back, jaw clenched. "Meaning?"

He rubbed his neck. "They ran a cardiac tox screen when her heart stopped, but I suggest we test for poison."

The word hit like a defibrillator to the chest. Because, goddammit, he was right. The scattered symptoms, the clean tests, the progressive deterioration ... it could all fit.

Someone might be poisoning her.

How had I not considered this? How could I have been so reckless?

Because you can't imagine anyone ever trying to hurt her.

But someone had hurt her and was actively threatening her with letters. And sadly, there could be other suspects. The creepy voyeur neighbor. Her ex-boyfriend. Scarlett, as charming as she might've seemed, well, you just never knew with people. Who knew who else might be on the list, too, or what access they might have to Tess?

Even if she continued to stay with me—and that was a big if —she'd leave the sanctuary of my place daily to plan that godforsaken wedding, running errands, putting herself in the crosshairs of anyone who wanted to slip a little toxin into, well, her skin, her food, her clothing. You name it.

I pulled out my phone, already dialing. "Order a comprehensive toxicology panel. NOW."

The sound of my footsteps echoed through the hall as one

thought hammered through my mind: I had to get to Tessa and warn her. Because if someone was doing this to her, they might succeed before I could figure out who or why. I'd spent years fighting my feelings for her, had finally tasted what we could have, then walked away like I always do. But I couldn't lose her. Not like this.

44

TESSA

"What do you mean, you can't talk to me?" I paced the length of my office. Well, the office Blake had created for me.

After his plea last night to stay and think things through, I'd agreed to one more day, though I was no closer to a decision. The penthouse had been empty when I woke this morning, Blake already gone, which suited me fine. I'd gotten straight to work, and now here I was, wedding planner portfolio clutched to my chest like armor, making my thirty-seventh call to yet another florist who was trying to end our conversation before I could even mention what services I needed.

"I'm sorry, we're all booked up." The woman's voice crackled through the phone, too rehearsed to be genuine.

My spine stiffened. "I haven't asked you a question yet." All I'd done was introduce myself with my name and my company.

"Right, well, I have a customer in the store, so I'm afraid I need to hang up."

Click.

The silence rang in my ear like an angry hornet. I stared at my phone, my reflection in the black screen showing the exact moment realization dawned on my face. They wouldn't dare go this far, would they? By now, everyone knew the wedding date had been moved up. The blogs had made sure of that. Social media was buzzing with speculation about why the "wedding of the year" was suddenly just six and a half weeks away.

Maybe the florists were just stressed about the timeline?

No. Any florist in Chicago would kill for this opportunity. The commission alone would be thousands, not to mention the media coverage that could make their career. There could only be one reason why every florist in town had proactively shut me down.

Time to prove my theory. I dialed number thirty-eight, this time swallowing my pride and withholding my name.

"Hi." I kept my voice honey sweet. "You guys do weddings, right?"

"We sure do!" The enthusiasm was jarring after so many cold shoulders.

The conversation flowed easily, with a possible opening that date until the moment of truth arrived.

"My name is Tessa Kincaid," I said, bracing for impact.

The silence on the other end was thunderous. Then came the throat-clearing, the backpedaling, the sudden discovery of a "booking conflict."

Unbelievable.

Thirty minutes later, I pushed open the shop's door, bells jingling overhead. The scent of roses and lilies hit me like a wall of perfume as I approached the counter where a woman arranged a bouquet.

"Hello," I said, keeping my voice steady. "Can I speak to the owner, please?"

"That would be me." She smiled, setting aside a stem of baby's breath. "How can I help you?"

"My name is Tessa Kincaid." I watched as recognition flickered across her face. "I called earlier."

The woman tried to keep her poker face, but she was terrible at it. Her smile faltered, shoulders stiffening, as if someone had replaced her spine with steel.

"Ah, right, about the wedding," she stammered. "Yes, I'm so very sorry, but we are booked up that weekend."

I kept my voice gentle, my smile genuine. "What did they offer you?"

She dropped her gaze, her fingers nervously arranging and rearranging the flowers before her. "Pardon me?"

"Once Upon a Lifetime," I clarified, watching her face pale. "What did they offer you?"

Her smile vanished completely.

"We're both businesswomen," I said, my voice firm but measured. Unfortunately, my lungs seemed to constrict without warning, so intensely that I had to take slow, shallow breaths, praying she wouldn't mistake my symptoms as nerves. This wasn't nerves. Emotionally, I was cool and calm. "I came all the way here to understand what I'm up against."

She studied me, fingers absently arranging a spray of baby's breath. "How would that information be pertinent?"

"I'm running a small business." I softened my tone. "There's a massive corporation trying to cut me out before I even have a chance to get my legs under me. You remember what that was like, don't you?" I gestured to the beautiful shop around us. "When you started this place, surely, there were some bumps along the road."

She regarded me carefully, something shifting in her expression.

"Tell me," I continued, trying to keep my voice strong in the face of an onslaught of nausea, "when you were starting up, did the biggest flower shop in Chicago try to shut you down before you even opened? Did they call every supplier in the Chicagoland area to blacklist you?" I leaned forward slightly. "Small businesses need to have each other's backs. Today, it's me they're targeting. What if, next year, some massive florist starts coming after the local flower shops?"

Her shoulders dropped.

"If you truly can't handle another wedding, that's one thing.

But don't blackball me." I held her gaze. "I might be small today, but I don't intend to stay small. And when I grow, I intend to bring other small businesses up with me. That's the difference. I won't use dirty tactics like they do to get ahead."

She sighed, her entire body softening as she placed her palms on the counter. "Look, I'm sorry. They're the biggest wedding planner in the area. They gave me an ultimatum: work with them or work with you. They give me over a dozen weddings a year."

"They do," I acknowledged. "But do you really want to be in business with someone who employs these tactics? Who actively tries to crush the little guy? Companies like that can't be trusted. They might give you business today, but if they're willing to stoop this low to hurt me, they might do it to you in the future."

The owner regarded me for several seconds, seemingly digesting my words, and then she retrieved a three-ring binder from beneath the counter. As she flipped through the pages, her posture seemed to shrink with each turn. "I have eleven weddings booked with Once Upon a Lifetime this year alone. Do you know how much profit that is for a small business like me?"

"You're right; it's substantial. They have that advantage." I nodded. "But I would venture to say I have one advantage they don't: I won't keep you at the mercy of corporate terms. I suspect they've demanded pricing that barely puts you above profit margins."

The sudden straightening of her shoulders told me I'd hit the mark.

"Every bride deserves the wedding of her dreams," I added, "not just the ones who've hitched their wagon to a corporation trying to bully their way to a monopoly. A wedding isn't supposed to be a battleground for businesses to try to destroy each other. It's meant to be a beacon of hope, a reminder that love is worth fighting for." I paused, letting my words sink in. "I'm not asking you to give up those eleven weddings. *They* are. I'm simply asking you to add wedding number twelve. I have a beautiful bride who's going through some really difficult personal problems right now. She doesn't deserve to have her wedding sabotaged by corporate greed."

She drew in a slow breath, uncertainty still clouding her features.

I placed my business card on the counter. "I'm not a big corporation. I don't have dozens of weddings to offer you. Not yet. But I'm an honest businesswoman who intends to grow with respect and dignity for all the companies I work with. I will never strong-arm anyone to get my way, and I will never put small businesses in the impossible position they've put you in." I stepped back from the counter. "I'm sorry they did this to you."

She glanced down at my card, her fingers hovering over its edge.

"Think about it," I said softly, grateful that the worst of the breathlessness had passed, though my stomach still churned. "I appreciate you giving me a call either way."

The bells chimed behind me as I stepped into the Chicago afternoon, my phone already buzzing in my pocket.

It was Blake.

45

TESSA

Blake: Answer my call. We need to talk.

Me: On my way to watch a bride try on Vera Wang. Rain check.

Blake: It's about your health.

Me: I assumed as much. If you wanted to talk about, you know, other things, you'd have done so before fleeing in the dark of night.

Oof. Turned out, my hurt feelings were gripping the wheel and accelerating the bitchy pedal. But seriously, I woke up, discovering he'd already left without a word. Evidently having no problem getting through his day with no closure.

Blake: I didn't flee. I'm at WORK. And you need to come here. Now.

Me: I have four appointments in the next three hours. Afraid it will have to wait.

Blake: It's urgent.

Me: Define urgent. Is it "aliens have invaded my bloodstream" urgent or "Blake needs to avoid an awkward conversation" urgent?

Blake: Something's come up.

Me: Unless my lab results have shown I need a medication in the next ten minutes or else my soul will permanently detach from my body, I'm afraid it'll have to wait.

Blake: Please come to the hospital. There, see? I said PLEASE.

Me: Slow clap. I know that word has eluded your vocabulary for quite a while.

Blake: This is serious.

Me: So am I. I'm seriously looking at $3,000/hour photographers after this fitting.

Blake: This wasn't our agreement. Our agreement was you'd come in for testing when I said so.

*Me: A) So, this is just about more testing. *eye roll emoji* Got it. B) Never agreed to "when you said so." Check the terms and conditions.*

Blake: If I'm right, you could be in danger, Tessa.

Me: From what? Whiplash from your constant mood changes or my medical condition?

Blake: You won't let me explain this request in person, WILL YOU?

Me: NO. P.S. I KNOW HOW TO USE THE CAPS TOO. SEE? THIS IS ALL CAPS.

Blake: Tessa.

Me: Dr. Morrison.

Blake: You want to be mad at me? Fine. But you need to take this seriously.

Me: Got it. Thanks for the mansplaining.

Blake: Tessa.

Me: Now, as for said testing, I'm happy to come in tomorrow morning at eight o'clock.

Blake: I won't be here tomorrow at eight.

Me: Darn. I'm sure someone else knows how to jab needles into my flesh. Now, if you'll excuse me, I have to run.

Blake: Tessa.

Blake: Tessa!

Blake: Fine. You win. You want to hear what I had to say OVER TEXT? I think someone might be trying to kill you.

46

TESSA

"You're leaving." Maria's words were not a question, but rather a quiet acknowledgment, wrapped in disappointment. She set down the dinner plate she'd brought, the china making a delicate sound against the dresser's top. Her gaze lingered on the suitcase I hadn't bothered to unpack since last night's argument with Blake.

Now, I was grateful I'd never unpacked because, holy hell, he was officially going off the deep end, suggesting someone was trying to end me. I mean, really? What true crime podcast had this man been bingeing? I was witnessing his rational thought crumble right in front of my eyes like a cookie left too long in hot coffee. Between my bleeding heart (which really needed to learn some boundaries) and his hemorrhaging paranoia (which needed serious medical attention), living together was definitely, absolutely, without a doubt the worst idea since that time I decided bangs would fix my life.

I smoothed a wrinkle from the blouse I was folding, buying time.

"It's been wonderful, staying here. Thank you for everything, Maria." My voice was steady, even if my hands weren't.

"Tessa ..." She twisted her apron between worried fingers. "I know it's not my place, but—"

"I have an important event to plan." The words came out brittle as winter ice. "I'd be more comfortable working from my own home." More comfortable away from him, away from the way my heart forgot its job description whenever he was near.

"Blake explained that you're staying here to avoid your home." Her voice was gentle, maternal.

I caught my reflection in the bedroom's mirror with flushed cheeks, eyes too bright, looking every bit like a woman running away. "Turns out, I don't think mold's my issue after all."

"No?" Maria stepped closer, concern etching deeper lines around her mouth. "What makes you say that?"

My gaze darted to the bedroom door, and I was grateful that Blake wouldn't be back for hours. His shifts at the hospital regularly stretched to thirty hours or more, he'd said, so thankfully, I would be gone long before he returned, leaving nothing but empty rooms and the ghost of what could have been.

It was better this way. To leave the same way he'd left me this morning.

"The whole point of staying here was to eliminate variables that might be making me sick. But between us?" I folded the final shirt, placing it carefully on top of the others, as if organizing my clothes could somehow organize the chaos in my head. "If my home was the thing that made me ill, today wouldn't have happened. Today, I felt worse than I have in months, and I've been sleeping here. So." I shrugged, aiming for casual despite the tremor in my hands. "Can't be from mold there."

The ancient floorboard behind me creaked with that distinctive sound of weight settling onto wood, and the fine hairs at my nape rose in recognition. I didn't need to turn to know it was him; my body had already betrayed me, every nerve ending singing with awareness, the air growing heavier with his presence.

"You've been feeling sicker today?" His deep baritone voice rolled through the room like distant thunder before a storm.

My traitorous heart didn't just flutter; it performed a full flip.

"I thought you'd still be at work," I said, proud that my voice didn't shake. Much.

"Left early." He stepped into my bedroom, his eyes sweeping over me with that intensity that made me feel like I was the only patient, the only person, in his world. "Talk to me about your symptoms."

Maria muttered something about checking on dinner and slipped out, leaving Blake and me alone. The air crackled with unspoken words and that damned electricity that always sparked between us.

"Same story, different day." I latched my suitcase closed. "As promised, I'll be at the lab in the morning. Now if you'll excuse me—"

"Tessa." Just my name, but the way he said it made me pause. "We need to talk about this."

"About what?" I tried to step around him, but suddenly, the room swayed treacherously, all those symptoms I'd been fighting rushing back at once: nausea, stomach cramps, and that terrifying shortness of breath.

His hands caught my upper arms, steadying me, and for one merciful moment, he said nothing, his gaze locked on mine.

"Don't," I whispered.

"Don't what?"

"Don't look at me like that. Like I'm one of your patients."

"Trust me." His voice roughened, his grip gentling, but not releasing. "Nothing about how I'm looking at you right now is professional."

My pulse jumped, and I wasn't sure if it was from the dizziness or his words.

"Let me go, Blake."

"No." The word was short, but its meaning stretched between us like a lifeline I wasn't sure I wanted to grab. "You want to prove you're healthy enough to leave? Fine. But first, you're going to be honest with me."

"I am being honest," I said, pushing away from him, needing

distance to think clearly. "Obviously, you heard what I said to Maria. If my place had mold that was making me sick, I'd be feeling better here, not worse today."

"You were feeling better when you arrived."

I lifted my chin, trying to sound stronger than I felt. "Point is, the only reason I was staying here was to avoid potential triggers." And this place? Was a land mine of triggers. All of them Blake-shaped. "Why are you really home early?" I asked, narrowing my eyes.

He rolled his sleeves up to his elbows. To distract me with those lean forearms, I bet.

"Your heart rate was elevated today. Irregular."

I blinked, processing the fact that even during his busy work-day, he'd been monitoring me.

"I'm fine," I claimed, though the room's subtle spinning suggested otherwise. "And I need to go."

"Tess, you don't look good."

"Gee, thanks."

"Let me at least examine you before you leave. If you leave and something happens ..." He grabbed the back of his neck. "I'll never be able to live with myself. Do this for me. Let me examine you."

Surely, he knew this was a waste of time; one exam wouldn't uncover what had evaded medical science for a year.

"And if you do find something concerning?"

My home was calling my name, but if I left like this, he'd never stop calling and texting and maybe even showing up. I needed to be able to focus, and the only way to do that was to convince him I wasn't about to die. Imminently.

"Then you trust me enough to help you. Not as your doctor, but as your ..." The word hung between us, unspoken. "As your friend."

Okay. I'd just pretend that the word *friend* didn't just slice my gut in half and try to remind my bitchy heart that this was his idea of a peace offering.

Part of me wanted to push him away. Specifically my bruised ego and heart, but I had made the decision to reclaim control of my life, and part of that was getting to the bottom of the symptoms so I could be in control all the time.

If I kicked Blake off my medical case now, how long would it take to find another doctor as determined as him to get to the bottom of this? Was it wrong of me to accept his help though when I was upset with him? Was that selfish? Or was it stupid to blow this opportunity to have him see my case all the way through?

"Fine," I conceded, ignoring how his relief made my stomach flip. "You can examine me, but only if you do it here." I wasn't letting him drag me to the hospital right now.

Blake nodded, his expression unreadable.

"Sit," he said, guiding me to the bed. "I'll get my medical bag."

As he left the room, I pressed a hand to my racing heart, wondering which would end me first: whatever mysterious illness was plaguing me or the way Blake made me feel when he looked at me like that.

The moment he stepped back through the doorway, medical bag in hand and stethoscope around his neck, I knew I was about to find out.

47

TESSA

I perched on the edge of the bed, hyperaware of his presence as he settled beside me, the mattress dipping under his weight. He reached for his stethoscope, the movement bringing a whisper of his body wash to me—clean and masculine, achingly familiar.

"I need to listen to your heart." His eyes met mine, dark and intent. "Try to breathe normally."

As if that were possible with you so close.

Blake pressed the stethoscope above my left breast, near one of the heart monitor nodes because, apparently, he needed to hear my heart with his own ears, too. There was something so intimate about this moment, knowing he was listening to my heartbeats, wondering if he knew that each beat of my heart pulsed for him.

It hit me then, with devastating clarity, why his rejection had wounded me so deeply. For one perfect moment on that terrace, all my dreams had aligned like stars. My business was open, and despite its complications, I was building something real, something mine, brick by precious brick. And there was Blake—the man who had haunted my teenage fantasies—finally touching me the way I'd always hoped. Like I was his everything.

For a handful of heartbeats, I'd held the world in my hands. Then it had all crumbled to dust.

"Good," he murmured, his voice honeyed and low. "Now your lungs. Deep breath."

I inhaled deeply, my chest rising and falling as he moved the stethoscope, first left, then right. His free hand rested lightly on my shoulder, steadying me. Or maybe himself.

"May I?" He fingered the hem of my shirt, eyes questioning.

I nodded, not trusting my voice, and the cool metal slid up my back beneath the fabric, followed by the ghost of his knuckles against my spine.

"Deep breath, Cupcake."

Ugh, would my pet name rolling off his tongue always make my skin tingle like this?

"Again ... once more."

When he finally removed the stethoscope, draping it around his neck, his frown sent a different kind of shiver through me.

"Your lungs sound diminished."

"What does that mean?"

"Lie back, please."

I complied, trying not to think about how many times I'd imagined being in this bed under vastly different circumstances. Blake stood over me, his expression unreadable as his hands moved to my abdomen. When I flinched, his eyebrows drew together in concern.

"Does that hurt?"

"A little," I admitted.

His lips pursed as he continued the examination, his touch still setting my nerve endings alight. Every point of contact felt like a reminder of what we were trying so hard to deny.

"Okay, you can sit up," he directed, stepping back to create distance between us.

The loss of contact felt like a winter chill.

His gaze drifted to my packed suitcase by the door, and something flickered across his face. Regret, I think. He pulled a hand to the back of his neck for a few seconds.

"You should stay," he said quietly. "At least until your breathing improves."

I slid off the bed, squaring my shoulders. I refused to be that girl who fell apart just because the man she wanted didn't want her back.

"I think we both know that's not a good idea."

The silence stretched between us, heavy with everything we weren't saying, until he finally broke it.

"Listen, I didn't mean to hurt your feelings," Blake said, his voice rough with emotion, but then he just stopped. At a loss for words? Or presuming that was the only explanation he thought I deserved?

"One minute, you're telling me you wanted to do more than just kiss me. Then you're burying your face between my legs like you've imagined nothing else, but the very next minute, you push me away."

"I made a mistake." The muscles in his jaw clenched, his eyes fixed on some point over my shoulder.

"Which part? Going down on me? Or making me assume it meant more than just sex?" I hated how small I felt in this moment.

"It did mean more than just sex." His eyes finally met mine, dark with pain. "That's the problem."

"He said, as if that sounds clear," I muttered.

Blake dragged a hand through his hair. "Tess, even if I could get past my issues—"

"Which I can only assume are some flavor of *fear of losing me*, but I wouldn't know what those issues are. Being that you won't open up to me." A bitterness in my voice crept out.

"Even if I could get past my issues, Ryker is my best friend. I promised him." His shoulders sagged, as if the weight of that promise physically pressed down on him.

"*That's* what this is about?" I balked, heat rising to my cheeks. How insulting. "We're grown-ups, Blake. We're not teenagers anymore."

"I don't expect you to understand."

"Try me." I lifted my chin, challenging him.

His expression shifted, and for a moment, I saw the teenager I'd first fallen for years ago.

"Ryker saved me, Tess. When I was drowning, if I didn't have his friendship, I wouldn't have had your family. Wouldn't have met you." He swallowed hard. "The only thing he ever asked of me was to never date you. I don't expect you to understand, but that matters to me. I made a commitment to always have his back as he's had mine. I can't betray him like that, Tess."

Something in his voice made me press harder. "That's not the only thing this is about though, is it?"

He looked away. "I have issues letting myself ... love."

"Why?" The word came out barely above a whisper, hope blooming in my chest that, finally, he might tell me what this was really about. Because, sure, the Ryker thing? I understood. But rejecting a lifetime of happiness without even trying to reason with Ryker? That wasn't passing my test. Whatever this issue of loving was—that was the biggest issue of all. The rest was just more justification to himself.

"But even if I didn't have issues, I'm not the stand-up guy you think I am, Tess."

"I know you have demons or whatever." My hand twitched with the urge to touch him, to smooth away the crease between his brows. "But you literally save lives every day. How can you still see yourself as a bad guy?"

"I don't. I accept who I am." He scrubbed his jaw. "But even if I could get past my issues and even if I could break the only promise I'd ever made to Ryker, you deserve someone better, Tess."

His words suspended between us, weighing down the air in my lungs, making it harder to breathe.

"You're fighting this though," I said, recognizing the torment in his eyes. "I can tell. You're trying to convince me as much as you're trying to convince yourself."

The silence that followed was answer enough. His eyes flickered with concern as he studied my face, changing the subject.

"Walk me through your symptoms today." His voice shifted to that professional tone, throwing up yet another wall between us.

"Blake."

"Walk me through them." His tone was clipped with the unspoken meaning behind them. The one that said *I'm done talking about this.*

Would I ever find out the other reasons he was fighting this hard to push me away? I needed to understand because this felt like ... like watching everything I ever wanted burning down in front of me, without knowing what started the fire.

My eyes stung, but I bit back the tears. I'd wait until later, when I was back at my home, where I could fall apart in private, where he couldn't see how thoroughly broken I felt.

"Nausea, stomachache, shallow breathing. I was particularly stressed today though."

"From the wedding planning?" His voice carried an edge.

"That and ... everything else." I risked a glance up at him. "So, maybe this is just stress."

Blake dragged a hand through his hair again, mussing it in a way that made him look less like the polished doctor and more like the man who'd devoured me on that terrace.

"Stress can wreak havoc on the human body," he acknowledged. "But this isn't stress, Tess. Something's wrong, and I need you to tell me everything about your day. From the moment you woke up until now."

"Why?"

"Please." The word carried weight, heavy with something that made me look up sharply. "Indulge me."

I studied him, noting the tension rolling across his shoulders, the way his muscles coiled like he was preparing for a fight.

"Well, I woke up, had breakfast—"

"What did you eat?"

"Pancakes. Extra syrup."

His eyes rolled skyward, and for a moment, a ghost of a smile played at his lips. "Of course you did."

The familiar banter tried to make me smile, but my pain kept it at bay.

"Then I had my morning tea and those supplements you gave me while making calls from the office. The office you created for me," I added.

"Did you touch anything new? Cologne? A cleaner? New body soap?"

"No."

His mouth fixed into a line. "Keep going."

"And then I left to run to a florist. That's when I started feeling sick."

His expression darkened. "Did you touch anything at the flower shop?"

I thought back. "No."

"Did you make any stops before the florist?"

"I ... yes. I stopped at my place for business cards. It was literally five seconds. If breathing in mold got you sick after five seconds, then sleeping there for the last year and a half would've killed me."

"Did you see him?" Blake's voice dropped dangerously low.

"Who?"

"Your creeper."

"My neighbor," I corrected, though something cold slithered down my spine at his choice of words.

"Was he waiting for you again?"

I swallowed hard. "He was on his porch."

Something shifted in Blake's expression. Something that made me glad I wasn't the focus of that barely contained fury. "Tell me exactly what happened."

"I was distracted, angry about the florist situation. I grabbed my cards, and when I was closing the door ..." I faltered, remembering. "He came up behind me, put his hand on my shoulder."

"He touched you." The words came out like ice cracking.

"Asked how I was feeling."

Blake's hand clenched into a fist. "When did the symptoms start?"

My breath caught as realization began to dawn. "Maybe ... fifteen minutes later."

He moved closer until his face was inches from mine, eyes fierce with protective intensity.

"These symptoms aren't random," he said, voice barely above a whisper. "After all our tests, I think someone's hurting you deliberately."

My heart stuttered. "Blake—"

"And when I find them," he continued, one hand coming up to cup my face, thumb brushing my cheekbone in a touch that was anything but clinical, "they'll learn exactly how much damage a doctor can do."

The promise in his voice sent ice water down my skin, but whether from fear of the threat or the way he was looking at me, I couldn't tell. And as his words sank in, a more terrifying question surfaced.

What if Blake was right? What if this whole time, someone had been making me sick?

No. That was lunacy. People don't get poisoned to death very often, and they certainly don't get poisoned slowly for over a year.

What if my illness was making Blake come unhinged?

"Stay here," he said. "I'll be right back."

"Where are you going?"

He left me here. Alone with my torturous thoughts, and just like last time, he didn't even bother to explain why.

I stood up and exited the room, and as I stepped into the hallway, a sliver of light caught my eye. The mystery door stood ajar, golden light spilling onto the hardwood floor like an invitation.

Blake must have gone in there. Whatever was in that room had drawn him away from me. Urgently.

But what could it be? It was silly and irrational to wonder if the room held the answers to why he pushed me away, why he'd crushed any hope of us being together, why he'd chosen his promise to Ryker over me. Chosen his unspoken demons over the possibility of love. Those answers lay in his guarded heart, not some mystery room.

And yet my feet inched closer to it.

He was probably just looking up some latest test result. Nothing to do with our non-relationship situation.

God, I hadn't realized how deep the roots of hope had grown until he'd ripped them out. All these years of maybes and what-ifs, of lingering touches and heated glances—gone. And all I had left was *friend* Blake. *Medical* Blake.

What if I wasn't sick? Would he even be talking to me right now? What if I was mistaking some of his care as feelings when it was nothing more than doctor stuff?

My hand trembled as I pushed the door open.

And then I took a step back.

"Oh my God."

48

TESSA

My heart pounded against my ribs. Papers. Dozens, no, hundreds, of papers covered every inch of the walls, and as I moved closer, my stomach dropped. These weren't just any papers.

They were mine. Every lab result. Every doctor's appointment. Every symptom I'd mentioned over the past year, meticulously documented and arranged like evidence in a murder investigation. Red strings connected documents, creating a web of my illness. Post-it Notes in Blake's precise handwriting were everywhere, covered in questions: Stomach inflammation? Connection to headaches? Environmental triggers?

Above the chaos were carefully printed headers: Immunology. Neurology. GI. Autoimmune possibilities.

"Tessa ..."

"What is this?"

"I can explain."

"When did you have time to do all this?" Why was *that* my question right now? There were much bigger ones to ask!

"At night," he said absently, as if missing sleep wasn't significant. "Here." Blake's voice was tight as he moved to another wall, which was also covered. "Look at this."

A timeline stretched across the surface of this wall, each date connected by more red string. First symptoms. First GI complaint. Unexplained hives. But it wasn't just medical data. He'd noted every major event in my life around that time. The day I moved into my townhouse. How many days passed before the symptoms started. Things I'd jotted down in that notebook I'd given him, which lay open on the table in the corner.

"This is when your neighbor moved in." Blake's finger jabbed at the timeline.

My mouth fell open as I took in the full scope of his office. This wasn't just a doctor trying to solve a case.

This was obsession.

This was a man who'd been combing through my medical history like a detective who couldn't let go of an unsolved crime. Evidently making other phone calls, too, to find out facts like when my neighbor moved in. Surrounded by Blake's obsession, I felt my heart drop and pain wrap around my ribs, seizing them in its grip.

He *was* unhinged.

And worse, all this time we'd spent together, all those looks I'd interpreted as romantic? Must have been nothing more than him studying me, like a goddamned science experiment!

"Is this all I am to you?" The words escaped before I could stop them, thick with tears I refused to let fall. I should have been grateful. Wasn't this what I'd wanted? A doctor who finally took me seriously? Who went above and beyond to help me? But standing in what felt like a shrine to my illness, my heart was shattering for an entirely different reason. "Is that why you've been spending time with me?" My lip trembled traitorously. "Because doctors love a good mystery, right? Is that all this was?"

With enough time, I could've handled his rejection. I could have handled his reasons that we couldn't be together. But I couldn't handle it if our relationship had all been in my head.

"Tess—"

"God, I'm such an idiot." I placed a hand over my stomach. "I actually thought … I thought you were interested in me. Not my symptoms. Not the medical puzzle. Just … me."

"That's not—"

"The way I've always been interested in you." The confession ripped from my throat, years of buried feelings suddenly spilling out. I turned away, unable to look at him. "How pathetic is that? The teenage girl who never grew up, who spent years wishing you'd look at me the way I looked at you. And then I end up in your ER, and we're finally talking again, and I let myself hope—" My voice cracked. "But this whole time, I was just a case study."

I fled to my room, yanking my suitcase and speed-walking down the hallway.

I had to get out of here before I completely fell apart.

Blake caught up to me though because I wasn't even allowed to have my final emotional breaking point in peace.

"I appreciate everything you've done," I managed, jabbing the elevator button repeatedly. "But this is too much. Every wedding I've ever planned, every centerpiece I've designed, do you know what I was thinking? *Would Blake like this? Would Blake choose this?* God, it's humiliating." The words wouldn't stop now. "And then miracle of miracles, you're finally in my life again, and I think maybe, maybe this time … but no. I'm just your medical mystery of the month."

"That couldn't be further from the truth."

"That room says otherwise."

"That room?" Blake's jaw clenched. "That room isn't evidence that I don't care about you, Tessa. It's proof that I'm terrified of losing you."

I froze.

"How dare you accuse me of not caring!" He stepped closer, radiating fury and something else, something raw. "I care so much that it fucking scares me. Do you want to know the biggest reason I pushed you away? Because everyone I've ever loved has left me, and the thought of you leaving …" His voice broke. "I couldn't survive that. Not *you*."

"Blake—"

"That wall? That's me trying desperately to keep you safe. Every time I hear about you suffering, it feels like someone's ripping my heart out. And this, solving this, was the one thing I thought I could do for you. Your family took in this pathetic, emotionally stunted kid who didn't know how to be a friend, who still doesn't know how to do relationships, and you ..." He raked a hand through his hair. "You've always been there. Always. And I've never earned that."

My heart was hammering so hard that I could barely breathe.

"So, don't you dare think this obsession means I don't care about you." He closed the distance between us, eyes blazing. "It means I love you, Tessa. I have always loved you, no matter how hard I fought it. I will always love you."

For a heartbeat, time stopped.

Then Blake's gaze dropped to my suitcase. With a growl of frustration, he yanked it from my hand and hurled it aside. It hit the wall with a crash that echoed through the hallway.

Before I could process what was happening, his hands were cupping my face, and his mouth crashed into mine. The kiss was desperate, hungry with years of denial and want and love pouring out all at once. I clutched his shirt, pulling him closer as his fingers tangled in my hair.

And then ... fueled with rage and pain, Blake pushed me against the foyer table.

"You think I don't care about you?" he growled, biting my lip slightly. "I'll show you how much I fucking care, Tessa."

He reached for the hem of my shirt and pulled.

49

TESSA

Blake's lips explored mine with an intensity that spoke of years of imagining this moment. Years of staring at my mouth, imagining it on his, all while I noticed the soft planes of his body and the strength of his hands, wondering what they'd feel like on my skin.

"Maria." Blake's eyes never left mine.

"Yes?" In my peripheral vision, I saw Maria appear tentatively, her voice and body language screaming, *Please let me get the hell out of here; I so do not want to hear my boss having sex.*

"Leave," Blake commanded. "Now."

"Done." She said in a *thank God* tone, scurrying to what I could only presume was a back door to the penthouse.

Meanwhile, Blake's mouth reclaimed mine, and unlike our passionate encounter on the terrace, this was fundamentally different. It was different in the way he devoured my mouth, like he'd hungered for it all the days of his life. It was different in how his hands roamed over my body with a fiery mix of tension and soft gentleness that spoke of something deeper and more meaningful than just sex. And it was different because of his profession. On the terrace, he'd admitted to wanting me physically all these years, but this time, he professed his love for me.

This was his soul recognizing mine.

I could feel it everywhere, like electricity charging through my body. Our connection sparked and pulled, transcending mere attraction, and each touch carried the weight of countless moments. Stolen glances across rooms, breath catching when we'd brush against each other, hearts racing in shared elevator rides.

Blake tugged my shirt over my head, his movements precise around the monitoring electrodes stuck to my skin. He disconnected the thin, flexible wires from the lightweight device with practiced ease, setting it aside as his mouth blazed a trail along my jaw. His bruised knuckles—evidence of his earlier protective fury—were surprisingly gentle as they worked at the buttons of my jeans.

I was tugging too. Tugging at his shirt, pulling it as high as I could before he reached behind himself—holy hell, was that sexy, when a guy could reach behind his shoulder blades and strip his entire shirt over his head—and pulled it off in one fluid motion, tossing it to the ground.

We fumbled with remaining clothes, hands desperate and greedy, mouths clashing and breaking apart only long enough to shed the last barriers between us. Standing nude in his foyer—surrounded by priceless art and that coveted statue that represented everything he'd achieved—Blake pulled back to look at me, his gaze raking over my body with such hunger that I felt cherished.

"You're beautiful, Cupcake."

So was he. Muscles, woven into a fabric of art on his body, ink that I knew concealed his scars, physical remnants of a past he'd shared only with me.

My finger traced along the roughest line, feeling the raised tissue beneath. "Does it hurt?"

Blake captured my hand, pressing my palm against his heart. "Not anymore." The simple words carried layers of meaning about his past, about us, about everything that had led to this moment.

Something crashed through his features then. A softness, a

light that looked like it had been trying to turn itself on for years in an unending storm and finally miraculously broke free.

My lips crashed to his, pressing my bare chest to his torso. When Blake, never breaking our kiss, reached down and picked me up, placing me on the foyer's glass table, I let out a delighted giggle.

The table was a delicate thing, only two feet deep and four feet long. I had no idea if the glass could withstand my weight, but the danger didn't bother me. Not one bit, not when Blake's hands were on my breasts.

Squeezing until I gasped.

His mouth blazed a trail down my jaw, pausing to press a tender kiss against the scar on my collarbone, the one that had driven him into a fury, before his tongue found my nipple. My head fell back against the wall as I ran my fingers through his hair, a bolt of heat charging between my legs until it throbbed with such intensity that I wasn't sure I could wait for foreplay. I needed him. All of him, buried deep inside of me.

"Birth control?" The question was a growl against my skin as his mouth continued its sweet torture.

"IUD," I managed breathlessly.

"Thank hell." Blake's voice was rough with need. "Because I want to feel every inch of you with my bare skin when I take you, Cupcake."

Take me. Two words alone that had the power to make me come undone. I wanted to submit to Blake, to let him worship my body until neither of us had anything left.

On the floor, Blake's pager beeped. My heart clenched. Surely, he would have to leave now, just when he'd finally professed his feelings, just when my body was so alive with want that I felt like I could lose my breaths if he stopped.

But he didn't stop. He kept going.

"Don't you have to get that?" I asked breathlessly.

Blake kissed me deeply, as if to silence the very question. "Hospital is full of doctors. They can manage."

His lips worked down my throat, making me smile despite my curiosity.

"Have you ever ignored a page before?"

"Not once," he admitted, licking up my throat, trailing his tongue along my lips.

"Don't you want to see what it's about?"

Blake's response was to drop to his knees, staring at my sex like he'd dreamed of licking it for years, like the taste he'd gotten on the terrace was nothing more than one drop of water to a dehydrated man.

"I'm too busy getting everything I ever wanted, Tessa."

He flattened his tongue and licked a long, slow stride up my folds, making me jerk.

My sudden movement as he pleasured me caused his prized statue to wobble—the caduceus that symbolized his dedication to medicine, the career that meant everything to him. In that suspended moment, as his most valued possession began to tip, it would have only taken an instant to save it, yet he didn't hesitate. His hands never left me. Instead, he let it crash to the ground, shattering its pieces along the floor like confetti while Blake buried his face between my legs, moaning as he licked in circles around the most sensitive flesh.

"Blake ..."

"I've dreamed about this for so long," he murmured against my skin.

No one had ever worked my body like this, like Blake knew it better than I did. He swirled his tongue around and around, making my hips jerk, and as the heat intensified in my lower belly, he added two fingers. Plunging them slowly into me.

Up to his knuckles, then pushing past the resistance until they were all the way inside of me.

Again, I let out a breath. Again, I held the back of his head as he brought his tongue back to my core while he curled his fingers and pumped them to the heat of our passion. I could feel myself clenching around his fingers. Damn, if his fingers felt this good, imagine his massive girth filling me completely.

Blake was still in his boxer briefs, but his erection pushed against the fabric, showing me how big Blake was. Bigger than I'd dreamed of, that was for damn sure.

Pumping his hand, Blake sucked and swirled my bud to the rhythm of my breaths, and when I'd clench his hair tighter, he seemed to know that meant he was hitting me just right. He worked my sex with his mouth while an orgasm began to build in my lower belly.

Good Lord. Blake Morrison was on his knees, devouring me. Licking me, working his thick fingers as my thighs began to quiver, his shoulder muscles tensing with each pump.

"Just like that ..." I moaned.

"Mmmmm ..." He curled his fingers, locking his eyes with me, making it clear that Blake knew exactly what he was doing.

When his tongue licked another long, torturous circle around that bundle of nerves and he sucked it into his mouth, I came undone. I crashed around his fingers. I crashed on his mouth, holding it between my legs as I jerked and twitched, my toes curling as my legs pressed against his ears.

My orgasm was so strong that the table rocked harshly, banging against the wall, threatening to shatter like I was shattering on Blake's face. But Blake never stopped; instead, he let out moans of his own while he pumped his fingers and sucked every last quiver out of me.

Then he stood, tugged his boxer briefs off, and my breath caught at the sight of him. Long, and thick, and deliciously pulsing with need. My tongue darted out to wet my lips, but before I could drop to my knees and take him to the back of my throat, Blake's hand encircled my wrist and pressed it against the wall above my head.

The moment his grip tightened, something flickered in his eyes like regret or fear, and he instantly released me.

"I'm sorry—"

"Don't be," I whispered, cradling his face between my palms. "I feel safe with you."

The truth of those words resonated deep in my bones. This was trust incarnate. I felt so secure in his hands that I could surrender completely, knowing he'd catch me if I fell.

Because this was Blake. My Blake. My body recognized him on a cellular level, reaching for him like a flower turning toward the sun.

I didn't want him holding back. And I certainly didn't want that past taking anything else from me. Especially not this.

Uncertainty creased his brow. "I don't want to trigger—"

"You won't."

"But—"

"If anything feels wrong, I promise I'll tell you immediately." I held his gaze, willing him to understand. "Blake?"

He stilled.

"I've dreamed of this for years. Please. I want you to devour me. Ravage me."

The change in his expression was electric. Uncertainty melting into relief, then blazing into raw hunger.

His lips found my jaw as his fingers teased my nipple. When he positioned himself at my entrance, his voice was rough velvet against my skin. "You're mine, Cupcake." He pushed forward, claiming me inch by exquisite inch.

A sharp bite of discomfort made me tense momentarily, but it melted into pleasure as he waited, letting my body adjust to him while he sank slowly into me. Claiming me. Filling me, my body stretching around him, him holding my arm captive above my head as he pushed all the way inside of me.

The look on Blake's face made fresh heat pool in my core; it was possession and tenderness, dominance and devotion, all mixed together. He pulled out a couple of inches and thrust inside again, this time harder, this time making me gasp with the intensity of his movement.

His whiskered jaw scraped against my skin as he found his

rhythm, and, holy hell, I loved submitting to him like this. My legs spread wide, arms pinned above me as he claimed me as his own, right here among the symbols of his success and power.

The glass table protested with each thrust, banging against the wall in a steady rhythm. Any thrust could shatter it, sending shards slicing into our skin, but neither of us cared. All that mattered was Blake's mouth on my throat, his body filling me as another climax began to build.

"I've wanted to bury myself in you for so long." He bit my lip, a little too hard. Like he was angry he'd been forced to wait for this.

I smiled and bit him back, rocking my hips with each of his thrusts. Which were growing more desperate, angrier even. How long I'd wanted this. Him on top of me, taking me, claiming me as his own.

When I finally crashed again, Blake released my arms to grip my hips, driving deeper as my muscles pulsed around him. Without warning, he wrapped my legs around his waist and carried me to an artful cushioned chair in the living room, never breaking our connection as he lowered us into it.

Straddling him, I kissed his jaw, his throat.

"Take control, Cupcake."

My lips paused on his skin at his words. This was Blake. Control-freak, never-willing-to-let-himself-submit-to-anything Blake, giving me complete control over him.

Giving me the reins was the sexiest thing he'd ever done, and as an added bonus, the wraparound windows of his plush living room didn't just offer a view of the city falling into darkness; they reflected us like a mirror. Blake's muscular, tattooed body sprawled in the chair, my thighs straddling his waist as I began to move. Each roll of my hips pressed my most sensitive spot against him, and the sight of us in the window's reflection had me building toward release again almost immediately.

My breasts bounced as he cupped them, my hair flowing behind me as our bodies moved together in perfect synchronization. Blake let me have this moment, surrendering control completely, perhaps sensing how much I needed this after feeling like my life had been so out of control for so long. As I found my own rhythm, I rocked and writhed until I felt his muscles beginning to tense beneath me, the tightening of his jaw and the roughening of his breathing telling me he was close.

Just before he found his release, Blake groaned out words that made my heart soar. "I love you, Tessa."

His declaration hung in the air between us as he came undone, the raw vulnerability in his expression unleashing something warm and wild in my chest that had been caged for years. We stayed like that, pulses gradually slowing, trading soft kisses that felt like promises neither of us had dared make before.

When we finally stood to dress, I caught Blake watching me like I was something precious he'd found after searching his whole life.

"I've loved you for a long time, Cupcake."

I stilled, one arm through my shirtsleeve, as the weight of those words settled over me. All those years we'd circled each other, both of us pushing away what we wanted most.

I knew my reasons. Some I'd never shared with another soul. But his ...

"Why didn't you tell me sooner?" The question slipped out before I could stop it. "Why didn't you let me love you?"

Blake pulled his shirt on, the fabric settling over the tattoos that hid the scars of his past, just like he'd tried to hide from his feelings all these years. His movements were measured, deliberate. The way he got when he was trying to maintain control.

"It's because of your parents, isn't it?" I ventured softly, remembering the pain that would flash across his face whenever family was mentioned. Whenever the first snowfall hit with a reminder of that winter night he'd lost them both.

"No." He stepped into his pants, one leg at a time, still not meeting my eyes. "That's not it. Not entirely."

Something in his tone made me pause. We'd just shared our

bodies, our hearts, crossed every physical boundary between us, but I feared he'd retreat now, pulling back behind scars, where dark corners of his soul cast shadows over his life. Shadows that stretched longer and deeper than I'd imagined. Whatever had stopped him from reaching for love all these years, it was something that still had power over him, even now.

"Will you tell me?" I whispered, my heart in my throat. "Why have you always pushed love away?"

50

BLAKE

The distant city sprawled out like a constellation of stars, its lights twinkling in the velvet darkness, while up here on the terrace, the air was just chilly enough that I'd wrapped Tessa in a cashmere blanket. Our wineglasses caught the soft glow from the string lights overhead, casting ruby shadows on the small table between us.

"Tell me why you've always pushed love away?" Tessa repeated her earlier question softly, her voice barely carrying over the muted hum of traffic.

I felt my shoulders tense, that familiar wall rising while my fingers pulled her closer against me, buying time.

"You already know some of it," I began. "About my parents ..." I trailed off, taking a slow breath while Tessa's fingers brushed my wrist in a gentle anchor to the present.

"The basics, yes," she acknowledged. "But not everything."

I nodded, fixing my gaze on the city lights. "I learned early on how quickly life could change." I paused, swallowing hard. "The first lesson came on Christmas Eve when my sister and I were baking cookies with our grandmother." My voice grew distant, lost in memory. "Mom and Dad had gone out for some last-minute shopping." Another pause, longer this time. "I can still see my grandmother's red apron turning white with flour as she wiped her hands to answer the doorbell. But what I remember most is the sound she made when she collapsed after learning her only child had died in a car accident."

A slight tremor ran through me then, but, as if sensing she needed to be steady, Tessa's hand stilled as it rested on my leg.

"With my Grandmother's death, we didn't have extended family who could take us in," I continued, hearing the clinical tone in my own voice, using it as armor against the raw emotion threatening to consume me. "So, Faith and I entered the foster system." I took a long sip of wine, trying to wash away the bitterness of the words. "That first night was when reality hit. I was lying in a bed with a green comforter instead of my football one. Breathing in artificial vanilla instead of the familiar scent of home."

My head went back in time to that first night.

Lying in bed, I counted the shadows on the ceiling that the streetlight made through the weird-shaped tree outside. That's when I heard her tiny feet padding down the hallway, the creaky floorboard by my door giving her away. Faith's shadow looked even smaller than a five-year-old girl's in the doorway.

"Blake?" Her voice was wobbly, like when she tried not to cry at the doctor's.

"Hey." I sat up, clicking on the lamp. The one that wasn't mine, in the room that wasn't mine. "Bad dream?"

She ambled closer. "I want to go home." Her eyes kept jumping around like scared butterflies, not landing on anything in this foreign room for too long. She hugged Mom's old sweater tight against her chest. The pink one she wouldn't let the social workers take away.

"I know," I whispered because what else could I say?

"When can we go home, Blake?" She said it like it was simple, like maybe we just got lost and needed directions to get back.

My throat got tight and scratchy. I patted the space next to me, and she climbed up, her hair still smelling like the baby shampoo Mom used to use. I held her close, trying to be brave enough for both of us, trying to find words that wouldn't hurt so much.

"We're never going home again, Faith."

She pulled back to look at me, her forehead all scrunched up, like she hadn't fully understood the conversations that preceded this one. Of course she hadn't. She was only five. How do you understand death at five?

"Never?"

I shook my head. "We have to be each other's home now."

Her bottom lip started doing that wobble thing, and her grip on Mom's sweater got so tight that her knuckles went white. I wanted to fix it so badly. To make everything okay again. But I couldn't even fix my own heart, let alone hers.

"I miss Mommy," she whimpered.

Three little words, and everything inside me crumbled like a sandcastle in the rain. Faith's sobs shook her whole body and mine, too, as I held her. The sweater between us still smelled like home, but home wasn't a place we'd ever experience again.

A cool breeze brought me back to the present, rustling through the potted plants surrounding us, carrying the faint scent of jasmine.

"Down the hall, my parents weren't sleeping in their room. They'd never make us breakfast again or take us hiking through national parks like Dad loved to do. They'd never ..." My voice dropped, and Tessa shifted even closer, nestling her head onto my shoulder.

How did this woman know exactly what I needed? Her presence, her warmth, a sedation to my pain.

"It was like Faith and I had been launched from a cannon and landed on a different planet. Nothing felt real anymore." I met

Tessa's gaze briefly as she looked up at me, the compassion in her eyes almost too much to bear.

"Externally, I maintained composure, primarily for Faith's sake. The first foster family was decent enough." I worked my jaw silently for a moment. "After a few months, we'd adapted to their routines, their way of life. But grief has a way of seeping through the cracks."

I rubbed Tessa's arm, pulling her tighter to my body to remind myself I wasn't alone anymore. "Six months later, they said goodbye."

Tessa took a deep breath, perhaps bracing herself, sensing the worst was yet to come.

"I convinced myself it was my fault," I admitted, each word feeling like it was being dragged from somewhere deep inside me. "That my demeanor had been too somber, too damaged. So, at the next placement, I became the model foster child." A bitter smile crossed my face. "I did chores unprompted, maintained perfect manners, followed every rule. But after a few months, they turned us away too. Claimed it was just part of the foster family process, but I knew better. Foster families were allowed to apply for adoption; they chose not to. Eight homes in six years, each one falling somewhere between awful and barely tolerable." I swallowed. "Then came the worst placement."

My voice dropped, the words feeling like gravel in my throat. "The one with a predator hiding behind a smile. The one who chose substances over basic human decency."

Beside me, I heard Tessa's sharp intake of breath, the soft rustle of the blanket as she shifted, wrapping her arm around my waist, like she was the one who needed the reminder that I'd made it out.

"Who weaponized our fear of separation to ensure our silence. I didn't know then that his threats were empty, that he couldn't actually separate us. That manipulation kept us there far longer than we should have been. Maybe if I'd reached out for help ..."

I stilled and braced myself to reveal something I'd never wanted her to know. But if we were really doing this, she needed to know what I meant when I said I was damaged. That I'd always be damaged.

"Tessa, there's something else I've never told you. Something I'm terrified to say out loud because ..." I swallowed hard. "Because I don't want you to be afraid of me."

Or reject me.

"What is it?"

I laced her fingers with mine, memorizing how they fit together in case this was the last time she'd let me hold her hand.

"One night, that foster dad was beating Faith worse than ever before. I tried to stop him, got between them. For a minute, he turned on me instead. Which was what I'd wanted. But then he went back to Faith. He was high on something. I could tell because his eyes were wild, movements erratic. And I knew ..." My voice cracked. "I knew I was watching my little sister get beaten to death."

Tessa's hand tightened, but she didn't pull away. Her eyes held mine, steady and present, giving me strength to continue.

"When I picked the baseball bat up, I just wanted him to stop. But after that first hit ..." I closed my eyes, the memory visceral. "I couldn't stop. I saw every bruise he'd left on Faith, heard every scream, felt every terror she'd lived through. Blood sprayed across the walls, across the dresser. By the time I stopped ..." My voice dropped to a whisper. "There wasn't much left of his face."

I forced myself to look at Tessa, expecting horror, revulsion. Instead, I found tears in her eyes. Not of fear, but compassion. She released my hand and touched my cheek.

"That's the darkness you've been carrying?" she asked softly.

"Ryker and the guys know. Told them one night after too many beers. They know what I did, what I'm capable of." I turned my face into her palm, still amazed she hadn't pulled away. "Telling someone you deliberately took a life ... it changes things. Tests everything. But they didn't run. Instead, they accepted me."

My body tightened, thinking of Knox. "That's what made me bond with them like brothers."

And why I cared so much about Knox. He was sitting in prison for murder while I walked free. Different circumstances, same deadly outcome. The guys stood by me when they learned my darkest truth, so how could I do any less for him?

"That darkness ..." My voice roughened. "It's still there, Tess. I wear the white coat now. Took an oath to do no harm. But if someone tried to hurt anyone I love ..." I broke off, jaw clenching.

"You'd protect them," she finished, her voice steady. "Like you protected Faith."

The acceptance in her tone warmed my body. I'd hoped she might understand, like the guys did, but this was different. Here was a woman who'd been attacked herself by a man who overpowered her. Trying to now trust a man twice her size who'd not only admitted to killing a man in the past, but who'd admitted he was capable of doing it again.

Not just capable. The moment I'd learned about Eric Voss, my mind had gone to dark places with vivid, detailed fantasies of finding that piece of garbage and making him suffer. My medical oath meant nothing when I thought about what he'd done to her.

"Faith survived because of you," she said. "You were just a kid, Blake. A kid protecting his baby sister the only way he could."

I buried my face in her neck, breathing in her familiar scent. "Faith survived," I murmured against her skin. "But then they separated us, pending the investigation. For months, I didn't know if she was safe or if I'd ever see her again. When I was finally cleared ..." I tightened my hold on Tessa. "It felt like something changed between us. There was this ... distance that wasn't there before."

"Have you ever talked about it?"

I shook my head. "By the time we were allowed to resume talking, it was mostly surface-level stuff. I was too afraid to rock the boat, and after a while, that just became our norm. Still is."

"So, you still talk to her?"

"Not as often as I'd like."

"Maybe you should try to talk to her about it now?" Tess suggested.

I considered this. "Yeah … I guess if I learned anything from you coding in my ER, it's to assume tomorrow is no guarantee."

Tessa allowed a few seconds to pass before continuing our previous conversation.

"So, is Faith the reason you kept pushing love away?"

I took a sip of wine. "When the foster system separated us, the process of getting her back was taking forever. I was starting to lose hope when Sarah took me in."

My voice softened involuntarily at the name, some of the tension easing from my shoulders.

"By then, I'd built walls so high that I couldn't see over them anymore. Life had become a series of waiting for the other shoe to drop. But my foster mom, Sarah …" I shook my head, turning slightly toward Tessa. "She was different."

I felt warmth creep into my voice, despite everything that happened later. "She didn't just house me; she noticed me. She'd catch me searching the web for footballs, and I'd find the exact one in my bedroom a few days later. When I dozed off studying on the couch, I'd wake up with a blanket tucked around me and a glass of water on the coffee table. Little things that made me feel …" I cleared my throat. "Seen, I guess."

It was the small things, I'd discovered, that made you feel the most loved.

Tessa reached out, her fingers ghosting over my clenched hand. After a moment, I relaxed my grip enough to let her fingers intertwine with mine again.

"We'd spend hours out in her garden," I continued, my thumb stroking Tessa's skin. "Just talking while we worked. She never pushed, never demanded answers, but somehow, I found myself telling her things. About Mom's chocolate chip cookies. About Dad teaching me to throw a baseball. About wanting to help people the way the ER doctors had tried to help my parents.

And the way I used to care for Faith's wounds after our foster dad ..." I trailed off, the pain choking the rest of that sentence.

Tessa tried to hide it, but I heard her sniffle.

"One evening, I told her I wanted to be a doctor. Instead of dismissing it as impractical for a foster kid with no financial means, she immediately started researching premed programs and scholarships."

Tessa trailed a finger along my leg, patiently waiting for me to continue.

"She was also the first person I told about our previous foster father." I cleared my throat. "She tried to hide it, but I saw her shoulders shake, saw the redness around her eyes. She promised I'd never experience anything like that again. Said she ..." I swallowed hard. "She loved me."

Loved. What a powerful word, capable of bringing people together. Or starting wars.

"Besides Faith, I'd forgotten what love felt like. Having someone genuinely invested in my well-being, my future ..." My damn throat tried to clench again. "For the first time since that accident, I started to believe that everything was going to be okay. Sarah was actively working the foster process to get Faith into our home so we could be together again. I joined a baseball team where I met Ryker, and I started to hang out with him. A lot. Like any ordinary teenage boy and his best friend." My breath hitched. "But then one day, I came home from school ..." Tessa pressed closer, her body a gentle warmth against my side as my voice grew distant. "There was a stranger at our kitchen table with Sarah. A new foster system administrator."

The memory of what happened with Sarah brought me back to that pivotal day.

I walked into the kitchen, and my entire world stuttered to a stop. The air still smelled like the chocolate chip cookies Sarah had made yesterday. Cookies she'd promised we'd make together every Sunday once Faith came home. But instead of warmth, I found a stranger sitting at our kitchen table with a manila folder. My gaze darted from that folder to Sarah, who sat opposite the woman, red-eyed and already crying at the sight of me. My stomach caved in on itself.

"What's going on?" I stepped forward, my pulse spiking. "Did something happen to Faith?"

"Sit down, Blake," the stranger said.

"Is she okay?"

"Faith's fine."

"Then what's this about?" I questioned Sarah.

I didn't like the tragic look on her face. Didn't like the apologetic, pleading stare she was giving me. Didn't like how the room felt like a funeral waiting to happen.

"Faith has to live with me," I said, my voice cracking. "She's the only family I have left, and we need each other." My chest constricted like it was caught in a trap. "Please. Whatever must've happened with the paperwork, please fix it. Please get Faith here."

The lady folded her hands. "I'm afraid that won't be possible now, Blake."

My heart crashed to my feet. Faith had to live with me. What if she was with another abuser? What if she was scared or hurt? She didn't even go to the same school as me, so I'd have no idea it was happening. I had to be able to protect her, and she needed me as much as I needed her. Being separated from her was absolute torture, like my soul was split in half, and the only way I got through this was knowing that we'd been getting closer to having her come live with us. For good. But suddenly, that was coming to a halt?

"Why?" I slammed my fist on the table, the impact sending tremors up my arm.

"Blake, sit down," Sarah pleaded.

But she no longer resembled the mom I'd come to know. Something was different about her. Just last month, she'd helped me paint Faith's room pink, her favorite color.

"Your sister will be home soon," she'd promised, squeezing my shoulder with paint-stained fingers.

Now those same hands trembled in her lap.

"Just tell me. Don't sugarcoat it, just spit it out."

"Blake, this isn't something to just blurt out," Sarah reasoned.

I looked between them, and somehow, I just ... knew. Maybe it was the pity in their eyes or the way Sarah looked so damn guilty. The truth hit me like a blood-soaked bomb.

"You're not adopting us," I deduced.

Her lip quivered.

"You're sending me back."

Sarah sniffled. Gone was the woman who'd wrapped her arms around me and given me a safe haven, a promise that life would be better. That she loved me, that she'd fight for me and Faith and give us a home forever. In her place was ... whoever the hell this traitor was.

"You're sending me back," I repeated, pathetically hoping she'd tell me I was wrong. My voice came out small, like the kid I'd been when I first entered the system.

"I'm sorry."

I huffed an angry laugh, and, goddammit, my eyes welled with tears, my throat betraying me by starting to close. The familiar sting of rejection burned through my chest, but this time, it went deeper, carved out places I didn't even know could hurt.

"Why?"

"Blake, let's talk about—"

"Why?" I slammed my fist on the table again, harder this time, welcoming the pain.

Sarah swallowed. "I'm sick."

"Sick," I repeated.

She didn't look sick. Not in the least.

"Doctors think I have a degenerative illness, Blake."

"And that disqualifies her from fostering us?" I snapped at the lady, tasting copper as I bit the inside of my cheek. It was selfish to

ask about me first rather than Sarah, but this wasn't about me. It was about saving Faith.

"It doesn't, but—" Sarah started, but I cut her off.

"It doesn't. So, you could keep fostering me. Us. You're just choosing not to."

"It's not that simple."

"I'm sure it's not."

"Blake."

"I get it. Your 'illness,' " I snarled, using air quotes around illness, *"is enough on your plate. I'll go pack my bag."*

"Blake, don't ..."

But I was already gone. Down the hall. Grabbing my backpack and shoving the little I had in this world into the duffel bag in my closet. The whole time, Sarah was trying to talk to me.

"I don't want you to watch what's about to happen to me," she said.

"Got it. Thanks."

"Blake, I'm doing this to protect you."

"Protect me?" I got nose to nose with her now, close enough to see the tears clinging to her lashes. "By throwing me out? By taking away the best and probably only chance I have at getting my sister back? You're doing that to protect me?"

"Blake, I'm sick."

"So you say."

"You don't believe me?"

"At least the other foster parents were honest about why they rejected me."

"I'm not rejecting you!"

"Move."

"Blake!"

I moved around her, taking the extra second to grab the picture frame—the one where Sarah had written Family Forever *across the bottom in her loopy handwriting, the one that had me and her at the beach, smiling, thinking I'd found my happily ever after—and threw it across the room. The shattered glass rained down onto the carpet.*

God, I was so fucking angry. How dare she do this to me? How dare she lead me on and promise me, repeatedly, that she would never turn her back on me? That she'd get me my sister back? How dare she pretend to care about the hell I'd gone through, only to do worse to me than anyone else had?

The pain was unbearable. The betrayal.

But beneath my anger at Sarah and the hurt, I was angry at myself. I should have known better. I let her in. I let her get my hopes up. I let myself smile again. And then I gave her the knife to cut my happily ever after to shreds.

Part of me wanted to turn around, to let her explain, to believe one more time. But I'd learned my lesson. Hope was just another word for poison.

"Blake!" Sarah cried.

I slammed the door behind me, leaving behind the scent of chocolate chip cookies and broken promises.

"Did you ever hear from her again?" Tessa's question yanked me back to the present.

I'd gotten so lost in telling her about Sarah that the memory had felt real all over again.

The clinical tone returned to my voice. "She tried to reach out. But I refused to talk to her."

I swirled my wineglass, watching the rim of red as it carried out its predictable pattern.

"I replayed every interaction, searching for the real reason she gave up on us. Was I too expensive to feed? Did I forget some crucial chore?"

Tessa reached up, her palm warm against my cheek. Her eyes were glassy, the tip of her nose slightly red.

"And now," Tess whispered, "do you believe she was sick?"

I considered this. "That day I slammed the door, I never

looked back. Couldn't bear to. But thinking about it now, in hindsight ... what if I'd been wrong? What if she really had been sick?" The thought slammed into my ribs. "What if I didn't believe her, just like all those doctors who'd dismissed you?"

"Maybe you should reach out to her."

"Maybe I should."

Maybe it *was* time. Assuming she was still alive, that was. Fuck, what if I was too late?

"And Faith? Did you and she ever get fostered together again?"

I shook my head. "No."

"So, that's why I never met her?"

"Faith's home was in a different school district. And while I worked to save money to fight for her when I turned eighteen, Ryker's family, your family, became my only taste of normalcy. Playing video games, shooting hoops, having dinner conversations that didn't revolve around foster-care hell. They never pried, and I was grateful."

My voice softened. "To be honest though, I started to feel envious. Bitter even, at how unfair it was that Ryker had this awesome family, stability, and love when I didn't. I started pushing him away, isolating myself. But by that point, Ryker knew me too well." A ghost of a smile crossed my face. "I can still picture Ryker's face when he snapped and said, 'It's not fair, what's happening to you, but you're my best friend, and I need you. So, don't you dare push me away because of what those bottom-feeding trash pandas have done. I'm like a stubborn piece of gum stuck to your shoe. You're not getting rid of me that easily.' "

I finally met Tessa's gaze fully, my voice quiet but firm. "So, I didn't push him away. But watching him navigate relationships in college, I remember thinking how grateful I was to never have that kind of vulnerability again. Why would anyone willingly give someone else the power to break them?"

The city lights sparkled, endless and indifferent, as Tessa's thumb brushed away a tear on her cheek.

"Why didn't you get Faith when you turned eighteen?"

My gut coiled at the memory. "It turned out the foster system was harder to crack than I thought. But once *she* was eighteen, we've stayed in touch."

Unfortunately, as I'd said, it was surface-level only. Maybe Tessa was right; maybe it was time Faith and I had that long-overdue talk about the night I'd killed my foster dad.

"Thank you for telling me," she murmured.

"I feel like you're the only one who'll ever understand me fully," I admitted. After a few seconds, I added, "Now, your turn."

51

TESSA

The terrace's bubble lights caught the angles of his face, reminding me of high school, watching him laugh with my brother. Back when he was happier, before Sarah broke his soul.

"Tell me about another memory that changed you," Blake said.

He already knew the biggest one: Eric Voss. But I was more than that attack, and it meant a lot that Blake wasn't defining my entire existence by one traumatic evening.

I settled my head on his chest, clutching the cashmere blanket tighter. "There's nothing I could say comparable to what you just told me."

"Tessa, I just want to know you. All of you. Every human has moments where they learn something about themselves or the world."

I studied the city lights flickering against the ebony sky. "Okay. Well, I've always wanted to be an entrepreneur." I smiled, remembering childhood dreams. "I marveled at Oprah and other successful women. I wanted my own business. Nothing too big, just a staff of twenty, where I'd be the idea person while others handled the day-to-day."

"I remember the time you started that cake-baking business out of your mom's kitchen."

I laughed. "I learned to create realistic business plans after that. But it wasn't about cakes. It was about female entrepreneurship. Then when I was sixteen, I confided my dreams to Mom." I glanced at Blake. "She mentioned she once had business aspirations too, but after starting a family, it wasn't feasible."

Those words became a little bomb on my self-confidence.

"Until then, it never occurred to me I'd have to choose between love and success. If Mom couldn't do both, how could I? After, I felt I had something to prove, that you didn't have to choose. But this nagging doubt kept whispering, *Think about all the statistics that are against you*."

I sipped my wine, wondering if that was another reason I hadn't dated for years. Not just the assault, but that earlier fear.

"I couldn't imagine life without love, but I also couldn't imagine giving up my dreams to get it. After graduation, I worked a safe job to save seed money, then started my business." I took a shaky breath. "That's when I met Eli. The real test of whether I could have it all. I struggled with both the relationship and the company. Eli tried to be supportive, but I wasn't giving him enough of my time, and my business wasn't getting enough of my time and energy either. When I broke things off with him, I just remember thinking, *I guess it's true; you can't have it all*."

"To go through that, on top of being sick without knowing why." Blake shook his head. "You should be proud you kept fighting for your business and for answers to your health."

Somehow, Blake understood me better than I understood myself.

"Do you still feel you have to choose between dreams or love?"

I considered this. "I'm scared," I admitted. "Here I am, in my thirties, with a struggling business and ..." My pulse pounded. "I'm terrified I'll lose it. Or you. Or both."

He picked up my hand, tracing long lines over my skin.

"You're not going to lose me, Cupcake," Blake assured me, his lips curving into that devastating smirk. "Unless it's to murder. When your brother finds out about us, he's going to kill me. Like, cement shoes, sleeping with the fishes, full mob hit."

My heart swelled at what this meant. By bringing up Ryker and future complications, Blake was telling me this was more than physical. This was a relationship worth facing my brother's wrath for.

"He won't kill you," I teased. "He's a criminal defense attorney."

"Exactly. So he'll know how to hide the evidence. In case my emotional baggage wasn't enough of a disincentive," Blake explained, "Ryker spent a decade making it crystal clear that if I ever touched you, he'd remove parts of my anatomy I'm rather attached to."

I laughed. "High school Ryker was trying to be badass with his backward baseball caps."

"It wasn't just high school. Three years ago, at that Fourth of July barbecue? When you wore that red bikini? He caught me looking and threatened to feed my eyeballs to the neighbor's Chihuahua."

My cheeks warmed at the memory, and how Blake couldn't take his eyes off me. "He was drunk on Mom's sangria."

"The Christmas before that, completely sober, he reminded me he knows how to make bodies disappear. While decorating cookies. With tiny candy canes." Blake shook his head. "When he finds out about us, it'll make the Red Wedding look like a tea party."

"Well then, we'd better think of a way to tell him. Sooner rather than later. Somewhere public. With witnesses and security cameras."

Blake groaned. "You want to tell him soon? I was thinking more along the lines of waiting until we're eighty. Or dead."

"We need a plan," I said, fighting a smile. "He's called several times when I couldn't pick up. When I call back, he might question why I suddenly sound so happy."

"I have a plan. It's called moving to Argentina. How do you feel about mastering Spanish?"

"Be serious."

"I am, mi amor." He pressed a kiss to my palm. "Though if we're going to die, we might as well face it head-on. But if Ryker asks, you seduced me. With that lip-biting thing, I was helpless."

"We'll figure it out," I promised, tracing his jaw. "Together."

I'd enjoy this night a little longer, but my hormones were already revving up for round two. Turns out, when you've had fantasies about a guy for years, it takes a lot to satisfy those desires …

52

TESSA

“Teenage me would be squealing right now,” I admitted, letting out a soft laugh. “Remember how you used to come to our house from your workouts, looking like you’d stepped off of a magazine cover?”

The distant city sparkled, while a quiet hum of traffic drifted all the way up here, to the terrace. Strands of soft bulbs criss-crossed overhead, casting a warm amber glow across the plush patio furniture, while ivy climbed the weathered brick walls like nature’s own decoration. The night breeze carried the last warmth of the day, playing through my hair, while Blake tucked me tighter against his side, the soft cashmere blanket caressing my skin.

I could hear a flicker of joy in Blake’s voice. “You used to watch me?”

“Like a live-in stalker.”

He chuckled.

“I used to have this fantasy that, one day, you’d spend the night with Ryker, and you would wait for him to fall asleep and sneak into my room.”

“Your brother would have castrated me.”

I shook my head, smirking. “We would’ve been quiet.”

Blake's eyebrow arched playfully. "And what did you fantasize about doing with me?"

"Everything."

When Blake shifted, I could tell that my words were already reactivating the launch sequence.

Same, Blake. Same.

My body apparently had plans to make up for lost time after all those years of stolen glances and careful distance. Now that I knew how his hands felt on my skin, how his breath caught when I kissed him, would I ever be able to look at him again without wanting more?

"At first, my fantasies were pretty vanilla. You know, missionary, that sort of thing, but the older I got, the more ..." I wobbled my head. "Sophisticated my fantasies became."

"I'm going to buy you an entire library of romance novels."

I smiled.

"Meanwhile, give me an example."

"So many to choose from. Where would I even begin?"

"Somewhere. Anywhere. Urgently, please."

I grinned wider, sifting through the millions of fantasies I'd had of Blake all these years.

"One of my fantasies was pleasuring you."

Blake groaned. A good groan. A *holy crap, that is hot* groan.

"I used to imagine that I would, like, hide beneath the table, where nobody else could see me, and you'd be sitting there, trying to be all serious and dark and brooding, but beneath the table, I'd have you in my mouth."

He shifted his hand against his now-bulging front.

"Everyone else would see you being normal, but they wouldn't be in on the secret. That beneath the tablecloth, you'd be buried in my throat."

When Blake shifted his hips again, visibly uncomfortable with his growing erection, I shrugged the cashmere blanket off my shoulders and knelt between his legs. His smile expanded as he set down his wine, and I worked his waistband, pulling his pants to his ankles.

But just as my fingers reached for his boxer briefs, his cell phone rang. Blake's face transformed with a clenching jaw and eyes narrowing. He stared at the screen like he was contemplating how satisfying it would be to chuck his iPhone off the roof. Then a look of resignation settled over his features, like his duty as a doctor was cockblocking his personal life.

"I'm sorry, Tess." The words came out through gritted teeth. "I have to take this."

He jabbed the button. "Dr. Morrison." His voice was professional, but barely masking his frustration. "Is the patient stable?" Pause. "Good. That means he's not critical. Walk me through what you've done so far."

Blake muted it for a second, running a hand through his hair. "Intern," he explained, the word dripping with both sympathy and irritation. "The other ER doc is working a critical case, so I have to walk him through this. Sorry, it might take a while."

I caught the important details in his explanation like breadcrumbs: patient stable, not critical, other doctor just busy.

That sounded like something he could ... multitask. Right?

I tugged his boxers.

"What are you doing?" Blake whispered, covering his phone's microphone.

"Take your call, Dr. Morrison. I'll find a way to entertain myself."

I smirked mischievously and rolled my tongue along the crown of his head.

Blake's eyes darkened, but he reached for the thread of resistance.

"Stop," he whispered.

Giving him another mischievous smile, I trailed my tongue down along the shaft and then slowly drew it up, performing swirling circles on the crown, watching as Blake's mouth hung open in ecstasy. I repeated the moves several times while Blake struggled to keep his voice level and even, answering a series of questions from this intern. All while boring his hungry stare into me.

It occurred to me that Blake was this powerful doctor who other people called for advice. But here he was, at the mercy of my tongue. After one long final swirl around the tip, I drew him into my mouth slowly. Methodically. His girth made it difficult, so I pulled back up and then took him in, one inch at a time.

I wasn't sure if the intern could hear the change in Blake's tone, but I definitely did. I definitely felt his fingers lock on the back of my head as I took him deeper into my mouth until I hit a gag reflex.

My eyes watered, so I pulled back, but focused on relaxing my throat until I took him all the way in.

That made his head roll back, his voice becoming more impatient with the intern's never-ending list of questions. While he spouted a bunch of medical jargon, I began bobbing.

I liked tasting him. I liked having him in my mouth, and I liked being the one that was secretly pleasuring him.

The conversation seemed to go on for an eternity, but I loved every moment of it. Every stroke, every lick, every finger tug at my hair, and all the while, I was getting hotter and hotter, an aching pulse demanding attention between my thighs.

Freeing myself of my clothing from the waist down, I climbed on top of him and glided him into my warm, aching need.

When I accidentally moaned, Blake covered my mouth with his hand.

But he didn't stop me. Not when I began to move, not when I found my rhythm, and not when I moved his hand from my mouth to my sex, biting my lip as he performed slow circles with this thumb.

I couldn't even make out what Blake was saying, but his eyes ... His eyes were glued to my sex taking him in me. This was so much hotter than any of my fantasies, a wave of pleasure rising embarrassingly quickly. As it finally crashed around me, he had to abandon circling my sensitive bud to clamp his hand over my mouth again while I twitched and jerked from the orgasm. Burying my face in his neck.

Suddenly, he clicked the red button on his cell phone, chucked it aside, and said, "Up. Now."

He tugged my body away from him.

"Sit on the sofa."

It was actually a patio couch, but I wasn't going to correct him.

"Now turn around, throw your legs up over the back, and dangle your head down."

I realized instantly what he was doing. He was positioning me upside down, my head and mouth dangling off the edge, in the perfect position for me to deep-throat him.

I happily obliged, opening my jaw as he knelt in front of me.

And thrust so deeply and quickly into my mouth that I gagged.

Pulling back slightly, Blake grabbed the back of my head. And started pistoning in and out of my mouth.

"Want me to pull out?" he asked.

With him finding his rhythm, I shook my head slightly. My answer made him groan and thrust his hips harder. I relaxed my throat, taking every inch of him until, finally, he stilled and roared. I could feel the warmth of his climax in the back of my throat, could feel him quivering as he caught his breath and then, after several seconds, freed himself.

"My turn," he announced.

I blinked. I wasn't expecting him to return the favor, but when he lay down on the ground, I wasn't going to argue with him either.

"On my face, Cupcake. Now."

The throbbing between my thighs was almost unbearable as I

positioned my knees on either side of his head, and then he pulled my sex to his mouth.

I ran my fingers through his hair as his skilled tongue found its tempo. My hips began to move, gyrating and quivering as he locked eyes with me, bringing me to the brink and holding me tightly until I crashed around him. Around my Blake.

53

BLAKE

PRIVATE MESSAGE

*Ryker: Any news about our friend? *thinking face emoji**

Me: Are you seriously putting this in writing? Did you have a stroke?

Ryker: Wow, someone's extra charming today.

Me: YOU. The actual lawyer. The one who gave me a two-hour lecture about "electronic paper trails" when I'd texted what Knox said in one of my visits.

Ryker: Relax. I've had this app since law school. Military-grade encryption.

*Me: Right. Because no one's ever hacked anything "military-grade." *eye roll emoji**

Ryker: Speaking of people avoiding my questions ... heard from my sister lately?

Me: ...

Me: ...

Me: Why would I have?

Ryker: Interesting response time.

Me: What's interesting is how smoothly you just pivoted from friend to Tess.

Ryker: You just called her Tess.

Well, shit.

Me: This is stupid. I'm hanging up on this text.

Ryker: That's not even a thing.

Me: Watch me.

Ryker: Blake.

Ryker: Blake?

Ryker: Fine. But if you're lying to me about either of them, they'll never find YOUR body. That's not a threat. It's a promise from your lawyer.

54

TESSA

"This is a terrible idea." My steps dragged against the sidewalk as we approached my front porch. "I still don't see the point."

"We've been over this," Blake's voice carried that infuriatingly calm doctor-knows-best tone that made me want to simultaneously strangle him and kiss him.

"Even on the one in a million chance you're correct ..." I shot him a look when he dramatically clutched his chest at my lack of faith. "There's no way we're going to find it."

"Stop. Your confidence is making my ego too big."

"We're not drug-sniffing dogs. This is pointless, and I'm worried."

For the first time since this wild theory of his took root, Blake's spine stiffened. Something dark flashed across his eyes, and I watched his unwavering certainty crack, just for a moment.

"You should wait outside," he declared, placing his hand over mine on the doorknob.

"And leave you alone in my townhouse? I think not."

He smirked, but there was steel beneath the playfulness.

"I'm not worried about me. I'm worried about you. If there's even a chance that what you're saying is right and you stumble across it, you could get sick. You're a doctor; you can't afford to get sick."

"Let me get this straight." Blake stepped closer, his presence making the air feel suddenly warmer. His fingers brushed against my cheek, sweeping away a fallen strand of hair. "Faced with the very real possibility that someone has been poisoning you, your primary concern right now is that *I* could find it and get sick?"

"You find that amusing?"

Blake shook his head, something soft and wondering crossing his face. "If kindness was a disease, yours would be so extreme that it'd be fatal."

"I disagree. Don't you remember my grade-A bitch phase when I was mad at you?"

The lock clicked open beneath my fingers, the door creaking on its hinges.

"Tessa?"

My stomach dropped. No. Not him, not now. Not when Blake was on high alert, convinced someone was trying to murder me, for crying out loud.

Last night, Blake had made me go over everyone in my life like I was the star witness in some true crime documentary. He'd even brought out a pad of paper and created two columns, methodically listing everyone who might have even the smallest reason to dislike me.

That list included:

Eric Voss. Top of the list, obviously, what with his creepy-ass letters and prior violence. Though how he'd get poison into my system was a mystery. Blake sent the letters to some testing facility to see if they contained poison, but so far, they hadn't come back. And Blake hadn't gotten sick after touching them. But I digress.

Once Upon a Lifetime, my business competitor. Though I'd pointed out that successful companies don't usually resort to murder to eliminate tiny competitors. Blake had written it down anyway, his doctor's scrawl matching his determined expression.

My neighbor, or "the creeper," as Blake dubbed him, who

apparently had means, access, and a "concerning fascination" with my comings and goings.

Sure, the guy was odd, but murder? No. I think not.

Eli, my ex-boyfriend. Blake pointed out that plenty of love stories end in death. #Romance. I'd reminded him Eli was more of a golden retriever puppy. The only pit bull in my life currently was Blake.

Scarlett, my best friend, whose name I'd scratched out so viciously that I'd torn through the page. Blake had the audacity to suggest that "deep-seated jealousy can hide in the most unexpected places." I'd nearly thrown the notepad at his head.

And after all that speculation of who might be trying to kill me (assuming someone was trying, which was still a far-fetched if) now here was Eli, standing on my porch with a pink wedding planner I'd completely forgotten about, while Blake's entire body tensed like a guard dog spotting an intruder.

"I thought that was you." Eli smiled, but it faltered when he caught the look in Blake's eyes.

"What are you doing here?" I tried for surprised rather than horrified, but given Blake's current murder-mystery obsession, I might as well have invited a cobra to afternoon tea.

"You asked me to drop this off." Eli held up the binder like a peace offering.

"Oh, right." The binder, once my pride and joy, filled with wedding planning ideas. In the chaos of this moment, I'd forgotten I'd asked for it back days ago. Not that I'd point out he was late ...

Blake shifted beside me, his shoulders tensing. "Interesting timing."

"Blake," I murmured, touching his arm.

"Just returning her things." Eli's casual tone had an edge to it now.

Blake's eyebrow arched. "And you just happen to show up the first time she's been home in days?"

"I didn't realize I needed to clear my schedule with you." Eli's smile stayed fixed, but his knuckles whitened around the binder.

"Just seems like quite a coincidence." Blake's voice was deceptively calm. "You holding on to her things this long, showing up right when she returns ..."

"What exactly are you implying?"

"I think you know exactly what I'm implying."

"What the hell is your problem?" Eli snarled.

"An ex lingering outside her place? Ever look up the word *stalker* in a dictionary?"

"You think I'm stalking her? That's rich."

"If the shoe fits ..."

"You pretentious piece of—" Eli's hands balled into fists. "You're lucky I don't rearrange that face of yours."

Blake's laugh was cold. "I'd love to see you try."

"Guys, stop." I pressed my palm against Blake's chest, but he was like granite under my hand.

"Maybe you're the reason she's been sick." Blake's accusation to Eli cut through the tension like a knife.

The words hung in the air for a moment before landing. Eli's face transformed from anger to stunned disbelief.

"You think I *poisoned* her?" He stared at Blake with wide eyes. "What, are you out of your fucking mind?"

"Do you have access to poisons?" Blake's voice was emotionless now, which somehow made it worse.

Eli's eyes ping-ponged between us. "Poisoning you? Really?" The hurt in his voice slapped me across the face.

"He's just trying to rule out all possibilities," I explained. "That's all."

"That's all, huh?" Eli's laugh was bitter. "Sounds to me like you're stumped, Doctor. You thought you were so smart, that after a year of other doctors failing to diagnose Tessa's symptoms, you'd swoop in and figure it out in no time. And when that didn't work, you couldn't admit that you're not smarter than all those other doctors. So, you had to concoct some other explanation to keep her hooked and relying on you to figure this out for her. How convenient that your explanation drives a wedge between her and everyone else she trusts."

"Eli!" I chided.

"No, Tessa, you need to hear this. If you ask me? There's only one person in your life that's toxic. This guy." Eli turned to me, his eyes soft with hurt. "After all we've been through, I can't believe you would even *think* I would do that to you."

Shame burned my cheeks.

"I was the one encouraging you to pursue a diagnosis when you wanted to give up," he continued. "I was the one who would drive you to your appointments and take off work. At the risk of sounding like a jerk, your illness negatively affected my life and our relationship. So, what exactly would I have gained, Tessa?"

He was right. It made no sense.

Plus, if he really wanted me dead, I'd be dead by now.

"Eli ..."

"Goodbye, Tessa."

The pink binder hit the porch with a hollow thud, and Eli stormed off. His car door slammed, tires screaming against pavement as he peeled away.

"He's right," I whispered, the words tasting like defeat. "Looking at everyone in my life like a suspect is unhealthy, Blake."

"Tessa ..."

"Look, my relationship with Eli didn't work out. Part of that was because he was *encouraging* me to figure out what was making me sick. In your theory, that would've put him in jail, so it doesn't make sense. Even though Eli and I broke up, we were on good terms. *Were* being the operative word."

"I'm sure he'll come back."

"It's not just him. I won't let this happen to everyone else in my life. There is no coming back from accusing someone of trying to murder you, Blake." My voice cracked. "If I were Eli, I would never want to talk to me again either. I'm ashamed of myself for entertaining this idea."

"Tessa ..."

I spun around, anger and hurt making me bold. "You will not confront anyone else in my life with this accusation, do you hear me?"

"And what if I'm right?"

I paused. "In the unimaginably, unlikely event that some kind of toxin is found in my veins, we'll cross that bridge when we come to it. But you're a doctor. You know as well as I do that doesn't necessarily mean someone in my life is poisoning me. There are outbreaks all the time at food processing plants or supplement companies. Think about all the areas within the supply chain where something we ingest or come into contact with can be inadvertently contaminated. Groundwater, medicine, food, supplements, cosmetics. You name it. So, keep that in mind because we are not speaking this thought aloud again, do you hear me?"

"What are you doing?" Blake asked, his attention fixed on my hand as I locked my front door.

"After careful consideration, this wild goose chase of visually inspecting my place for possible poison is fruitless and dangerous. We both have busy days ahead of us."

Blake's chest puffed up, squaring his shoulders like he was facing down a difficult patient as he glanced at my front door. I could read the proposal forming on his face—that he would go inside alone, play detective in my townhouse. But he was an emergency room doctor, for crying out loud, not a poison control expert or a drug-sniffing canine. What did he realistically think he would find?

Nothing. That was the problem.

Blake's anxiety over my illness was unraveling into irrational thoughts and wild theories. Again. For that reason alone, I prayed the latest round of testing would reveal an answer.

We walked back toward the car in silence.

"I know you mean well." I softened my tone, watching his shoulders slowly unknot.

Blake grabbed the back of his neck, looking uncertain. "I do, but you're right. I'm sorry. The last thing I want to do is sabotage your life, Cupcake."

A smile crept across my face, and just like that, my anger toward Blake melted away like morning frost. I wrapped my hands around his neck, reminding myself that Blake was, well, less than seasoned when it came to relationships. He was my pit bull, barking and snapping at the fingers of anyone he perceived as a threat.

I reached up on tiptoe and planted my lips to his, getting lost in the kiss as his mouth opened, my fingers exploring his back while his found my hair. The world narrowed to just us, just this moment—

"What the fuck?"

A car door slammed like a gunshot, making me jump. We pulled apart and turned toward the sound, only to find my brother, Ryker, storming toward us, his face a thundercloud of rage.

Before I could even process what was happening, Ryker's palms slammed against Blake's chest, sending him wobbling backward.

55

TESSA

Ryker charged like a freight train, his shoulder connecting with Blake's stomach with enough force to send them both sprawling into my landlord's prized hydrangeas. The flowers never stood a chance.

"Ryker!" I yelled.

My brother's tattooed fist connected with Blake's jaw, the crack echoing off the brick townhouses. The same fist that used to threaten my high school dates was now trying to rearrange his best friend's face.

"I told you to never touch my sister."

"You knew I was protecting her," Blake snapped.

"Protecting. Not fucking." Another punch.

"RYKER JAMES KINCAID!" This time, I channeled our mother's voice, which was about as effective as trying to stop a hurricane with an umbrella.

I lunged forward, wrapping my arms around my brother's torso, trying to restrain six foot two of pure rage. But it was like a miniature dachshund attempting to tackle a Great Dane, and as an added bonus, my timing couldn't have been worse. As I grabbed him, Ryker was already pulling back for another punch.

His elbow caught my temple, sending me stumbling backward onto the grass.

Blake's eyes darkened dangerously as he watched me fall. He shoved my brother with enough force to flip their positions, landing a solid punch that was definitely going to leave Ryker with a black eye that'd be hard to explain to his clients. You know, criminals who were on trial for violent crimes.

"And here I thought, board meetings were violent." The dry voice cut through the chaos.

I looked up to see Jace standing at the edge of my lawn, impeccable in a charcoal suit despite the early hour, one eyebrow raised in amusement. He must have been in the car with Ryker?

"Gentlemen," he said, voice deceptively calm as he strode toward the brawl, "I believe this is what we call a PR disaster."

With shocking efficiency, he inserted himself between Blake and Ryker, using his considerable height and strength to separate them with one arm each. They continued struggling against his grip like rabid wolves, but Jace held firm, the only sign of exertion a slight tightening around his jaw.

"Lockwood, get the hell out of my way," Ryker snarled, trying to maneuver around him.

Jace's grip only tightened. "You two realize there are at least seven people filming this right now?" His voice remained conversational, but something in his tone made both men pause. "And that at least three of those videos will be on social media within five minutes? Tell me, Ryker, how will your clients feel about their attorney being filmed assaulting a doctor? And, Blake, I'm sure the hospital board will be thrilled to see their chief of emergency medicine applicant participating in a lawn-wrestling match."

They stopped struggling, though the murderous glares continued.

"Now," Jace continued, "as entertaining as this is—and believe me, watching two grown men destroy their careers over testosterone is truly fascinating—perhaps we could continue this discussion inside? Unless you'd prefer to complete your mutual destruction in public."

My head throbbing, I scrambled to my feet.

"I told you what I'd do if you ever touched my sister!" Ryker growled at Blake, ignoring Jace completely.

"This isn't some random hookup!" Blake shot back, dodging another attempt by Ryker to get around Jace. "I'm in love with her, you fucking idiot!"

Those words seemed to enrage Ryker even more. A one-off hookup was one thing. A complicated, long-term relationship? That was exactly what Ryker was trying to avoid this whole time between me and Blake, and Blake defied his warnings.

"I'm going to sell your organs on the black market!" Ryker started struggling again.

"Fascinating business model," Jace remarked dryly, "but I'm afraid medical ethics committees tend to frown on organ harvesting from living donors."

Blake and Ryker lunged for each other, arms around Jace.

"STOP IT!" I shrieked. "You guys are middle-aged!"

They all froze, like someone had hit pause on a very violent movie. Three heads swiveled toward me in perfect synchronization, wearing matching expressions of horror.

"I'm not middle-aged," Ryker said, looking genuinely wounded. "I'm thirty-five."

Blake shoved away from my brother and Jace, brushing grass from his now-ruined dress shirt. "Middle-aged is, like, forty-five."

"I don't even have gray hair yet," Jace added quietly, looking legitimately offended.

I stared at them in disbelief. "Seriously? THAT'S what got you to stop?"

"We're not middle-aged," Ryker muttered again, wiping blood from his split lip with the back of his hand.

"For once, I actually agree with your brother," Jace said, straightening his tie, which had almost remained perfect despite the physical intervention.

I planted myself between Ryker and Blake, arms spread between their chests, just in case they started acting like morons again.

"A) You're not teenagers anymore, so stop acting like them! And B) in case either of you needs a reminder, I'm thirty-three years old. You." I jabbed a finger at Ryker. "Lost the right to express opinions over my dating choices when I stopped wearing braces, and you"—I turned to Blake—"are not helping your case by rolling around on my lawn like a WWE reject!

"And you." I turned to Jace, who actually took a step back, hands raised in surrender. "What are you even doing here?"

"Ryker and I had plans. He took a detour, to check on you." Jace shot an accusing look at Blake. "Seems multiple people have been worried about you lately, Tessa, and that role should come with a warning label."

Good God, people were still recording us. Probably posting videos online as we spoke. I could imagine the headlines now.

Emergency Room Doctor Practices Bone-Setting Technique on Best Friend's Face.

High-Profile Criminal Defense Attorney Discovers Assault Charges Are Less Fun from the Other Side of the Courtroom.

"Till Death Do Us Part" Takes on New Meaning at Wedding Planner's Home.

Billionaire CEO Referees Lawn Brawl. Stock Prices Soar!

"Get in the house," I hissed, pointing at my front door. "Now. Or I swear to God, I'll be the one selling all your organs on the black market."

They maintained their alpha-male staring contest for a few more seconds, muscles tense, like two tomcats deciding if another round was worth it. Finally, they trudged up my sidewalk, leaving a trail of grass clippings and wounded pride in their wake.

I followed behind them, already mentally composing an apology email to my landlord about the decimated flower bed.

"What are you doing here?" I snapped to Ryker once inside.

"You haven't been returning my phone calls. Decided to pop over and make sure you're okay."

"I've been busy," I said apologetically.

"So it would appear." My brother's gaze attempted to incinerate Blake.

"Not like that."

Jace moved to the kitchen, inspecting the five-dollar coffee maker I'd snagged at a garage sale like he wasn't sure what he was looking at. His coffee maker was probably a shiny silver thing with three hundred buttons. Mine had a crack, a chip, and a stained carafe that hadn't been truly clean since the 1980s.

He poked at it dubiously with one finger. "This is ... fascinating. Is this what they used to brew coffee before electricity?"

My brother's gaze returned to my face, then wandered south, to the little wire attached to the small black box clipped to my waist.

"What the hell is that?" Ryker barked.

The heart monitor felt heavier on my waistband.

"What are you, going undercover? Trying to get somebody to confess to a crime or something?"

Such a typical thought for a lawyer.

"No, it's ..." Crap. I squared my shoulders. "It's a traveling heart monitor. A cardiologist asked me to wear one for four weeks."

My brother's attention snapped to my eyes. Jace went completely still by the coffee maker, his gaze sharpening as he looked between me and Blake.

"A cardiologist," Ryker repeated, his tone shifting into concern. "Why do you have to have your heart monitored?"

Ladies and gentlemen, it was time to buckle up and return your tray tables to their upright position.

I had thought long and hard about how I would break the news to my older brother that I had been battling a medical mystery, and whenever I thought about it, I imagined a calm conversation organized by me, after I had plenty of answers to reassure him. But you know what they say about the best-laid plans.

Blake reached into my fridge, rummaged around, and found an ancient beer left by Eli, popping the cap off and handing it to Ryker.

"Here, man." Blake put the bottle in Ryker's hand.

"It's not even noon," Ryker balked.

"Trust me. You're going to want a drink for this."

56

TESSA

Ryker slumped at my kitchen table, a bag of frozen peas on his punched eye, looking less like the tough-guy big brother I knew and more like the scared kid who used to check under my bed for monsters. His beer sat half empty, probably warm by now.

In the corner, Jace was obviously trying to stay out of this conversation. Currently, he was staring at my ancient refrigerator, the kind with manual defrost that occasionally made sounds like a dying whale. The way he studied it, you'd think he was contemplating whether it belonged in a museum of American history.

"Jesus, Tessa." Ryker's voice was rough. "Why didn't you tell me sooner?"

"Are you kidding?" I gestured toward the front door, where he'd nearly killed Blake twenty minutes ago. "Exhibit A in why telling you anything is a terrible life choice."

"I wouldn't have beaten anyone up over you being sick." He actually managed to look wounded.

"You're a control freak, Ryker. The second I told you, you would've swooped into my life like some demented helicopter parent and tried to micromanage everything from my doctor's appointments to what brand of toothpaste I use."

"That's not true."

I cocked my head and channeled our mother's patented *really* expression.

"Okay, fine," he grumbled, "it's true. But you still should have told me. I'm your brother, Tess. Finding out like this ..." He shook his head, and the hurt in his eyes made my body ache.

"I know you mean well, but I didn't have the capacity to manage your bulldozing skills. I had enough on my plate, trying to launch a business and juggle medical appointments."

Ryker tossed the peas on my table, pushed to his feet, and started pacing, his tall frame making my kitchen feel suddenly smaller. Each heavy footfall matched the pounding in my head.

What ensued was a follow-up interrogation that would've made the FBI proud. More details around my symptoms. What tests had been run. Which doctors had I seen. Had I gotten second opinions? Third opinions?

Jace, meanwhile, was holding up a manual can opener as if it were an archaeological find. Our eyes met briefly, and he quickly set it down, returning his attention to the unfolding drama with the composure of someone used to high-stakes situations, if not outdated kitchen tools.

Blake remained surprisingly calm throughout the inquisition, respecting my need to handle this conversation without his doctor mode kicking in. He only spoke up when Ryker fired medical questions his way, otherwise staying quiet, a silent pillar of support while I peeled back the layers of this mess for my brother.

That was, until we were almost done.

"There's one more thing," Blake said, his voice careful.

My stomach dropped. "Blake, don't."

His eyes met mine, full of apology and determination. "He deserves to know."

"Know what?" Ryker's pacing stopped dead.

"There's nothing to know," I cut in quickly. "It's just a theory, and Blake's the only one who believes it."

"Actually, I'm not," Blake said. "Another medical professional brought it to my attention first."

"Why are you telling him this?" The words came out sharp. "Are you trying to wind him up?"

"Wasn't that the point of this conversation? Getting your brother up to speed on everything?"

Betrayal burned through me, my hands clenching into fists. The rational part of my brain knew Blake meant well, but right now, that part was being steamrolled by the urge to throw something at his stupidly handsome head.

"Somebody had better tell me what the hell is going on right now." Ryker's voice had dropped to that dangerous octave that usually preceded someone getting their face rearranged.

"It's just a slim possibility," Blake hedged, choosing his words carefully. "But in covering all our bases, we're currently testing for toxins in her blood."

The kitchen went dead silent. I could practically hear the gears turning in my brother's head as he processed that bomb.

"Are you saying that someone might be intentionally hurting my sister?"

"It's possible," Blake answered. "It's also possible a toxin could have come from another source. We'll know more once we have the results."

"And how long will that take?" Ryker's words came out harsh.

"We stopped at the lab before coming here. I put a rush on it. We should have results by end of day."

"So, by tonight, we'll know if someone's intentionally hurting her?"

The tone alone came off like a death warning.

The way Blake's jaw tightened sent a chill over my skin.

When he spoke, his voice was pure ice. "We will. And if it comes back positive ..." He didn't finish the threat, but his eyes said everything.

I'd seen that look before, in the ER when he was fighting to save me. It was the look that said he'd move heaven and earth to fix this.

What scared me most wasn't the possibility that someone might be poisoning me. What scared me was the knowledge that if those tests came back positive, I'd have two men—a brother who'd do anything to protect me and a doctor with a dangerous, dark side, who knew exactly which nerve endings caused the most pain—hunting down whoever was responsible.

And now, based on the way Jace was quietly locking eyes with the boys, I feared there could be a third hunter in the pack. One with virtually unlimited resources and connections.

And God help anyone who got in their way.

57

BLAKE

SINNERS & SAINTS GROUP CHAT

*Axel: Why does Ryker look like he got in a fight with a doorknob and lost? *fist emoji**

Jace: When did you see Ryker?

Axel: Just dropped off the money I lost at poker because our esteemed lawyer hates Venmo. Something about money trails. Now spill. Who redecorated his face?

Ryker: You do realize I can read this, genius?

Axel: [has removed Ryker from the chat]

Jace: [has added Ryker to the chat]

Axel: [has removed Ryker from the chat]

Jace: [has added Ryker to the chat]

Ryker: Are you fucking five?

Axel: Seriously though, who'd you piss off? Please say opposing counsel.

Me: Maybe we should discuss this never.

Axel: HOLY SHIT. Blake knows something.

Axel: WAIT.

Axel: Did our good doctor finally snap? Did years of suppressed rage emerge in a beautiful display of violence?

Me: Axel, if you value your ability to walk, drop it.

Axel: OH MY GOD, HE DID

Axel: DOCTOR BLAKE WENT FULL HYDE

Ryker: Shut up. Now.

Axel: Was it in the library with the candlestick? The study with the rope? THE KITCHEN WITH A MEDICAL TEXTBOOK?

Me: Can't make poker night. Busy.

Ryker: Same.

Axel: Cowards.

Axel: Next week, I'm bringing:

Popcorn

Boxing gloves

A medical kit (just in case)

My phone to record everything

Vegas odds (My money's on Blake. He's got that quiet serial killer energy.)

Me: I know where you sleep.

Axel: Threats only prove my point, Dr. Jekyll.

Ryker: I'm getting too old for this shit.

Jace: You're 35.

*Axel: And apparently still young enough to get his ass kicked by a doctor. *crying-laughing emoji**

Ryker: [Ryker has left the chat]

Axel: COWARDS.

Axel: Hey, Jace, what's the over/under on them killing me in my sleep?

Jace: I'm not taking that bet.

Jace: But I'd clean up your will, just in case.

I shoved my phone back into my pocket and resumed rounds.

"Room eight needs an attending," a resident called out, handing me a tablet.

The screen nearly shattered in my grip as I stared at the name of the patient—*the* name—at the top.

Eric Voss.

My vision tunneled, the rest of the ER falling away as those letters burned into my retinas. After days of searching, of hitting dead ends, of watching Tessa jump at shadows, of imagining every horror he'd unleashed upon her that night, and every letter he'd sent since, here he was, delivered right into my web.

A savage sort of joy unfurled in my chest. Fate, it seemed, finally gave me a break.

Each step down the hallway felt charged with electricity. The antiseptic hospital smell faded beneath something darker, the metallic taste of vengeance coating my tongue. Every tear I'd wiped from Tessa's cheeks, that time she'd woken screaming, that flinch when Chuck had moved too fast ... it all crystallized into this moment.

Stepping into the room and shutting the door, I drew the privacy curtain closed with deliberate slowness, savoring the screech of metal rings against the rail. Like a shark circling its prey.

"Mr. Voss." I stepped forward, letting my lips curl into the kind of smile that made grown men uncomfortable. The smile of a predator who'd finally cornered its prey. "I can't tell you how very happy I am to see you here."

58

BLAKE

Eric Voss.

I forced myself to breathe, to maintain some semblance of professional calm, but images started flashing through my mind like a horror show I couldn't stop.

Tessa's nightmare-twisted sheets. That scar on her collarbone—jagged, angry—where the bottle had cut her as she fought. How she'd curl into herself whenever she talked about that night.

After I set the tablet down, my fingers curled into fists, uncurled, curled again. In my mind, I could see it all: his weight crushing her small frame into the mattress, her desperate gasps for air, the sound of glass shattering. Her blood pooling across her chest.

He laid hands on her. He hurt her. He violated her.

I'd sworn an oath. First, do no harm. But other oaths stirred in my blood. The ones I'd made to Faith all those years ago, watching her bruises heal. The silent promise I'd made to Tessa, holding her through her nightmare. The darkness that lived in me, which had been waiting since that night with the baseball bat, recognized this moment for what it was.

A reckoning.

Inside, that familiar rage was building. The kind that had painted walls with blood. Only this time, it wasn't for Faith.

It was for Tessa.

For every time she'd woken up terrified.

For every flinch.

For every tear she'd shed.

For every moment she'd felt powerless.

The oath I'd taken as a doctor seemed very far away now, replaced by something older, something primal. Something that remembered the weight of that baseball bat and knew exactly how to make someone suffer.

I stepped closer.

Voss lay there, blood seeping from a knife wound dangerously close to his femoral artery, along with a compound fracture to his shin, his face already glazed with pain and fear.

"You know who I am?" I snapped on a pair of fresh latex gloves, accentuating the snap.

The guy tried to muster his arrogant swagger as he cocked his head, clearly disturbed by the tone in my voice. "Should I?"

I made a show of ambling up to his bed, glancing down at his very injured shin. "If you did, I'd venture to guess you would've gone to a different ER." Look at that slight shiver of fear mixing with confusion in his eyes. "I can't remember the last time blood brought me this much joy."

What a delicious sight, seeing his face go pale.

"My, what happened?" I visually examined the compound fracture, his shinbone escaping his leg cavity like it couldn't stand being attached to his body. "Tell me." I drew my hand closer to the wound, savoring the way he flinched. "Did your latest victim fight back?"

His eyes darted to the curtain, but no one could save him now.

"I don't know what you're talking about."

"Did she stab you first? Or kick your shin first?"

"I want a different doctor."

"You were angry, weren't you?" I leaned down, my face close to his. "When your company was sold. When social media painted you as the predator you are." When the Sinners and Saints destroyed every facet of his life while I called dibs on dismembering him. "So, you found another vulnerable woman to take your anger out on. But this one?" My lips curled. "This one was armed. Smart girl, going for the dick." I glanced at the blade spearing from his flesh. "Shame she missed."

"I don't know what you're talking about—"

My hand found his wound. Applied pressure. His words dissolved into a choked gasp.

"How many?" I asked quietly.

"What?"

I pressed harder. "How many women, Eric?"

"None! I never—"

"Wrong answer." I shifted my grip, feeling him bite back a scream. "Want to try again?"

Sweat beaded on his forehead. "You can't do this. You're a doctor!"

I met his eyes. "You picked the wrong woman to hurt."

"Please," he whimpered. "I didn't mean to—"

"How. Many?"

I pressed against the bone protruding out of his skin.

He groaned and then curled his lips at me. "I'll tell them what you're doing."

"Your word against mine. Poetic, isn't it? Her word wasn't enough to put you away. And yours? A ruined man accusing a respectable doctor of hurting you? Who do you think they'll believe?"

Besides, you won't have the chance.

I moved my hand to the blade of the knife. "One wiggle, and this will puncture your femoral artery. You'll bleed out before we can get a bag of blood to your room."

Beads of sweat formed on his upper lip. "Fine. I ... I lost count."

"You lost count?" The words came out as ice.

"I ... I don't want to do this. It's ... I can't help it, okay? But I never hurt them."

He means stabbed them. He just used this knife to scare them, to force them into compliance. This was probably his knife. And this woman, bless her soul, turned it against him.

"So, it's okay, is that it? Because you don't kill them?"

"I never meant to—"

"Death isn't always about stopping a pulse. Sometimes, it's about shattering someone so completely that the person they were dies. You didn't just attack her body; you murdered the woman who used to walk home alone at night without checking over her shoulder. The one who didn't flinch at shadows or wake up screaming. That's the real death sentence you handed out. And for that? Your pulse is a fair trade."

"You're out of your mind!"

"Any other victim, I'd have handed you to authorities. But the day you laid a hand on Tessa?" My fingers found the knife's handle. "That was the day your tombstone was engraved. The day I became your Grim Reaper."

Recognition flooded his face. "You're one of them. The ones who destroyed my company."

"We buried you, Eric Voss." I twisted the knife, just slightly. Just enough. "And my face will be the last one you see."

I watched blood pool beneath him, dared him to scream. If he did, he'd just confessed to multiple sexual assaults, and with everything Axel's PR company had dug up, he'd go to prison for the rest of his life.

"Consider yourself lucky," I added as his terrified eyes began to fade. "If I'd found you outside these walls, your end would have been much messier."

His breaths became shallow, desperate. I stood there, watching his face go pale, until his pulse faded to nothing.

Only then did I reach for the code blue button, when I was certain it was far too late.

"Time of death," I murmured, "is when I say it is."

59

BLAKE

I sat across from my sister in the corner booth of the busy coffee shop, wrapping my hands around my latte. The rich scent of espresso mingled with the sweetness of freshly baked pastries.

"Look," I started, tracing the rim of my cup, ready to move on from the small talk to the point of why I'd asked her to come. "I think it's time we talk about what happened that day."

Faith's eyes widened, but I caught something else: shock giving way to relief. Like maybe she'd been wanting to talk about this too.

"I feel like everything changed after that," I said.

"We got separated," she murmured, fidgeting with her cardigan sleeve.

"It was more than that." The espresso machine hissed loudly. "We always had each other, and then something shifted. When they were finishing the investigation, you seemed a million miles away."

She frowned at the untouched muffin between us. "I suppose I was processing everything."

"When we'd see each other, I got the impression talking about it would only upset you more. So I kept quiet, but looking back,

I'm not sure that was the right call." Because look at her. I could still see the shadows trying to claim her.

"That's what we do, isn't it?" Faith tightened her grip on her cup. "Put the big stuff in a box. Pretend it didn't happen."

"Trauma has a way of silencing people," I offered.

She nodded. "Having someone try to kill you, then witnessing you kill him instead..." The coffee grinder whirred during her pause. "Not exactly casual conversation material."

The memory of it sliced through my gut. "I did it to protect you."

"I know." Her eyes met mine, glistening. "You did what I couldn't. What I wanted to do so many times."

Not many people would admit to fantasizing over killing their foster dad. That alone both made me worry for Faith, and feel closer to her all at the same time.

What had that tragic day done to her? What demons had it unleashed?

Something moved behind her eyes when she spoke about it, something dark and shadowed.

I hoped I was wrong.

Her voice dropped lower. "You saved my life, Blake. I've never properly thanked you for that." She wiped a tear. "Without you, I wouldn't be here."

Relief settled into my heart that the distance I'd felt between us wasn't, in fact, some deep-seeded fear of me or something.

"I wish we'd talked sooner," I said.

"Me too. But we're not exactly great at that." She pushed her coffee aside. "It was easier to just lock it away."

"Still. I'm sorry," I said.

"For what?"

"For not talking about this years ago." I met her eyes. "But mostly, I'm sorry that I didn't smash in his skull sooner."

Faith paused, but then, her lips tilted up on one side and she reached across the table to clasp her hand on mine.

"My big scary brother."

"No more distance between us," I ordered. "Can you live with that?"

"I can live with that."

My turn to smile. "Good. Because I want you in my life, Faith."

"Well, then." She sat back, taking a sip of her coffee. "Catch me up on everything I've missed."

60

BLAKE

I drummed my fingers against my desk, the familiar knot in my stomach tightening when Thomas entered with that look on his face—the one that meant another dead end.

"Nothing?" I asked.

Thomas shifted his weight, his usually confident demeanor softening with sympathy. As the head of toxicology and our most senior clinical pathologist, he wasn't used to being stumped.

"Not one trace," he said, running a hand through his salt-and-pepper hair. "I ran every test twice."

"Let me see it." The words came out rough, but Thomas didn't flinch. He'd known me long enough to recognize when my edge came from fear rather than anger.

He handed me the report, and I scanned the neat columns of negatives, each one a door slamming shut on another possibility. Arsenic, lead, mercury—nothing. Every common drug, every predictable poison—nothing. The paper trembled slightly in my hands.

"We must have missed something." I pressed my palms flat against my desk, leaning forward. "There have to be other possibilities, other poisons we haven't considered."

Thomas's expression turned grave.

"Unfortunately, we're looking at over a thousand recognized toxic substances that could cause poisoning. Metals, drugs, industrial chemicals, biological toxins, pesticides, plant-based poisons—"

"A thousand." The word poisoned the air between us. A thousand ways someone could be slowly killing my Tessa while I chased shadows.

"I tested for the most likely suspects," Thomas said carefully. "Even threw in some less common ones. But, Dr. Morrison ... are you still convinced poisoning is behind her symptoms?"

I stared at the sheet until the words blurred, then pressed my fingers against the bridge of my nose, trying to ward off the headache I could feel building.

"I don't know anymore," I admitted, hating the defeat in my voice.

Thomas leaned forward. "If it were me, I'd review her chart again. Fresh eyes."

"Go back to ground zero." I didn't bother hiding my frustration.

"Medicine is detective work. Sometimes, the most important clue is the one you overlooked because you were looking too hard in the wrong direction." He paused, choosing his next words carefully. "It's a marathon, not a sprint. Most doctors don't have the stamina for cases like these."

"And if I still can't shake this feeling about poison?"

Thomas stroked his beard thoughtfully. "Based on her symptoms, we'd be looking at metals, pesticides, or plant-based toxins. We could cast a wider net, dig deeper into the obscure ones. It would mean specialist tests, external labs." He held up a hand before I could interrupt. "But," he continued, "it would be helpful if we knew who might be doing this to your patient."

"Why does that matter?"

His eyebrows shot up. "Knowledge. Access. Resources. A chemistry expert would have very different capabilities than a truck driver. Understanding the suspect helps us understand the weapon."

"This shouldn't be so hard." I put my hands on my hips, anxiety crawling under my skin. "Why do I get the feeling that if I don't figure this out soon, she's going to die?"

Thomas studied me for a long moment. "This patient means a lot to you?"

My throat tightened. I turned to face the window, but I could still feel Thomas's gaze on my back. "She means more than anyone else in my life." The admission felt like ripping off a bandage. "I have this gut feeling I'm missing something. I've saved countless lives, but what if ... what if I'm about to lose the only one that's ever really mattered to me?"

That wasn't fair. My sister mattered to me. Greatly. Ryker and the other guys, too. But Tessa ... she was on a different level from all of them.

"You can only do your best, Dr. Morrison."

My best, apparently, wasn't enough.

"Think about it. Let me know how you want to proceed."

Alone in my office, I forced myself to view the suspects through Thomas's new lens, with intel Tessa had shared with me about each. Eli, the real estate agent. Scarlett, the marketing expert. The creepy neighbor. The wedding planning company. None of them fit the profile of someone with access to sophisticated toxins that could evade detection. And ending Voss? Hadn't stopped her symptoms.

I read the report again, then a third time, as if sheer willpower could change the results. But the knot in my stomach told me what I didn't want to admit: I was missing something.

And whatever it was, it might cost Tessa her life.

61

BLAKE

How could I have known that the clue that would solve everything was right here at this dinner table?

"Maybe it's time we put this behind us," Tessa suggested, her voice soft but determined. She twirled her fork in the fettuccine Alfredo—her favorite comfort food that she'd barely touched—while I watched her from across the candlelit table, cataloging every micro-expression that crossed her face.

Our first dinner party as a couple should have been perfect. Maria had outdone herself with the table setting. Crystal glasses caught the warm glow of candles while elegant floral centerpieces added splashes of color, but something about the formal arrangement, the careful positioning of every fork and knife, reminded me more of a wake than a celebration. Tessa's wake, specifically, if I couldn't figure this out.

"I told you when I first started that I would never give up until I got an answer," I said, trying to keep my voice gentle, even as my hands clenched beneath the tablecloth. "End of conversation."

Scarlett suddenly found her wineglass fascinating. She took a long sip, her usual sharp wit momentarily dulled by the tension crackling across the table.

"I don't like what this is doing to you." Tessa's eyes pierced straight through me.

"Ditto." The word came out harder than I intended.

Her fork hit the plate with a clash that made everyone jump. "Blake—"

"Tessa." I leaned forward, memorizing how the candlelight cast highlights in her hair. "You've been staying with me. I see what this is doing to you. By dinner, you're so exhausted that you can barely lift your head from the couch."

"I'm running a business; of course I'm exhausted." Her chin lifted in that stubborn tilt I'd come to both love and dread.

"That's not what this is, and we both know it."

"You knew fatigue was one of the major symptoms," she countered.

"There's something fundamentally different about seeing the word *fatigue* on a patient's medical chart and watching that person struggle to make it through each day." I had to pause, swallowing past the tightness in my throat. "Seeing you on that couch each night ..." *Breaks my heart.*

"You're not letting Blake give up on this," Ryker suddenly announced, his tone pure courtroom authority. My best friend might be Tessa's older brother, but right now, he was in full lawyer mode, treating the dinner table like his latest case.

Although Axel was right; Ryker was, in fact, sporting a slight black eye. One Tessa aggressively ignored. And one that Scarlett, sensing something between me and Ryker, smirked at.

"Oh, I'm sorry. I forgot we're back in the seventeenth century, when my older brother was allowed to dictate my life choices," Tessa snapped, fire dancing in her eyes.

Even through my worry, I couldn't help but smirk. This was my Tessa—five feet three inches of pure determination. She might be dealing with a mysterious illness, but she compensated for every moment of vulnerability with twice as much spirit. Any hint that someone saw her as fragile, and she'd launch what Scarlett called her "verbal flare gun," reminding everyone that beneath the nausea, muscle weakness, and constellation of other symptoms was a force of nature who wouldn't be controlled. Or pitied.

The moment I showed any sympathy, she'd redirect the conversation to cancer patients or terminally ill children. This, she'd insist, was just an inconvenience. It would not define her.

"Now, seeing as how I planned this dinner party, with Maria's help, of course, I would greatly appreciate it if we changed the subject." Her tone left no room for argument.

Scarlett smirked and winked at me, as if to say, *See? Terrifying Chihuahua.*

"How's work?" Tessa asked her best friend.

"Work's great," Scarlett offered, though something flickered behind her usual confidence. "I'm putting my hat in the ring for a promotion."

"Good." Tessa brightened, attempting another bite of pasta. "You deserve it. You've worked your ass off for that company. When do you apply?"

"Soon." Scarlett's usual swagger dimmed. "There are some ... complications going on at work right now though."

"What kind of complications?"

Scarlett's trademark smirk vanished. She suddenly became focused on straightening her already-perfect silverware. "You know how corporate America can be."

Scarlett didn't meet Tessa's worried eyes. Eyes that glided to me with a silent question. Like I'd know why her best friend was suddenly acting elusive and upset?

I shrugged.

Tessa evaluated her friend, and evidently, she decided not to push Scarlett to explain why this confident woman was suddenly avoiding eye contact.

The conversation drifted to safer waters after that, but I barely registered the words. I was too busy watching the way Tessa pushed her favorite dish around her plate, taking microscopic bites. The wineglass she kept lifting to her lips without the level ever changing. The slight hunch of her shoulders that told me she was hiding another stomachache.

When her gaze met mine across the table, I mouthed, *You okay?*

She nodded with a smile that didn't reach her eyes, and something inside me cracked. The love of my life was drowning right in front of me, and I was just standing on deck, watching her slip beneath the waves.

Later, while I was gathering after-dinner drinks, Tessa found me in the kitchen, my palms pressed against the counter as I tried to steady myself.

"Hey ..." Her hand was warm against my back.

I forced a smile, hating that she was wasting energy worrying about me when she should be resting.

"Are you having fun?" I managed.

Look at her beautiful smile.

"I love this. Having friends over for dinner ... I've never gotten to do stuff like this before. It's ..." She ran a hand through her hair, and that's when I saw it. "Nice."

I caught her hand, extending her arm to examine it in the kitchen's overhead light. The flesh near her elbow was angry and inflamed, a scattering of hives spreading across her skin.

"How long has this been here?"

Her furrowed brows told me she was taken aback by the sharp tone in my voice. "It kind of comes and goes in different spots. This time, it's been there a few hours, I think?"

This time ...

A slight sniffle caught my attention—something I might have missed with anyone else, but these days, I was attuned to Tessa's every emotion.

"Have you been crying?"

"No." She frowned. "Why do you have such a weird tone? It's creepy."

I dropped her arm as my mind raced. "So, you have nasal congestion."

"I'm not sick if that's what you're worried about. It's just allergies."

"Yesterday, your skin looked flushed in the morning."

"It did?"

My eyes darted from left to right. "Flushing. Hives. Nasal congestion consistent with histamine response. Skin. Gastrointestinal. Lungs."

The pieces were finally, finally clicking into place.

"Blake? Where are you going?"

But I was already jogging to my home office, my heart pounding with possibility.

"I heard a lecture last year," I called over my shoulder.

Footsteps followed. Tessa, then Ryker and Scarlett, drawn by the commotion. They crowded the doorway, muttering expressions of disbelief at the wall of medical data I'd compiled.

"What in the ever-loving hell?" Ryker whistled. "And I thought my murder boards were intense. This is like if WebMD had a baby with *CSI*."

"Her symptoms," I said, yanking papers from one wall and pinning them to another section with trembling fingers. "At first glance, they seem unrelated, but they're not."

"If I didn't know you, I'd think Ted Bundy and a stalker had a baby," Ryker observed, trailing a finger over a Post-it that read, *HEART! Pulse!*

"Please tell me this lands in the top five weirdest things he's done," Scarlett asked Tessa.

"Like any chronic illness, it's put stress on your heart for over a year. No wonder you've been having issues."

The pieces were falling faster now, a medical jigsaw finally taking shape.

"I've worked with seasoned homicide detectives," Ryker said. "They've never had a case board like this."

"But the heart isn't the primary problem. That's why the cardiologist hasn't found any typical cardiac anomalies."

"Should we be worried about him?" Scarlett stage-whispered to Tessa.

"When he gets like this, you just need to let him finish his thoughts," Tessa answered.

"This is it." I turned to face them, my pulse racing. "This has to be it. I saw a conference presentation on this last year. It's notoriously difficult to diagnose unless you know exactly what you're looking for."

"What is it?" Tessa's voice was barely a whisper.

I met her eyes, seeing all our possible futures reflected there. "One last blood test. Come on."

She hesitated for just a moment, then reached for my outstretched hand. As our fingers intertwined, I made a silent promise that this time, I wouldn't let her down.

Behind us, I heard Scarlett whisper to Ryker, "Ten bucks says your sister's dating either a genius or a serial killer."

"Twenty says it's both," Ryker muttered back, but I barely heard them.

I was already pulling Tessa toward the door, toward answers, toward hope.

Please, I thought, *let this be it.*

62

TESSA

"It came back positive?" My voice trembled with disbelief.

"See for yourself." Blake handed me the results, his eyes bright.

For over a year, not a single test had shown anything. Not one. I stared at the paper in my hands, the letters blurring as tears threatened.

"Oh my God," I whispered. "What does it mean?"

We sat in Blake's office at the hospital. Well, I sat. Blake was too anxious to stay still, wearing a path in the floor as he paced. It was strange, seeing him like this. The usually composed Dr. Morrison was practically vibrating with barely contained energy.

"This is why I wanted my colleague, Dr. Benjamin Hayes, to join us," Blake said, gesturing to the other doctor. "He's an expert in this particular area."

Dr. Hayes leaned forward in his chair, his manner gentle but direct. "Tessa, you recall we took your latest round of blood two weeks ago?"

After the dinner party.

I nodded, my heart hammering against my ribs.

"And then we followed that up with a urine test to confirm our suspicion."

"Right," I said, placing the paper down so I could twist my fingers on my lap. "But no one told me why because they didn't want to get my hopes up." Especially since I'd been feeling downright lousy lately.

"That initial blood test showed an elevated level of tryptase."

"Tryptase?" The word felt foreign on my tongue. "No doctor has ever mentioned tryptase to me before."

Dr. Hayes smiled slightly and nodded. "It's not something doctors typically test for unless they're specifically looking for it. When that test came back elevated, we followed it up with a urine test, looking for 11-beta-prostaglandin F2α, prostaglandin D2, and leukotriene E4. They're specific markers."

He started to list off some complicated medical terms, but Blake cleared his throat gently when he saw the confused look on my face.

"Right, sorry." Dr. Hayes softened his approach. "Tessa, after all the tests we've run, with these positive markers, we finally have some answers. You have something called mast cell activation syndrome, or MCAS. It's a rare and complex disorder, and I want to walk you through what that means."

The words hit me like a tornado. I hadn't been overreacting. There was something wrong with my body. This was real.

My vision blurred more as additional tears welled up.

"Mast cell activation syndrome?" My voice cracked. "I've never heard of that, not even in all my hours of research, trying to self-diagnose on Google."

Dr. Hayes remained patient, his smile gentle. I glanced at Blake, catching the relief cascading through his shoulders, the slight upturn of his lips. Whatever this was, it must not be fatal then. The knot in my chest loosened slightly.

"Your body has immune cells called mast cells that are supposed to help fight infections and respond to injuries," Dr. Hayes explained. "They release chemicals like histamine, prostaglandins, and leukotrienes to protect you. But in MCAS, these cells become overly sensitive. They activate when they shouldn't and release too many compounds, causing a cascade of symptoms all over your body, even when there's no real threat."

"Symptoms like mine?" The question tumbled out before I could stop it. This felt too good to be true. Tears spilled down my cheeks before I even knew what this meant. For crying out loud, I should wait to feel this elated until he confirmed I shouldn't go pick out a coffin during my afternoon errands.

Dr. Hayes nodded. "Mast cells live throughout your body, but they're concentrated in your GI tract, your lungs, and your skin. Symptoms vary with patients because of that. They can mimic allergies, autoimmune disorders, or even anxiety too."

"But you're confident I have this?" I pressed, hardly daring to breathe.

"I am."

A sob caught in my throat. "Why didn't anyone else diagnose it? I've seen so many doctors over the last year, and none of them even mentioned this as a possibility."

"MCAS is notoriously difficult to diagnose," Dr. Hayes explained. "One of the biggest reasons is that its symptoms can overlap with other conditions, sending doctors chasing the wrong illness."

I glanced between Blake and Dr. Hayes.

"So, why did you guys figure it out?" They exchanged an amused look, and I rushed to clarify, "I didn't mean that like it sounded. I just meant ... why now? Why did you test for this?"

Blake stopped pacing, running a hand through his hair. "Remember that dinner party a couple of weeks ago, when I noticed that red mark on your arm? I noticed you sniffling?"

"Yeah, you were worried I had been crying."

Something softened in Blake's expression. "That's exactly it. I noticed because I was worried about you." He paused, seeming to wrestle with something. "The sniffling, the allergies, the hives, the gastrointestinal issues, the fatigue ... I remembered a conference presentation about MCAS last year. Something clicked, and when it did, I called Dr. Hayes."

My heart squeezed. This was the Iceman, who normally kept his distance from everyone. The only reason he'd figured this out was by allowing himself to become emotionally invested.

#Irony

"So, what does this mean?" I asked, my voice small. "Is it terminal? Curable?"

Dr. Hayes shook his head. "It's not terminal. MCAS can't be cured, but it can be managed. The goal is to stabilize your mast cells and block the chemicals they release through antihistamines, H2 blockers to reduce the histamine in your stomach, mast cell stabilizers, and potentially Leukotriene Inhibitors to block inflammatory chemicals. Now, the trick with mast cells it that *something* is triggering them. It can be triggered by all sorts of everyday things: allergies, certain foods, fragrances, even mild illnesses. Our first step is to get your current flare under control. Then we'll work on identifying what specific triggers are causing these reactions. Once we understand those patterns, we can look at tapering down your medications, potentially using them only when you experience flares."

I nodded.

"We'll monitor your symptoms and adjust your medications as needed."

"You're positive I have this?" I repeated.

"I am."

"And you think this is why I got sick a year ago?"

"What I've typically seen with cases like this is that there is some inciting trigger in your body. Typically, that is a virus or bacteria that activates your mast cells. It's likely you had an infection over a year ago, and that's what started all this. And once your mast cells were angry, for lack of a better word, they have been misbehaving ever since."

Yes. I was sick with that flu/lung thing right before this all started.

"Do you have any questions?"

"Probably," I admitted. "Not that I can think of right now; to be honest, this is a lot to digest."

After Dr. Hayes left, promising to send in prescriptions and schedule a follow-up, I sat there in stunned silence. Blake moved to sit across from me, his eyes intent on my face.

"I didn't realize how much I'd given up until now." My voice paused on account of thick emotions strangling it. "After everything ... I convinced myself that freedom meant accepting I'd never get answers." I swallowed hard. "But avoiding my health—that wasn't freedom. Getting this answer, facing it head-on ... that's the only way I'd have ever been free." And now, at long last, I had it. I smiled. "You have no idea what this feels like."

"I don't," Blake said softly. "But I want to. Please try to describe it to me."

I eyed him curiously. "Why?"

"First of all, anything to do with you, I want to understand completely. Understanding what you're going through helps me support you better."

My heart stumbled in my chest. How did he manage to say exactly the right thing with such simple sincerity?

"You said, 'first of all,' which means there's something else?"

He scrubbed his jaw, settling more deeply into his chair. "I suppose the doctor in me needs to hear this too."

"Really? From what Ryker always told me, you keep an emotional distance from your patients and their cases."

So, why would the medical professional in him wonder what this feels like *emotionally*?

Blake was quiet for a long moment, his eyes distant. When he finally spoke, his voice was raw with honesty. He told me about the teenage patient he'd lost, about how his belief that it was his emotions that resulted in her death that shaped his approach to medicine.

"But I only found this diagnosis because I let myself care. That night, it wasn't medical training that made me notice your sniffling; it was the thought of you crying alone that kept me listening. All these years, I've been fighting against the very thing that led me to the answer." He scratched his temple. "Makes me wonder if maybe I got it wrong. If caring isn't a liability at all, but something that makes me see what the tests and textbooks might miss."

I could see the change in him in the softening of his features.

"Please," he said finally, his eyes finding mine, "tell me what this feels like for you."

I took a deep breath, running a hand through my hair. "I think I'm in shock." Behind that shock was a tsunami of emotions. I could feel it pricking the back of my eyes with tears, constricting my throat, making my chest ache as I replayed the last year of my life.

"It's weird," I continued, my voice wavering. "You'd think right now, all I would feel is elation. And I do. God, I do. I finally have a diagnosis, a treatment plan. I finally have hope that I'll feel better."

My hands twisted together in my lap. "But there are so many people out there right now who are suffering, being told by the medical community that nothing's wrong with them. My heart breaks for them."

Blake leaned forward, his elbows on his knees, waiting for me to continue.

"You know, after my experience, I've come to believe there's a bell curve of doctors. The vast majority are good, doing their best. But there's a small percentage that give everyone else a bad name, and when you meet those doctors ..." My voice cracked. "It's soul-crushing."

Blake's hand found mine, his thumb tracing circles on my palm.

"Most people are incredibly busy," I continued. "If someone's going out of their way to set up appointments with doctors, it means something's wrong. They're reaching out for help. If the doctor doesn't have the answer, that's okay. What's not okay is tossing them around like a hot potato with no follow-up. What's not okay is implying, or downright telling them, that there's nothing wrong with them, that it's all in their head."

Blake's entire body stiffened. "Someone said that to you?"

I nodded, the memory sharp as glass. "Six minutes. That's how long I was in his exam room. He spent the first minute telling me all my tests were normal, that he found no physical evidence of my symptoms. He spent the next five minutes telling me it was all in my head, that he thought I had psychological issues, in the most patronizing, condescending tone imaginable."

Blake's jaw hardened, his eyes midnight dark. "What was his name?"

"I'm not telling you this so you can avenge my honor." I wiped a tear. "I'm telling you this because as a doctor, you need to hear what some patients go through before they land in your emergency room. A lot of patients are fighting a war with their bodies, with the medical system, with medical professionals who make them feel hopeless or like their concerns aren't valid." My voice dropped to barely above a whisper. "And when enough people don't believe you, it starts to take its toll. There's nothing more isolating than having the very people who've taken an oath to protect you be the ones who hurt you."

Blake's shoulders rose with a deep, angry breath.

"You start to wonder if maybe it *is* all in your head. And you go through your days, getting sicker and sicker, those words echoing in your mind: that you're doing this to yourself." The tears were flowing freely now. "I spent over 365 days in this battle, and there were times when I'd lay my head down at night, alone in my bed, sobbing, wondering if I could cope with another day of it."

I wiped my cheeks with my free hand. "By the time I landed in your emergency room, I had decided to give up fighting for answers. Not because I wasn't a fighter, but because I couldn't take it anymore. I needed to get off that roller coaster. It seemed no one believed I was sick anyway. But thankfully, you encouraged me to keep going. One last time. And now, it's finally over."

Blake stood, pulling me up with him and into his arms. I pressed my face into his chest, breathing in the familiar scent of him.

“Thank you,” I whispered against his shirt. “For giving me my life back.”

His arms tightened around me, and I felt him press a kiss to the top of my head. We stood there in silence, the weight of the past year finally beginning to lift, replaced by something light, something beautiful.

If only it could have lasted.

63

TESSA

"You look so much better." Scarlett's tongue poked out in concentration as she applied the topcoat to my pinkie nail, the fresh polish gleaming under Blake's kitchen lights.

"Do I?" I wiggled my other fingers, admiring her handiwork.

"Girl, you were starting to resemble the Crypt Keeper there for a hot second."

I shot her my best death glare, which only made her grin wider.

"Only for a hot second!" She held up her hands in defense. "But now? Your skin's all glowy, and your eyes are bright again. You look amazing."

"Well, I feel amazing." The words came out almost reverently. After so long of feeling horrible, it still felt surreal to wake up every morning feeling like myself again.

"So, the medications are working?" Scarlett capped the polish, the familiar scent of acetone mixing with the coffee brewing behind us.

"Like a dream." I couldn't keep the smile from my face. "No more symptoms, and my energy's back. It kind of feels like I've been dragging an anchor behind me for the past year, and now it's finally gone."

"And how does Blake feel now that you have this diagnosis?" Scarlett questioned.

I frowned a little. "He seems great, but he's still a little concerned that we don't know all the triggers. He keeps saying he feels like he's missing something. I'm recording everything I eat or drink, and I've gone down to the bare minimum again, just so we can start with a clean slate." I met her eyes and managed a small smile. "We'll get there."

"So, are you fasting tonight then?" she wondered.

"Hell no. The bride paid for the most expensive meal in probably planet Earth history, *and she splurged for* Krug Grande Cuvée 172ème Edition. That's like $450 per bottle. You can bet your ass I'll have more than one glass of that champagne."

Scarlett chuckled. "I love it. Learning to live with your condition without missing out on the good stuff." She waved air onto my fingers to make the nails dry faster. "Speaking of Dr. Hottie." Scarlett waggled her eyebrows. "Where is he?"

"Working."

"Will he make it to the wedding?"

I frowned, trying to ignore the little pang in my chest. "Unlikely. But that's okay. Today is a success story."

She shook her head. "I still cannot believe you planned a wedding in seven weeks. How did you pull it off?"

"Some of it was luck, with vendors having openings from cancellations and things like that. Some of it was just ..."

"Incredible business skills," Scarlett cut in. "I saw your website. Making sure every vendor got their own landing page with contact info and glowing testimonials about pulling off a wedding in record time? Genius."

I shrugged, but couldn't hide my smile. "Anyone willing to work with us in such a compressed timeline deserved a shout-out."

The elevator announced its arrival with a soft ding.

"I thought you said he had to work?" Scarlett's eyebrows shot up.

"He did." I slid off the stool and padded toward the foyer in my bare feet, noticing the conspicuously empty spot where the medical statue had stood before Blake and I ... well, broke it, having sex. My cheeks warmed at the memory.

I stopped short at the sight of three people standing in the entryway. A woman with cotton-candy-pink hair held an elegant garment bag, a man with flowing silver-streaked hair carried what looked like a professional case of some sort, and another woman juggled two purple cases that practically screamed expensive.

"I'm sorry, can I help you?"

"Where should we set up?" the man asked, as if this was all perfectly normal.

"Set up for what?"

They exchanged knowing looks.

"Dr. Morrison didn't tell you we were coming?"

The pink-haired woman's smile widened. "We're here to transform you into Cinderella for your ball."

She breezed past me, setting her things down in the kitchen while I stood there, mouth agape.

"Blake sent you for *me*?"

"I have other options downstairs if this one doesn't suit you." She unzipped the garment bag, revealing an emerald-green gown that looked like it belonged on a red carpet. The silk caught the light, flowing like liquid jewel.

"Holy crap!" Scarlett practically floated toward it, her hand hovering over the fabric without quite touching it.

"Why?" My voice came out barely above a whisper. "I mean, I told Blake I'd bought a gown."

"Off the clearance rack, I know." The pink-haired woman, whose name was Lily, I'd learn later, softened. "Dr. Morrison said, and I quote, 'Tessa's about to show the world what she's capable of. Make her feel as extraordinary on the outside as she is on the inside. Whatever she wants, the sky's the limit.' "

My throat tightened as warmth bloomed in my chest.

"Nope, no crying." The hairstylist tsked. "We can't have those pretty eyes getting puffy. Now, where can we set up? I still need to bring up your shoe options."

The next hour passed in a whirlwind of pampering. Scarlett perched on a nearby stool, thoroughly enjoying the show as the team worked their magic. I kept my best friend's perfect manicure but accepted a heavenly pedicure that had me practically melting into the chair. The makeup artist, who apparently worked for the city's top fashion magazines, transformed my face with expert touches that somehow made me look like myself, only ... more. My light-brown hair, usually falling in whatever way it pleased, was styled into elegant waves that caught the auburn highlights perfectly.

And then there was the gown.

"Holy shit," Scarlett breathed as I emerged from the bedroom.

The emerald silk hugged every curve like it was made for me, which, given that Blake had somehow gotten my measurements during last week's shopping trip, it probably was. The fabric cascaded to the floor like a waterfall, a daring slit revealing glimpses of the crystal-studded heels below. The sweetheart neckline made my neck look longer, more elegant, while the off-shoulder sleeves showed off collarbones that were no longer sharp with illness.

I barely recognized the woman in the mirror. Gone was the tired entrepreneur who'd spent a year fighting her own body while trying to launch a business. In her place stood someone who radiated health and confidence. My skin glowed with vitality, my eyes bright with possibility rather than fever. The mistakes and setbacks of the past year didn't feel like failures anymore; they were just steps on the path that led me here.

Until this moment, it hadn't really bothered me that Blake had to work today. I told myself I'd be busy the entire time at the wedding and reception anyway. But now, looking at my reflection, I wished we could have had one dance together tonight. Just one.

To celebrate the end of one chapter and the beginning of another in my career, my health, and us.

"Ready?" Lily asked, smoothing an invisible wrinkle from the dress. "Dr. Morrison hired a car for you. It's waiting downstairs."

I took one last look in the mirror, seeing not just how far I'd come, but how far I could go.

"I'm ready."

It wasn't until I took the elevator down and stepped outside into the crisp air that I saw him.

Dressed in a tuxedo, looking handsomer than I had ever seen him, Blake pushed off from the black sedan behind him and walked up to me.

"You made it," I whispered. "I thought you had to work?"

"I rearranged my schedule a week ago. Do you really think I would miss the most important moment of your career?"

My eyes stung.

"I was given strict instructions by your makeup artist to not allow you to cry. So, suck it up, Cupcake. We have a wedding to get to."

"I guess you *can* have it all," I mused to myself. Your dreams *and* love.

64

BLAKE

SINNERS & SAINTS GROUP CHAT

Axel: HOLY SHIT, HOLY SHIT

Axel: Our boy Blake is trending on Instagram???

Axel: Dr. Death actually owns a tux and knows how to smile???

Me: It's called a wedding, jackass. Rich people post everything. You, of all people, know that.

Axel: I wasn't invited to a wedding with hot, emotionally vulnerable women in formalwear??? This is a crime against humanity.

Axel: Wait.

Axel: IS THAT ...

Jace: Tessa. On Blake's arm.

Jace: Looking very ... not sisterly.

Ryker: My sister's catastrophic taste in men has finally reached apocalyptic proportions.

Axel: WHAT

Axel: THE

Axel: FUCK

Axel: So ... that black eye makes a lot more sense now.

Ryker: He got lucky. I was distracted by the shock of finding out my best friend and my sister have been lying to my face.

Axel: That's it? No murder? No grave? What happened to "touch my sister and die"?

Ryker: Tessa threatened to tell our mother about spring break, freshman year, if I interfered.

Axel: This is bullshit. I was promised violence. I had money on someone losing teeth.

Me: Your disappointment in the lack of bloodshed is genuinely concerning.

Axel: Says the guy who's been secretly dating his best friend's sister while treating patients. Very serial killer origin story of you.

Ryker: Don't push it, Axel.

*Axel: Or what? You'll give him another chance to punch you? *eye roll emoji**

Jace: Are we just going to ignore that there's apparently a spring break story that's worse than Ryker's sister dating his best friend?

Axel: Yeah, why don't we remember that?

Ryker: You two were both blackout drunk that night, thus your convenient amnesia.

*Axel: NEW MISSION ACQUIRED *target emoji**

Ryker: I will end you.

Me: Now who's making death threats?

Ryker: Shut up, sister kisser.

Axel: Would this be a bad time to mention I finally got that rash to go away? Turns out, it wasn't an STD!

Everyone: SHUT UP, AXEL.

65

TESSA

"The wedding was magnificent, Tessa." Shelly's eyes sparkled as she raised her crystal flute of champagne, the bubbles catching the soft glow of thousands of twinkling lights overhead.

I breathed in the magic of the moment, letting myself finally, finally, take it all in. The grand ballroom had been transformed into an enchanted garden, with cascading wisteria and delicate white orchids creating ethereal archways overhead. Crystal chandeliers cast prismatic rainbows across the marble floors while vintage mercury glass votives flickered like captured starlight on every table. The string quartet's melody floated through the air like silk, wrapping around couples as they swayed on the dance floor. Every detail, from the hand-calligraphed place cards to the towering cake draped in sugar flowers, was exactly as I'd dreamed it would be for Shelly.

Then there was Blake—handsome, sexy Blake in his tux—respectfully staying away from me so I could do my job but flashing me moments of encouragement throughout the event.

"I hope it's everything you imagined," I managed.

Shelly laughed, the sound as effervescent as her champagne. "Are you kidding? This looks like it took years to plan, not weeks. I still can't believe you pulled it off."

"We had the vision," I reminded her. "It was just a matter of getting the right vendors to execute it in a ... compressed timeframe."

"You say that like moving heaven and earth is just another day at the office."

When I gave her a small smile, she reached out and gripped my hand.

"I know what you went through, Tessa."

My heart stuttered. "What do you mean?"

"Everything. The sabotage from Once Upon a Lifetime. How they tried to destroy you every step of the way." She squeezed my fingers. "And you never said a word. You just kept fighting, all while dealing with your own health crisis."

"How did you—"

"Find out about the sabotage?" She took another sip of champagne, her eyes knowing. "Remember that first meeting when we discussed moving up the date? We talked about the risks, about how Once Upon a Lifetime might play dirty. But you never mentioned it again, and I thought ... well, I thought surely no one could be heartless enough to try to ruin a wedding. I was wrong."

My throat tightened. "I just wanted you to have your perfect day."

"And you gave me that, despite everything they threw at you." Shelly's eyes danced. "But now, it's your turn. Check today's online issue of *To Have and To Hold*."

My heart stopped. *To Have and To Hold* was the wedding industry's bible, the magazine I'd dreamed of being featured in someday, maybe years from now, if I was lucky. When Shelly's groom appeared with his phone, the page already loaded, I had to blink back tears to read what I was seeing.

There I was. Front page. A full exclusive, complete with photos from the wedding that was still unfolding around us. My hands shook as I read, certain phrases leaping off the screen.

"... the event planner to watch ..."

"... transforms dreams into reality with unparalleled dedication ..."

"... a diamond in a sea of stones, Tessa Kincaid's Wildest Dreams Events stands apart through genuine care for clients and unwavering support of local businesses ..."

The article then shifted, exposing Once Upon a Lifetime's systematic sabotage of small businesses, complete with vendor interviews and damning evidence. Screenshots. They were under investigation, so now, they couldn't hurt anyone else.

"How?" I whispered.

"I asked one of my influencer friends to write about you as a thank-you for making this wedding happen so quickly. She used to be an investigative reporter, and when she started interviewing vendors ..." Shelly's smile turned triumphant. "Well, she uncovered quite a story. David versus Goliath. And, Tessa? There are three dozen more influencers posting about this wedding right now. Each one has at least fifteen brides already asking about you."

My throat swelled to the point that it was hard to choke out words.

"Shelly, this is your day, not—"

"I got my day," she interrupted softly, her eyes filling with tears. "Thanks to you, I got to have my father here for it."

She gestured across the room, and I turned to see her father making his way toward us. Despite the cane that supported his frail frame, despite the hollow cheeks, his eyes shone with a warmth that made my own tears spill over.

"Ms. Kincaid," he began, his voice fragile.

"Please, call me Tessa."

He nodded, taking a shaky breath. "Tessa. You know, from the moment they placed Shelly in my arms at the hospital, there was one day I dreamed about more than any other." He paused, collecting himself. "Walking my little girl down the aisle. It's ... it's more than just a tradition. It's a father's final act of love. That moment when you guide your child from the life you helped build for them into the life they'll build for themselves."

His voice broke, and Shelly pressed closer to his side, her own tears falling freely now.

"When I got the diagnosis, I thought ... I thought that moment had been stolen from us. But you—" He reached out with trembling fingers to grasp my hand. "You gave me that gift. That precious, irreplaceable moment with my daughter. There aren't enough words, enough ways to say thank you for that."

I tried to speak, but emotion clogged my voice. Shelly wrapped her arms around her father, both of them holding each other as their shoulders shook with quiet sobs. When they finally separated, Shelly wiped her eyes and managed a watery smile.

"Oh, and one more thing. Daddy and I added a thirty-five percent bonus for moving heaven and earth to make this happen."

I blinked, stunned. "That's ... that's incredibly generous."

"And, Tessa?" Shelly's eyes turned serious. "Raise your rates by at least fifty percent. You're about to have your pick of clients."

As I stood there, surrounded by the fairy-tale wedding I'd created and the lives I'd touched, I finally let myself believe it, that all my dreams weren't just possible; they were coming true.

And there was one person I wanted to share them with.

66

TESSA

"Guard the door." Holding an open champagne bottle in one hand, Blake handed a staff member a stack of hundred-dollar bills with his other.

The waiter opened his mouth to protest, but when he realized the bills in his hand were hundreds, he complied. Immediately standing in front of the ballroom's only exit into these gardens.

"I really should be in there for the cake cutting," I said.

That's why this outside area was currently clear of guests. They'd all gone inside to watch the twenty-thousand-dollar cake be cut and served because who wouldn't want a slice of twenty-thousand-dollar cake?

Answer: Blake Morrison.

After spending the entire evening undressing me with his eyes, he'd waited as long as he could to make his move.

With hunger in his gaze, Blake led me along the cobblestone path, beneath the bubble lights strung over flowers, and into a secluded garden gazebo. In here, you couldn't even see the building, what with all the ivy and flowers draped inside the crisscross pattern of wooden walls. In the moonlight and surrounding soft light radiating from nearby bulbs, it took on a fairy-tale quality, like being inside an ornament decorated with ivy and flowers.

"I've been dying to get you alone all night," Blake said, nibbing on my earlobe. "The venue staff has the cake cutting covered. Your part is done until the send-off."

I smiled. I'd casually told that to Blake a few minutes ago—that I could step away during the cake cutting since the venue staff knew exactly what to do—and he'd gotten a ravenous look in his eyes, vanished, and returned with a bottle of champagne. Bringing me out here.

"Take off your dress," Blake said.

Good Lord. The way he commanded that shot a bolt of electricity between my legs, and my sex started to throb instantly.

The traitor.

"We're in public."

"Not really." He kissed my neck again, and my damn hormones responded by making my nipples harden. "We have a highly compensated guard to ensure no one interrupts us, and no one can see us in here."

While true, it still felt risky.

"It's unprofessional," I protested, even as Blake slid his free hand into the slit of my dress, drawing it closer to the space between my thighs. Which was now aching like a heartbeat.

"Two lovers in a secluded garden gazebo. Even if the bride caught you, I bet she'd find it romantic."

She would. But that wasn't the point. The point was, "I planned the wedding and—" My words cut off when two of his fingers slipped inside of me.

"No panties," he groaned, pulling them out slightly. "If I knew you weren't wearing panties, I would have taken you on the drive to the wedding. And again during the ceremony." He pushed them in with punishing force. "And again during the dinner."

I could barely focus on his words though, my sex throbbing around him as he pushed deeper inside, and began slow, torturous circles of my sensitive bud with his thumb.

"We shouldn't ..." I breathed in one final, pathetic attempt at protesting.

But after quickly looking around, I realized he was right. The only opening to the ivy-and-floral-covered gazebo faced the lake, and not a soul was out here. Nor would they be, thanks to our guard. Out here, it was just the two of us.

"Want me to stop, Cupcake?"

In response, I rocked my hips, rolling myself on his hand.

"Good girl," he cooed, rewarding me by curling his fingers inside of me and thrusting them at the perfect angle.

But I wanted more. Needed more, all of him filling me.

Suddenly, his hands were on my designer dress, which he bunched up to my waist, exposing my sex.

"Lean back," he demanded, pressing my back against the wall at an angle where my sex was closest to him. "Now hold this."

I grabbed the fistfuls of fabric, holding them up, eager to find out what he was about to do because the glisten in his eyes told me he had something fun planned.

"Higher." He pushed the fabric up until it was at my belly button.

Swallowing, I couldn't help but check one last time that no one was at risk of seeing me, completely exposed to Blake, before watching him take that bottle of champagne and tip it down my lower belly.

I sucked in a breath, the chilled liquid dripping down my skin, to my sex.

Blake's confident eyes met mine, a smirk tugging at his lips. "I'm going to drink you, Cupcake."

And then Blake Morrison, still fashioned in a three-thousand-dollar tux, got down on one knee. Not to propose, though that would come in the future, I'd be certain. But to position himself to my sex, which was dripping with champagne.

His tongue started on my lower abs, lapping up the sweet, sticky residue before trailing a long, aching path toward my thighs. He stopped though, flashing a mischievous grin at me as he made me wait, dripping more bubbly down my stomach.

Blake's gaze seemed mesmerized by it, watching the liquid drip around my folds, and then he fell to the wooden floor. Finally, gloriously, Blake flattened his tongue and swiped a slow line up my sex. My eyes shut, my mouth falling open in a groan as he lapped up every drop of champagne around my sex and then, propping my right foot up on the bench beside us, dipped his tongue down my folds and penetrated me.

Standing here now, an offering to Blake, I immediately wondered why I'd fought this. His tongue plunged in deeper, then pulled back and began thrusting in and out. When he finally returned to my bud, he gave it all the attention I could have asked for. Swirling, circling, and sucking while I looked down at the man I loved, my heart exploding with joy. And passion. It wasn't long before I came undone on his mouth.

Shuddering and shaking, I rocked my hips against him, riding every last tremble until, finally, my muscles went weak with exhaustion.

Blake stood, turned me around, and pulled me further away from the wall, guiding my hips out and legs apart as he unzipped his pants.

"You're so beautiful, Cupcake."

He lined himself up at my entrance, my thighs throbbing with ache as he pushed himself inside in one forceful thrust.

Filling me. Stretching me. Burying himself in me.

Already, a fresh orgasm began to climb around him, and as he found his rhythm, I bit my lip to suppress a scream of ecstasy.

Blake Morrison—ER doctor, fantasy of every sex dream I'd ever had—was in a tuxedo, taking me from behind, while I was in a designer emerald gown. He buried himself inside of me in a gazebo of flowers, grabbing my breast as he slammed himself into me over and over. I used one hand to keep the fabric out of the way and the other to brace myself.

Especially as he got rougher and rougher with his thrusts.

When he slapped my ass so hard that a bite of pain preceded the pleasure, I had to bite my lip harder to keep from making too much noise.

And then I began quivering.

"Not yet," Blake demanded.

"Blake ..."

"I'll tell you when you can come on me, Tess. Not yet."

I moaned, unsure if I could hold it in. He was hitting that perfect bundle of nerves.

"Almost, Cupcake," he promised. "I want you to come on me when I come inside of you."

Holy hell.

When Blake started breathing heavier, I could tell he was close.

"Now, Cupcake."

I came harder than I ever came in my life, throbbing around his shaft. All while he thrust into me hard and fast, until, finally, he stilled. Spent.

It took us a minute to get our breaths, and when we were done, Blake immediately helped put my gown back into the right position.

Miraculously, we hadn't spilled champagne or fluids on the outside of the gown.

"We're having another round of that at home," Blake said, kissing my forehead.

As we stepped out of the gazebo, we gave our clothes a few last adjustments. Anyone watching would know what had happened, what with two lovers emerging from a romantic, secluded spot in the garden. My lipstick was surely smeared, and I could feel the slight sheen of sweat on my neck while Blake's dark hair was still slightly mussed. My plan was to make a beeline for the ladies' room, but after just five steps, I froze.

Because there, standing just around the corner, was Eli. How he'd scored an invitation to this wedding and how he'd gotten past the waiter still guarding the door, I couldn't be sure. But what I could be sure of was the look on his face, which was absolute pain. His usual confident posture was gone, replaced by something smaller, more fragile.

I could read the devastation in his eyes as he scanned me, then Blake, who wrapped a possessive arm around my waist. I wanted to say something to him, but before I got the chance, Eli walked off, vanishing into the sea of people inside the ballroom.

"I need to talk to him," I said.

Because I owed him an apology. I couldn't imagine how heartbreaking it was, not only to get broken up with, but to see me truly in love, knowing I'd just shared an intimate moment with my new boyfriend.

All after being accused of poisoning me.

67

TESSA

Eli walked up to me.

"Can you give us a minute?" I asked Blake.

He didn't like my ex, that much was obvious, but after flashing a possessive glare at Eli, he pressed a kiss to my temple and nodded.

"I'll be at the bar," Blake said, reluctantly ambling off to give us space.

"Champagne?" Eli offered, somehow having materialized two flutes without me noticing.

I accepted one with a polite smile. "I didn't realize you'd be coming today."

"Sold a house to the groom's mom." He took a sip. "She was so appreciative that she offered me an invitation. Said she wanted to help me drum up business."

"So, this was a business event for you too?"

"Passed out business cards," he admitted with a sheepish grin. "Felt dirty, doing it."

I laughed. "Don't. I'm happy for you, Eli. Your career is really taking off."

"Yours too," he said, clinking his glass against mine. "Cheers."

As I took a sip, I noted how the reception was winding down.

The dance floor had thinned, leaving scattered couples swaying to the music. Through the windows, the city lights twinkled like warning signals I couldn't quite read.

"So, it's official," Eli said, his voice taking on an edge I'd never heard before. "You chose him."

I frowned. *What a weird thing to say, given it had never been a competition.*

"I'm sorry it didn't work out between us."

"Don't be." He waved his hand dismissively, but his knuckles were white around the stem of his glass. "I'm happy for you, Tessa."

The strain in his voice, the odd tension in his posture, told me he was still hurt. Of course he was.

"I'm sorry Blake accused you of trying to poison me," I offered, trying to clear the air.

Eli's laugh held no humor. "Can you imagine? Real estate agent by day, toxicology expert by night?"

Something niggled at the back of my mind, a warning I couldn't quite grasp.

"Actually, turns out, I have something called MCAS." I explained the diagnosis.

"Geez." His eyebrows shot up, but something flickered in his eyes. "And here your boyfriend thought I was the one that got you sick that first time."

First time? The words swirled around my mind, trying to decode his precise word choice, the peculiar emphasis.

"I was the one who took you to most of your appointments," he continued, his voice softening to something almost wistful. "The one who tucked you into bed when you were feeling sick."

"I'm grateful for everything you did."

"I liked it," he admitted, and the raw honesty in his voice chilled me.

Liked it? My symptoms *haunted* Blake. While, of course, he wanted to take care of me, he took no pleasure in it because it meant I was feeling awful.

I took an instinctive step back, my body recognizing the danger before my mind could process it. Red flags were screaming, even if I couldn't pinpoint why.

"When we first got together, you were so strong, so independent. But after that first bout of bronchitis ..." His eyes took on a faraway look. "You needed me. For the first time, you actually needed me."

My eyes darted between his, horror dawning as pieces started clicking into place. The edges of my vision began to blur, and I looked down at my champagne flute with growing dread.

Meanwhile, his mouth curled up into a pitiful, victorious smile.

"I wasn't trying to kill you," he clarified, as if that made it better. "I just ... I liked being needed. When you were sick, you let me take care of you. Let me be the strong one."

The room started to tilt, preventing me from running off. All the while, my mind fought against this new reality because it didn't fit.

Did it? Then again, I recalled the doctor telling me all the things that can trigger your mast cells. If medications could trigger them, then surely poisons could too.

"But I still kept getting sick after we broke up." My voice was wobbly.

His smile turned proud. "You're always trying to save money. That's why you bought your tea bags in bulk. It wasn't difficult to lace them with low doses of thallium."

My stomach plunged to the ground, suddenly assaulted with nausea.

"It's tasteless, slow-acting, with a nonlethal accumulation. By the time you started feeling sick, you wouldn't connect it to your morning tea. And I only doctored some of the bags, scattered throughout the box. Just enough to keep you dependent, never enough to raise suspicion."

The same box of tea I'd brought to Blake's. The one sitting in his cabinet, untouched since my diagnosis, because the doctor worried about histamine reactions to certain foods.

"I wanted to spend the rest of my life with you." His words came out like an accusation. "Taking care of you. Being your hero."

"Blake ..." Through my blurring vision, I saw him at the bar, his back to us as he talked to some man.

Eli stepped closer, his cologne, once so familiar, now suffocating.

"He's about to suffer the same fate as you," he growled, his facial expression finally matching the evilness in his actions. "But don't worry, Tessa. I took pity on you. The poison I chose for you tonight is fast-acting." His voice dropped to a whisper. "I considered choosing an excruciating one. So, you should feel lucky."

"How ... how did you ..." My tongue felt too heavy for words.

"Research poisons?" He caught me as I stumbled, pulling me against his chest like we were lovers sharing an intimate moment.

If Blake's back wasn't to me, he'd know something was wrong.

"It's amazing what you can learn online. Like how effective cyanide is. Symptoms begin almost immediately if a lethal dose is ingested because it blocks oxygen utilization at the cellular level, effectively causing internal suffocation. Within thirty minutes, you'll be dead. Oh, and the best part is that your hero boyfriend won't be able to save you. Even if he somehow survives what I have planned, which he won't, rushing you to the emergency room won't help. Want to know why?"

Eli pressed his lips to my ear, whispering like he was saying something sexy. "Cyanide requires a specific antidote to save you. But you'll be dead long before he figures out which poison you ingested."

He did that on purpose, I realized. Wanted to kill me in front of Blake, in a way where Blake would know I was dying and wouldn't be able to do anything about it. Wouldn't be able to diagnose it fast enough. All while slipping Blake poison too.

I tried to pull away, but my muscles had turned to water. Through dimming vision, I watched the man and Blake continue talking, unaware I was actively dying.

He shoved me away suddenly, and I felt myself falling. The edges of my vision went black, and as I crashed to the ground, one last coherent thought raced through my heart a second before everything went black.

I need to warn Blake.

68

BLAKE

I glanced back at Tessa, praying my face didn't betray my raw disdain for Eli. I didn't want to be that guy. The perpetually threatened boyfriend who couldn't handle his girlfriend's past. Yet here I was, wrestling with an inflammation of jealousy I couldn't seem to suppress.

That's what this had to be, right? Jealousy?

Having never been in a relationship before, I had no reference point for this visceral urge to insert myself between them, to create distance. This burning need to separate them.

Okay, fine. I also had the urge to relocate his teeth.

"What can I get you?" the bartender asked.

"Two glasses of champagne."

"Dr. Morrison." Dr. Elias Vaughn, chief of surgery, appeared to my left. His steady hands, more accustomed to scalpels than scotch glasses, held his drink with the same precision he brought to the OR. Even here, amid the wedding's exuberance, his presence commanded attention—the kind of authority that could make or break careers.

Case in point: he was a commanding force on the committee choosing the new chief of emergency medicine.

"Dr. Vaughn," I said. "I didn't expect to see you here."

"Father of the groom and I go way back." He swirled his scotch, ice clinking against crystal. "You know how it is. Hospital board, country club, the circles overlap. You?"

"My girlfriend is the wedding planner." I motioned toward the vision in emerald.

"Girlfriend." His eyebrows lifted, but his expression remained calculated. "I was under the impression the—what do they call you, Iceman? —didn't have a girlfriend."

"I suppose things change."

"They certainly do." He studied me over the rim of his glass, gaze sharp despite the casual setting. "The committee has been following your career closely, Blake. Your outcomes data is exceptional. Lowest mortality rate in the ER's history, and your residents' success rates are unprecedented."

"Thank you."

"You know what impresses the board most? Your consistency. Crisis after crisis, you maintain absolute clarity. Take last month's bus accident. You orchestrated that response like conducting a symphony. No emotional decisions, no protocol exceptions. Pure, clinical efficiency." He leaned closer, lowering his voice. "Do you know how rare that is? Most chiefs eventually crack. They start making exceptions, letting emotion cloud their judgment. One tearful family member, one child that reminds them of their own, and suddenly, they're bending protocols, reallocating resources based on heart rather than head. Bad for the bottom line. Plus, they expose the hospital to liability. One emotional disclosure to a grieving family, one promise we can't legally keep. The ripple effects are devastating."

"And that strict adherence to protocols, does that drive better patient outcomes?"

Silence. For several seconds.

"One could assume so," he allowed.

Unbelievable. *Assume* so. Why hadn't they studied patient outcomes to the extent they did the financial benefits? Weren't we here to serve patients first?

I took a slow sip of my drink, buying time to choose my words carefully. "And if that approach isn't always what's best for the patient?"

He studied me for a long moment. "Are you suggesting your methods haven't been effective?"

"I'm suggesting that medicine isn't one size fits all. Sometimes, protocols need adaptation. Sometimes, listening to instinct, or, yes, emotion, leads to better outcomes."

"Interesting perspective." His smile didn't reach his eyes. "Especially given that your emotional detachment is what sets you apart from the other candidates for chief."

I kept my expression neutral. "Is that the primary factor?"

He set his empty glass on a passing tray. "The board believes your ... traditional approach is exactly what Mercy Harbor needs right now. In fact," he continued, "barring any surprises, you're our top choice for the position."

My spine stiffened. This was the most coveted promotion in the hospital system, one that I had wanted more than anything.

Pride and happiness flickered within me, but it was unexpectedly muted, like a television with the volume low. The achievement I'd dreamed of felt hollow, a shell of what I'd imagined.

What the hell did that mean?

"I appreciate the committee's confidence," I said carefully.

"Just maintain that legendary composure of yours, Blake." He clapped my shoulder. "Don't give us any reason to question our assessment of you."

In one night, Tessa and I both had our career dreams come true. I should take her out to dinner and celebrate, and I would celebrate *her*. But why did I not feel like celebrating *my* career accomplishment?

Because you're not sure your career is enough anymore. Because for the first time in your life, you've found something that matters more than medicine.

"Thank you, sir." I managed to hide my inner conflict. For now. "Can I ask you something?"

He nodded.

"Do you know Dr. Tristan Rhodes?"

Dr. Vaughn scratched his chin, a fresh crystal glass the bartender offered dangling casually from his fingers. "Name doesn't ring a bell."

"He's in private practice, affiliated with Mercy Harbor." My ribs tightened. "When my girlfriend, Tessa, was at her sickest, she saw him, desperate for help. She had an array of physical symptoms, but when the first labs came back normal, you know what he told her?"

Dr. Vaughn waited, his expression neutral.

"He told her he didn't believe she was actually sick. Said her problems were all psychological." My voice turned to ice. "This from a doctor with zero psychological training."

It had taken every ounce of self-control not to beat Rhodes to a bloody pulp. After Tessa refused to give me his name, I'd scoured through her medical records and found the evidence in black-and-white, Rhodes's own damning notes in her chart. I'd even driven to his house, my fist itching to reshape his facial bones, but something stopped me at his front door. A beating would only last minutes. He deserved something far more devastating: the end of his medical career.

I'd planned to escalate this to the medical director, but sometimes, you can't pass up an opportunity like this. Dr. Vaughn's power in the hospital system was massive.

His fingers tightened around his glass. "Perhaps Tessa's case was uniquely complicated."

"Complicated?" The word sliced like a surgeon's ten blade. "So, anyone whose symptoms are tricky to figure out, who comes to us for help at their physical and emotional worst, deserves to be dismissed as delusional?"

"No," he agreed, but his tone remained diplomatic.

"I looked into Rhodes's cases. In the last six months, he's told twenty-eight percent of his patients their problems were psychological."

Dr. Vaughn's features hardened slightly.

"I wonder how many of those patients never sought another doctor." My voice dropped lower. "And I wonder how many might die because they don't."

"I'd have to look at those cases individually before forming—"

"Doctors having each other's backs? Really?"

"What, exactly, are you hoping to gain from this conversation, Dr. Morrison?" His diplomatic veneer cracked. "Because I can assure you the decision for chief of emergency medicine isn't in ink yet, and the board doesn't look kindly on people who—"

"Who hold doctors to ethical standards?" I cut in. "Mercy Harbor is a world-renowned level-one trauma center. Any doctor affiliated with it should represent excellence in patient care. Period."

"Do you not find this somewhat hypocritical?" His eyes narrowed. "I've heard about your bedside manner. You're harsh and uncaring."

"While that's true, I respect my patients. I believe them." I leaned forward. "And this isn't about me; this is about a doctor who's a bad seed, and you know it. Before I consider accepting chief of emergency medicine, I'd like to understand Mercy Harbor's position on doctors like these."

"Are you giving me an ultimatum?"

"I'm giving you facts. Now I'd like to see what Mercy Harbor does with them."

In that moment, I wondered what the old me would have done. Would I have pushed Dr. Vaughn to take action against a doctor treating patients unfairly? I'd like to think so. But all I knew for certain was that my experience with Tessa had transformed me, both as a human, and as a doctor.

Dr. Vaughn released a deep sigh, his shoulders sagging slightly. "I'll look into Rhodes. We can't afford the liability of patients getting sick or dying."

Not the heartfelt reaction I'd hoped for, but it would achieve the same result.

"Thank you, Dr. Vaughn. It's important—"

A woman's shriek sliced through the evening's gentle murmur. I spun away from the bar, my heart already climbing into my throat before my mind could process why.

Tessa wasn't where I'd left her. Instead, a light crowd was gathering, their formalwear a black sea around something on the floor. Exactly where she'd been standing minutes ago when I'd turned to order our drinks.

No.

My feet moved before my brain could catch up, medical training warring with primal fear. The crowd parted as I approached, and the sight knocked the air from my lungs.

Tessa lay sprawled on her back, the emerald silk of her gown pooled around her like spilled paint. Her skin had taken on an ashen quality that made my medical instincts scream. To her right, a shattered champagne flute glinted among droplets of pale gold liquid.

"Tessa." I dropped to my knees beside her, muscle memory taking over as I pressed two fingers to her carotid artery.

Dr. Vaughn appeared, already shrugging off his dinner jacket. "Pulse?"

"Weak." My voice came out clipped, professional. *Focus on the medicine. Don't think about how still she is. How pale.* I pointed to a woman clutching her phone. "Call 911. Now!"

"Oh God, Tessa?" The bride appeared at the edge of the crowd, her voice pitched high with panic.

"Did anyone see what happened?" Dr. Vaughn—thank God he was here—began his own assessment.

"I think she fainted," someone offered.

"She was talking to a guy and just ... collapsed."

Eli. The name crashed through my ears like a record scratch. Where the fuck was he? My eyes swept the ballroom, finally landing on him at the far end. He wasn't concerned. Wasn't rushing to help or even asking if she was okay.

No. The bastard was smirking.

Our eyes locked across the space, and in that moment, I knew.

"He did this to her." The words came out as a growl.

I turned back to Tessa, my hands moving in practiced patterns as I checked for obvious trauma: stab wounds, injection sites, anything that could explain this. Nothing visible, but that might mean ... my gaze fell on the scattered champagne.

"No one touch that glass," I ordered.

Dr. Vaughn gave a sharp nod, understanding immediately the way two seasoned doctors can.

Something in the drink.

Sadly, a number of women wound up in our emergency room each year from date-rape drugs, but this time, I suspected the toxin was lethal.

"Her pulse is deteriorating," Dr. Vaughn reported, his fingers replacing mine at her throat.

I glanced back at Eli, who still hadn't moved. Still wore that knowing smirk. "I think that man poisoned her. We need to know with what, or ..." I couldn't finish the sentence.

Eli's smirk widened as he backed toward the ballroom doors, his movements deliberate, taunting.

"The paramedics are four minutes out," a woman in the crowd called out.

Four minutes. Without knowing what poison was in her system, those four minutes could be the difference between life and death.

I started to rise, but Dr. Vaughn's hand shot out, gripping my arm.

"Where are you going?" he asked with an edge of horror.

"I need to know what he gave her."

"And you think he'll just tell you? If you're right, he's dangerous, possibly armed, and he just poisoned someone in a room full of witnesses. What do you think happens when you corner him?"

"And what if he hurts other people tonight?" Admittedly, that fell far second to saving Tessa's life, but it was there. "If I can identify the poison before we reach the ER—"

“The police are on their way,” Dr. Vaughn pressed.

“Keep her in recovery position,” I said, already rising. “When the paramedics arrive, tell them suspected poisoning, onset within minutes of ingestion. Symptoms suggesting neurotoxin.”

“Blake.” Dr. Vaughn’s voice darkened. He wasn’t used to someone not obeying him, evidently. “You walk out that door, you can forget about chief of emergency medicine.”

His intentions were good. I knew that. He wanted to protect me from what he saw as a dangerous mistake. And maybe protect himself too. After all, a prominent doctor at his hospital couldn’t be caught assaulting someone who might be innocent. That’s why he tried using what he thought was my weakness against me. But he’d miscalculated.

I met his eyes. “Then I forget about it.”

As I sprinted toward the doors, one thought hammered in my head: this was exactly what Eli wanted. He’d orchestrated this whole scene. The dramatic collapse, the lingering smirk, making sure I saw him leave.

He was separating me from Tessa.

And I was letting him.

What choice did I have?

To save her, I’d gladly give my life.

69

BLAKE

I jogged toward the vestibule where Eli had vanished, my pulse spiking through my eardrums. Confronting him wasn't a choice; it was a necessity. The bastard might not confess what he'd given her, but he might have something on him: a vial, a pill bottle, hell, even a receipt that could point us toward the poison slowly killing her. Every second we spent in the ER playing diagnostic roulette with a thousand possible toxins could be the difference between life and death.

Time wasn't just ticking away; it was bleeding out like a severed artery.

But if I had any hope of saving Tess, I needed to be smart here. Clinical. Precise. Eli was obviously baiting me into a trap, and while I'd gladly share whatever hellish fate he had planned if she didn't make it—while every fiber of my being ached to hunt him down and beat him until his pulse flatlined—right now, her survival hinged on this deadly confrontation.

So, at the last second, I pivoted left and slipped down a long hallway, approaching the vestibule from the opposite direction Eli expected.

Predictably, the coward was crouched behind the doorway he expected me to walk through, his body angled to watch that entrance. As I crept closer, my attention locked on to his right hand and the syringe it gripped.

Fresh, boiling hot rage clouded my vision as the pieces snapped into place. That lying bastard had played the concerned friend, pacing the halls outside her hospital room, pushing doctors to figure this out, acting devastated as her condition deteriorated. All while knowing he'd caused this. Snapshots of her suffering flashed through my mind: her body trembling as she retched on the bathroom floor, those haunting dark circles beneath her eyes, the way her cheekbones had grown sharp as her strength ebbed away until, at times, she wanted to give up the fight. And through it all, he'd stood there, pretending to care, probably savoring every moment of the hell he'd created.

Just past the open doorway, a handful of people gathered their belongings, preparing to leave, preparing to create a brand-new problem. If they chose *this* side exit over the front door, they'd walk straight into Eli's path. I had no idea what depths of depravity Eli would sink to, what mistakes his desperation might drive him to make. Or how many chemicals he might have on him.

One wrong move, and this could turn into a mass casualty incident.

An ambulance siren wailed in the distance while panicked voices from the crowd gathering around Tessa masked my footsteps as I advanced toward Eli.

Three feet behind him, my heart slammed against my ribs. I'd been in fights before, but never one where someone I loved would die if I failed.

One deep breath.

Then I lunged.

In that fraction of a second, Eli turned. His eyes went wide, but it was too late. I locked my left arm around his throat in a choke hold and seized his right wrist in an iron grip.

Eli thrashed wildly, fighting to free his arm. The awkward angle and his desperate jerking threatened to break my hold, but I tightened my elbow around his throat, trying to resist snapping it.

"It was you," I growled. "All along, it was you hurting her."

A piercing shriek cut through the air.

"Let him go!" An elderly woman burst into the vestibule, her oversize purse clutched against her chest. Her eyes blazed with misplaced righteousness as she took in the scene. Me, the apparent attacker, my arm locked around Eli's throat.

More faces appeared in the doorway, a wall of horrified onlookers.

"Stay back!" I shouted. "He has a syringe!"

Either the old woman didn't hear me or didn't care. Her focus locked on to my arm around Eli's throat, and to my horror, she charged forward, ramming her heavy purse against my back.

"Stop!" I roared. "He has a fucking needle. If it jabs you, you're dead!"

Eli took advantage of the commotion, twisting until his arm slipped through my fingers. The old woman hovered just inches away, perfectly positioned for him to strike her, and now, a middle-aged man lunged into the kill zone too. His arms were outstretched to drag her back so I could regain control.

But it was too late.

Eli slithered through my grip like a snake.

He stumbled back, brandishing the syringe like a knife.

"Everyone, leave," I commanded the frozen crowd of five.

"No one leaves," Eli snarled.

When they didn't move, I bellowed, "For God's sake, he doesn't have a gun! You can outrun a syringe!"

But fear does strange things to people. They huddled together, wide-eyed and trembling. I positioned myself between them and Eli, becoming a human shield.

"Leave. Now," I ordered over my shoulder, never taking my eyes off Eli. "This might be your last chance."

The sirens grew closer. Finally, mercifully, the five spectators scurried away, leaving me alone with the monster who'd tried to kill Tessa.

One snap of his neck, and he'd be dead. Even if he injected me, I might be able to end him before I lost consciousness.

"What did you give her?" My voice was deadly calm.

Eli's lips curled into a sneer. "Come closer, and I'll tell you."

"Tell me what you gave her, and I'll let you live."

"Am I supposed to be scared?"

"But if you don't tell me." I let ice creep into my tone. "I will make your death unimaginably painful."

"You're a doctor." He scoffed.

"Being a doctor gives me the exact skills I need to make your death excruciating."

For the first time, a flicker of uncertainty crossed his face. Evidently, the monster cared about his own survival.

"This is your last chance, Eli. Tell me what's in that syringe, or I end your life."

"You think you've won, don't you?" Something unhinged seeped through his tone. "Your perfect life, your perfect job. She was supposed to be mine." His fingers tightened around the syringe. "Everything was perfect until you showed up. And now?" A cruel smile twisted his lips. "Her organs are already shutting down. Ticktock, Doctor."

He thought he was taunting me. And he was, but every word was a tell, narrowing the list of possible toxins.

When I'd been worried Tessa was being poisoned, I'd spend hours researching toxins, giving myself a fresh course on these agents.

"You chose a fast-acting agent this time then."

I watched his reaction carefully while, inside, my heart thrashed against my ribs violently. Because fast-acting confirmed we needed answers now, and the only way to get them was through Eli.

"Smart doctor." His voice dripped with contempt. "Always thinking you know everything."

I let my voice crack with the desperation I'd been fighting to hide. "Just tell me what you injected her with."

"Injected?" A cold smile spread across his face.

The poison hadn't been administered via syringe then. Dermal absorption or ingestion. My mind raced through the possibilities and landed again on that flute of champagne she'd had. Something in it that could overwhelm her system before she even realized what was happening.

"She could be in agony right now," I said, letting my mask slip further. "Tell me what you gave her so I can help her."

"By the time you figure out what it was ..." His lips curved into another cruel smile. "It'll be too late."

Figure it out. The words hit like a diagnosis. This wasn't just any poison; it was something that needed its own antidote. Something specific. And whatever it was had to be accessible enough for a real estate agent to get his hands on.

I stepped closer. He raised the syringe.

"You've been poisoning her all along."

This was what he craved: watching me suffer. So long as I fed that need, he'd keep talking. I slumped my shoulders, ran a trembling hand through my hair. The devastation inside me was real, but for the first time in my career, I was deliberately letting it show.

"How long does she have?" I choked.

"She'll be gone in thirty minutes."

"So, it's not arsenic then. That causes organ failure and takes hours to kill. I'm guessing strychnine." I watched his face, hunting for tells.

Eli smirked.

Not strychnine.

The sirens grew closer.

"I doubt a guy like you would have the skills to deliver ricin. One wrong move, and you'd be the one dying."

"You think you're smarter than everyone." He leaned forward, eyes fever bright. "But right now? The woman you stole from me is dying. Her cells are cutting off oxygen, and there's nothing you can do to save her."

Cells cutting off oxygen.

"You gave her cyanide."

The color drained from his face.

Bingo.

My mind raced with sudden, brutal clarity. Elation, that I knew the poison, knew the antidote that could save her. But right behind that surge of relief came the crushing weight of medical knowledge. Cyanide was burning through her cells. Every second it coursed through her bloodstream was pure agony. And if she didn't get the antidote soon, knowing the answer wouldn't matter at all.

At the far end of the ballroom, doors burst open. A gurney raced toward Tessa.

I could run now, but Eli was a rabid animal. He might attack someone else out of spite, might even take another shot at Tessa while the paramedics worked to save her.

I eyed the syringe, decision made as I pulled my phone up, firing off a quick text to Dr. Vaughn. *Cyanide. Call ER. Have antidote ready.*

His thumbs-up reply came instantly.

With Tessa in good hands, I could focus on the monster in front of me. I shoved my phone away, met his gaze ...

And launched forward.

I seized his right wrist with both hands, spun so my back pressed against his chest, and grappled for the syringe. He sank his teeth into my shoulder, hooked his leg around my knee, and slammed me to the ground.

I rolled, but he was already on me, straddling my hips, needle poised to plunge into my neck. I grabbed his wrist with both hands, but he had the leverage.

The needle inched toward my skin.

"Tessa was mine," he spat.

The point crept closer to my throat.

I bucked, but he didn't budge.

"She trusted you," I snarled. In college, a guy had violated her, and it took her years to carefully, methodically let anyone in. Each smile, each casual touch, each moment of vulnerability had been hard-won. "She let you in, and you violated her trust."

"We were perfect together." Spittle flew from his lips. "She was going to take me back. Until you came along."

He leaned forward, putting his full weight behind the needle's descent. But his shift in gravity was his mistake. When I bucked again, he tilted right, allowing me to roll with the momentum.

I flipped him onto his back and knocked the syringe from his grasp. His eyes went wide as I drove my forearm into his throat.

In my peripheral vision, I saw the stretcher with two EMTs racing toward the front doors. They had Tessa. My heart soared.

I snatched up the fallen syringe, pressed it to his neck, and pushed the plunger home.

"Enjoy the fate you planned for her."

70

BLAKE

I burst into the emergency room, where a swarm of medical professionals surrounded Tessa. ER doctors, nurses, and Dr. Vaughn. A sea of hands moved with practiced efficiency, the kind of orchestrated mayhem that only happened when death lurked at the edges of possibility.

Tessa's skin had gone ghostly pale, her lips tinged with an all-too-familiar blue that made my chest constrict.

"Get an ECG and increase her on oxygen to fifteen liters per minute. Vitals every two minutes. And get toxicology down here now!" Dr. Calder barked. My rival for chief of emergency medicine—thank God he was the one on duty tonight because he was amazing—pressed his stethoscope to her chest, his face carved in concentration.

"Dr. Morrison, you should leave," Dr. Vaughn said quietly.

"I'm not leaving." The words came out raw.

"Heart rate's dropping. Forty-seven beats per minute!" a nurse called out as she hung a saline IV.

"You could be a distraction." Dr. Vaughn's voice was gentle but firm. "We need to work on saving her life."

"I want to help." My voice cracked.

"I know you do. You're emotionally compromised, and we can't have that in the ER. Out. Now."

It wasn't until then that I realized the room had gone blurry. My eyes were burning, my throat so tight that it felt like I was swallowing fire. For the first time in my career, I understood what it meant to be on this side of an emergency, to be the one watching, helpless, as someone you love balanced on the scalpel's edge between life and death.

Like that family member I'd shooed away the day Tessa had landed in my ER.

"At least tell me how she's doing."

"She's barely responsive," the nurse reported with no filter. "BP is crashing. Seventy-five over fifty."

Dr. Calder grabbed the IV tubing. "Push atropine, 0.5 milligrams IV. Now."

"Antidote?"

"Given the second she arrived." Dr. Vaughn guided me into the hallway. "We're working on stabilizing her vitals to give the antidote a chance to work. You're positive it's cyanide?"

My hand—gloved, thanks to the EMTs—trembled as I held out the syringe I'd used on Eli along with a shard of glass I'd collected from the broken champagne flute on the ground. "It might have trace amounts. We should confirm."

Dr. Vaughn took the items carefully with gloved hands, passing them to a waiting intern. "Toxicology. Stat." He leveled his eyes on mine. "She's in good hands, Dr. Morrison."

After discarding my glove, I pinched the bridge of my nose and began pacing, feeling more useless than I had in my entire medical career as the frantic voices from Tessa's room became a brutal symphony.

I texted Ryker. *Come to Mercy Harbor. Now. 911.*

He tried to call, but I couldn't tell him his sister might die over the phone. He deserved better than that.

Oh God. What if she died? What if I was too late?

It was strange, how I'd imagined my life full of solitude all these years, but now, the thought of a world without Tessa felt like contemplating life without oxygen. Impossible, devastating, void of any meaning or joy.

My eyes burned hotter. I couldn't remember the last time I'd cried, let alone in public. Probably in one of my foster homes, maybe the last time my foster father had beaten Faith.

"Dr. Morrison?"

I spun to find Collins, the intern I'd once lectured for showing emotion. I'd dragged him aside and torn him apart for crying in the hallway.

"Pretty poetic, huh?" I managed a weak smile. "I gave you hell for crying over a patient."

"You're allowed to cry over this patient." His voice was gentle as he looked to the room. "I heard she means a lot to you."

"Some people would gloat right now."

Collins showed me his true colors. Again. "I would never gloat over a patient fighting for their life," he said softly. "I'm really sorry you're going through this. If there's anything I can do to help, please let me know."

I nodded. "Thank you, Collins."

He gave me an understanding look and turned to leave.

"Hey, Collins?"

He paused.

"How about you shadow me next week?"

Assuming I came in next week. Assuming Tessa survived. I couldn't even let the thought in that next week wouldn't be an ordinary, normal week ...

His face brightened. "Really?"

"Really. In fact, let's make it a month."

His smile widened, and I recognized something I'd missed before: the pure compassion that made him not just a doctor, but a healer.

"It's not just for your benefit," I added. "I think I could learn a lot from you."

Because as it turned out, caring about your patient didn't make you a dangerous doctor. It made you a better one.

71

BLAKE

When two uniformed police officers entered the sterile hospital hallway, heading toward Tessa's room, I realized my time had run out. I caught Ryker's arm—he was still processing everything I'd told him about Eli's attack—and pulled him into a quiet alcove near the emergency stairwell.

I pressed a twenty into his palm. "Need to hire you as my criminal defense lawyer."

Ryker glanced at the bill, his expression sharpening. "Why?"

Because I hadn't yet told him what happened *after* Eli poisoned his sister.

"The man who attacked Tessa is dead." I lowered my voice. "Before I say more, I need you to officially be my lawyer so we have confidentiality."

Ryker studied my face for one heartbeat, then shoved the money into his back pocket with decisive force. "Take me somewhere more private."

I led him down the fluorescent-lit corridor, past rooms filled with beeping monitors and hushed voices to a small consultation room. The door clicked shut behind us.

"Tell me everything."

"I killed him." The words exploded from me. "On purpose."

After I laid out every detail, Ryker's face had gone hard as granite.

"When I had him in the choke hold, the immediate threat was neutralized. The needle was out of play. I could've held him for police. But I didn't." I swallowed. "It wasn't self-defense."

He chewed his cheek, processing this. "Have they questioned you yet?"

"No. But they will. Soon."

Ryker's jaw worked. "How do you want to handle this?"

"What do you mean?"

"Are you telling me this because you want to be noble?" His voice took on an edge. "Turn yourself in and spend the rest of your life in prison? That's door number one. I strongly suggest door number two."

"Which is?"

"First, you give the police minimal information. You answer nothing without me present." He stepped closer, his voice dropping. "You describe a violent confrontation, where control of the needle was constantly in flux until it found his skin. You explain the threat to my sister and everyone else in that room. You stick to those facts. Period."

"It's not the whole story." I had a choice to stop.

"Enjoy rotting in prison if that makes you feel more noble." His eyes flashed. "The man tried to murder my sister. Twice. You really think I'm letting you go down for taking him out?"

I clenched my jaw.

"After I talk to them, then what?" I asked.

"You let me handle the entire legal process." Ryker's voice carried absolute certainty. "Statistically, charges are highly unlikely. There's no evidence except your word, which you'll keep to yourself. Your prints on the syringe are explained by the struggle. Hell, everyone in that ballroom owes you their life. Any one of them could've died if you hadn't stopped Eli." He gripped my shoulder, his voice softening. "Now let's go talk to the police."

72

BLAKE

I just confessed to murder, and Ryker didn't even blink.

Walking toward Tessa's ER room, I watched my best friend—a criminal defense attorney whose entire career was built on upholding the law—process what I'd done. What I'd become. Again. This time, a killer who'd stopped a man's heart to avenge his sister.

But instead of turning away in disgust, Ryker gripped my shoulder, his fingers digging in with fierce loyalty. "Whatever happens, Blake, I'm with you. All the way."

My throat tightened. This was what family felt like. Not the emptiness I'd known as a child, but unwavering support in the darkest moment of your life. The knowledge that someone would walk through fire with you, no matter what sins stained your soul.

The cardiac monitor's steady beep pulled my attention back to Tessa as they wheeled her gurney down the hallway. Sinus tachycardia, 130 beats per minute. Oxygen saturation dropping to 88%. The doctor in me cataloged every detail with clinical precision, even as my hands trembled with fear.

"Where are you taking her?" My voice cracked, betraying the terror I'd been trying to contain.

"ICU," a nurse called over her shoulder, not breaking stride.

Dr. Calder appeared beside us, his face grim. "We have her on 100% oxygen with a mask right now."

"Partial pressure of oxygen?" The question came automatically, my medical training kicking in like muscle memory. But while my mind raced through protocols and procedures, my heart screamed that this was Tessa. Not just another patient with cyanide poisoning.

"65 millimeters of mercury and falling." Each of Calder's words felt like watching a patient flatline on the table. That moment when the monitor's steady rhythm dissolves into a single, merciless tone.

As a physician, I knew exactly what those numbers meant. As a man in love, I felt the weight of each digit crushing my chest.

"Early intubation would prevent further tissue hypoxia." The words tumbled out, mechanical and desperate. "Have you started—"

"Hydroxocobalamin is running wide open," Calder cut in. "Sodium thiosulfate as a secondary treatment. IV fluids for pressure support. Anti-seizure prophylaxis. Activated charcoal since ingestion was recent."

I nodded along, my doctor's brain ticking through the treatment algorithm, even as my heart threatened to shatter. Every detail was textbook perfect, exactly what I would have ordered myself. But knowing the medicine didn't help. Not when I could see the cyanosis tinting her lips blue, not when I knew exactly how cyanide was stealing oxygen from every cell in her body.

My medical knowledge wasn't a comfort; it was torture. I understood with horrifying clarity exactly how the poison was destroying her from the inside out.

"Current lactate levels?" I heard myself asking, even though I didn't want to know. Even though each lab value was another dagger in my heart.

"12.4 and rising."

The number pierced through my chest like an OR scalpel. Metabolic acidosis. Cellular death. My medical mind translated the values automatically while my soul rebelled against their meaning. I pressed my palms against my eyes, trying to erase the textbook predictions of mortality rates associated with numbers like these.

"Will she be okay?" The question came out raw, stripped of all medical pretense. In that moment, I wasn't Dr. Morrison, trauma doctor. I was just a man terrified of losing the woman he loved.

Calder's hesitation became a fresh blade between my ribs. "At this stage, there's a lot of uncertainty. We'll be monitoring her in the ICU."

"Time to consciousness?" I barely recognized my own voice.

"If she regains consciousness," he emphasized, and the word *if* shredded what was left of my composure, "it won't be for several hours, maybe a day, as her body recovers from cellular damage caused by oxygen deprivation."

The unspoken prognosis hung between us. I knew the statistics. Knew the likelihood of anoxic brain injury, of permanent cardiac damage, of multi-organ failure. My years of medical training painted vivid pictures of every possible complication. A thousand ways to lose her, each one more terrifying than the last.

I'd spent my entire adult life in a prison of isolation, its walls built from fear, each brick cemented in the belief that if you loved anyone, they'd choose to leave you. That caring for someone was just volunteering for pain. I'd been my own warden, my own sentencer, my own executioner.

But Tessa had slipped through the bars like sunlight through clouds, her affection seeds promising to take root and grow. She chose to love me, showing me through her actions that she'd never leave.

And now I understood. All that darkness that had poisoned me, that had turned me bitter and withdrawn, had a cure all along.

She was the antidote.

I'd wasted so many years fighting this love. But now that it coursed through my system, it transformed everything it touched. Each beat of my heart pumped it deeper, dissolving years of calcified pain. Where I'd built walls, light began to crack through. Where shadows had pooled, warmth began to spread.

Love wasn't a prison sentence. It was freedom.

But only if she lived.

Ryker's hand found my shoulder again, anchoring me as my world spun out of control. That's when I heard heavy footsteps approaching from behind.

"Dr. Morrison." The police officer's voice was steel wrapped in false courtesy. "We need to ask you some questions about Eli Porter's death."

In saving Tessa, I might have damned myself. But I'd do it again. A thousand times over.

Some prices were worth paying.

73

BLAKE

As I sat in the chair next to Tessa's ICU bed, I shoved my face in my hands.

Ryker, once again, squeezed my shoulder. Something he'd been doing on the hour since Tessa arrived at the hospital.

The ICU room had become my new prison cell, my penance for failing her.

Earlier, the police had questioned me—with my lawyer present, of course—and for now, they'd left. If they suspected I'd done something nefarious, they'd done a good job of hiding it. They had searched Eli's apartment and found a bathroom jar filled with toxins. Based on entries they had found and hand-scribbled notes, it seemed Tessa and I were the first targets on his hit list. The guy had absolutely flipped a switch, been rejected too many times in his life, I guess. Next on that list was his boss. Followed by two of his coworkers and then God knows who else.

But those details washed over me like white noise. There was only Tessa, lying still as death in the hospital bed.

"Why don't I get you some food?" Ryker's voice broke through the fog. "My parents are in the cafeteria." He paused, studying me. "They're relieved you're here with her, Blake. They know you'll make sure she gets the best possible care, but you need to eat."

I pressed my palms against my eyes, this time guilt a poison in my veins. "I should never have left her side."

"There's no way you could have known—"

"That doesn't matter." My voice cracked. "I left her alone and unprotected. Might as well have handed her to her killer on a silver platter. I suspected him, Ryker. The test results said no toxins, but ... I never should have left him alone with her."

"I could stand here and talk for an hour, but nothing I say will get through right now. You need rest and food."

"I can't possibly sleep."

"Then we'll work on item number two. I'll get you something to eat."

As Ryker's footsteps faded, silence crept in like a fog. Only the steady beep of monitors broke through, each sound a cruel reminder that she should have woken up by now. Unable to stay still, I paced the length of the ICU room, my eyes fixed on the shallow rise and fall of her chest.

At her bedside, I brushed my knuckles along her skin. Too cold. The kind of cold that meant her cells had been starved of oxygen because I hadn't protected her.

"Most everyone I've loved has left me, Tessa." My voice was barely a whisper. "Don't you dare leave me too. If you do ..." The words caught in my throat. *I'll follow you. I'll drink that same poison and chase you through whatever hell you're experiencing until my heart stops beating.*

My eyes burned at the sight of her. My fierce, independent Tessa, lying there helpless.

"You have to wake up." The words spilled out, raw and desperate. "So I can tell you how I've always felt. I wasn't sure I believed in love at first sight, but if it exists, I remember the exact moment it hit me: watching you walk past me as a teenager. The way you ran your fingers through your hair, how the sunlight caught those auburn highlights.

Then your green eyes met mine, and my world just … stopped."

I gripped her hand, her skin winter cold against mine. "You offered me this shy smile, but somehow found the courage to introduce yourself. Your voice was so light, so … undamaged. The world hadn't been cruel to you yet, the way it had been to me when it took my parents. The way it would be when Sarah walked away. All I knew in that moment was that I wanted to protect you from the darkness in this world."

Her eyelids didn't flutter. Mouth didn't open.

"You're going to wake up." My voice was raw from exhaustion and pain. "You have to."

But the silence stretched on, broken only by the steady, mocking beep of machines. Hours bled together, marked by nurses' quiet footsteps and the shadows crawling across the wall. Nothing changed. Nothing moved.

The hope I'd been clinging to finally cracked, piece by piece, like ice splintering beneath my feet—

Something fluttered against my palm.

My gaze snapped to her fingers, heart suspended between beats. Had I imagined it?

"Tessa?" My pulse hammered against my ribs.

Her lashes trembled, and my world narrowed to that tiny movement. Leaning down, I cupped her cool cheek, careful not to disturb her oxygen mask. Her breath fogged the plastic in steady rhythm—in, out, in, out—each exhale a gift.

Then, like dawn breaking after the longest night of my life, her eyes fluttered open. Emerald green. The color of life, of hope, of everything I'd almost lost.

"I'm here, Tessa."

She blinked slowly, her pupils struggling to focus in the harsh ICU lighting. Then her gaze found mine, and as her lips parted beneath the mask, the faintest whisper escaped.

"Blake?"

Relief hit me like a wrecking ball. For this one moment—this single, precious heartbeat—I let myself feel nothing but gratitude. She was alive. She knew my name.

She had come back to me.

But right behind it was terror of what came next.

What damage had the poison done to her brain, her heart, her organs?

74

TESSA

Consciousness came in waves, first the stabbing brightness, then the acidic taste in my mouth, and finally the steady beeping that meant I was alive. But it was the warmth of his hand in mine that drew me from the chasms of darkness into the sterile hospital room.

"Tessa?" His voice—that deep baritone I'd know anywhere—cracked with emotion.

Something pressed against my mouth and nose, heating with each painful breath. Through the fog, I made out Blake's face above me, his tuxedo shirt wrinkled, like he'd been wearing it for days.

"I'm here," he said softly, his composure warring with something raw in his eyes. "I'm right here, Cupcake."

That nickname. It pulled me further from the depths, even as my body cataloged each ache: the sharp pain in my lungs with every breath, the vicious throb behind my temples, the cool drip of fluids through my IV.

"Blake?"

He dropped his head, and I caught the slight tremor in his shoulders before he straightened. His fingers never left my skin, tracing small, soothing patterns on my palm, as if reassuring himself I was really there.

"Do you remember why you're here?" The professional tone couldn't quite mask the undercurrent of fury and terror in his voice.

My gaze drifted around the private ICU room, taking in the array of monitoring equipment. That's when it hit me. Eli. The drink. His threat against Blake.

"Did he hurt you?" I tried to sit up.

He stopped me from moving. "You're lying in the ICU after nearly dying, and you're worried about *me*?" His chuckle was rough. "That's so perfectly you that it hurts, Cupcake."

"But he said—"

"He didn't hurt anyone else." Blake's free hand curled into a fist at his side. "And he'll never hurt you again."

The clinical fluorescent lights cast shadows under his eyes, highlighting the muscle working in his jaw. I'd seen Blake angry before, but this was different.

"He's gone?" I managed.

Blake's gaze swept over me, cataloging every monitor, every tube, every mark Eli's poison had left on my body. Something dangerous flickered in his eyes. "He deserved a fate far worse than what he got. If you hadn't been fighting for your life ..." He left the sentence unfinished, but his grip on my hand tightened.

"The tea!" I jerked upright, or tried to, but he pressed a hand to my shoulder again. "It's in your house. You need to get rid of it before anybody touches it!"

Blake's features shadowed into an almost-unrecognizable version of himself. "He laced your tea?"

I nodded.

Blake's jaw hardened. "You consumed poison in my home."

It wasn't a question. It was a revelation, one of disgust.

"The whole time I was protecting you, he was still ..." He cut himself off, running a hand through his already-disheveled hair.

He stepped away to make a call to his staff, and I watched how he paced, his shoulders rigid with tension. Even across the room, he kept glancing back at me, as if afraid I'd disappear if he looked away too long.

When he returned, his fingers immediately sought mine again.

"They're okay?" I asked about his staff.

"They're fine. Police are on their way to my place to get it."

Good. That was good. God, if Maria had ...

"I can't believe this happened," I said. "I honestly never suspected him."

"I know." His other hand came up to brush a strand of hair from my face, lingering longer than necessary.

"I should have listened to you."

"This isn't your fault." His words came out fiercely.

"When you told me you suspected someone was poisoning me, I thought you'd gone off the deep end."

A ghost of a smirk touched his lips. "I had gone off the deep end a little. The mere possibility that someone was trying to hurt you ..." He shook his head. "It made me snap."

"How ..." I swallowed hard. "How did Eli die?"

Something shifted in Blake's expression, a darkness passing behind his eyes like storm clouds.

"He intended to poison me," he said carefully. "There was a scuffle. He was the one who ended up poisoned."

I searched his features. The tight line of his mouth, the way his eyes met mine steadily but with a silent warning. *Don't ask any more questions, Tessa. Let me protect you from this.*

In that moment, I understood. Eli could have gone to prison, but Blake had chosen a more permanent solution. I should have been horrified. Instead, I felt a deep sense of security washing over me. This brilliant, complicated man would tear the world apart to keep me safe.

I laced my fingers through his, accepting everything that went unspoken between us. His eyes watched my gesture carefully, understanding dawning in their depths that I accepted him, all of him. The darkness. The light. The morally gray lines.

He leaned in, close enough that I could see the gold flecks in his brown eyes. "Do you want to know why I've always called you Cupcake?"

Hope bloomed in my chest as I nodded.

Blake paused.

"Because there was this one moment when my world changed forever." His voice dropped lower, meant only for me. "It was after Sarah, after I'd shut down from everyone. I heard singing coming from the kitchen. Your voice. You were dancing while you baked cupcakes, completely lost in your own happiness. Your back was to me, so you didn't even know I stood there, watching you."

His thumb brushed across my knuckles as he continued, "For the first time since Sarah left, I felt something crack through the darkness I'd surrendered to. There you were, this pure light, reminding me that good people existed. And as I watched you dance and sing, I found myself smiling for the first time since Sarah left me. It was like your joy was contagious, and in that moment, I wondered if it was possible that, one day, I might feel happy like you. That maybe, someday, I could feel whole again."

Blake swallowed hard, his Adam's apple bobbing. "That was the moment I fell in love with you, Tessa. I didn't even know if you'd ever look at me that way, and afterward, I tried to bury it. I was too broken, too hardened. But every time I said that name, Cupcake, I was back in that kitchen, watching you dance, falling in love with you all over again."

Tears pricked my eyes. "Why didn't you tell me?"

He trailed a finger down my cheek. "Because I couldn't plant those seeds of possibility in me. The closest I came was two years ago, and then I let fear take the wheel. But it's always been you, Cupcake. Through everything, it's only ever been you."

My soul devoured his words, wanting to eat them, imprint

them into my DNA. Words that I wanted to call up anytime I wanted them to sing to me. I wanted to snuggle with them at night and drink them on days when I felt sad.

"I love you, Blake," I whispered. "It's always been you too."

75

BLAKE

“Surely, you can hire movers for this,” Jace argued, his CEO status practically oozing from every pore as he struggled with a chair.

“What fun would that be?” I grinned. “Besides, Tessa has spoken.”

For someone still adjusting to the whole wealthy lifestyle, Tessa had some interesting rules. Four sweaty men hauling her belongings? Totally fine as long as she knew at least two of them. But professional movers? God forbid.

So, here we were. Sinners and Saints, reduced to common laborers, all because she batted those big green eyes at us.

Okay, fine, she batted her eyes at me, and I strong-armed the guys into helping. The things we do for love. Or in my case, the things we make our friends do for love.

In a swift move that widened Tessa’s eyes in surprise, I captured her waist and drew her body to mine. Her breath caught, and I felt that familiar surge of satisfaction. At least I could still throw her off-balance as much as she did me.

I grabbed her chin between my finger and thumb. “I expect to see more of that fire in our bedroom tonight.”

Our. The word soared through my soul.

Her green eyes darted from my left to my right, and then I

claimed her mouth with my own. As always, kissing her made me lose track of everything. The guys, the moving van, all of it. It wasn't until Axel stomped past us with a chair that we pulled apart.

"Jesus, Morrison. Seeing you in love is all sorts of unsettling."

After wrapping my arm around Tessa's shoulders, we followed him back inside.

"You'll find love too, Axel," Tessa assured him.

He glared at her. "I'd rather chew my arm off with no teeth."

"Axel isn't a relationship kind of guy," Ryker explained. "His longest commitment was to a houseplant, and it died in record time."

"That plant was defective," Axel protested. "And I'm not afraid of commitment. I'm committed to avoiding it."

Jace checked his phone again, his knuckles white around the edges.

"Everything okay?" I asked quietly.

Jace shoved his phone into his pocket like it burned. "Yeah."

"Here, I can take that—" Tessa started.

"Touch that, and we'll die," Axel barked.

Tessa's brows furrowed.

"He's being dramatic," Ryker assured her. "But Blake did threaten us if we let you lift a finger, so do us a solid and go sit down. I can't have a black eye at my next court date. The judge already thinks I'm suspicious after the last one."

"I'm not an invalid," Tessa protested, reaching for a box.

All three men formed a wall between her and the boxes, arms crossed.

"Did you just—" She glanced between them. "Are you actually creating a human barrier?"

"Think of us as your personal Secret Service," Axel said. "Except our mission is keeping our favorite doctor from going full drill sergeant on us. And trust me, if he does, he'll hold a grudge that'll ruin at least eight poker nights. Man's a nightmare when he doesn't get his way. Takes all our money and doesn't even have the decency to pretend he's not doing it on purpose."

Later, when we finished moving Tessa's stuff, Jace pulled me aside, pressing a paper into my hand.

"Current address confirmed."

I'd had his guy check it; return addresses could be outdated.

The paper felt heavy in my hand. After years of wondering why I wasn't enough, of building walls so thick that even Tessa had to fight to scale them, I might finally uncover the truth.

"You going to go there?" Jace asked.

I took a deep breath, folding the paper with deliberate precision. "It's time," I said. "Time to bury some old wounds."

Jace nodded, then looked up and down the street with guarded features, like a man expecting shadows to come alive.

I'd noticed it before, how Jace's normally sharp wit seemed to dull around the same time each year. At first, I'd assumed it was grief. The anniversary of his mother's death had nearly broken him in college. The guy who'd built an empire from his family's ashes after his father's murder had almost crumbled when cancer claimed her too.

He'd recovered on the surface with cutting remarks and brilliant business moves, but something remained guarded about him. Until falling for Tessa, I'd never questioned why Jace lived alone. But watching him check his phone again with that haunted expression, I suspected something darker lurked beneath the surface.

And I started to worry that whatever ghost was hunting him, it was getting closer.

76

BLAKE

When I walked up the concrete steps of the faded gray bungalow, my feet felt encased in lead. The peeling paint matched the broken pieces of my past: worn down, neglected.

My knocks echoed accusations.

You. Left. Me.

You. Broke. Me.

When a short woman in scrubs opened the door, my stomach dropped.

"Does Sarah Vega live here?"

She nodded. "Who's asking?"

Who indeed? Her former foster son. The boy she'd discarded when he needed her most. Because she claimed she was sick.

Claimed. The word evaporated as I stared at this woman who was obviously a nurse.

"Blake Morrison."

Her eyes widened with recognition. "Oh, come in."

The door creaked open to a living room converted into a hospital room. And there, in a bed that dominated the space, lay a ghost of the woman who'd haunted my memories.

The unexpected sight made me freeze for a moment.

Sarah's once-vibrant eyes were sunken. But what caught my

doctor's attention was the central line port in her chest for long-term IV access.

The realization hit me all at once, making me feel instantly ill.

"You really were sick."

Every word I'd dismissed as an excuse had been true. Years of anger crumbled to reveal something worse: Guilt that while I'd cursed her name, she'd been fighting for her life.

"Misdiagnosed back then." She waved a skeletal hand, her smile weak. "Wasn't a degenerative illness after all. Just a tumor mimicking the symptoms. I fought it for many years."

Jesus. I couldn't miss the parallel to Tessa's illness. If I'd stayed in touch, could I have helped her?

I eyed the gray color of her skin. "How long do you have?"

A coughing fit racked her fragile frame. The nurse rushed to help, offering water, and after a minute, Sarah waved her off.

"I'm fine. If you wouldn't mind, I'd like to be alone with my son."

Son. One word. Three letters. It shattered something inside me.

Once the nurse left, Sarah motioned me closer.

"Doctors can't be sure. Best guess, a week."

A *week*. God, I'd almost put this visit off for another month.

"I've been hoping to see you since..."

"The day you left me," I finished.

Her eyes filled with torment I knew too well.

"That was the biggest mistake of my life." Tears spilled onto her hollow cheeks. "After, I tried to petition the foster-care system, but they said it was too late." She'd tried to get me back? "Said I wouldn't be allowed to contact you until you turned eighteen."

"That's when your letters started."

"I don't blame you for never responding. When you make the biggest mistake of your life, you can't assume people will listen to your apology."

Still. "Why didn't you tell me you had cancer?"

"I thought about it. But it wasn't appropriate for a letter. And your silence told me a visit would be unwelcomed." She squeezed my hand. "I'm sorry, Blake. I should never have left you. At the time, I thought about how you and your sister had already lost your parents. I didn't want your heart broken, watching my degenerative illness take me too. I thought I was protecting you, but I was wrong. I'd give anything to go back and change it."

Her words untangled years of resentment.

"The day you left," she continued, "my world collapsed. And when I tried to get you back, it gave me reason to live. I couldn't die until I got you back. So I fought. First with the foster care system. That one I lost. But cancer?" She smiled. "Beat two recurrences over the years."

While I'd been building walls, she'd been fighting to stay alive. Fighting for a chance to see me again.

Something broke inside me, a dam letting healing waters rush through. I wished I could go back to that teenage boy all those years ago and tell him everything would be okay, tell him not to waste years on bitterness.

"I love you, Sarah."

I stayed with her every night after. Four days later, as I held her hand, Sarah took her final breath.

Some might see that as tragic. And in terms of years lost between us, it was. But Tessa helped me see the blessing. All Sarah wanted was to see me again. To apologize. And to be forgiven.

She'd gotten that. And my wounds had healed too.

Life could be both tragic and beautiful.

Like Sarah teaching one final lesson: sometimes, the bravest thing is to let love in, even knowing it might hurt.

77

TESSA

The scent of fresh paint mingled with the comfort of old books as I arranged another stack on my custom shelves. My library. God, I still got a little thrill just thinking those words. My very own library, complete with that rolling ladder I'd always dreamed about since watching Beauty and the Beast for the first time.

"You missed the boys," I said. "I can't wait for you to meet them all."

"I still can't get over what Eli did," Scarlett said, lost in thought.

I blushed, remembering Blake's whispered confession about Eli. About protection and love and the lengths someone would go to keep their family safe. And when Eric Voss died in Blake's ER, I had my suspicions about that too.

Police now had their own suspicions about missing women in the area. That knife in Voss's thigh? His latest victim had survived to tell detectives that Voss had bragged about other women who hadn't been so lucky. Women whose bodies hadn't been found.

If Voss hadn't "succumbed" to his injuries that night, those women's families might never have known what happened to their loved ones. The investigation had already found evidence linking him to three missing persons cases.

I knew how this should feel. I should be horrified that Blake might have crossed a line, taken justice into his own hands. But each time that thought surfaced, I remembered what the women had gone through and what their families had lost. How many more would there have been while police built their case? How many more families destroyed?

I couldn't bring myself to feel anything but relief that he was gone, even if Blake had helped him along.

"I mean, you dated a monster who systematically poisoned you," Scarlett shuddered.

"Tell me about it."

"So, were you sick all along, or was it the poison?"

"Both. My specialist said my original lung infection threw my mast cells into chaos. But when they'd start to calm, I'd unknowingly ingest thallium in a one-two punch. I'd get sick from the poison, which would inflame my mast cells."

"Bloody hell."

"Hell is right."

"And now? Do you still have to get treated?"

"I'll have to manage it my whole life, but it's totally doable."

"And the cyanide? Any permanent damage?"

"Thankfully, I've made a full recovery." I ran a hand through my hair. "So, have you officially applied for that promotion?"

She twisted a strand of hair around her finger. "I have my final interview coming up."

"But?" I abandoned my shelving and sat in the chair beside her.

"I have this... weird feeling."

"Like you won't get the promotion?"

She tossed aside her magazine. "No. Maybe. I don't know."

"Scarlett—"

"How are the bookshelves coming?" Blake's voice from the doorway made us both jump. He leaned against the frame, radiating that quiet intensity that made the earth stop spinning for me.

Scarlett stood, smoothing her pants. The mask of confidence slipped back into place so fast I almost doubted I'd seen it falter.

"And that's my cue." She gathered her things, then kissed my cheek. "I'm glad you got your happily ever after, Tessa," she whispered, then saluted Blake. "Dr. Morrison."

"Scarlett." His lips twitched.

"Thanks for saving my bestie." She headed for the door.

"You're welcome anytime," Blake called after her.

"I'm going to hold you to that!" Her voice floated back.

Blake's arms slipped around my waist, and I leaned against his chest, breathing him in.

"Did you find out what's wrong?"

I shook my head. "No. But whatever it is, I have a feeling it's bigger than she's letting on."

78

BLAKE

"What exactly am I looking at?" Tessa stepped out of the car, her head tilted back to take in the full Gothic glory of the mansion. The stone gargoyles leered through the evening fog, their weathered faces telling secrets in shadow. "Because this is either the world's most dramatic man cave or the setting of every horror movie ever made."

I wrapped my arm around her shoulders. "A club of sorts."

"When you said 'club,' I thought you meant metaphorical. Not a physical haunted mansion."

I pressed a kiss to her temple, breathing in the honeysuckle scent of her shampoo.

"Ryker never breathed a word about this place."

"Against the rules," I explained.

"Rules?" Her eyebrows shot up.

"You're the first nonmember to see this place," I said, unlocking the heavy door.

"If there's a secret handshake," she whispered, stepping inside, "I expect to learn it immediately."

We entered the main living area, where Ryker, Axel, and Jace sat around the poker table.

Ryker looked up from the spread of cards in his hand and smirked. "Told you he wasn't kidding."

"This place is supposed to be for club members only," Axel muttered. "You never let me bring one model. Not one."

"Tessa's one of us now," I declared.

All three guys stilled.

"You know what this means," Jace said.

"He knows." Ryker pushed up from his chair and put his hand on her shoulder.

"You've always had my protection," Ryker said, "but now you have all of ours."

"What?" Tessa managed, confused.

"These aren't just ordinary men," I explained. "They're your guardians now. A client gets too handsy? Axel knows people who can have their company bankrupted by morning. Legal trouble? Ryker will have a team of lawyers at your door before you hang up the phone. Business complication? Jace owns so many businesses that I've lost count and has specialists on speed dial."

Tessa evaluated the men, still struggling to digest what I was saying to her.

"Day or night," I continued, "one call to any of us, and we'll help you. That's what family means to us. And, Tessa, you're their family now too."

Tessa's eyes watered as Ryker, Axel, and Jace each patted her shoulder, acknowledging the unspoken promise.

"Come here." I drew her through the mansion's back door into the garden.

The setting sun painted the roses in amber light, and Tessa's eyes sparkled as she took in the cascading flowers and ivy-wrapped trellises. Her fingers twitched slightly, like she was mentally arranging centerpieces and wedding arches.

I pulled her close, her small frame fitting perfectly against mine, like she'd been crafted just for these moments.

"I've spent my whole life feeling uncertain," I admitted, the words flowing easier now than they ever had before. "Like I was standing outside a snow globe, watching everyone else find their happiness while I pressed my hands against the glass. Deep down, I never thought I'd find it. And when it came close, when you came close, I pushed it away." I traced my thumb along her cheekbone. "Until now. Now, I've never been more certain of anything, Tessa. You're my reason for everything. I promise I'll protect you as we build our future together. I love you."

Drawing her mouth to mine, I couldn't believe this was my new reality. These lips, these moments together had become my heartbeat. I'd get to watch her empire grow, her wedding planning business already bursting with A-list clients and a wait list that read like a who's who of Chicago society.

And watch I would, protecting her as she soared.

As for me, I'd decided to turn down the promotion and continue my current role in the ER while I pursued my board certification in internal medicine. After seeing what Tessa went through and getting a glimpse behind the curtain of how many patients struggle to get diagnoses, I felt called to something new, something bigger than emergency medicine. I planned to open my own clinic one day, where I could spend more time with patients, more time listening, and more time helping them get to the root of their medical mysteries.

"I love you, Blake," she whispered against my lips.

I kissed her again, gentle, but eager to get back to our penthouse later, where we could be alone. Where we could make love, like we did every night and most mornings. My staff loved Tessa, more than they loved me, I think, and everything was finally falling into place.

With one exception.

After getting lost in kisses, I brought Tessa back inside and waited a few more minutes before pulling Jace away from the others.

Something was wrong with the billionaire who transformed failing companies by prioritizing employees over profits, giving raises instead of pink slips. Fortune called him the Santa Claus of

CEOs, measuring success by lives improved rather than dollars earned.

You'd think the guy wouldn't look so damn haunted.

"We're all worried about you," I pressed. "We can tell something's going on, but for the life of us, we can't imagine why you won't tell us what it is."

He was silent for several seconds, but I studied him, making it clear that this time, I wouldn't accept "I'm fine" for an answer. I'd wait. For as long as it took.

Finally, he cleared his throat, looking to the ground. "There's something I never told you guys."

I cocked my head. "We don't keep secrets from each other."

"Well, I did." He flipped his phone over repeatedly. "We went through enough shit together. Last thing I wanted was to add another burden."

"The whole point of our club is to be there for each other. Through everything."

"And I needed that." He met my eyes. "Maybe I was worried you guys wouldn't have my back if you knew what I'd done."

"Knox was convicted of murder, and we stood by him. What could you possibly have done that would make you think we'd support Knox, but not you?"

He rubbed his eye. "Let's just say I have a dark past."

"We all have a dark past."

He leveled me with a glare. "You have to trust me." His voice dropped. "We all have our sins and secrets, and mine are better left buried."

With that, he turned and walked away, leaving me alone with the unsettling realization that the man I considered a brother—the billionaire with a heart of gold—might be hiding something darker than any of us could imagine.

EPILOGUE

TESSA

"You slept with your boss?" My eyes bugged out as I grabbed my wineglass for support.

The light in our dining room flickered across Scarlett's face, highlighting something I'd never seen there before. Was that fear mixed with desire?

"On accident." Scarlett took a long sip of her Merlot. "And not just once." A blush crept up her neck as she leaned closer, lowering her voice. "I've never felt anything like it. With him, it's like everyone else disappears."

"How does one accidentally sleep with her boss?"

"Easy." Scarlett's laugh held a hint of hysteria. "You meet a hot-as-sin guy, spend a no-strings-attached weekend with him, and then when you go back to work on Monday morning, you discover he's the new owner of your entire company." She traced the rim of her wineglass. "Jace Lockwood."

I nearly choked. "Blake's friend?"

"The one and only." She drew her fingertips to her lips. "I've tried to stop thinking about him because every time I do, my skin heats up. And whenever he's near me, it's like he electrifies all the particles in the air. And when he looks at me with those intense green eyes? It's like everyone else disappears. Like he can see right through me." She shook her head. "And now he wants more. A lot more."

"Well, that doesn't sound so terrible," I ventured.

"It is when there's someone at work who's hurting me." Her fingers trembled around her glass. "Every day at work is a battlefield because Jace is obsessed with finding out who it is. And when he does ..." She left the sentence hanging.

"Why don't you just tell Jace who he is?"

Scarlett met my eyes, and in that moment, I saw real fear there. "Because the man hurting me—the one Jace is hell-bent on destroying—isn't just dangerous. He's Jace's best friend. And if Jace finds out the truth, everything could burn."

The color drained from my face as her words sank in.

Before I could respond, Scarlett's phone lit up. She glanced down, and I watched her entire body freeze.

"What is it?" I asked.

She turned the phone toward me, her hand trembling. It was a text from Jace:

Just got some shocking information. We need to talk. Now.

Scarlett's eyes met mine, wide with panic. "I think he just found out."

As she rushed out, I couldn't help wondering what secrets remained untold. And I had no idea if Scarlett or Jace would make it out unscathed.

Looking for more of Tessa and Blake? Get an exclusive bonus scene:

Also_by_Kathy_Lockheart

Immerse yourself in this **bestselling, unputdownable romance series** where desire and danger collide. Four couples, four **stand-alones interconnected** by a deliciously dark thread of romance, action, mystery, and shocking twists...

⭐ **Deadly_Illusion** ⭐ She was able to hide the bruises from everyone...until an MMA fighter came along. Now he'll die to protect her, maybe even kill...

. . .

☆ **Fatal Cure** ☆ She'll risk everything to annihilate the enemy who decimated her family. But what happens when that dangerous enemy turns out to be the man she's fallen in love with?

☆ **Lethal Justice** ☆ Chicago's most wanted criminal has fallen for the wrong woman. She's his hostage in a heist, and if he leaves any witnesses, his colleagues will kill them both.

☆ **Grave Deception** ☆ Her new neighbor is a scorching hot police detective—one she has a massive crush on, but she never wanted to get his attention like this: as the apparent victim of an attempted murder.

Equal parts rapturous and intense, this roller-coaster series will leave you begging for more. **Binge these stay-up-all-night romances if you dare...**

☆☆☆☆☆ "An amazing, gut-wrenching...out-of-body experience."

☆☆☆☆☆ "Raw, emotional, and beautifully written."

☆☆☆☆☆ "T*his* is the kind of fairytale that would change our lives."

DUETS:

☆ **Secret Vendetta** ☆ I've become the obsession of a killer with serious stalker tendencies.

☆ **Crossfire** ☆ In my defense, I didn't know he was sent to kill me when I fell in love with him.

ACKNOWLEDGMENTS

I'd like to thank you, the reader. Your time is limited, and I can't tell you how grateful I am that you chose to spend it in the Lockheart Universe! From the bottom of my heart, THANK YOU.

I want to thank Skye Warren and all the presenters and contributors to Romance Author Mastermind. I attended my first conference in 2024 and I've never experienced anything like it. Everyone there wanted to share with each other and help each other grow. There was a sense of camaraderie and support that was overwhelming and beautiful. It was at this conference that I discovered the next stepping stones of my career, and I can truly say I learned so much as an author. Thank you for sharing everything you learn with others!

I also want to specifically thank Jill Ramsower and Hannah Shield. I cannot express how much I appreciate you going above and beyond to share best practices with me, encourage me, and help educate me. Your support, encouragement, and wisdom have helped me grow as both an author and an entrepreneur. Thank you!

To my friends and family: your love and encouragement are something I feel grateful for every single day of my life. I love you more than any words I could ever write on a page.

Thank you to Susan Staudinger. Your developmental and content editing made this book far better than it ever would have been without you.

To Amy and Kristen, my formal beta readers. Thank you for helping make this story even better.

To Valentine and the entire staff at Valentine PR! This book wouldn't be what it is without you. Thank you!

To my editor Jovana, your attention to detail polished this story and made it the best it could be! To my cover artists, Hang Le and Sherri with Wild Love Designs, for bringing such beauty to this novel!

To all the authors who came before me—your success paves the road for new writers to do what they love. Thank you.

~ *Kathy*

LET'S CONNECT!

The easiest way to connect with me is to go to my website, www.KathyLockheart.com, and find my social media links. I interact with readers, so don't be surprised if you see me reply to your post or invite you to join a reader team!

Xoxo

Kathy

amazon.com/Kathy-Lockheart/e/B08XY5F2XG
bookbub.com/profile/kathy-lockheart
facebook.com/KathyLockheartAuthor
tiktok.com/@kathylockheart_author
instagram.com/kathy_lockheart
x.com/Kathy_Lockheart
pinterest.com/kathylockheart

Printed in Dunstable, United Kingdom

77135750R00245